THE
TEMPLE
OF MUSIC

ALSO BY JONATHAN LOWY

Elvis and Nixon

THE
TEMPLE
OF MUSIC

A Novel

JONATHAN
LOWY

Crown Publishers
New York

Published by Crown Publishers, New York, New York.
Member of the Crown Publishing Group,
a division of Random House, Inc.
www.crownpublishing.com

CROWN is a trademark and the Crown colophon is a
registered trademark of Random House, Inc.

Printed in the United States of America

DESIGN BY BARBARA STURMAN

Library of Congress Cataloging-in-Publication Data
Lowy, Jonathan.
    Temple of music : a novel / by Jonathan Lowy.—1st ed.
    (Hardcover)
    1. United States—History—1865–1921—Fiction.
2. Czolgosz, Leon F., 1873?–1901—Fiction. 3. McKinley,
William, 1843–1901—Fiction. 4. Presidents—United
States—Fiction. 5. Czech-Americans—Fiction.
6. Assassination—Fiction. 7. Assassins—Fiction. I. Title.
PS3562.O94T46   2004
813'.6—dc22   2003024165

ISBN 0-609-60819-3

10 9 8 7 6 5 4 3 2 1

First Edition

Acknowledgments

I would like to give my continued thanks to my agent, Deborah Grosvenor, for her editorial judgment and dedicated representation; to friends and family who read earlier versions of this book and provided much-needed encouragement and advice: Dawn Nunziato, Judy Lowy, and Chris Knott; and to my editor, Rachel Kahan, and everyone else at Crown.

PART ONE

THE
PARTY

I · LEON · 1873–1901

His mother should not have come here; the trip was arduous, she was getting on in years, and Leon was in her womb, a stowaway on the ship to the new world. Childbirth would kill her, eventually, though that was a few years away. Still, she had had enough of regeneration.

Imagine her family seeing her off at the dock, peasants in the old country, sturdy Slavs, thickset and ruddy-cheeked, and her husband's, Paul's, hardscrabble Poles. They have ridden donkey carts to get to the shipyard, they have walked, they have hitched rides in the backs of wagons. Crying for the son and daughter they will never see again. She is standing high on the deck of the ship, rocking in the water. Her bony fingers—that is what Leon remembers about her, her fingers: delicate, elongated, so light, so sharp, clenched tight around the rail as if someone she cannot see is hell-bent on denying her station on the deck. Babies are tugging at the hem of her dress; Leon's father is silent as their families watch the impossibly large ship slip away from them only to vanish into a speck, then merge with the sun until they all disappear over the horizon. That empty space somewhere in front of them all, that nothingness out there they could only imagine, that was America.

And so Leon Czolgosz arrived in this country an embryonic being, and he was born in this new land. That was 1873.

. . .

Then blink your eyes and let time reemerge twenty-eight years later: October 29, 1901. Men in uniform are marching in lockstep down the corridor on either side of a prisoner, their movements efficient, coordinated, precise. When they reach the chair, they turn and push him into the seat, though it isn't necessary; he does not resist. Immediately other men strap in his arms, shackle his legs, buckle belts around his neck and head. In the death chamber, everyone has a job to do. There are the men who tape electrodes to his skin, the man who shaves the circle of hair from his head, the man who wrenches water from a sponge onto the bald patch. One man will raise his hand to signal to another that it is time to pull the switch. There is a priest, though the prisoner has insisted he wants no representatives of an organized church; there are witnesses in chairs facing the electric chair as if it were a theater stage. It's not a simple thing to execute a man but they do it well. There's an economy of movement, procedures stylized as ritual. It's a testament to the prison personnel, the efficiency of it all. You do something long enough, you perfect the process. It's a testament to science, to engineering, the management of the place.

A man raises his hand, slow and deliberate, like taking an oath, a priest in some secular American faith. The switch is thrown and an eighteen-hundred-volt charge sends the body of the prisoner into sizzling convulsions, a frenzy of such intense motion that his matter seems atomized, his form transported. The witnesses in the room can smell the burnt skin; how could you not? Then the body becomes definite again, something real, and settles back in the chair. A doctor places his stethoscope on the heart, listens once, twice, then nods to a man who throws the switch for the second charge.

Again: the precision. The swift sequence of commands and response.

The corpse is taken from the chamber, and a saw cuts the top of the prisoner's skull, his brain is scooped out, his ears and face are measured again for evidence of dementia. The brain was not the cause, the doctors determine. But still it must be destroyed; whatever it is, all of it must be eradicated.

So they strip him of his clothes and carry him outside. Men take his arms and legs and swing his limp naked body into a pit they have dug in the night. A man lifts a metal canister and pours its contents in.

The liquid sizzles, then smokes. The men watch as the skin melts into nothing and the acid—it is sulfuric acid they have poured in—works through the layers of muscle, fat, tissue, then bones. There is a heart, a liver, a stomach, intestines, organs that are no longer identifiable as the acid devours what remains.

More signals. A man in a beaver pelt hat on the edge of the pit nods his head, another carboy of acid is poured in until there is no body there, only mist at the bottom of the hole that rises up . . . up . . . up. . . .

And Leon Czolgosz vanishes into a speck, that nothingness out there on the horizon.

Blink your eyes again. He reappears.

2 · THE TIMES

This was the Gilded Age, the Age of the Robber Barons; the Gay Nineties fell within it—Leon's years. The age of the giants, the money gods. Bell invented the telephone. Edison invented the phonograph, recorded voice, recorded music. Edison invented electric light. Edison was working on moving picture shows. Industry was taking over. Railroads were covering the nation in long lines of track; forests were hacked down to form roads that would never end. Fathers who had traveled west in horse-drawn wagons now stepped into a railway car in San Francisco and stepped off in New York. This thing, this organism, America, was growing more complex: there were trolley cars over ground to take you through the cities; tunnels and pipes coursed underneath. And there was talk of horseless carriages, automobiles. The cities were taking over. The work was in the factories. Children worked, women worked.

Giants made of money were written of but never seen, gods of the new industrial age. They owned everything and lived in some magical place beyond human imagination. Carnegie was the god of Iron,

Rockefeller was Oil, Jay Gould and Leland Stanford were Railroads. J. P. Morgan was Steel. Horatio Alger wrote of Ragged Dick transforming himself from street urchin into millionaire, armed only with ambition, wits, and know-how; in one hundred books he pulled the trick, but in truth the gods had already snapped up all the money. There wasn't any left. That is why we needed to churn out silver money. That is what Bryan said. Silver was for the workingman, the ones who got to the table too late, after the goodies were eaten.

3 · THE PARTY · December 17, 1892, 7 P.M.

And there were parties, galas the likes of which had never been imagined.

Back then . . . in New York . . . music is playing, a string orchestra, men in white jackets so pristine they shimmer like moonlight in the night. Men in silk suits and women in silk dresses swirl on the ballroom floor, spin in unison, in rhythm with the violins, the harps, the falsetto crooning some song that was auditioned last Saturday night at Lucy Vanderbilt's and is fast becoming all the rage. From eye level, if you are a dancer on the floor, or a young man sipping martinis at the bar, the silk swirls in circles, wrapping round, waiters' corkscrews. But if you are gazing from above, if you are Andrew Carnegie, J. P. Morgan, if you are Jay Gould, or John Rockefeller, or some other god gazing down, the men and women, rich as they are, beautiful as they are, flowing to the music like champagne, would seem like cogs in a machine just invented to manufacture steel tubes at twice the speed and a third of the cost.

Or you may be Morris Vandeveer, beaming up at the musicians *(angels of sound! the finest New York City has to offer)* as they tune up on your balcony. You have had the balustrade completely redone for this party: last week a band of Italians straight off the boat finished sculpting a line of gargoyles who now poke out from the rails, laughing and crying and howling, all in gold foil *(Price be damned! Just tell me how many zeroes)*, proud of this party you are hosting, this celebration *of life! of America!,* brushing a speck off the epaulette of a waiter strolling by, bending over to sneak a peek at the French maid, herself bent over *(quite!)* dusting. The mansion you have recently purchased, then refurbished, repainted, reupholstered, and reappointed, from the newly stocked wine and champagne cellar in the basement to the glass-roofed atrium on the penthouse floor. It is four buildings, really, tunneled together underneath and merged by removing the interior walls and planting a courtyard in the middle that is a patch of woods and pasture and gardens smack in the center of the fast-growing city. Morris is wearing a black silk suit covered by a white silk robe as he waltzes from guest to guest, holding a crystal goblet that is always filled with champagne and yet he is always drinking it. (As the knocker sounded, marking the arrival of the first guests, Morris was naked as a babe, innocent in thought and—if one took a liberal attitude toward the efforts being made by this girl, Lily, who lay next to him in bed, using an experienced tongue and gentle nibble of teeth—*deed.*) His garb gives the appearance of pajamas, something ludicrous and silly, which is how Morris Vandeveer appears, kissing each newly arriving guest on each cheek, directing the servant to hand over a glass and fill it to the brim.

Money is everywhere. It is fruit that falls from the trees, it is manna, something you pluck from the ground and stuff in your mouth as you run, a waterfall that rushes down the curving grand staircase of the Vandeveers' mansion on Fifth Avenue where this party is being held. It must be a waltz the orchestra is playing. A perfect world, purchased for an evening.

The visitors to Château Vandeveer have arrived in lavish carriages that wait for them on the avenue outside. Every man—drivers and guests—wears a hat. Most wear a mustache. The guests wear tails, black ties, top hats made of beaver pelt. The drivers outside pull wool caps over their ears to fend off the cold as they chat over cigars and pipe tobacco, strap onto their horses burlap feed bags stuffed with oats. Those garish futurists who use the horseless variety will tinker with the engine, unscrew a bolt or a nut, try to figure out how the magical machine is able to transport them without legs. Someone starts a fire in a pail and they warm hands, toss apple cores to shoe away the bums, the street urchins gazing at their grubby, unshaven faces in the polished glass, rubbing mud on as if it were makeup, slicking back their hair as if their refurbished image would transport them into the cab of the owners, their clothes, their lives. . . .

While the guests linger and wait for the meals and the usual, unusual festivities, there is the customary chatter, of strikes and immigrants, anarchists and moral decline.

"We are becoming a nation of swarthy Europeans, of Jews, of Negroes," someone says.

"At the Van Pelts' last month the anarchists tried to beat down the doors during the ball. We were trapped inside and on the last bottle of champagne."

"That's rich," says Morris Vandeveer, floating by, tossing out, like pansy petals, toast wedges dolloped with caviar, flights of champagne just carried like newborn chicks from the cellar.

"We are doing our damnedest to turn Darwin on his head; by water we bring beasts to our shores."

"Are we not a Christian nation?"

"Rockefeller had it right," someone howls. "God gave me my money!"

"Here! Here!" and the clink of glasses.

4 · LEON · 1879

Transportation is slow and cumbersome but getting faster all the time. From the Vandeveers' you would walk down Fifth Avenue, if you care to, or jump a trolley, or ride a carriage or just a horse, till you reach water where you can take a mule-drawn barge down canals newly constructed with the thundering confidence that for the next century American commerce will travel only over these narrow waterways; pack a box with bread, cured meats—it will be several weeks' journey to Alpena, Michigan, a town where immigrants go when they get lost on the way to Detroit. You walk down an alley with a butcher so near on one side you hear the chickens in the mornings when the man goes at them with the cleaver and on the other side's a place the men go to drink after work and in between there's this dusty shack where the Czolgoszes live.

He is just a boy, Leon, and you pronounce his last name like the noise of a train and the coal they shovel in it and what the women say when they see a mouse skitter cross the floor all mixed up: Choalgosh.

There's a game he plays with a can his brother stomped on to make it kinda like a ball and you kick it.

It is before work and the sun hasn't gotten up yet. Waldek would tap Leon on the back and wake him up and they'd slip outside quiet so their mom and dad wouldn't hear. Then Waldek would pull out from his coat pocket or from a gutter or Leon couldn't be sure from where but there it was, silver and glimmering in the streetlamps, and Leon could see his toothy smile in the bent metal, refracted in the angles. Waldek would lay stones on each side of the road at one end, and in between that was one goal, and then he'd lay two on the other end.

"You kick the can," Waldek says. "It's not a can, it's a ball and you kick it."

"I kick it with my foot," Leon says, pointing at the end of his leg.

"Yes," Waldek says. "That's your foot. You kick it. It's a ball."

On the weekends and at nights there were other kids, too, and the games were wild and the city was a field you could go everywhere. But in the early mornings before work it was only Waldek and Leon. Sometimes his mother is watching at the window and sometimes she taps on the glass and sometimes Leon can't see her but still he knows she is there.

Run toward the boy with the ball, you try a move, a jig, a sidestep to get past. Watch Waldek and that's how you learn how to do it. Nudge your toe under the ball and kick and it goes up in the air.

Waldek stands still and the ball flies over Leon's head, that's how high. Turn around and it's sailed through the goal, between the stones.

His mother's clapping those long delicate hands together, and she'll blow Leon a kiss when he scores one.

When you turn back around, Waldek's walking on his hands, upside down, laughing.

"Here's how," Waldek says. "First you crouch like a frog. Then you tip forward so you lean your shins against the back of your arms. Then lift your legs up."

You try to do it but it's hard so you watch. You don't know what your shins are and besides you tip over when you try.

"Here. Try it slow. I'll hold the back of your legs. I'll hold your shins."

So Waldek grabs Leon's legs and lifts him up and now he's standing, standing on his head. *Ha ha! The world's upside down!*

The sun is peeking out now, and the rooster cries across the street, and Leon wonders why, and there comes the fat man in the apron and the meat cleaver, but upside down—*ha ha!*—and the rooster runs out in the road and the fat man with the blood-splattered apron chases him, both upside down, they are dancing on a ceiling though they think they are right side up. The man swings the cleaver, and the rooster struts just ahead of the blade. Waldek laughs and the man steps toward him, but then the rooster struts close and this time the blade hits and the head of the rooster flies off, upside down, dancing on the ceiling; the rooster's head is in the sky, lying there, disembodied, blood trailing off from the neck, like some star, some constellation that the butcher looks up at.

And what they say about when you kill a chicken, that it still moves after it's dead? That it still talks and squawks and won't give up? That it doesn't recognize death like it's supposed to? It's true. Leon sees, upside down, Waldek holding his legs, the world tipped askew. *Look, Waldek. That's something they say that is true.*

5 · THE TIMES · 1877

This was the age of the Great Strikes. It was the age of America's almost revolution.

The strikes began in Baltimore with a single strike, one working unit, one employer, one trade. The Chesapeake & Ohio Railroad was demanding that its firemen take a reduction in pay, from $1.75 a day to $1.58. The workers refused. On their current wages they could hardly get by. They struck.

The railroad's demand hit a chord; the company had gone too far. Other workers joined the strike in solidarity: can makers, box makers. Union and nonunion alike. They shut down the freight lines. The strikes spread beyond Baltimore, to West Virginia, Pennsylvania, New York. They spread beyond the C&O, beyond railroads. There were demonstrations, rallies. Philadelphia, Columbus, Cincinnati, St. Louis. Buffalo, New York City, Syracuse. Albany, Pittsburgh, Trenton. Chicago, Fort Wayne. San Francisco. Plants were closing, workers were in the streets. Militia were called in. In Baltimore they killed two, wounded many more. Thousands—women, men, children—were amassing in the cities. In Pittsburgh, the Philadelphia militia killed sixteen. When the Pittsburgh militia saw the carnage, they joined sides with the workers. The mob raided stores throughout the city and seized hundreds of rifles and revolvers. Thousands were armed. They burned train cars. They took what they believed to be rightfully theirs, without regard for the property rules of the governing elite. Everywhere there were fights, gunfire. Soldiers were killed, workers were killed.

"The mob is a wild beast and needs to be shot down," one newspaper wrote.

"Chicago is in possession of communists," said another.

President Rutherford B. Hayes was urged to call in federal troops to put down the uprising.

The renowned preacher, Henry Ward Beecher, preached that a dollar a day was not enough for a man who insisted on drinking beer and smoking, but more than sufficient for a prudent family that practiced self-denial, who could make do with bread and water. After all, the Reverend said, the great laws of political economy demanded that the railroad companies reduce their pay. The communistic principles the strikers sought would destroy the individuality of the person, and individual liberty itself. The strikers' way was not that of the Lord.

The head of the Pennsylvania Railroad, Tom Scott, said what the strikers needed was a rifle diet for a few days. See how they like that kind of bread.

It could no longer be called a strike. It was not just a call for improved conditions or wages. Workers were now rebelling without specified demands. They could not be palliated with a few more dollars, an hour off each week. There was something more fundamental at issue, deeper concerns that needed to be addressed. And these were not demands. The workers were not *asking* for anything. They were out in the streets, ready to take what was rightfully theirs.

It had happened, finally, in America.

In months, if not weeks, the revolution would prevail. By 1878 at the latest.

6 · McKINLEY · 1870

To get from New York you take a series of trolleys in the city, then a train that runs on a new line of tracks heading south and west—if you stay on it will take you clear to Indian country—but get off when the land gets pasture-like, cattle grazing on farms where money trees do not grow but there is grain and corn . . . Ohio. Canton.

It must be close to midnight, but it's still warm out on the road midst the fields.

A girl who has wandered, without realizing it, into young womanhood, is seated on the bench seat of a carriage beside a boy who, tentatively holding the reins of the driver horse, raced into manhood too quickly.

"When did you fall in love with me?" Ida, the girl, says.

It is the sort of brash thing she always says, the young man thinks. That's what they teach them at Brooke Hall. William doesn't know of such schools but it must be where rich girls learn to act rich.

"I asked you a question, Major McKinley. Was it the first time, at the bank? Was it me or the smell of the money?"

He thinks she is serious for a moment, but then her mouth breaks out in a grin that giggles. She's too fast for him, too quick.

"I'm not certain, Miss Saxton, if a young lady should be asking such—"

"Well, Major, this young lady wishes to know. You were on line to make your deposit. The busy men were in the back puffing their awful cigars; I was sick with the smoke, it was terrible. You had never seen such beauty, unparalleled. Or was it later, at the church social?"

You are a beauty, McKinley wishes to say. In between Ida's fluttering lids he catches the moonlight reflecting in her dark eyes. The wonder of that image. Her smile beaming. He actually feels his breath stop for an instant, like that.

"Major?" she says. "I'm still waiting for an answer. And, Major, is that a smile I detect on your face, or is the moonlight playing tricks?"

Whoa!—A man stepped out in front of the buggy. McKinley had lost track of the road, that he was driving, where he was. He pulls the reins up, slowing the horse, then trots it to the side of the road to let the traffic pass.

"All right then, how close did you come to dying in the war? Did you see a dead body? Did you hold one? Did you see their spirits rise out of their corpses like ghosts on a foggy night like this one out in the fields? I believe in spirits; in Venice my sister Pina and I saw one, I swear to the Lord; on the Grand Canal one night our gondola passed a ghost rising out from the waters. We all have spirits; do you?"

Before he can even get a grasp of where this line of questions has come from, she has jumped out of the buggy and runs. There is a pasture of wheat; harvesttime is soon, so the stalks are tall and thick and the wind blows them away from her as she runs through the field like a wave rippling toward shore. She has seen the ocean; the major probably hasn't, and what's more, she imagines he never will. A quiet landlocked life in Canton is what she sees for him, successful, secure, but never far from home. Which is fine. She has had her travels, her months in Europe so vivid she will always be able to travel back in her mind to the foggy bogs of Scotland, the majesty of Saint Peter's in Rome, Michelangelo's *Captives,* mortals wrestling in constant battle with this life. So they can live in Canton, if that is how it shall be, and rocking in her girlhood chair she will travel back across the Atlantic.

She glances back as she runs. The major is following her.

"Do you see spirits in the field, Major McKinley?" she yells. "They're blowing down the wheat, letting us pass."

He staggers after her. No, he didn't see spirits in the battlefield. Antietam was the closest, he imagines. Even saw a cannonball land in a man's chest. The food wagon he was pulling out to the front lines got stuck, and as he was digging the wheels out of the mud the cannon fired in front of him. There was a soldier he had just handed coffee to, and he heard him scream and ran toward the scream. Colonel Hayes would take it for bravery, a heroic effort, but it was reflex. The boy's face he will never forget. Dark piercing eyes canopied by a thick stalk of eyebrows. Slavic if he had to guess. He was gurgling blood already, and when William picked up his head, the red dribbled out of his mouth like a baby, down his lap. The coffee still on his breath, the mug had been in his hand when he was hit. Then he was gone. There were no spirits. There is God in His Heaven and a better life than this but no spirits.

He looks up and doesn't see her, only an impress of wheat before him, the wave the wind leaves in its wake. There seems to be a funnel of dust rising up beyond the fields, on the edge of the horizon. Then a giggle, Ida's laugh, and as he runs on there she is, Ida, rolling, rollicking in the wheat, her silky brown hair no longer pinned up but wrapping round her face in a veil.

"I would think Brooke Hall would teach young ladies to be, how should I say, young ladies?" There, he has said it. He has never seen anything like this, her senseless frivolity. One simply does not—

"The major is a shy one," she says, again with a giggle. "Who could have known?"

"It's not— I'm not— it's just—. Where is your brother George, anyway? If your father hears of this, someone sees, hears, you, and the chaperone is—." He stops himself. She is beside herself with laughter now.

"You noticed that young lady at the store, where George said he had some items to buy?"

McKinley nods.

"I should think that George is painting a nude portrait of her at this very moment. Without paint or canvas."

Ida rolls to her feet and runs on. McKinley has never known a girl like this one. Never known a girl before, true, other than his sisters, but that is not the point. It is just this Ida Saxton. He is drawn to her, he cannot help it.

"You don't dance, do you?" McKinley yells, chasing her again through the field. "There are limits, after all. Or drink? The Lord does set His limits!"

As he runs he glances back to see if the buggy is still there, if anyone is watching. There is no one. She is running and the wheat is rolling down in waves and he is gaining on her and her laugh is riding the wind too, filling the field on this magical, moonlit night.

He catches up, runs alongside her. She is hitching up her long blue dress and petticoats so she can run, and he could rub her silken hair between his fingers, it is so smooth and fine. Ida is laughing; she is laughing enough to test the Lord on His limits. Despite himself, the muscles in his face relax, her smile infects him. The wheat is laughing, the moon, the stars.

"It was the first time," he yells out. "The very first instant I set eyes."

"Major?" she says.

"At the bank. I was certain the first time I saw you at your father's bank."

7 · THE PARTY · December 17, 1892, 8 P.M.

Back to New York . . . Fifth Avenue . . . inside the grand house that glowers down at the street below as if it were a moat, cordoning off invaders from without *(but what about from within?)* . . . the guests are presented with menus painted in gold on polished coconuts; they dine to a chorus of nightingales, blackbirds, canaries, and Neapolitan singers in native garb (Morris appears, from who knows where, in the same absurd Italian suit, silky and hanging loose, and mouths the words with the band; it's a hoot, everyone agrees, *pure Morris Vandeveer*). The diners drink *Mumm's Extra Dry* and *Moët & Chandon Brut,* and upon their golden plates and bowls find heaping servings of small Blue Point oysters, *lemardelais à la Princess,* green turtle soup, lobster, columbine of chicken (California style), roast mountain sheep (with puree of chestnuts), Brussels sprouts sauté, *amontillado pasado,* new asparagus with cream sauce and vinaigrette, diamondback terrapin, ruddy duck, fresh strawberries, blue raspberries, vanilla mousse.

In the center of each table is a lake in which pairs of swans glide above fish, bright yellow, blue, and black, and floating atop the water are blooming water lilies and tiny barges carrying smoked salmon and shad roe on toast. The waiters will net them for you if you like. Wave for them; clap. Ring the bell near the bread dish.

The men must have a paunch earned from excess. You must light a good cigar, puff, exhale, puff again. In one hand you loosely coddle the heavy crystal of a highball. You must have a brandy, have a whiskey. Your wife does not approve, but it is after dinner now and there are no ladies in this room; the men have retired to the den. The walls are lined with engraved oak and above the dark seasoned wood are paintings of barely clad maidens chased by lustful satyrs who grab at the ladies' flowing, diaphanous robes. There must be a fire raging in a fireplace large enough to fit the Columbia football team, burning logs so wide they must be from California, or some equally foreign state.

You think you hear a smash from somewhere, broken glass, a door that slammed, something, it startles you, but the party goes on so you ignore it. You find a plush leather chair, sink into the soft seat. Take a puff on your cigar, take another. Encase yourself in smoke.

Morris Vandeveer has spent $343,000 for this evening, you are told, to entertain fewer than one hundred guests for an evening. A shipload of immigrants, Italians, Jews, and Irish, *en masse,* will not see that amount of money in their lifetimes—in three lifetimes. You could fill this mansion with the wretches from those ships, stack their bodies like cords of wood in the Ballroom with its fifty-foot frescoed ceilings modeled after the Sistine Chapel (the Creation, Adam and Eve cast out from the Garden), the Great Room, the Foyer. . . .

Your friend, the great industrialist Henry Clay Frick, is there, the great man of iron and coke; he has just returned from England and France with a crateload of paintings. There is a reporter at the table, a man from California who wants to know how Frick got his money and how much his workers, the coal miners, receive for their troubles. Frick brushes him off.

"This is a party, Mr. Bierce," Frick says. "I was speaking of art. Of darkness, light and shadow."

The reporter, Ambrose Bierce is his name, ambles off in search of a fresh drink, and Frick continues.

"The Dutch have this way where the light emerges seemingly from out of nowhere on the canvas," Frick says. "It's done with earth tones, brown and gray and red, even black, and then there's a side of a face illuminated, a glow that looks like it emanates from within. Here is a girl with yellow flower petals reflecting in her cheeks. The artist captures a beauty not to be found in this world. It's the oils, the way the canvas absorbs the paint."

Frick's eyes are lit up too, as he says this; the recollection of the paintings brings their own glow.

"What are you saying, Frick?" says Morris Vandeveer, passing by. (Mark Hanna, his comrade in conversation, has gone silent and waved down a whiskey from a passing waiter.) "Are you saying man paints a beauty God cannot capture?"

"What I'm saying," says Henry Clay Frick, "is that man paints a beauty he can never be."

8 · EMMA · 1884

And in Russia . . . young Emma Goldman runs through a field of
light and flowers and shadows where a goatherd, an older, wilder
boy, has kissed her hard and they have embraced in the rolling grain
and now she is running back for dinner. Walking home from school
she had seen him, she lugging her books in a satchel, he skipping rocks
over the tips of the grass blades, along the perimeter of his flock, forc-
ing the stragglers back into the fold. He had looked back at her once,
and the next day they walked along together as the sun dashed over
the hills, hoarding its light. They would walk more each night, their
minds on parallel tracks, conversing silently, and then he said he had a
secret place where there was a hollow under the cliff; it was like a cave,
no one would see them inside.

When she returned home, it was dark and there was her father,
iron-backed at the kitchen table, potato soup oozing onto the gray
wires of his beard. Once Emma opened the door he sprang up; the
wind must have circled in and picked him up, propelled him toward
her. They merged to form one suffocating force, all-powerful and
seemingly invincible, the bitter Russian cold, the Goldman hovel, the
old man's piercing glare. A howl whistled from the swerving trees outside into her father's barrel chest, bulging out the metal staves.

The spoon he plunged into the pasty soup, and he opened his
mouth and Emma squinted her eyes and shut her ears; but even if she
could cut out the sound, she knew the words anyway. She could feel his
baritone through the wood planks of the floor, the message rebounded
up through her legs into her stomach, it made her queasy. Where had
she been, it was dark, what sort of girl, there was talk in town, they
were an honorable family, poor but strong in the soul, God sees all,
Emma, the rabbi, in temple you should see how he gives me looks.

What you did was stay motionless and try to drift from your body
so when he grabbed you by the shoulders and dragged you into your
room and glared at you in that way that burned and shook your nerves,

you weren't really there. Her sister Lena was snapping a branch to toss into the stove, then standing up to stir the soup. She turned and gave Emma a look that almost winked. There was a boat to America and Lena had saved some money, she knew someone, there were plans. She was older, she said, she could go now. To New York. That was all Emma knew—the words, *New York*. It was a magic place you dreamt of. Children in town heard from friends whose parents' cousins had been. There were castles there, circuses; there were towers up to the sky and contraptions you could hardly imagine. *Freedom* was what it was, though Emma wasn't clear what the word meant. Her Uncle Herschel, the one her father snarled was a nihilist—the Cossacks took him away and what do you expect when you say such things about the tsar, you can think them but to shout them to the world?—Herschel spoke of freedom, in English even. Maybe it was part of the magic, the heart of the dream.

Coming home from school, the goatherd boy had not brought her to the cave; Emma had searched him out.

They never exchanged names. She has given the boy the name Orpheus because their love in the fields is music and dance, something she can sing to herself hours later, alone in her bed.

And every night walking home there's this gnawing in her stomach; she labors to breathe—it's her throat, it's her chest, it's her nerves. When she opens the door at home, her father will grab her by the shoulders so close she will feel his beard scratch her face and there will be that look in his eyes. When she let the boy have his way with her, she saw that look in her father's eyes—she couldn't block it out—and she smiled fierce, but when she is home her father pushes her hard against the wall and those eyes burn down upon you and the door slams shut and she has the urge to run, to escape, she will run, once there is a way to escape, to gain passage. She will escape to America.

9 · HAYMARKET · 1887

There were heroes in America, ghosts who tried to remake the world. There were the Haymarket martyrs—Albert Parsons, August Spies, Louis Lingg, Samuel Fielden, Michael Schwab, Oscar Neebe, George Engel, Adolph Fischer—innocent men, wrongly convicted by the State of Illinois. They were poets too, Parsons and Spies anyway, at least when they faced death.

The speeches they gave after they were sentenced were prophecy and music; it was as if their ideals planted them high on a cliff where they could gaze out over the mountains, beyond the canyons in which their tribesmen lived, and there they saw another world.

And dead Albert Parsons and August Spies and the rest of the Haymarket martyrs were like ghosts, they *were* ghosts, after they were murdered by the State of Illinois on November 11, 1887. Their crime? Two crimes, actually. They were anarchists, they believed that America was a plaything of the wealthy, laws were wielded by the powerful to subjugate the weak, the system needed to be destroyed and replaced with . . . well . . . there were a range of options . . . freedom has its necessary vagaries . . . but if you demand an answer . . . then . . . basically . . . nothing.

And that was the message of those ghosts, those ghosts who spoke to so many, who spoke to Emma Goldman and Alexander Berkman.

And the other crime of Albert Parsons, August Spies, and the rest of the Haymarket martyrs? Besides their beliefs?

Wrong place, wrong time.

10 · THE PARTY · December 17, 1892, 9 P.M.

There are professors at your table too, from Columbia, Harvard, and Yale. If you are Marcus Hanna, a man of business, coal, then newspapers—a self-made man—you rarely hear talk in such intellectual tones. You are accustomed to dealing on the surface of things, wages and prices, supply, demand. But here you listen to the men of science, the philosophers, anthropologists. Scientists of the body, earth, the social organism.

"We are slightly less than three decades from the war," one professor says, an anthropologist from England, "when all the talk was slavery. Of course the Southern practices were depraved. You will not hear a defense of the slaver from me. And yet, one would have thought from all the abolitionists' prattle that once we loosened the Negro from his chains we would find our dark brethren climbing to all heights in society, in business and politics, what have you. But you see nothing of the kind. Here they are, no longer chattel, but still on the lowest rung."

"You must give them time, Professor," another chimes in. "And you still hear stories from the South. These lynchings and so on."

"Of course, of course," the British professor interrupts, "there are societal factors, I'm well aware. There always are. But as scientists, we must get to the root of the matter. Who are these Negroes? I have studied—"

"Professor," another whispers, motioning him to lower his voice while a colored waiter—a huge man, well over six feet—removes dishes from the table.

"No, there's no harm in a man knowing the truth about himself and his race. As I was saying," the professor raises his voice a notch now and turns toward the colored man. "I have studied them, and I have found the following. The Negro children may be sharp, intelligent, full of vivacity, but on approaching the adult period a gradual change sets in. The intellect becomes clouded, animation gives place to a lethargy, briskness becomes indolence. The reason, I have deduced, is that the growth of the Negro brain must be arrested by the premature closing of the cranial sutures and the frontal bone. There is no doubt the arrest or deterioration in mental development is largely responsible for the fact that after puberty sexual matters take the first place in the Negro's life and thoughts. You will not be surprised to find in the Negro a lowered morality, as evidenced by the higher rates one finds in our prisons. Contrast with the white, whose brainpan expands, allowing for proper development."

Mark Hanna, listening to the professor's discourse, thinks: balderdash. Mark Hanna says, loudly, emphatically, as he puffs a long stream of cigar smoke toward the face of the Brit, "Balderdash. Professor," Hanna says, "give a colored man money, facts, and opportunity, he'll latch on to it fast as a white. Faster, if I may, than your Irish."

"Mr.—"

"Hanna. Marcus Alonzo Hanna. We know this even in my beloved Ohio. I'm no scientist, I'm a man of business, but I'll bet I've spoken to more Negroes in a week than you, Professor, have studied behind a glass in your life. They can work you proud and thank you for the chance more than many of your college boys, I'd wager."

"Mr. Hanna, you misunderstand. This is not some theory I've picked up in the course of anecdotal wanderings, nor some personal bias. This is scientific fact. Mentally, the Negro is inferior to the white."

Hanna turns and walks away toward . . . a mayor, a congressman, a senator, somebody—Hanna isn't certain—and another businessman speaks to fill the void.

"And you see this as part of the evolutionary scheme, Professor?"

"Darwin took only the first step in the analysis," says a new voice, a professor from Yale.

"Yes, Professor Sumner, please explain."

"Put simply, the millionaires of the present day are the product of natural selection. The business world is the jungle of old, the swamps out of which we emerged long ago. Their success—your success, gentlemen—is the survival of the fittest" (the men listening pat their vest-covered bellies, slip open a button or two), "the working out of a law of nature and a law, if you will, of God."

To which, Professor Sumner having said all that needs to be said, there are nods and guffaws, a prayerful gaze heavenward, to the ceiling, and hurrumphs all around. Here's how, and the downing of drinks.

II · SHIPS

And there were beings who came to this country in droves back in those days, fully formed, gazing out at the nothingness, the blank dreamscape out there on the horizon, America.

One ship leaves Russia for Hamburg, then debarks across the Atlantic, and peeking her head out from the rails on the deck one early morning a girl sees a gigantic statue of a lady, arm raised, and she knows it is an image she has heard talk of. Here is the land of freedom, the girl believes this so much she is crying, sobbing as she gazes at the giant lady. 1885: Emma Goldman is sixteen years old.

And William McKinley's ancestors came over in 1743, on another ship. Its hold was not stuffed with Slavs or Russians, Catholics or Jews, crying babies, the stench of the poor, the clatter of foreign tongues. The decks are clean, the hands quick and able. The snap of fingers brings to the man seated on the deck sliced marbled beef, peeled orange sections, banana, apples, honey, assembled to form the image of man. There are Negroes dancing. The slave ship the dancers came from sails just behind them, still in sight over the waves.

Beneath the deck, in humbler quarters, lie David McKinley and his wife, Esther. Before leaving Scotland David has consulted with real estate men who assured him that the money he carries with him is sufficient to buy him three hundred acres or more in this new land.

And elsewhere on Emma's ship the water rocks suddenly, causing a young man to slip; the crutches that hold him up fall and he drops to the deck. He watches as the world lolls on its side like a dolphin frolicking in the waves, and his crutches slide down toward the water. He scurries after them on his knees, but how can he ever get there fast enough? And how, without them, will he be able to walk in this new land? So how will he find work in America?

But just as he crawls to the edge of the deck, at the rails his hands grasp a girl's wooden shoe. The girl, just younger than himself if he had to guess—sixteen, seventeen—leans down and catches his crutches just before they go over the edge. She hands them to him. He takes them, nods thanks, and pulls himself up.

And that is how Morris Steinglitz, long before he would begin to call himself Morris Vandeveer, met his wife-to-be, Amelia.

12 · THE PARTY · December 17, 1892, 11:30 P.M.

Back on Fifth Avenue . . . in the Hunt Room, which runs into a courtyard that is the intersection of the four buildings that make up the Vandeveer mansion . . . illuminated by gaslights and candles strung along wires attached at the opposing walls . . . where earlier this evening Morris Vandeveer, your host, closed the massive redwood doors and opened a secret hatch, out of which emerged a family of small deer, foxes, a bevy of doves, a dog, a warthog, a zebra, then had his boys hand you and the other guests rifles and . . . *have at it! The hunt was on!* The room was a forest, it appeared to be a forest, and somehow there was fog and a stream where there should have been a hallway. The trick was to bag the animals without doing in a fellow guest. . . .

Carnegie is there (one warthog: he hauled it before the fire by the tusks), and Frick (a zebra), and Marcus Alonzo Hanna, who bagged a pair of doves and the ear of a Negro servant. It was an accident: Hanna gave the man a dollar for his troubles.

. . .

Morris is no hunter; he can't stand the sight or feel of a gun. He refuses to touch any device, he says, manufactured for the sole purpose of destroying another life, or one's own. The men laugh when he says it, *pure Morris, so Vandeveer,* and imagine him a joker, but the fact remains that the firearms he has purchased solely for this occasion will be given to his guests as party favors to take home when the night's done.

Why does Morris Vandeveer sponsor a hunt when he despises the very idea so?

Because he loves irony.

Because he finds that contrast is what gives life color and tone.

Because his party planner promised him it was the one thing that had not been done this season, it would make news, be *all the talk,* on the social circuit.

Because he believes, at some level half-submerged below conscious thought, that his guests, in the midst of these cruel and reckless shooting games, will see the awfulness of it all, violence, killing, man's inhumanity and such, thus triggering the sort of revolutions that alter lives and history.

Because the idea just came to him one night and he ran with it.

Because some things are unexplainable.

13 · THE TIMES · 1885

At this time Sigmund Freud was a young doctor in Austria, just getting his hands wet, so to speak, in his explorations of the mind. It would be some time before his ideas, about the psychic repercussions of suppressing one's sexual impulses, for example, would become well known, at which time Anthony Comstock, the morality policeman of the day, would have been able to find someone medically trained with a couch, to whom he could hash it all out, what was really going on in his mind. It would be complicated and would be all about dreams. The idea was that truth was something you try to hide from yourself, a shell game, a three-card monte of the mind.

There was a lot of that going on back then: deceptions, shell games with the truth.

14 · THE PARTY · December 17, 1892, 2 A.M.

Upstairs, after the Hunt, the men are led into an auxiliary dining hall where they sit around a vast oval table of polished walnut. There has been much drink. Their wives have been brought to their rooms upstairs, they are assured. The men are awaiting something, some special surprise of their host.

Morris is nowhere to be seen, he has vanished who knows where *(so Morris! so Vandeveer!)*. The rumor is that there is a room upstairs with a costumed ball, where the dancers do not even know the genders of those with whom they frolic, much less their names. There is talk of bedroom suites adjoining the ballroom, dark but for flickering candle-light, jars of condoms in the entrance ways: *Help yourself, boys and girls! There's enough madness in the world!*

Morris pirouettes, his hands outstretched above his head, then disappears into another darkened room where a girl, flat-chested and boyish, awaits him on a feather bed.

And downstairs, the festivities continue, as if Morris is conducting them from some unknown, hidden post.

The doors open and a team of ten Negroes enters the room. They are huge, bare-chested, well-muscled, straight from an auction block of the era just past. On their shoulders they carry a platter that must be ten feet around, and on it sits a covered golden plate, equally large. They lay the platter on the table before the guests. Trumpets sound, a small orchestra appears on a balcony, and the cover is ceremoniously lifted.

As the Negroes stride out of the room, Morris Vandeveer appears, *who knows from where.* He waves his hand to display what lays on the huge golden plate: a pie, eight foot round, with a risen browned crust. Morris is holding a knife as long as he is. He tries to wield it, gathering all his mustered strength, as David might have, had he the good fortune to be so well-armed, before Goliath. The men around the table are hushed. Morris drags the knife to the edge of the table. Finally he is able to lift it over his head. Then the weight of it takes over, and the blade falls into the pie, leaving a gaping hole in the side. There is a flutter of wings, shrieks, chirps. Blackbirds and doves fly out, one after another, and the men, after initial shocked gasps, applaud.

"But *this,*" Morris Vandeveer says, "is not the dainty dish they set before the king!" Then he claps his hands three times. The musicians strike out some jazzy, vaudeville tune, all fiddles and clarinets.

And suddenly a hole pops in the crust. Then another. Then another. There are three girls, no more than eighteen or nineteen, a blond, a brunette, and a redhead, standing in the pie, stark naked.

PART TWO

THE
HOUSE ON
MARKET STREET

1 · LEON

Leon would wake up with this dream that he was running. There was this place he had to be, this thing he had to get there, but it was never fast enough, time was running out, or the thing, it wasn't there.

2 · LEON · 1885

This is the truth behind the dream:

He is running.

The sweat pours down his brow, salt burns his eyes. He runs and looks for an open door. He jags inside, down the hallways, through neighbors' bedrooms, kitchens. He is looking for people, for women. He knows what he is looking for; his father has told him, his brother Waldek has told him. He knows his mother's condition, and so he knows what he is looking for.

Back home they have called for the doctor; his father has sent Waldek out in the streets for the doctor. This is what his father tells his mother, when she screams and cries out, this is what he tells her.

"He is coming. Any moment he arrives here for you."

She has screamed so long now her voice is worn to a high scratch, wire stretched taut, then cut in the factory. The sheets are wet through, and her hair is as if a torrent of rain has soaked the Czolgoszes' basement apartment.

His father knows enough to tie her legs apart and to the posts. For other children no doctor came, but this he has never seen before.

Leon is still running. The Szeptickis chase him out of their cramped room. He scurries up the stairs and tries the next floor, and he is chased out again; women are in the stairwell screaming at him, looking up, looking down; an older boy, eighteen, nineteen, runs after him, then another boy. The older kids laughing, the fathers screaming.

"It is my mother," Leon says. "She is back home and I need—"

He is clutching the bottle in one hand, the nipple top in the other. The boys chase him out into the street, a horse rears up on his legs in front of him. He ducks down and runs across the street, and when another cab crosses the other way, that is how he gains on the boys for they get stuck behind.

He knows of a Jewish lady down the street.

His father ties her head down to the back of the bed, to stop the wrenching from side to side, the frantic heaving. The baby's hair he can see now, but when he reached inside her and grabbed it and pulled, his wife let out a yell and her hips and legs wrenched him into the wall, his head hit hard on the plaster. That is when he tied her head down. It is better that she does not see.

There is blood. He does not know from where.

"The doctor will not come," she whispers with the small voice that remains.

"He comes. In moments he is here."

"He will not come. We did not pay him. For the last there was no money."

"He said it did not matter. He tells me of an oath. That is money, this is life, he says this to me. The doctor."

"He will not come." Her voice so quiet now she is becoming a spirit, here in the dark room, here in the flickering candlelight. It was the priest then. It was the priest who told him not to come.

He grabs the baby's hair again and pulls.

. . .

Leon loses the older boys around the next corner. Still he runs, dodging the pushcarts, the cabs, the horses and the people passing by. He is past the rest of the Poles now, past the Slavs and Germans. Now he runs through the streets of the foreigners, Irish, Italians. Their clothes and caps are uniforms that identify them, that and the language that switches as he runs and the music, too—reels and fiddles and now a lady sings opera. There are Negroes in the windows. There are street kids he knows to stay away from in the alleys.

He is clenching the bottle in one hand, the nipple top in the other.

And now here are the bearded men, the hair in curls about the ears. Here are the Jews.

"You must remain still," Paul tells his wife. He is holding the baby's head now, the top of the head, but the rest remains hidden inside her. The baby's hair is thick and wet.

His wife says nothing.

He has sent someone to boil water, but he does not know what he will do when it comes, if someone finds water, a pail, if someone can start a fire. He does not know where anyone is. His wife has not said anything for some time.

"Now you push. I will pull and you— Yes, that is it, that is good. The baby is coming out."

It is as if she is saving her last strength to push this child into the world.

Leon has explained to the Jews who he wants, what he needs. He does not know the language or names, but they communicate. The bottle, he points at the bottle in one hand, the nipple top clenched in the other.

They point him up the street, then down an alley, through a door so low that he must bow to enter. There is candlelight, a cry. A baby.

A woman nursing, a mother.

Leon shows her the bottle, the nipple top.

"My mother. My father sent me here," he says.

The woman does not understand.

He holds up again the bottle, the nipple top.

"She is giving birth," Leon says. "Right now, while we speak. I will have a baby brother, a sister, I do not know."

The woman says something in Jewish words he cannot understand. The man who led him here, now standing behind him, speaks. "What she says is, 'Your mother will nurse him. Your mother's milk is best for her baby.' "

"But you do not understand," Leon says. "My father, he has told me that the baby will not live without." Leon holds up the bottle again. "The baby will die, my father says."

The woman speaks again, frustrated, as she continues to nurse.

"Then your mother will nurse him," a man in the doorway says. "You are a boy, you do not understand such things." The man taps the side of his head and circles his finger. The boy's confused.

"NO!" Leon yells so loud the man steps back, and the baby lets loose of her mother's breast and cries. The woman throws up a hand and shouts.

Leon is not confused. He is twelve years old, but he is not a boy. He has been working every day for six years, after school, instead of school, selling shoes, selling newspapers, pushing a cart, hauling water, shoveling manure off the streets, hauling manure, carrying scrap metal from the factory, pouring the molten metal so hot his hair singes from the heat.

His mother is ill and the doctor will not come. There is no money, and the doctor will not come. The baby must have milk, but his mother has no milk to give. He cannot explain it any clearer. That is all he understands. But he understands enough.

The woman shields the baby from him, covers it with her blouse, buttoning up.

Leon lunges at her. The bottle in one hand, he bites the nipple top between his teeth and grabs the woman's breast, tugs it away from the baby, and squeezes. A squirt of milk comes out and he slaps the open end of the bottle over it and squeezes again. The woman is screaming, and the man has turned to run. Leon pulls off the bottle and squeezes the nipple of her breast, the bottle catches the milk. Then again. Again. The woman is screaming and her baby is crying and there are men shouting outside, coming in.

Leon works frantically, squeezing, filling the bottle, then stuffing the bottle in his pocket as he grabs her breast with his teeth. When the men enter, he pulls the rubber nipple over the top of the bottle. The men grab him, but Leon shakes them loose and when they turn to the woman, the mother, he is able to run out the door.

When Leon comes home, his brother Waldek is in the street outside, kicking stones. There are neighbors about, women covered with black shawls and veils, men shaking their heads.

Leon has never seen his brother cry before.

The older men block the doorway, but Waldek parts the way. There are things the boy must learn. There are things you cannot hide from.

When Leon enters the room, he cannot see at first. The candle has burned out and the black stub of the wick floats in a pan of hot liquified wax. There is an odd smell. He hears a snuffle, a cough. His father, on his knees, his head collapsed on the bed, a pool of blood underneath.

A woman he recognizes from upstairs is holding a blanket and is rocking it in her arms. Poking out from the blanket is a head, matted black hair coated in a clear gel.

Leon looks for his mother in the bed, but there is only a white sheet in her form, a ghostly outline of her face, her shoulders, breasts, legs, and arms.

He knows his mother is there but he does not want to bother her just yet.

3 · LEON · 1887

The children are waving arms, shouting. A grown-up points at them, the teacher, a lady. Their mouths move, but it's silent; the window's shut. Flags—red, white, and blue—a map, this is America. A girl looks and sees Leon crouched in the bushes, head poking out on the far side of the glass, outside the classroom. She's seen him before. Her curls, her sky-blue eyes, a smile that twinkles.

After work, newspapers in the morning, toss on a porch, run through town, some customers want you to knock on their door, sometimes a man flips a penny at you, sometimes a lady bends over and her breasts smother you when she kisses you hard. Then when you're finished there's a rag man; you help haul his cart through town. Leon runs orders—we've got shirts, we've got coal, a lantern today, a wheel, we can bang it round for you no charge. You don't know what the words mean, but you say them; the man is a Jew and he tells you what to say. Run up to the stoop, up the stairs. Shout the wares, shout like you believe it. Leon knows enough to keep some coins to himself before, at day's end, he gives his father the rest. A woman is always around his father now and she seems to know, a way she looks at you.

After work, if he hurries, or when the rag man takes lunch, here he is, peeking in at the school. This is America, children. Sing, children. Hold your heart and sing. Silently, through the glass. Sing.

The boys and girls get up to leave and Leon meets them in the park. Running, jumping. The girl with the curls and the sky blue eyes, books lashed with a belt over her shoulder. The boys hurling dirt, sticks, stones, what have you. There are ballgames Leon doesn't understand—pigskin, rawhide, you hit the ball and run, you hit the kid with the ball, you wrestle somebody to the ground.

This time Leon is ready. He is kicking a can already when the kids get out of school and get to the park.

Pointing. Laughing.

"Look."

"What is it?"

"It's not a can," Leon says.

Pointing.

"It's a ball." Leon has pounded it under his feet like Waldek showed him.

"Where's your mother?"

"You're not from school."

"Go back to momma." Laughing. "If you can."

"Look, it's a can."

"Garbage from the ragman's cart."

Pointing. Laughing. And the girl with the curls is nowhere.

"It's not a can. It's a ball and you kick it."

Pointing.

Pointing.

Laughing.

4 · LEON · 1888

The ragman was taken away; there was a young girl, questions he could not answer. Women spat at him as the police shoved him in the paddy wagon, pointing, yelling names, laughing. Leon works in the factories now, spiderlike amalgams of metal that appear functionless and yet there is this rush to produce. More, more. Faster, faster. Economy's booming, what's made today is sold tomorrow. The days are longer, it's harder, but still Leon races to the school afterward; he pokes out of the bushes outside. One night he broke a window, so now he hears the teachers and the children. He does not show himself anymore, he does not play in the park. He listens.

With the money he saves, he buys books.

He learns to read. Waldek helps. His sisters help. There's a young man, Frank, who comes visiting one sister. Frank helps.

Leon can read.

He buys books.

Frank says, "Don't read history. History, you sense it here," tapping his chest. "And here," tapping the side of his head. "Your skull is glass all around. Look. Dream. Remake the world."

Leon listens. It's hard sometimes when there's this grating noise in his head and his stomach goes sour and stings his throat and he clenches his eyes it hurts so; he wonders did his mother feel this, is this how death feels, and then he wakes up and the school is empty. Waldek gives him pills for the pain, nostrums you order in the mail, they're just another type of hurt. Then the pain subsides.

His skull is glass all around. He floats, he sees things: pirate ships in search of buried treasure, street urchins turned millionaires, African safaris.

He listens.

One day the girl with the curls sees Leon in the window and smiles, but he doesn't return the glance. He has learned better.

He reads.

He listens.

He grows older.

5 · LEON · 1889

Leon is kneeling, silent; the priest was speaking. Our Father Was in Heaven. His Only Begotten Son Had Given His Life For You. For Leon. For Waldek. Their Father. Their Mother, he supposed, though he could not understand how that could be. His Was the Glory.

It was all shouted at him like the big print newspaper headlines he used to hawk on the streets of Detroit; you didn't read the articles so only got a vague sense, the gist. Glory. Life Everlasting. Damnation, Hell. Wages of Sin. Sacrifice.

The poor shall always be with us, so sayeth the Lord. There's our relief fund for the less fortunate ones, and did I mention the church renovations? The new organ on order all the way from Pittsburgh? Pass the hat, pass the cup. The poor shall always be with us.

You work through the week and then this is where you go; this is where the workingman, for a moment, is rich. The priest brings you to the kingdom, this is the land of gold. As long as he can remember they brought him to the church, his father, his mother.

The garments were beautiful, the organ was beautiful, the frescoes on the walls of the church.

The priest walks down the aisle waving the smoking incense back and forth, right to left, up and back. The smell is sweet, like a forest pine. It is the smell, and the thunderous organ pipes, that he loves best. It takes him away.

Leon had come to church from the glass factory. When you entered the factory, you saw the furnace before you, a wall of fire, flames tall as a city building, a church steeple, as T-shirted men thrust glowing tongs into the heat. The flames were faces, too, eyes and tongues and laughing mouths that snapped cackles at him. They licked the men's faces and turned them black.

You worked through the night. He would wake up still rubbing the previous day's work from his eyes, grab a slab of dark bread, and walk through the pitch-black streets to the factory, sleepwalking. At work you grabbed a steaming bucket of hot molten liquid and hauled it to the cooler. Don't spill it on your chest or legs or arms for it will burn the skin away. Don't look down at the bucket or the steam will get you. Leon would come home numb from the heat and the weight. Ten, twelve hours, through the night. It made you hard, quiet. Seventy-five cents a day.

The streets were empty. They lived in Pennsylvania now, but it might have still been Michigan. At the end of one alley, planks of wood were nailed across to make a shack, a sheet draped over the front to form a door, outlines of bodies inside, illuminated faintly by embers of a cigarette. The night was moonless, silent but for the occasional cry of a baby from an open window overhead.

The stars were bodies in the sky: a bear, a hammer thrower, a king clutching a thunderbolt in a tight fist. Waldek had explained them to him, but Leon could never make them out. The idea was that this is where the heroes lived past their time, where history is enshrined. There are worlds you cannot see, cannot touch. Time travels alongside us, so what happened before and what happens in the future is happening now, but like in another town, across an ocean, in the sky. Leon will travel there, he senses it, he knows it. At church sometimes he closes his eyes and the organ music fills his head and lifts him into that other land, and when Waldek rustles him awake he cannot recall where he has been or where he is.

"She could have been saved." It was Waldek speaking. Leon had forgotten his brother was there, walking beside him.

"Who?"

"You know. You must have sensed it. Or maybe you were too young."

"I don't—"

"Our mother. The doctor came, and he said there was a way she could be saved. She was too old."

"But the doctor, the money, he was not given the money and so he did not come. That is what Father said."

"That is part true. He would not come because of the money. But the last time he came, months before, he told us she was too old to have another child. There were problems with the baby; he wasn't certain but he had seen the signs before, and she was too old. He would not think that it would turn out. He said he knew a man, not him, but another man could solve such things. He gave a name. He wrote down where he could be found."

Leon saw the flames of the factory appear out of the dark. Then the smoke, thick gray clouds exhaling out of the chimney stacks, obscuring the stars, those gods in heaven, as they drifted to the sky. They walked on, Leon recalling that day, four years ago, running through the streets and then home, holding that rubber nipple on top of the bottle tight as if life depended on it.

The incense, the organ music, it took you away.

The priest spoke of the fires of hell. Leon wondered if he had worked in the factory, if Jesus had, if God. The snapping cackling flames in the dark, the devil.

This was the priest. An old man, gray-haired. The priest Waldek had told him of, the one who spoke to their father and mother days after the doctor's visit. Waldek had come with them, he had heard.

The doctor was tempting them with the devil's tongue, the priest had said to their mother and father. To take the life of the baby, to consider such a thing, guaranteed passage to damnation. It could not be spoken of further in God's house.

Yes, the priest understood she was beyond the best of her child-

bearing years. Yes, she had been ill and the doctor was a man of medicine, not he. He was a man of God, not science. Yes, all true. And all
lies. God asks for sacrifices. It is not ours to question. There was a picture the priest showed them of an old man holding a knife to his son's
neck. Abraham, Isaac. Then he pointed out the cross behind the altar;
the crown of thorns alone was as big as Leon, it seemed like.

Not ours to question.

The sweet smell of the incense filled Leon's nostrils. An altar boy
was swinging it. Leon realized he was alone in the pew. He looked up
and there was his father, on bended knee. His mouth was open. The
priest placed in, gently, expertly, a fragment of the body of Christ.

6 · LEON · 1892

He is on the line, cutting wires. They come at him in huge bales,
twenty-five metal strands bound together, each fifty, sixty feet
long, each suspended on a pulley and rolled at him waist high by the
man to his right: the metal glares against the window of his skull, daz-
zling him, blinding him. Leon grabs a bundle, swings it in position,
and hacks away, cutting as many wires as he can, then twirls it around
and cuts the other side. A boy moves the pulley, tugging the mass of
wires to speed it along. When the wires are cut into ten-foot pieces
and the stray edges are sawed off, Leon rolls them to the next man and
looks to his right in time to catch the next bundle. Four dollars: a fortune for a day's work.

The next bundle is the same as the previous bundle. Leon imagines that beyond his vision the boy reattaches the metal Leon has cut,
undoing his work. The pulley is a loop, there is no point to any of it; it
simply repeats itself.

He wakes when it is still dark; his father wakes him, his brother wakes
him. He finds himself in the room where they cook and eat, standing

before a metal pot. He cups his hands and spoons the cold, dirty water onto his face. If it is cold outside, the water is, too, and it shocks him into readiness. If he is lucky, there is a slice of stale bread to eat, a few sips of coffee, and then Waldek pulls him out the door. By the time he gets to work he is already exhausted from the walk. There's a numbness, a grittiness, a layer of skin he'd like to strip away. Then he finds himself standing before the pulley, grabbing the bales of wire as they are hurled toward him, cutting then shoving them along the pulley. For twelve hours he pushes the bale around the loop, cuts the wire that only regenerates itself like a lizard's tail.

When the day is over, his hands are too sore to grip, his feet have no feeling. He walks home with Waldek.

There are children who walk alongside them, ten years old, twelve years old. They work the same hours, the boys who pull the bales, who pick up the loose strands of wire and jam them back into the bundles. It is not heavy work, but it is dangerous. The bales sliding along the pulley knock them over; the wire is sharp. Eyes are gouged. Heads are cracked. There is no time to grieve the losses. We all have our losses. There is only time for work.

Leon must eat at some point or he could not survive these days, but he cannot recall what or when.

If it is Saturday, there may be a beer with his fellow workers down at the tavern. That he remembers. He does not work Sundays because Sunday is a holy day; they go to church.

He lies in bed to try to sleep and sees the wire spinning madly around the pulley loop; he is ducking and dodging, but the wire beheads him and as the blood begins to spout out of his severed neck, Waldek wakes him up though it is still dark. Time for work.

It is the same day, over and over.

They are in Cleveland, though it might as well be Pennsylvania.

He is thinking about what Waldek and he read together last night—the Polish Bible they ordered in the mail. It was Leon's idea. He wondered if it might be his English, what the priest would say to them in church: Jesus, a misunderstanding. He didn't trust the priest. It was his eyes, the way he didn't look at you when he gave you the wafer, when you spoke in the booth, when he nodded at you as you walked through the doorway. Messages unstated. Leon had decided he had to read the book himself, to see if it was the book, the priest, or his English.

And so they had ordered the Bible. Since it came in the mail Waldek and Leon would take turns reading it when they were not at work, discussing it over meals when their shifts overlapped. It was not what he had been led to believe. There was talk of working people, the poor. There were lepers. Money was not so good. There was talk of money changers, and though Leon and Waldek did not know what that meant, they knew it was not good. There was no talk of the church fund, repairs for the roof, for the organ, new vestments. Things were very different from what the priests here said. There was talk of a rich man blocked from entering an eye of a needle, blessed were the meek. This Jesus had no patience for the wealthy man, the owners, the bankers.

All of a sudden Leon feels sharp points rip skin on his forehead, down his cheek, and he is knocked off his feet. When he opens his eyes, he is looking up from the floor of the factory and there above him the bundle of wires is spinning in circles and the wire stings where it cuts you. He had not seen the bale when it came at him on the pulley and then it was too late, he was upside down *(Look, Waldek!)*; it just happens sometimes—things go askew, his mind was somewhere else.

He feels his face. It is wet and red. Blood pours out. He feels woozy.

When he opens his eyes next, Waldek is standing over him. They are outside of the wire factory, Leon on the ground, his head raised on a stone pillow.

"What were you thinking?" Waldek says. "We thought we had lost you."

"It was not my English," Leon says. "You see, Waldek, I have it figured out. It was not my English."

7 · BIERCE · 1897

A nd there were geniuses of irony roaming the nation back then, men of wry wisdom you would find in taverns slumped on a bar stool, gnawing on a cigar, cross-examining the world. In the age just passed there was Samuel Clemens and now there was Ambrose Bierce, who, at this moment, is combing out his thick black moustache with slender, tobacco-stained fingers, gazing at his reflection in a half-empty whiskey tumbler that transforms his face into a distorted cylindrical form with a reddish hue, a ghostly apparition that, as a writer of the macabre, he appreciates; a man who has been haunted by ghosts since childhood; a man who sees, in life every day, all around him, the extraordinary and the awful and the just plain silly—millionaires playing at sand castles the size of big city blocks, slopped together with the mud of Manhattan mixed with flesh and blood immigrants as mortar, moneyed men who suck life out of the masses like vampires, masses too ignorant to notice *(damned funny, really, with three shots of digestible rotgut in the belly)*; a man who learned, at the ripe age of nineteen when he enlisted and served in the War Between the States, that mankind has become expert in one thing alone: slaughtering his fellows *(the moneyed men had the good sense to purchase lesser souls to serve in their stead on the battlefield)*; a man who was shot in the head with a musket ball, whose head was punctured by a bullet ("Death is not the end," he would later write, "there remains the litigation over the estate") but lived, to write, to pan for gold in the Indians' sacred Black Hills in the Dakota Territory, to one day in 1887 hear a knock on the door of his home in San Francisco and let in a strapping young man with an air of half princely entitlement, half flame-throwing revolutionary, and another half, thrown in for good measure, awkward schoolboy, shy from growing too fast ("I am from the *San Francisco Examiner*"; "Oh, you come from Mr. Hearst"; "I *am* Mr. Hearst"); Bierce is hired on the spot to work for a man great enough to carry with him always his middle name, William Randolph Hearst, he is to report on the sinister interplay between the ruthless moneyed men who rule this great land ("used to be great, anyways; coulda been") like feudal lords, and the venal politicians who bed down with the barons like old diseased harlots ("Drop a dollar in our campaign coffers on the way out, love"), a web of corruption and bribery and selling of the soul by those rare souls with souls to sell: Collis Huntington of the railroads (who, seeing Bierce on the steps of the Capitol one day, beseeches Hearst to cease his incessant investigations and lambastings of the railroad trust, "Every man has his price, Bierce; name yours," to which Bierce replies, "My price is seventy-five million dollars. If, when you are ready to pay, I happen to be out of town, you may hand it over to my friend, the Treasurer of the United States"); John D. Rockefeller; and the bosses' hirelings on the Hill, Congressman William McKinley (about whom, years later, Bierce will write that "If bad institutions and bad men can be got rid of by killing, then the killing must be done," a sentence that his boss, the great Hearst, will never be able to live down), Congressman Thomas Reed, and more; a man who, when his mother dies, rather than go to the funeral, buys drinks all around at the Bohemian Club; a man who, when his father dies, rather than go to the funeral, buys drinks all around at the Bohemian Club; whose son walks in on his girlfriend's lover one day and shoots him dead, then kills himself; a man who writes and drinks and laughs, for all you can do in this world is laugh, laugh at everything; who, one day, years from now, sensing the end, will say his farewells and then ride a horse into the uncharted Mexican wilderness, into the teeth of a raging civil war ("Farewell, this civilized life—so called") and will never be heard from again; but now, at this moment, resting on a bar stool at Justus Schwab's saloon in New York City, he raises the tumbler that holds the sacrament that is what remains of his whiskey, and sings:

> *My country tis of thee*
> *Sweet land of felony*
> *Of thee I sing!*
> *Land where my father fried*
> *Young witches and applied*
> *Whips to the Quakers' hides*
> *And made them spring!*

8 · MORRIS · 1886

And there were nameless men, too, seated at other bars, immigrants so green from the boat they wouldn't be sure if his song was parody or truth. There was Morris Steinglitz, who downs a shot of cheap rotgut, slaps a coin on the bar, then stuffs his crutches under his armpits and labors out of the saloon. In his native Germany his education earned him a teacher's post (philosophy, history), but in two days visiting the local schools he has learned that he will have to try something new here in America. His crutches will keep him from most hard labor, and street peddling will be difficult.

Morris struggles to make his way down the street, his oversized crutches catapulting him up forward with each step. He stops in wherever he sees a WORK or HIRE sign, or lines of men waiting. At the end of the day he finds himself outside of some sort of slaughterhouse; what he knows is the smell of meat. Morris ditches his crutches under the fence beside him, then slides his right foot along the gravel when it's his turn to speak to the foreman.

"Foot's asleep," Morris says.

The foreman hadn't even looked up to see him; his eyes are on a paper in his hand.

"Grind meat before?" the foreman asks.

Morris pauses.

"I've dissected," he says. "Chopped things into pieces so tiny," Morris pinches his fingers close together, "a student can understand."

The foreman looks up and squints at Morris to get a look.

"Ever make sausage?"

"Let me tell it this way," Morris says. "In Germany I would gather miscellaneous items, then stuff them into tubes of casing, and tie the ends together for ease to consume."

9 · EMMA · 1889

Standing at the bar in Justus Schwab's saloon, Emma still has the feeling that overtook her the first time she walked through these doors almost six months ago, the day she arrived in Manhattan from her sister's place in Rochester. The bar is packed, patrons perched on every stool, others standing, crowding in between. The air is hot and loud with arguments exuding the passionate certainty that these debates will turn the course of history. There are others listening, heads nodding back and forth between the combatants, laughing between sips of cold beer. By now Emma knows the arguments without even hearing them. There are many strands (violence or pacifism? religion or atheism? incrementalism or radicalism?), but one overriding question: anarchism or socialism? It is beyond dispute within the walls of Justus Schwab's saloon on First Street that capitalism must and will fall, that the political hirelings of that debauched, immoral system will be removed, that the entire socioeconomic structure of these United States is rotten to the core and cannot stand. A system built on the backs of subjugated men, enslaved Africans, indentured Chinese, chatteled women, immigrants and children, whose lives are used as fodder, as fuel to be burned in a moneymaking contraption built to serve one purpose only: the grotesquely extravagant desires of Andrew Carnegie, John D. Rockefeller, Jay Gould, Leland Stanford, the Vanderbilt clan, to list a few notable devils. "Democracy"? "Representatives of the people" represent the moneyed interests, nothing more. A life is valued by its ability to produce product—*money! capital!*—for a man whose only worth, his only claim to superiority, is that he *owns*. Owns land, owns factories, owns stock. Owns people, truly. Families, lives, futures. A system in which the chance fortune of birth and ownership and the will to wield brute force against one's fellow man determines which children play and which shall work, who shall be healed and who shall remain ill. Who shall live and who shall die.

A man is standing on a chair and reading a scroll of paper. "Labor being the source of all wealth and civilization," he shouts over the rumble, "and useful labor being possible only by and through the associated efforts of the people, the results of labor should, therefore, in all justice, belong to society! The system under which society is now organized is imperfect and hostile to the general welfare, since through it the directors of labor, necessarily a small minority, are enabled in the competitive struggle to practically monopolize all the means of labor, and the masses are therefore maintained in poverty and dependence."

Glasses are raised, downed, and thumped loudly on the bar and tables.

"Since the ruling political parties have always sought only the direct interest of the dominant or wealthy classes," he continues, "endeavored to uphold their industrial supremacy, and to perpetuate the present conditions of society, it is now the duty of the working people to organize themselves into one great labor party, using political power to achieve industrial independence!"

And at that the young man ignites the scroll on a hanging gas lantern and waves the flaming manifesto over his head triumphantly, to the hoots of all, until Justus Schwab extinguishes the torch with the tossed contents of a mug of beer, and the hoots turn to laughs.

No, the question is not *will* the capitalist house of cards survive *(Never!)*, or when it will collapse *(Soon!)*, or who should rule the new society *(The workers!)*. The only question is what should replace the system, how the workers should rule come the revolution. In true freedom, or by a government ruled by and for the people. All are welcome at Schwab's, anarchists and socialists alike, and they agree on much, but these constant arguments, the pressing issue of what system to implement once capitalism falls—*any day!*—overshadows all agreements, transforms adversaries into villains more hated and feared than the evil railroad tycoon Jay Gould. For the adversary (the socialist; the anarchist) is willing to destroy America's—*mankind's*—last, great chance to create a Utopia here on earth.

And back in Rochester, Emma thinks, what was the overriding question? *Where is the salt?!* (her father bellowing at the kitchen table, glowering for service), *Lena, the soup's thin.* Emma's husband *(how could the woman who exchanged vows with that vacuous man, Jacob Kersner, have been the same Emma Goldman?)*, Jacob, staggers out from a bar, leans on a snowbank for support, a girl, perhaps, under a limp arm, cocaine in an envelope, a dull smile, vacant as a dog's. Her boss at the shirt factory, Mr. Gerstner, commands her to work late, then sneaks up behind her and his hands grope her breasts, slide under her waistband like snakes. And then she would return home to that cauldron of silent stares, resentments, and smoldering disgust; her sister and husband and sister's husband, meekly servile before the glare of her father, the gray iron wool of his beard like an armored breastplate, imposing, impervious. He had chased them there, after Emma had joined Lena in America, and Rochester was a place they had all *happened into;* it was Russia in a new land, transplanted. There was no choice. As if God, or the state, had placed them all there.

Emma now walks slowly through the bar, dancing to the battling voices, the violent chatter a symphony, Tchaikovsky or Beethoven, punctuated by emphatic booms on the kettle drum. Haymarket! Marx! Engels! 1848! The trusts! The railroads! Anarchy! Socialism! Anarchy! Socialism! God is dead! Nietzsche! Anarchy! Freedom I tell you! Only true freedom!

Emma knocks on the bar and Justus hands her a beer. *This* is New York. She begrudges herself for wasting her first months in Rochester. This is America.

"Emma!" As soon as she hears the deep, gravelly voice she knows it is Most.

"Johann." Before they had met she had seen crude sketches of him in the newspapers, caricatures of the immigrant radical devil, mouth foaming onto his beard, bottle rockets and dynamite clenched in his fist, and so her image of him was formed. Even now, at times, she can't help but see him as the stick figure come-to-life.

He grabs her shoulders and leans down to her, but she redirects his lips to her cheeks.

"Emma, my dear," Johann says, his arm around her, guiding her to his booth. She has never seen him dressed so dapper. He almost seems young, closer to her age than her father's. There are flowers on the table, roses in a vase, a bottle of red wine.

"Such riches," she says. "How could you afford this?"

"I thought you would be earlier and we could share a little aperitif." Most's mouth is askew when he says it. She cannot be sure if it is his scar and the disfigurement of his face, or disgust at her tardiness.

"I am sorry," she says. "Alex and I were preparing pamphlets for the rally. But we still have time for a glass."

His mouth twitches upward again, more violently than before, then he grabs her around the waist and pulls her away from the booth. He has shown her the wine to tantalize her, nothing more.

"Too late for that," he says. "We go. On we go."

A cab is waiting for them outside.

"To the opera," Most says, and the driver whips the horses to a fast trot.

The lobby of the opera house is a parade of silk and lace, dresses that flow like velvet rivers.

"That lady there," Emma says. A blur of giant rubies and sapphires dangles on a golden chain adorning a pristine alabaster neck. "Johann, how much does it all cost?"

"The dress and baubles? A year's wages for a workingman. Ten years perhaps. But the woman who wears it will never work a day in her life, nor will her daughter, or ten generations after. Yet it is beautiful, no?"

Emma expects they will have to climb to their seats, somewhere in the rafters, but Johann shows her to a balcony overlooking the stage. He nods to the tuxedoed man in the adjoining booth.

"How much did you pay for these seats, Johann?"

"They are beautiful too, yes? When one sees *Carmen,* one should be close enough to feel the dance. Not just hear it. It must be lived!"

"But the money for the tickets? Where could you get it?"

"You think beauty should be the private province of the rich?" Johann says. "Enjoy."

In the carriage ride back Johann quizzes Emma. "Hum the motifs, my girl, sing the arias! The high notes of the soprano, the deep lows of the baritone. Which hit you here?" thumping his chest. "Have you ever heard such before?"

"Back in Russia once I heard *Il Trovatore*, but it was nothing to compare."

Johann nods, and then he is upon her, a schoolteacher with eyes oozing lust. His hands grab at her breasts, her legs.

"Your blond hair," he says. "The blue eyes. You are a real American girl, no? I have only heard of such." He is laughing as his tongue pokes under her blouse.

"No, Johann," Emma says, shuffling away from him on the seat.

"You remind me of Carmen," he says, sliding toward her. "Tease and then run. I can play that game!"

"But Johann," she cries. "This is not love!"

"Love?" Most cackles. He lurches toward her as the carriage turns a corner. "What a girl you are! There is no love. There is only sex."

10 · EMMA · 1890

"The revolutionist, the *true* revolutionist, must be ready to die for the cause."

Alexander Berkman is stabbing the words with the butt of his knife as he speaks. His eyes are fixed straight across the booth, but he does not see Emma there.

"The true revolutionist feels the misery of the people, he bleeds it, he screams with their pain. And he sees, too—" now Berkman slices his steak and chews quickly as he speaks—"he sees the world to come, after the revolution. A part of him lives in this utopia."

Alex gulps his beer, hunches over his plate, a rabbi over his Torah, cutting his steak furiously.

"I am so sorry, Emma," he says in between bites, "you must have some. The porterhouse is delicious."

"No, Alex." Emma is picking on a slab of bread. Then she winces and grabs her side.

"Is it that pain again, my dear?" Alex points at her. "Did you go to the doctor finally?"

"No, no." Emma shrugs him off. "It's you and your extravagances. Would your true revolutionist spend such wages on food, on drink? And you talk of giving away your life."

"We all have our weaknesses, my dear Emma. I admit, I am no different. Your Fedya has his art. A day's wages we spend on oil and canvas. For what? A painting no one will ever buy."

"You sound like a capitalist, Alex. That is art. We cannot define beauty in dollars."

"My friends at the cigar makers, Emma, they could define it in dollars. Your Fedya's easel, his brushes, his canvases. That is food for a week, clothes, a roof. I did not place the price on these things, but there you are. Like your friend Most—"

"No, no, no." Emma slaps her hand on the table. "Johann is not my friend. My Fedya would never take money from the cause, money given for papers, for rallies, the people, for—." She is too flustered to speak. She lapses into Russian to explain, but Alex stops her. They are to speak only in English. They are here in America and you must learn to communicate.

"I know, I know," Alex says. He gnaws some gristle, then tosses his napkin over it, his plate empty but the bone. "I am sorry to compare them. I love your Fedya too. Not so much his art—it is no porterhouse steak—but let us not argue. Tonight we love, no?"

Emma and Alex walk to a theater that is not a theater but a meeting room Emma and Alex and Fedya and their friends use as a theater. There are no audiences, no admission required to enter. There is no script; it is all improvised. It is done for the experience. You take on personalities, act what you can then become. You find within yourself what you act.

Fedya has painted on the walls a mob scene, faces yelling, clenched fists raised, torches and scrawled signs: *Eight for What We Will!* Scattered amidst the mob are policemen clasping clubs, waving revolvers, blowing whistles. The theater is a square room and the paintings on the walls give it the illusion of a city. The buildings Fedya has painted in the background are familiar, they all know the scene it depicts: Haymarket Square, Chicago, May 4, 1886.

"Who are you today?" Emma says.

Alex is standing near the far wall, pumping his fist up at an imaginary crowd.

"Albert Parsons," he says. "Eight hours for work, eight hours for rest, eight hours for what we will!"

Suddenly he jumps backward and lands on the floor on his rear.

"The bomb is thrown," Alex says. "Parsons is as stunned as anyone. He is nowhere near the explosive, knows nothing of it."

Then Emma sashays toward Alex/Parsons, a handkerchief wrapped round her neck as if it were a silk scarf. She pulls her skirt up seductively, revealing thigh.

"Sonja," she says. "The heroine in *What Is to Be Done?* Earning money for the defense of her hero."

Alex places his hands behind his back, chafing in invisible cuffs, then follows a policeman who isn't there, then an imaginary prison guard. He looks up, prayerfully, at the ceiling. Everyone knows Albert Parsons is now on the gallows.

Someone else who sees himself, for the moment, as Louis Lingg, sits on the floor in a make-believe prison cell, toys with a makeshift bomb that accidentally detonates, then sprawls on his back, dead. It is a scene that makes them all a little uncomfortable, suggesting that Lingg was capable of making the bomb that killed the policemen at Haymarket.

About the room men and women receive their death sentences, give tearful speeches good-bye, solemnly submit to be hung at the gallows. No one pays attention to anyone else; they are each in their own theater, their own world, except Fedya, who, taking a break from painting, reads from the speech August Spies gave in the courtroom after being informed that the State had decided to kill him.

"I say that the preservation of this order," Fedya yells, "is criminal. Is murderous. It means the preservation of the systematic destruction of children and women in factories. It means the preservation of enforced idleness of large armies of men, and their degradation. It means the preservation of intemperance, and sexual as well as intellectual prostitution. It means the preservation of misery, want, and servility on the one hand, and the dangerous accumulation of spoils, idleness, voluptuousness and tyranny on the other. It means the preservation of vice in every form. That is your 'order,' gentlemen."

Alex closes his eyes, raises his neck as the imaginary gallows rope lifts Albert Parsons off his feet. Emma falls to her knees as Sonja cries for her innocent lover.

After the performances are over, Alex and Emma walk home to the apartment they share with Fedya and Helen Minkin. Alex works at the cigar makers, Emma and Helen sew piecework, Fedya paints his art. The money all goes in the pot. No one resents the other, no one feels she is getting the short end. This is the free state. This is man in his nature.

As Emma hangs up her hat, Alex comes up behind and slips his hands around her waist, embraces her, nibbles her neck. Spins her around and kisses her full on the lips.

Emma pushes him away gently.

"I cannot," she says.

Alex questions her with his eyes. He has already begun to kick off his shoes.

"You must go to the doctor, Emma. These pains might be serious. And a man and his woman—that's not right."

"I saw the doctor, Alex."

"What did he say?"

Emma dismisses Alex with a shrug. "It isn't that. I wanted to tell you tonight," she says. "It is Fedya. It is Fedya I love now."

Alex is silent for a moment, then shakes his head. He smiles and steps closer, places his arms gently over Emma's shoulders.

"So now it is Fedya," he says. "Did you think I would lay claim to your heart?"

II · EMMA · 1891

She travels throughout the East, the Midwest, speaking, lecturing, rallying. Cleveland, Pittsburgh, Philadelphia, Baltimore, Washington, Buffalo. Most has sent her on tour and she is becoming renowned, her fiery tongue, words that lash open the sores on the backs of the workingman. She has lost her schoolgirl looks, the gentle softness of her face. Now she ties her unwashed, stringy hair back with a strand of handkerchief. She is thicker around the waist. Still pretty, but one has to look harder to see it, if one cares to. She is becoming Red Emma.

She gives the speech that Most has taught her to give. The eight-hour workday will not make a man free. Increasing wages to more than a dollar a day will not address the root of the problem. The unionists and reformers are false prophets; they seek only to tinker at the margins of the system. The system is rotten. Unless the roots are pulled out, one is simply subsisting on a different branch of the same corrupt, enslaving tree. The tree must fall.

An old man comes up to her after a speech. This is St. Louis, or Kansas City, she is not sure where the train let her off.

"I have listened to all you say, Miss Goldman," the old man says.

His face is charred and smoky from a life of factory work. It is the furnaces, the heat of the smokestacks. There are diseases that will kill him which will not be understood until Emma herself is long dead, and yet she can see it, the burgeoning sickness. It's in his eyes, the smell of his sweat, the rattling timbre of his voice.

"Your words stir me, Miss Emma," he says, "in here," and he pats where the diseases will strike him, under his shirt. "The world you speak of, without bosses, where working folk like me make the rules. Ah, that's a pretty picture."

"It will happen," Emma says. "Sooner than you might think."

"But not soon enough, ma'am. You say the eight-hour day is not an answer. And that may be true in your world. But I will not live to see another. All I want is a day that ends before nightfall, so I can share a supper with my wife, so my grandchildren can know who I am before we meet again in the next world. You say another dime of wages is not the answer? But those dimes will buy my wife a dress that is not tattered, my family three square meals, some shoes without holes the rain puddles soak through to the socks. Is that too much to ask, Miss Emma? Must I be denied that, so that your wonderful future world can come, one day, after I'm gone, if you are so lucky?"

Emma is on a train now, coming home to New York. In the reflection of the window she sees the old man, then the doctor she saw how many months ago, staring at her with a somberness that says, I am sorry; it is nature, God, something grand that has doled out to you this sorry fate. The doctor said there is hope, an operation; it is new and success is uncertain, and of course there is risk, but there is no other choice if you wish to bear children. And looking back on it, perhaps it is the way the doctor presents her plight that leads Emma to decide immediately that she will not undergo the procedure.

No, she cannot enter the old man's mind, or his soul, but she knows how hollow her answers sound, answers that merely parrot Johann's words. *The tree must die so your grandchildren will live in a better world.* But the dark waters of his eyes held the unanswerable response: *An hour of sunlight is something. It is not everything, but it is something.*

When she is home, she will demand answers from Most. Answers he does not have, he cannot give.

12 · McKINLEY · What He Remembers

c. 1848–1851

There is a memory McKinley has of standing in church and his mother is kneeling beside him in the pew, his father is on the other side of her, and their eyes are closed. His should be too, but they aren't; he's just a boy and can't help but look around at the men and women, parents of his school friends and neighbors. Everyone knows everyone in Niles. Their eyes are closed and their lips are moving slightly in a silent, indecipherable conversation with that which cannot be seen, only sensed.

1852

At school a friend says there's a girl that gave him the eye; she's attractive and he thinks her name is Kate.

William is not certain why he can't bring himself to talk to her or even look. Then, as he walks home and sits down for dinner that night it strikes him. It's the sense that he is being witnessed, being judged. That the eyes of God are always upon him.

1858

At school again. He tells the cook the pudding's melting, and his classmates laugh at him something harsh. He can't help it; he's never seen ice cream before.

1860

And then he is seventeen and his father, who does not permit discussion of worldly matters at the dinner table—prayer, silence, and Pass the potatoes, please is the rule—asks for silence and a special prayer for the nation and our new president, Mr. Lincoln.

1864

He is back from the war and home, in church, and the organ is thundering, a Bach fugue, glorious notes raining down from the steeple, showering the pews.

There was a moment on a battlefield by a creek in Virginia where the fighting paused long enough for men to die and be carried off to their comrades, and the smoke from the cannon fire and rifles hung in the air over the grass, blanketing the soldiers, freezing them in position. And though William will never mention this to anyone in his life—he has vowed secrecy—he thought he heard the voice of God.

A hymn is playing and all rise, and William raises his voice. "Nearer my God to Thee," he sings with the chorus. "Nearer to Thee."

13 · McKINLEY · January 26, 1871

William leans on the windowsill, gazes out at the city. The pipes screech as Ida continues to wash up in the bathroom, so he opens the window, letting in a flood of chatter from the street. He looks down at the sea of hats below: bowlers, top hats, European workmen's caps, ladies' bonnets. Herds of people strolling past one another on the sidewalk. Oceans of the lower order—decent, hard-working folk, some; derelicts, others—but all a lower order. Such concentrated humanity. Irish, Italians, Hebrews, Negroes, Slavs of all varieties, other dialects he has never heard. Towers of Babel, truly. Canton and Cleveland are nothing to compare with New York. Other than the troops he marched with during the war, he has never seen so many bodies in so little space. So God intended. And so shall it be.

And the buildings! He had heard that in Manhattan the great moneyed men commanded that their homes and offices be built high enough so they could reach up to the heavens, but you cannot envision it until you are here, gazing out on Broadway. Carnegie, Rockefeller, they are lifting the nation up to the heavens on their broad shoulders and mighty arms.

And the people below, the oceans, they had laid the tracks his and Ida's train had ridden on; they had laid the brick of the hotel in which they now stayed, swept the streets of the manure left by the carriage horses, tunneled the sewers. How many of them did it take to lay the stone to build just one of the mansions they had seen today on Fifth Avenue? Then there were the architects who designed them, the artists who gilded the ceilings and walls, the engineers. The glass he had just opened, the bathtub in which his Ida now washed. This was America, what it had become.

So here they are. It is their honeymoon, their first night as man and wife since their wedding in Canton.

Ida slinks out of the bathroom in a silk robe, embroidered with yellow flowers and violet waterfalls and tied with a sash. As she walks across the room to the bed her robe parts, exposing her leg. It has to be Italian, William supposes, brought over from her trip two years ago with Pina. One did not wear such things in Ohio. They were brought over on their ships.

Her leg is white and smooth as ivory, he cannot help but notice. It stares at him from across the room. He has never seen such a thing. She crosses her legs and then he sees them both, bare naked to the thigh. She kicks off her slippers and now her feet are exposed. He rushes across the room and snuffs out the lights beside the bed, but the buildings across the street illuminate her. It is not right to look, but he cannot help but glance. She emanates a perfume that draws him to her.

Had he ever looked at her before, really looked? Her thick dark hair is combed out over her shoulders, the bun untied; it falls down her back. Her eyes flicker in the sparkling, dancing light darting in from across the street—the stars, the moon, he isn't certain. Her lips so full, crinkled at the corners in a slight, wry smile. He is her husband now. This is their honeymoon. He can kiss her.

She smiles, beckoning him. Between the buttons of her robe he can see the catches of her girdle. During the war, around campfires at night soldiers would talk of what lay beneath such underclothes. Soft breasts, nipples ripe as cherries. He had never listened, of course, but you could not help but hear a thing or two.

He sits beside her on the bed.

There was the way of the Lord, there was temptation, there was sin. And then there were husbands and wives. Propagation. The Lord spoke too of begetting.

The lights from the window grow fainter.

He closes his eyes, begins to fumble with the buttons of Ida's robe, the ties and latches underneath, but they are locks for which he has no key.

The smell of her perfume fills his head. *(Did it come here on a boat from France?)* This is what it must feel like to drink, what whiskey and wine can do.

She is smiling, beckoning. She helps him unlatch herself, disrobe.

There was Eve and the apple, there was sin.

But he is her husband now. She is his wife.

She tilts her head so when he opens his eyes next her lips are there, full red before him and he falls into them, his lips on hers. Was there ever skin so soft, so lush?

She was his wife. She was his wife.

"Do you have to leave?"

It is over and William is in the bathroom in an instant, the door slammed behind him. He has to get rid of the sweat, the seed—the sin—from his skin, his self, his soul. He steps into the bath and ladles water on himself. It is cold but he deserves no better. He rushes to quickly cover his nakedness, so the soap leaves a film on his skin. But he deserves no better.

"William, my love," Ida says. "Come back to bed, dear."

He doesn't answer. She had seen him in his nakedness.

He dabs himself with a towel, hurriedly pulls on his pants, his shirt, shoes, suspenders, grabs his hat at the door.

"A little air," he says. "A bit of business."

And he is out the door, onto the streets.

14 · IDA · January 26, 1871

It is not over William she cries. He is such a young man in some ways, will turn twenty-eight in days, but he is really just a boy. When it comes to love, anyway. He knows of death, learned of death early, but not of women. Ida has always found his shyness becoming, attractive. An innocence beneath the ambition, the seriousness of purpose. A naiveté.

He will walk the streets and return.

She has pulled out from the bottom of her suitcase a letter, stiff and yellow with time. The stamps are wondrous, they tell a story in themselves. From the Confederate states where it was mailed, then

France, finally Italy where the letter tracked her down. She was in Venice when she opened it.

I am a soldier. Ida knows the words by heart now. *You have always known me as a soldier. I dare say, if I may be so bold to suggest that you may have loved me, may love me still in a fashion at least, you have fallen in love with a soldier.*

And if you ever held love for me it was for a Confederate man. I am a Virginian, body, heart and soul. That you know well. There is a mountain in the Shenandoahs I have always yearned to share with you. There is a spot where the woods vanish into meadow and you can see the deer lap at the creek, the bears slap-boxing their cubs, cardinals serenading. As busy as your Northern cities but no one is going anywhere, an idle, ambling sort of busyness. I always imagined our front porch overlooking that spot.

How is Paris? How was London? Where to next? Rome? Venice? I confess I forget. I tried to keep up with you but you spoke of your plans so quickly.

What I am getting around to saying is this: I have no nation anymore. I am a defeated soldier. Imagine coming awake to find yourself an alien, a rebel in a country not your own. I have lived four years now in this nether nation, where my land and the land of my father's are in enemy soil. I am guilty of the sin of loyalty only. I lost my nation for love of nation, my home for love of home.

My Ida, you deserve better. Was there ever a young lady in all the North or South the like of you? I recall when we were out picnicking and you took my prize rifle and when I turned my back you shot at the tree and swore to me that the Northerners had come back for me. I could have ravished you (after strangling your slender, pretty neck). You were joshing me, but you told truths you could not know.

Death hounds me. Disgrace makes his bed with mine. I carry shame on my back as I move from town to town.

My Ida. You are worthy of kings, not the conquered; of victors, not the vanquished.

I wish you the kingdoms you so richly deserve.
Good-bye.

. . .

When she had received the letter in Italy, she had already been given word that John Wright was dead. She had been informed that it was an illness, though the details were a touch unclear, a hint of tales one dare not speak. *Death hounds me.* She could still hear John speak those words, in his beautiful Southern lilt. *Death hounds me.*

Ida does not even realize that the door has opened. William has placed his hat on the peg, sat beside her on the bed. She quickly folds the letter and slips it under her leg.

"My darling," he says. "I am sorry. I should not have left you, but I couldn't help but do it."

He wipes away the tears from her cheek, gently pats her hair.

"It is God's will," he says. "We will be all right."

15 · IDA · December 1872

They are falling down the rabbit hole. Together, arms waving high over their heads, tangled in hair that is one mass of curls, all undone. Mother and daughter, Ida and Katie.

They are lying together on Ida's bed, on their backs, gazing up at the ceiling. Falling through the rabbit hole.

"Take the Smaller pills, Katie love. Just like Alice. The tunnel gets narrow here so take your Smaller pills." Ida giggles as she pops the pill in, covering it with her hand because there is no pill. Katie watches her mother, then places her two little fingers in her mouth, still watching.

"Who is smiling there?" Ida points at the flowers painted above the chair rail. "Katie, when you are three, and little Ida" (she pats her round belly) "is your age, you can move into your own room and we will paint this room together, Katie and Mommie, and it will be Wonderland. That point on the wall there, just below the mirror, will be a Cheshire cat."

Katie doesn't see the cat, but she sees her mother smile and so she smiles, too.

Ida has worked it out with Katie, plans for the whole house and the front yard and the garden out back. There's a plank of the fence on the walkway out front, the bottom half of it was kicked off by some kids, and that's where the white rabbit hops under, you chase him up the walk, onto the stoop, then round the front porch, ducking under the glider, then round through the door, sliding on the long gray rug (a hunting scene, if you care to look) in the living room, sliding in your socks on the hardwood floors of the dining room, momentum almost carries you into Daddy's den, then up the stairs and through the bedrooms, Ida's, Daddy's, to Katie's room, where they are now. The house is like Ida's childhood house, the images have merged in her mind: a child should have a maze of hallways and bay windows and secret passageways to tunnel through and explore, and a lush lawn out front and a flowery garden out back and trees to climb too. There's even a rocking chair Ida's father gave her as a child.

"And when we land at the bottom of the hole, we ROLLLLLL!!!!!" Ida grabs Katie around the waist and rolls with her to the edge of the bed. Ida has pulled the veiled canopies down on all sides so the world beyond the bed is barely visible, a vague outline of dressers, a vanity, family portraits on the wall.

"This is your world," Ida whispers, to herself and to Katie and little Ida inside her belly. "Nothing out there is real."

"And we ROLLLL BACK!!!!!" Back and forth, from side to side they roll on the bed and Ida is laughing and Katie is laughing too.

There is a knock on the door.

"Must be the Mad Hatter," Ida says. "Shhhhhh! Or the March Hare."

The door opens.

"Missus Ida."

It is Ester. The help.

"Missus Ida, it's time to get Miss Katie ready for bed. Bath time, Miss Katie."

Ester has walked in and opened the canopy, and light rushes onto the bed and blinds them, so much of it rains in.

"Must we, Ester? Must we now?"

Ester smiles, shakes her head. "You take care of that baby in there,

Missus Ida. Mr. McKinley's boy's coming out any day now, and I wouldn't want him—"

"It's a girl, Ester. I know it's a girl. There will be three of us—and you, Ester. Four. I know. This one will be little Ida. The one after will have to be little William."

Katie grabs her mother's cheek with two little fingers and rubs and there's this way she kisses the skin that's between, a suckling and a cooing all at once. Ida wants time to stop then, let the moment never die.

Then Ester grabs Katie in her arms, and Ida kisses her on the forehead.

"Mother and Father will kiss you goodnight. After your bath, love."

And the child is taken away, out of the room.

16 · McKINLEY · March 1873

William is downstairs in his den. He is not where he hoped to be at thirty. He had been on the right track, district attorney at twenty-six, but then after he married Ida he fell short, one hundred and forty-three votes between a second term as DA, a rising star in Republican politics in the county, and where he is now—pushing loans at his father-in-law's bank. The very bank where even Ida worked, back when they met.

But this is not an end. A diversion, a setback, but not an end of the road. Even poor boys reach the heights in this great nation, in those Horatio Alger books everyone is reading. And William McKinley is no Ragged Dick. His is no rags to riches story. He was never quite in rags, and it is not riches he is after.

You keep your eye steady on the beam. Keep your temperament solid as a fence post. Never too high nor too low. On the beam, William. The beam.

It is helpful to review his credentials like a business's prospectus, take stock of the past, chart plans for his future. There are men it pays to pay attention to, friendships to fertilize with compliments, favors, and talk.

At this moment, at his desk, he is writing a letter to his old army colonel, Rutherford Hayes.

17 · LITTLE IDA · August 22, 1873

William finishes another letter to now-Governor Rutherford B. Hayes. In correspondence they can relive their Civil War days together. Embellishing their accomplishments, magnifying the glories, they allow each other to become heroic. The governor insists now that at Antietam young Major McKinley's hat was knocked off by a cannonball when he fearlessly drove a wagon full of supplies into battle, for the third (or was it the fourth?) time, bringing food, water, bandages to the soldiers. There are rumors that one of Stonewall Jackson's boys had McKinley in his rifle sights but Jackson stopped him before he could pull the trigger, telling him, "A boy that brave should be spared." The governor has made sure not to correct the story.

McKinley reciprocates with his own elaborated recountings of his superior's heroics, then lets slip a hint that he may be reentering the political circus. If he were to dip a toe back into those waters, would the governor have suggestions, advice?

The governor, McKinley knows, is planning a run at the presidency next election, and his chances are good. In Ohio Hayes is a king.

The governor advises that a run at Congress in a term or two would not be ill-advised. No, McKinley's razor-thin loss for county prosecutor was not a fatal wound. His recent maneuvers have been clever. Joining the Masons is admirable. Heading the local chapter of the Young Men's Christian Association is sound. Keep in touch with the legion, the veterans' groups. A job in James Saxton's bank is respectable, and with his legal background and war record, McKinley will make a formidable opponent for whoever the Democrats can field.

(The suggestion, McKinley reads, is that Hayes will assure him the Republican slot.) In politics, resiliency is all. You get off the floor, off the battlefield, off the bad end of an election return, and fight again.

McKinley seals up the letter, rings the bell at his desk, and when Ester arrives he hands it to her to bring to post.

Pulls the watch out of his vest pocket. Almost midnight.

There is a knock and McKinley opens the door of his den.

"I'm done, Mr. McKinley," says Doctor English, slump shouldered, snapping up his bag. The doctor is a gaunt man whose hair has grayed before McKinley's eyes, in the past months alone it seems. "There is nothing more to be done. I'm sorry."

"There is prayer," McKinley corrects him. "There is always that."

The doctor shakes his head. "Things are not as clean as they once were," the doctor says. "It is not the same country our fathers built. The peoples, the vast mix. What came over on the ships. I'm sorry but I've lived too long, I think."

McKinley escorts him to the foyer.

Ester has appeared and she opens the front door and the rain whips in. The doctor looks at her, shakes his head as he wraps himself in a thin cloak.

"I've done my best."

"We thank you for it, Doctor English," McKinley says. "You will be in our prayers."

The idea has come into Ida's head that God has banished her. When her mother died and little Ida was born six months later, there was the sense of an exchange, that she had bargained life for death and this was not something that God approved of. That was the beginning of the end.

This is what she thinks, rocking in her chair beside little Ida's bed. The doctors have come and gone and they will come again, but there is nothing they can do. A child of four months is too weak to fight back the disease. Even adults fall prey, but little Ida, she came into the world weak. The girl was born with beauty, a wondrous equanimity, but not physical strength. The sickness may have entered her in the womb. Or soon after. There is talk of the hired help, have the servants been ill, other children who may have visited, but none of it goes anywhere but in circles.

. . .

Katie wants to play with her baby sister. She cries at the door, "Ida."
She may be calling for her sister or her mother; Ida is not certain, for
Katie has been deprived of both since the sickness set in. Since little
Ida was born, in truth.

The baby's crib is sealed in a makeshift box made of white sheets, with
steam piped in from the top. This is the latest doctor's idea, to steam
out the illness, boil the body clean, as Ida understands it. It makes it
impossible for Ida to even hold her little daughter's hand, gaze into her
blue eyes, stroke her blonde hair. One morning she purchased a pink
ribbon to wrap round the girl's hair and had sewed it onto a hat, with
matching slippers, and when she returned the girl was hidden from
her, boxed in these sheets. Ida is still holding the slippers, the little
bonnet.

Will the box merely keep her daughter bound up with the illness?
If the devil has entered her girl, if God has done this thing, will it be
trapped inside?

She knows she should not think such things. She must stay
strong. Prayer, faith. Trust, not disillusion.

The child has not moved for several hours now. She is sleeping peace-
fully, though her forehead drips with sweat, her nightshirt is drenched
to the skin. Her clothes must be changed. On top of whatever this illness, this fate has wrought her, she will catch cold. A mother should
not be cordoned off from her child. Ida snatches the sheet curtains, the
box, the living coffin—steam be damned—and reaches in. The baby
rustles. When Ida gently cradles her head, her child wriggles away
from her.

The door opens—it is William—and the baby begins to thrash.
She has little control of her neck, so her head rocks wildly about.

"My dear, my dear," William says, patting his wife's hand. "How
long—?"

"Just now. She was so—. It's horrible."

The little girl's head is slithering now from side to side, on her
back in the crib.

Ida reaches in again and grabs her, holds her firm around her middle. Little Ida's head frantically lurches a bit, almost sliding out of her mother's grasp, but Ida holds on tighter, lifts the girl out of the box, clutches the tiny body to her chest. That seems to settle her; the lunging stops.

The baby looks up, her eyes roll back a bit, showing whites. Ida thinks the child is communicating, she is certain of it.

You must be strong, Mama. You must carry on. I love you, and Daddy too. I would have been like you, dark and beautiful and free. I am like you. I am you, Mama. We are one.

"Did you hear that, too?"

Ida feels herself come out of a deep sleep. She has no idea how much time has passed since she rescued little Ida from her boxed crib. Must have collapsed on the bed. William is lightly touching her shoulders. She hears singing, quiet, behind her.

> *Nearer my God to Thee,*
> *Nearer to Thee.*
> *Or if on joyful wing, cleaving the sky.*
> *Sun, moon, and stars forgot, upward I fly,*
> *Still all my song shall be,*
> *Nearer my God to Thee*
> *Nearer my God to Thee,*
> *Nearer to Thee.*

The singing continues, the same hymn repeating. She opens her eyes, turns around.

It is William standing over her. William who is singing.

She looks down but the baby, little Ida, is not there in her arms.

"But what, she was— Didn't you— I was—."

"It is God's will," William says. He is holding a blanket in his arms. Ida had crocheted it before the child was born.

Ida pulls the blanket off and there is the girl's pink face. Her eyes are closed, the tiny arms and legs hanging down limply from her father's arms.

"My God." Ida screams, she howls. Ester runs in, the nurse, the doctor.

Katie steps inside. "Mommy! Mommy!" William nods to the maid and she grabs Katie, pulls her out of the room, screaming into the hall.

Ida falls to her knees, head in hands, then collapses, sobbing on the floor.

William kneels beside her. "There there," he says. His voice is faint and cracking as he speaks. "It is God's will."

Ida turns toward him; stares. She has never seen him cry before.

"My God," she says. "What a horrible thought."

18 · LEON · 1893

Leon's father has bought a saloon at Third and Tot Streets in Cleveland, and Leon sits upstairs where the men talk and drink. A man named Frank presides over a discussion group he calls it, a workingman's association, but it is just the men who don't work talking and drinking, the men who have had their jobs taken from them, Frank says. His hair looks like the butcher chopped it as Frank fled from him.

Leon serves the men drinks and sausages and cheese. Frank takes him under his wing, an arm draped over his shoulders and angry words soaked in whiskey and beer; Leon can smell the resolve.

"There is an order to your education," Frank says. "First you open your mind with Jules Verne, the world of possibilities. There are other worlds. Take boats to the center of the earth. Armies from other planets do battle. Fly to the moon."

Leon's father looks at him askance—there are tables to clean—but Waldek covers for his brother when he sees Leon's eyes grow big with Frank's words. Leon's sister carts a tray of drinks, sausages, bread wrapped in smoke from the oven.

"Time is like space. It can be laid out on a map, we can plot trips from here to there, future and past. Leon, where have you come from? Your parents left Poland, sailed to America. You came from Michigan, Alpena and Detroit, then Pennsylvania, now Cleveland. So you traveled through space. And in time, from past to present. But we can go the other way, backward to the past, or forward to the future.

"You do not need to understand all at once. More later.

"Next, the facts. Leon, let me tell you what you have lived but do not know. Let me spell it out for you. Wages and prices. The factory worker earns five cents an hour, seven cents, ten cents. Twenty cents. The workday is twelve hours, fourteen hours, sixteen. A bag of flour costs almost two dollars. Rent is four dollars or more. The numbers, they do not add up. You live in the cellars, stuffed in sweaty rooms, on cots, with two families, three, four. Or the corporation owns the home, owns the store where they take back the meager wages they have given you. You work for your keep and are never the better for it. It is slavery, yes?

"Listen, Leon. There are twelve and a half million families in America. Eleven million are as I described. A dollar a day or slightly more. Three hundred fifty, four hundred dollars each year they earn, these families.

"You know Marshall Field, who owns the great department store in Chicago city? Every hour he makes six hundred dollars. Every hour of every day. Six hundred dollars an hour, the one man, twenty-four hours every day. A single day: fourteen thousand four hundred dollars. A working life in a single day. I do not say he *earns* that money. Yet he takes that money home. His best workers, what does he pay them? Twenty cents an hour.

"Andrew Carnegie? Twenty-five million dollars in a year."

Leon's sister swaggers past with a tray, and Frank pauses for a glance.

"Capital is organizing, consolidating, pooling their strength. Their money, their power is not enough for them. In their eyes we have too much. The disparities I have described are too slight for them. Our very existence threatens them. We are like spirits to them, a conscience they do not have. A soul. Our crime is that we breathe, that we look with eyes. That the cries of our babies disturb their stroll through the gardens.

"Next, the concepts, the ideas. Karl Marx, Engels. Bakunin, Bellamy. It does not have to be this way. There are other futures, other paths. Possibilities. Alone we are nothing. Powerless. But together, we hold the keys to the capitalists' millions. The mills that churn out Carnegie's twenty-five million? If we refuse to work them, they grind to a halt. Without us Mr. Gould's railroads do not run; they have no tracks, no stoked coal. Mr. Rockefeller's oil ceases to pump. The capitalist will never soil his hands with the grime of labor, the labor that is necessary to keep him alive. The great cities, New York, Chicago, Boston, they will turn silent as the grave if we stand united and refuse to work until our demands are met.

"Yet we continue to work, and the capitalist feeds off our labors. We run on his treadmill to carry him from place to place, not realizing that his own legs can no longer walk from disuse. We hold the keys.

"The system need not be as it is. There is socialism. There is anarchy. There is a better way to run a world."

19 · MORRIS · 1886

"The way you do it is you take the scrapings of meat, what is left of the pig after we're done slicing and chopping. It all goes in the vat, see?"

The foreman pokes his head in and Morris does, too, but the stench makes him bounce back just as fast.

"Detritus," Morris says, trying out the word. He read it in an English dictionary on the train into work.

The foreman glances at him funny. "Gristle," he says. "Their insides. Ground up bone, muscle and some meat hanging on."

The foreman walks on through the factory, and Morris follows as best he can, dragging his left foot behind like a convict's ball on a chain. The cleavers make a sharp grating noise that pierces through your head, but Morris forces the sound out; he is working through philosophical parables all around him. When he learns English well enough, he will teach this to his students: Kant, Kierkegaard, Hegel. It's all here in the slaughterhouse.

"Stones that the builders rejected," Morris says.

The foreman shrugs. "Bones mostly. But yeah, maybe the spare pebble now and then, but it's the workers bring it in, we tell 'em wipe their boots but do they listen?"

Morris shakes his head. "We listen to what we tell ourselves was said."

"They pulverize it here," the foreman says, pointing to a crew of men standing around a metal vat, their T-shirts dark with sweat. Men are pounding with huge mallets while others position an anvil hanging from a cable that then drops down, splattering blood and bone all around.

"Thor's hammer," Morris says. "But man-made. By the same men who made Thor." Morris laughs, but the foreman only scowls and stares.

"Not your business," the foreman says. "I was just trying to give you some context, to see your place in things. Here," stepping quickly through the factory, "this is where they prepare the casing."

Men are unraveling intestines, scraping the tubes, stretching them, pumping water through to rinse.

"Here's what you do," the foreman continues. "One of the boys wheels a vat to you. Someone else hands you the casing. Division of labor it's called. Modern business practices. All you gotta do is take a handful of meat and stuff it inside. You won't need to move, so your legs shouldn't bother you. It's simple. Just leave a little room in the tube so the next guy can twist the links and tie the ends up."

Morris watches the process. The vat is full of a pulverized mess, bloody and putrid but malleable, easy to grip and mold. The knots on the ends of the sausage links shield the intestines, blood, organs, and bits of bone from the eater even after the contents enter his own intestines. From sausage to sausage.

"I get it," Morris says, finally. "I disguise the truth for a living."

20 · CARNEGIE · 1892

On the other side of the ocean there is a rocky cliff the townspeople call the mountain lion. The lion overlooks the water and when the waves propel rocks at the island, he darts out his long sandpaper tongue and pulverizes them into pebbles he then devours. The lion is voracious; he eats what is before him, not knowing that he, the lion, is the mountain rock. He is devouring himself.

The cliff is in Scotland. On top is perched a castle carved out of the rock of the mountain. There are rumors that, years ago, men smashed the boulders from the mountain into stones, cleared the forest to make a road, carried the stones, then laid them at the end of the road and built the castle. But in the mythology of the place, what stands for truth in Castle Dulsinore, these men did not exist. The mountain lion formed itself into the castle that captured the spirit of its present owner, Andrew Carnegie.

Carnegie maintains his vast holdings in America but has entrusted his mines to managers, part owners, lesser men. Carnegie has reached that point in life where he can leave the day-to-day operations to others while he retires to his ancestral Scotland. He left this island when he was a boy and had nothing. It was in America that he earned his millions. In America he became a god.

Not a ruthless god; he sees himself as gracious. He decrees that the people shall have a library, so workingmen might read a book or two, and libraries are built. He commands that the people shall have knowledge, and a university is built. He will leave the world a better place for lesser men.

He has left Henry Frick in charge of his steel mills at Homestead, Pennsylvania.

21 · EMMA · July 6, 1892

"It is no longer a strike," Alex says. "It is a war."

They are in Massachusetts now, in Worcester. Emma and Alex have opened an ice cream shop, and Fedya runs a photographic studio. The plan was to earn money for Alex's passage back to Russia, where revolutionaries can best serve the cause at the moment. But now all that will have to be rethought. News has come from Pennsylvania, from the Homestead mills.

They close the shop, spread out newspapers on the table before them.

"Frick is the iron hand," Alex says. "Carnegie is the smiling public face, his philanthropy is a show. But while Carnegie luxuriates in his Scottish castle, Frick, his dark soul, wreaks his will."

"How could he hire Pinkertons?!" Emma exclaims. "How could they fire on workers?"

"They are hired soldiers," Alex says. "Maybe Pinkerton supplied them, but these aren't detectives or bodyguards. These are mercenaries. This is a war. The war between labor and capital!"

"The tariff is the vehicle," Emma says, reading the paper. "Congress makes the duty as high as the millionaires want it, but Carnegie had McKinley place a special provision into the bill that allowed Carnegie to lower the price of his steel, knowing that the workers' wages at Homestead were tied to the price. The steelworkers' wages fell. They wanted twenty-four dollars a month. Frick offered twenty-three, knowing full well they would reject the cut in pay. When they did, they struck. Then Frick laid them off, prepared for battle, wrapped the mills in barbed wire, and locked them out. The workers knew what Frick was up to, that he wanted a chance to destroy the union."

Fedya knocks on the glass door out front and Emma lets him in.

"Have you heard?!" she says.

Fedya does not say anything. His eyes are red and bleary, circled in rings. He appears even slighter than usual, more gentle and weak. He is holding a scrolled-up newspaper. He unwraps it, removes the canvas inside, and spreads it on the table in front of them.

"Fedya," Emma says, "it's beautiful."

It is a painting of a river. Boats are floating upstream, all filled with Pinkerton soldiers. Their rifles are raised, and smoke fires out of the barrels and forms clouds that float up and shade the sky dark as the smokestacks surrounding the factory before them. On the banks of the river stand the workers and their families. Women and children have been shot; you can see them bleeding on the grass. Others are trampled by the mad rush to escape the soldiers' guns, up the banks of the river.

Henry Clay Frick stands on a balcony atop the steel mills, stroking his mustache, laughing as he overlooks the battle. And in the sky, in the clouds, there are other winged capitalist sprites: President Harrison, Congressman William McKinley. Andrew Carnegie is watching, too, serene as a divine spectator in control of all that transpires beneath them.

Alex hugs Fedya, kisses him on the cheeks, and Emma does the same.

"I call it *The Battle of Homestead*," Fedya says.

"This is only the first battle," Alex says. "The war has begun."

22 · IDA · 1875

Katie is playing out in the front yard of the McKinleys' Market Street home in Canton. She was chasing a cat until it escaped from her and ran up a tree, where it happened upon a robin's nest. Before the mother bird could do anything to protect her family-to-be, the cat had knocked the eggs down from the limb to the grass below. Katie found the shells cracked and empty. The cat dashed off, then stopped on the road to lick its paws. Katie picked up shards of the spotted shells.

She turns toward the house and looks up at the drawn shades of her mother's room.

"Mother," she says, jumping as she opens her hands. "Look!"

Ida, looking down from her rocking chair, upstairs in the house sees her, she sees it all. *All she sees are the shells. The beauty of the shards.* Katie is three years old and does not know what was inside them.

All Katie sees is the dark form of her mother nod her head on the far side of the window.

Uncle George arrives on his bicycle. He is not with the pretty lady with the yellow curls and the kittenish giggle this time and Katie wonders why. He is with a pretty lady with bobbed black hair and a cackling laugh.

"Katie Pumpkin," Uncle George says. He embraces her and gives her a kiss on the cheek. "How is your mother today, Katie love?"

Katie points up at her mother's window, and George waves.

"How would you like some ice cream, Katie Pumpkin?"

"Where?" she says, looking at the basket on the handlebars in front.

"We'll ride into town. A big girl like you can ride on my bicycle. I forget, do you like chocolate or vanilla? Oh, I remember. Both!"

Katie shakes her head. "Can't," she pouts.

"Can't? And why is that, my ice cream girl?"

"Mommy won't allow it."

"Won't allow it? The shop is just down the street. I'll talk to her."

"Mommy says I can't leave her sight," Katie cries. "Uncle George, why does God punish my mommy so?"

23 · EMMA · July 15, 1892

Emma is on the streets. The night has taken that imperceptible turn toward morning and emerged in the dim nether zone in between. Must be one, two o'clock now. She has paced up and down the sidewalk for hours, until time has become stuck, as if Alex's train had halted on the route to Pittsburgh.

They had closed up the ice cream shop and Fedya's studio, sold what they could and left Worcester to rush back to New York. Friends of Justus put them up—Alex, Justus, and Fedya in a pile on the floor—but still they had to borrow money to pay for Alex's train ride to Pittsburgh and one night's lodging outside the Homestead mills. It was up to Emma to earn the rest, enough for the expenses Alex needed to execute the plan.

Now on the streets of New York, trying to dream . . . she is dreaming . . . *Alex arrives in Pittsburgh and the working people welcome him like some anarchist messiah; hushed but not bowing, they draw strength from him. They show him the way to Homestead, to the corporate offices: "Here lie the strikers," the workers say to him, "good working men gunned down by the Pinkertons. Frick, Henry Clay Frick laughed at the sight as Andrew Carnegie sat in his Scottish castle on the other side of the sea and laughed too; his laugh was heard here at Homestead when the Pinkerton spies lifted their rifles and fired. And there, Mr. Alexander Berkman, up there sits evil Frick, counting money and corpses. . . ."*

A carriage splashes mud from the road, splattering her dress and face. Emma curses reflexively as she wipes her mouth. It is then that she sees herself as if she were looking from the outside; it is as if someone dressed her in a harlot's costume while she was asleep, then placed her on a street corner to be illuminated by the seductive red lights. From a carriage (she now has the good sense to walk away from the large puddle on the edge of the road) a man is leering at her, lascivious, all eyes and open mouth, and she thinks it is her father. Though she knows that her father is still in Rochester, she also knows that this beady-eyed man in the gilded carriage *is* her father: veins flowing with American money and Protestant blood—no poor Russian Jew—but still, the eyes. The hands on her skirts. The searching mouth. Her father.

The heart and body and soul are separate, she tells herself. She makes herself become a character she has read: Sonja, renting her body for the sake of the cause, for the working people. Alex is giving his life. Emma is giving a fuck. It is not a word she uses—it is Victoria Woodhull's word, it is Voltairine de Cleyre's—but that is the word for it. She runs through the men she has slept with, from her girlish imaginings of beautiful Orpheus in the fields back in Russia, to Jacob Kersner in Rochester, to the mangled, snarled face of Johann Most. Alex. Fedya.

Alex is giving his life. A bargain he has struck: Frick for Berkman. A fuck is a small price.

The man in the carriage is beckoning.

The gun, the bullets, postage to send them to Alex in Pittsburgh.

The man still beckons; he leers from the window of his carriage. Emma tries to fix on a smile and walks toward him.

24 · KATIE · June 25, 1875

Her skin is scarlet, as if her slight body cannot contain the torrent of blood coursing inside her. It is the typhoid that is causing her color to darken, the doctor says, not the vicelike grip Ida is keeping on her daughter's hand.

Katie is lying on her bed, eyes closed, rocking her head back and forth, slightly and rapidly, as she tries to rest. Ida leans over and squeezes cool water from a hand towel onto her forehead and she thinks Katie almost smiles as it sizzles off.

"Mommy?"

"Yes, I'm here, love."

"Where are we going, Mommy? It's hot. So hot."

"Down the rabbit hole, my love. It's hot down the rabbit hole."

"Do you have the Small pills, Mommy?"

"Right here, my darling. I shall never forget them."

"Stay with me, Mommy. It's so hot."

Ida squeezes more water on her daughter's forehead. "I shall never leave you, love."

Katie is three and a half. She has lived ten of her little sister's lifetimes already, poor little Ida. Is that a full life? Are their lives meant to run quickly, time that is compacted? Still full, complete, stories with beginnings, middles, and ends, though not as long as one might imagine, as a parent might hope.

The doctor has told her Katie is near the end, most likely. The fever will break soon, or her body will no longer take it.

Ida has never known Doctor English to be so curt in his words, so cruel even. He is tired, he says. He cannot do battle with the typhoid. It outmatches him. The typhoid, to Doctor English, is no longer a disease but has taken on a form. The typhoid is a Gatling gun, and he is armed only with a knife, an Indian's arrow. It is a beast, a monster that has stowed away on ships with the unwashed immigrants, slept in their pens, their dirt-ridden cots, feasted on rotting sausages brought by the swarthy Italians, the fetid beef of the penurious Jews, whiskey of the raucous Irish, Polish vodka, Russian vodka, Slavic goulash. The typhoid burrows itself into the wombs of the immoral sluts who walk the streets, is passed on to the worthless tramps who ride the rails, the shifty Chinamen with their ill-gotten railroad money. The typhoid must be the devil's handiwork, for why else would it visit itself on such decent, moral families as the McKinleys and the Saxtons? It is what this country is coming to. A sign of the collapse, the end. "The bastard immigrants," the doctor says, biting his lower lip hard.

Ida grasps her daughter's hand. She thought Katie had left her, but then she felt a rubbing on her cheek, so faint it was almost imperceptible but there it was, and a coo from the bed that faded into silence and then Katie was asleep.

"How is she?" It is William.

"I do not want that doctor in here."

"My dear, it is not his fault—"

"Perhaps not. But I do not want him here. He is a vile man."

"He has worked so hard, my dear. He was here all night. You are tired, too; we all are. Did you sleep?"

Ida rubs the wet towel on Katie's forehead. Opens the girl's blouse and moistens her chest and arms. The skin is so white now, the limbs slight. She has eaten so little over the past weeks. She is a strong girl—

she would not have held on so long otherwise—but her body has little left to fight the typhoid.

Ida's eyes are closed, she forces them shut to try to rest some herself. She must be fresh when Katie awakes; she must be ready. Ida is still grasping her daughter's hand hard when her head drops to her shoulder, nodding off.

She finds herself in the darkness, an open space with a cool breeze gently blowing her hair. She hears singing, a man's quiet voice. She is in the front yard, the grass is tall here on Market Street. The girls are holding hands with her, all in a circle, dancing, laughing. Little Ida must be five or six, Katie is eight. Katie has her mother's long, dark hair; Ida has retained her blonde locks, her blue eyes. Mommy, Mommy! More, more! Ida leads them around faster, holding hands, running, the circle spinning wildly until the girls are in the air, still holding hands, spinning, dancing, laughing. Little Ida is happy, little Katie is happy. They are in the clouds. Her mother is there, too. John, her Confederate love, too.

Suddenly there is no laughter, no dancing; they are gone. Ida is alone, adrift in the clouds. No anchor, no rudder. She is rocked by the wind, here, there. A leaf. A storm rages in the clouds; in this world everywhere a storm is raging, and Ida is a helpless shard of a leaf. Alone. Adrift. Surrounded by death.

She feels she is beginning to shake. Thunder from afar, not here yet but fast approaching. Her body is so weak that it cannot even control itself, her limbs, her mind.

Alone.

There is still William. He is her love that remains.

She is still holding Katie's hand, but now she realizes it is no longer warm. Katie's forehead is dry, her face still, eyes shut.

William is kneeling beside her, holding Katie's other hand, pressing it against his lips as he sings.

25 · LEON · 1893

When he is on strike, Leon attends the workers' meetings. Frank is now his sister's husband and he organizes them. They meet in the mornings. It is Frank's idea that they gather early, so they will not think of the time off from work as a vacation, they will not grow soft.

Frank insists, too, that they meet in the woods, not in the taverns as the other men wish. "It is not only religion that is the opiate of the masses," Frank says. Frank knows his Karl Marx, his Bakunin, his Engels. "It is liquor," he says. "Whiskey and beer. In the woods the air is clean. There is room to run, to wrestle and box. Stay fit, strong. Let off steam.

"The capitalists are looking for excuses to get rid of us. You sleep in one day, it makes it easy for them. They will not need to get out their Pinkertons, their hired guns."

One man brings his pistol and posts the boss's picture on a tree, target-shoots holes in the temple. The men laugh. Frank does not object. This Frank is a leader.

There is a clearing in the woods, and Frank stands on a tree stump while Leon and the other men sit on the grass and the low-hanging tree limbs. Frank's figure is elongated unnaturally, magnificent; his voice emanates a glow. Leon's eyes go watery listening; he can't help it—a tear drips down, but he wipes it away quick.

At the first meetings the men are angry, ready to storm the factory, take it over by force. Soon the scabs will be hired; they will not be hard to find. They must be fought.

Frank says, "For a workingman to take food from the plate of his fellow is a greater sin than the capitalist's theft. Will a capitalist ever betray his class for us? And they have the money, the police, the Pinkertons. We have so little. But throw a few crumbs, too tiny and rotten for rodents to subsist on, and there will be workers ready to stab us and our families, snatch our jobs. We cannot stand for it! We will not! Our only strength is in numbers! In solidarity!"

The men cheer. Pistols are waved, torches lit. Frank waves them quiet. It is a delicate matter, balancing emotion and reasoned thought: the stoking up, and then the calming down. It is another reason Frank insists they meet in the woods.

The bosses hire scabs to replace the striking men. Frank leads the men to the factory gates the next morning. "Your job is your property," he says. "You have a right to work, to feed your family."

At dawn they form a blockade, two deep, arms linked, in front of the entrance of the factory. But before they see a scab, the cops come at them with clubs, beating down on heads, smashing apart their linked arms.

"What is our crime?" Frank shouts. "What are we charged with?! We want a dollar and a quarter for a day's work! We want an eight-hour shift! Are these crimes in America?"

Leon's arms are linked with Frank's when they are both knocked down. Leon feels something hard hit the back of his head, then he is trampled by boots so can do nothing when they drag Frank away in the paddy wagon.

Leon and the rest of the men agree to meet that evening in the woods. There is no one to take Frank's place; no one wants to. Someone says that his wife's father runs a saloon and will feed them sandwiches at the next meeting. After all, there is no work, there is no money for food. The others agree. They decide to meet at lunchtime, to take full advantage of the free meals. Besides, in the mornings they can look for other jobs, though few will mention this aloud.

Days pass and no one hears from Frank. One night Leon walks to the jail and a guard tells him he can join Frank in another cell if he cares so much.

At the next meeting there is talk of returning to work. There are men with four, six, seven children, and there is nothing for them, no money for food, clothes, coal. Some of the children have kept their jobs, but it is not enough to pay even the rent.

"The factory will go on without us. Each of us is a lump of coal they shovel into the furnace to fuel the factory. More where that came from; just dig deeper."

"There is nothing else we can do. It is unfair, it is unjust. It is criminal, vile, evil. Yes, it is all those things and more. But we have no choice. We have done what we could."

Then Leon speaks up, for the first time. "We cannot betray who we are," Leon says. "Remember what Frank said to us? We are working people. Our only strength is in solidarity. Have we forgotten?"

"Do you have a wife?" someone shouts. "Do you have children?" says another. "Do you even have a girlfriend?" someone else says, and there is much laughter and banging of glasses.

A tomato hits Leon in the face; it stings him in the eye. More laughs.

Within a week the men have decided that they will go back to work wherever they can find it, whoever will hire them.

Leon tries again to speak to Frank, but he is told they have moved him to another jail.

Some days he walks through the streets and lets his mind go: he climbs under his mother's white sheets—this time he lifts the covers and crawls in—she is smiling and warm, she welcomes him into a den and holds him snug; you don't talk, just lie there, gazing up at the stars at a place that isn't there (that's it: this place, it isn't there), the world's upside down. He doesn't know where he is when finally he sees a bar and walks in and watches the girls, too beautiful to speak to.

He walks home in the dark alone.

Leon stays out of work another week. He is living with his father, his brothers, his sisters, his father's new wife. The wife wants to know why they must feed this man, this Leon, just who does he think he is. A twenty-year-old man not working, living off the toil of his old father, his brother. "This is not right," she says. "In the old country you would never hear."

Leon begins to tell her about the strike. A boy he worked with in the factory, one day the bin of liquid metal tipped and poured over him, coated him in the molten silver. Leon thought he could see his bones glow, his skeleton. Another boy, his arm was sliced right off at the shoulder when a bundle of wire caught hold and wrapped around and was pullied away too quick. Eyes are poked by a stray wire, you should hear the screams. This for seventy-five cents a twelve-hour day, for a dollar. If the doctor will see you, they will take all of your wages, you will never see them again. If the doctors will see you.

Leon looks at his father, but his father says nothing.

"And so," his father's wife says, waving him off, "in this country you go to the city and work you become rich. They say this in the books. America, land of opportunity. You must work. Even the oxen he works for his food."

26 · LEON · 1893

The next week Leon returns to the factory. He has learned from the other men that it is not so easy to get your job back. The factory is hiring new workers, but they have a list of the strikers, and the strikers will not get their jobs back.

At the gate Leon is directed to the hiring man, just outside the doors to the factory. There is a line of men, and the hiring man has a list he is checking off. Leon cannot recall the man's name—he may never have known it—but he recognizes him. The day when the molten metal spilled on the boy, the hiring man immediately grabbed three workers to right the barrel and shovel what had spilled on the floor back in. The boy screamed and writhed, but the man urged them to work on. The metal that spilled, it was so precious.

The man in front of Leon is told he is not needed, not now or ever, and now Leon is first in line.

"Name?" the man asks.

"Nieman," Leon says. The name just comes into his head. It is nothing: No Man. "Fred Nieman," he says.

"What sort of name is that, Nieman?"

"I— it's—" Leon shrugs his shoulders.

"Ever worked here before?"

"Never."

"Experience?"

"There was a glass factory in Pennsylvania. And a wire factory in Detroit. Or near there, in Alpena."

The man has been writing things down, but now he stops and looks at Leon.

"You a striking bastard, No Man?" he says.

"No, sir," Leon says.

"Not only are you a striking bastard," the hiring man says, smiling. "You are one lying bastard who will never work again."

27 · VICTORIA AND IDA · December 1875

Ida is in her room upstairs, rocking on the chair Daddy gave her. A wedding present, it was from her childhood, it was before everything. Rocking. At the window. There is light outside, there must be, the shade is drawn which is the way she likes it; it leaves shadows, only shadows, people transformed into shadows. We transform into shadows. Rocking.

Ester brings her lunch. She knocks and spoons the soup. "Where is Mr. McKinley today, Ester? What is today in the world of my William?" And Ester's words take form, the light streaming through; she is transported, Ida is. She is not a recluse. She travels. "What today in the world of William?" *The where, the who.* "What today, Ester?"

"A rally on temperance. A woman, Victoria Woodhull, is visiting from the East to speak."

"Who is she, Ester? You blush when you say the name."

"I shouldn't, Miss Ida. It's just what people say is all."

"You must, Ester. Tell me all."

"Well, Miss Ida. If you say."

That is the pattern; Ida knows it and smiles. Whether Ester embroiders or spoons out reality unadulterated Ida cannot be sure, but she will tell all.

"This Victoria Woodhull, ma'am, they say she doesn't believe in marriage, she says men and women should do their—you know, be familiar—with whom they like. They say she or her sister is close with one of them Vanderbilts, that she ran for president even. Frederick Douglass wouldn't even be seen with her, and he was supposed to be running with her! She's sold stocks and raises the dead and everything in between. Miss Ida, the woman's a scandal."

"Ester," Ida says. "Tell Mr. McKinley to bring her to the house after his business with her is through."

Ida is not certain how much time has passed when she hears a knock on the door. She had dozed off, she must have. "Yes, yes," she whispers, and the door is opened.

"I—da," she struggles to say as a woman approaches her, "Mc—Kinley." She offers a hand that falls limply from her wrist.

"Victoria Woodhull." The woman first grasps Ida's hand but then is compelled to embrace her about the shoulders, hold her close. Perhaps she can transfer some strength to this weak sister, that is the message: massage muscle, bone, and will into her with a warm hug.

"I am told," Ida continues slowly, "you are quite renowned."

Ida sits back down in her rocking chair by the window, surrounded on either side by piles of wool and slippers. Victoria pulls up another chair and sits across from her.

"You ran for president," Ida goes on. "An ex—, extraordinary thing for a lady. My husband wishes to run, too. One day."

"He has many ready advantages," Victoria says. "Privileges."

Ida nods her head.

"Is he prepared to make full use of them? Has he read Marx? Have you?" Victoria does not wait for answers. "The system of capital degrades, and it is the woman who bears the brunt of the degradation. Man is struck so low he must turn woman even lower. Domination and hierarchy are the only structures he has learned and so that is the game he plays. But there is another way. Where the mind blossoms and the heart is full."

Victoria scoots her chair closer. Victoria grabs Ida's hands gently and holds them steady on her lap.

"Are you free, Ida?" Victoria says.

Ida looks at her, her head either nodding slightly or twitching. Victoria is not certain.

"This is not a nation in which women are free, by and large," Victoria says. "We have freed the Negro, but left womankind in chains. Marriage can be an enslaver."

"And circumstance," Ida says. "The turns of life can form a prison. God . . ."

Victoria waits for her to complete the thought but that is all of it.

"Sexuality can be shackled by the church and its vows," Victoria says. "It doesn't have to be."

"You would appreciate my brother George," Ida says, and her mouth crackles into a smile. "Never let anyone stand in the way between himself and," she pauses and lowers her voice, "a bed."

The smile lapses, and soon Ida is gazing at the pictures on the wall: the little girl, the baby.

"Those are yours," Victoria says. "You have lost them."

Ida is silent.

"Have you spoken with them?"

Ida turns to Victoria, a spark of brightness in her eyes.

"I can help you," Victoria says. "It used to be my profession. Séances, communing with the dead."

"You can summon them?" Ida's eyes are wide open and her voice is trembling.

"Close your eyes, Ida. Hold my hands tight."

Ida does as she's told.

"Tell me their names."

"Katherine. I called her my little Katie. And Ida. Ida was just a baby. She couldn't speak when . . ."

"That doesn't matter. Now stand up with me, Ida. Let me open the window. Hold my hands again. Stand close. Your eyes must be closed. What would you say to Katherine? When you wanted her to come to dinner, what would you say?"

"I would—"

"Not out loud." Victoria massages, with a fingertip, the side of

Ida's head. "And what would you sing to Ida? In your mind, Ida, in
your soul. Let them come to you. Katie. Ida. Come to your mother.
Katie, Ida. Speak."

The two women stand in silence. Then, suddenly, Ida clenches
Victoria's hands hard. The room is very cold. The curtains rustle, the
shades slap against the windowpane. The wind swirls, wrapping them
both in a spiraling cocoon of spirit. Victoria knows the feeling, though
it has been many years since she led a séance, years since she beckoned
back the dead.

There are sounds that are voices only Ida can hear. There are
flashes of light that are images only Ida can see. There are rushes of
wind that are sensations only Ida can feel. An embrace, a song, a kiss.

Ida is standing rigid, her eyes closed. She feels cleansed, suddenly,
by the water pouring down her cheeks like a river.

28 · LEON · 1891

He has two names now. At work he is Nieman. That is enough for
the foreman, the men on the new factory floor. "Nieman?" "Here.
We need a body." If someone asks, after work with a beer, it's Fred.
Fred Nieman. At home he is Leon. Waldek works with him and sees
both.

One day they are forging buckets; the steam burns you, then you
submerge the hot metal in water to cool. The grating in his head, the
harsh taste in his throat. His eyes clench shut. Survive the pain; it will
pass. Shut your thoughts down, space travel. This is the thought that
seeps through: he is molten, like the metal he lugs in the vats steaming
up at him on the factory floor. God pours us into casts, stamps names,
families, fates. Every life has an arc. Leon, Nieman. Waldek, Frank.
Shuffle them like cards. You are every man. You are no man.

"You are all right tonight, Leon?" Waldek is walking home with
him, after work.

Waldek has a girl. She has a sister, but it did not work with her and Leon; there were silences she did not want a part of.

Leon goes home and lies in bed. At night he sees his mother, her long fingers, alabaster white, a smile that fills the ceiling, sparkles moonlight.

"Don't worry, my precious boy. You are headed for great things."

The pamphlets Frank brings him, the books, Leon reads.

His mother fills the sky.

He lies alone.

His mother's smile is the moon. She speaks the future. She is in a place now where history is laid out before her and she is reading it to her Leon, telling him the story. At night she turns the pages of this book, what time will bring.

He reads.

He is alone.

He listens to the sound of the moonlight.

29 · HANNA · June 1876

At first he is not visible. There are just clouds of smoke emanating from a space the other spectators have left open on the bench seat in the courtroom. As if he were not a man but a coal refinery, a factory. As if he were what he has built, what he has paid for, what he owns. A hot, fiery spirit of the modern age.

Then a hand appears, stubby fingers grasping an even fatter cigar. The clouds drift apart for an instant and are sucked inside, back from whence they came, and it is then you see the ruddy cheeks, the narrow beady eyes, the corners of his thin lips flirting with the hint of an impish smile. His arms are spread wide along the tops of the bench back, his legs are splayed out to allow his vast belly to drop down without hindrance.

The belly is the focal point. It is coated in a silky white dress shirt and a black vest, highlit by a sparkling gold chain that holds the watch tucked away in a pocket. It is not the clothes or the watch where the eye is drawn but the belly, round as a womb, full term, near ready to burst. To burst with many things. With this afternoon's lunch of roasted goose bathed in a cherry Madeira sauce, baked red potatoes lathered with sweet melted butter, hunks of black pumpernickel bread lathered with more butter, dipped in honey, bread pudding, peanuts and wine.

Bursting with money, too, gold coins and paper dollars and endless credit. That is what flows through the umbilical cord, fueled by the goose and potatoes and bread pudding, fired by the Cuban cigar in his fist. And still, though there is money in the full-bellied womb of Marcus Alonzo Hanna, much money, that is not what he is about. That is not the focus of his small, balding head. That is not why his mouth flirts with a smile that might just as likely emit a curse, suppressed but ready to dart out like a serpent's forked tongue. That is not the child he feels he is carrying, that is not what he yearns to bring into the world, to give to Ohio and America. There is something else.

The prosecutor is wrapping up his examination, or so Hanna supposes. He cannot be sure for there is no crescendo, no logical end to the line of questioning; but the silence after he last spoke seems a minute or two longer than his customary pauses brought on by stammering and confusion. A district attorney lost in his own courtroom. The dolt is a servant, salaried by the tax dollars of Marcus Hanna.

"Mr. McKinley," the judge says as the prosecutor finds his seat, "are you prepared to proceed for the defense?"

"Yes, Your Honor." McKinley stands up from the defense counsel table.

"Thank you, Your Honor," the prosecutor mumbles. "That will be all."

"Sergeant McGarrity," McKinley begins, "you were discussing the arrest of the striking men, my clients."

McKinley stands up, tugs down his vest to straighten it, then remains erect behind counsel table. He is not a lawyer to pounce on the witness stand, to stalk about the courtroom as if seeking prey. His tone is even, respectful.

"Sergeant, these are hardworking men, would you agree?"

The officer nods. "I know nothing to the contrary."

"They work the mines?"

"I believe."

"Every day."

The sergeant nods.

"They are fathers?"

"So I've come to learn."

"They have never been known to be part of the troublesome lot? They follow the righteous path, not drink nor other sins?"

The judge coughs. "Move along, Mr. McKinley." And a louder cough is heard from the spectators' bench seats, a cough emitted from amid the clouds of cigar smoke, something between a laugh and a scream.

"These men, before their wages were cut, they did not ever run astray of the law?"

"To my knowledge."

"Before their wages were cut, they did not even strike, isn't that the truth?"

"As I know it to be. Yes."

"When their wages were cut, and they struck, it was then that the mine operators replaced them, yes? Filled their jobs with other men, good men with families too, but jobs my clients had held and worked?"

"I believe that is the case."

"And were it not for their wages being cut, and the strike, and their jobs being replaced—"

The prosecutor stands. "Objection, Your Honor. That is speculative, legal conclusion—"

"Move along, Mr. McKinley," the judge says.

"Well then," McKinley says, "*before* they struck, and their jobs were replaced, you never knew these men to commit an act of violence against their fellow man?"

The officer gazes up at the judge's bench, shrugs to ask whether the lawyer can continue this irrelevant line of questions.

Hanna searches his vest pockets for a scrap of paper to scrawl a note to the doltish prosecutor: *Object, you fool! The men were strikers, they destroyed property on their employer's grounds, the property of Marcus Alonzo Hanna. They were arrested. They are guilty!*

Hanna can find no paper so he pulls himself up from his seat, stumbles into the aisle, and steps toward the prosecutor's table.

"You may be seated, Mr. Hanna," the judge says. "Answer Mr. McKinley's questions, Sergeant. They are proper."

"I forgot the question."

"Well then." McKinley steps on the officer's words now. For the first time in the trial he is firm, loud, as close to angry as his understated way allows. Hanna senses it: submerged outrage. Hanna does not like the turn. The men of the jury, all can see, have stirred out of their postmeal slumbers and are nodding their heads at attention.

No, Hanna does not like it. This attorney, McKinley, is a puzzle. He is not a workingmen's lawyer, not a Eugene Debs or even close. Hanna has had him investigated a bit. The man's politics are, from all accounts, acceptable Republican. Sound money, sound respect for the dominion of capital. Not unlike Hanna's. Nor is he wanting for clients, or money. His wife's family are Saxtons, of Saxton's bank in Canton. A steady font of funds there. Respectable. Active in veterans' groups, member of the Masonic Lodge, head of the Canton YMCA, superintendent of the Sunday School at the First Methodist Church. Attorney William McKinley is a man of modest tastes and modest wants. No children. Which all makes this case, these clients, an odd choice. An odd choice for a man who seems not the type to make odd choices. Unless he seeks revenge on the prosecutor who defeated him at the polls, who threw him out of office by a sparse few hundred votes. But Attorney McKinley does not seem a man who stokes the embers of revenge in his heart. Hanna has learned that he is a churchly man and wonders if that explains it.

He thinks not. He has heard that Attorney McKinley has his sights set on Washington, on the Congress. Hanna picked that pearl up by himself, in the den of his club.

"Let me repeat it for you then, Sergeant," McKinley shouts. "You made the arrests. The men, these men, my clients, were outside of the mines. There were police. There were men entering the mines to work. Some called them names. Some shouted Scab! There were worse names I cannot repeat in the presence of ladies. These men were workers. They worked an honest day or night in the mines. Some brought their children to exercise their God-given right to toil alongside their fathers in those same mines. You saw them, Sergeant. Yet you never saw them do a single act of violence against their fellow man? As God is your witness, Sergeant, is that not the truth?"

The officer looks at the prosecuting attorney across from him, who is staring uncomfortably at the jurors, then up at the judge again, who again nods: "Answer the question." There is silence for a moment. The jurors follow the officer's eyes around the courtroom as they gaze everywhere but at the man to whom he is supposed to be speaking, the defendants' attorney, William McKinley.

Hanna does not like it one bit. *Damn the judge:* he should stand up and explain it all to the jurors. The prosecutor, the dolt, will never get the point across. Mark Hanna, owner of those mines, the man whose operations were slowed down, almost stopped for a day by this—*illegal breach of contract!*—strike, whose profits were, essentially, truth be known, taken from him—money rightfully his; earned of his labors!—to the owner goes the profit; he who risks, he who builds—*property destroyed!*—Hanna should have a right to speak.

He would put down his cigar and say, were he addressing the jury, that this McKinley is missing the point. He may seem a decent, God-following type, this William McKinley, and perhaps he is. But still, it is a sly lawyer's trick. For these men are not charged with an act of violence against man! They are not charged with assault or murder! They were striking! They destroyed fences and gates! Illegal! A crime! Does not a piece of metal have rights?! Or its owner?! Marcus Hanna was robbed of his profit! Robbed, gentlemen of the jury! As clear as were an urchin to pick your pockets on the streets of Cleveland!

Hanna puffs his cigar violently, emitting more clouds, then coughs, drawing the judge's eyes to him. He begins to stand again but the judge waves him down.

"Yes, Mr. McKinley," the sergeant finally says, quietly. "That is the truth."

Once the trial ends the jury does not take long to consider. Hanna knows that the strikers will be let off. It is a battle lost.

After the jury delivers its verdict Hanna waddles down the aisle.

As McKinley places his files into his briefcase, Hanna grabs the attorney's shoulder and offers a hand to shake.

"McKinley, is it?" Hanna says.

McKinley looks up at him.

"You just beat the bejesus out of that poor prosecutor, McKinley. Why Stark County tossed you out the other year—well, it doesn't add up to much sense. But that's the Democrats. They fight tooth and nail for power and position, but once they get it, damned if they have a clue what to do with it. Am I right?"

McKinley nods his head cautiously. Around him the defendants, his clients, are embracing their families. A reporter approaches when one of the men asks how they can ever repay him.

"No need to worry about money," McKinley says, as the reporter jots down his words on a pad. "The honor of representing you good men was enough. Good luck to you all. God's speed."

Hanna laughs, shakes his head as the reporter walks off.

"Not that they were good for a dime anyway," Hanna mutters. "What you've been paid is all you were going to get, am I right? Smart move."

McKinley begins to walk down the aisle of the courtroom to the door. He waves to his clients, gestures to another reporter that they can speak in a minute. When he hears a loud bang he turns back; Mark Hanna has bent the floor with the tip of his cane.

"Those were my mines, Mr. McKinley," Hanna shouts. "The striking bastards—your clients—my workers—were trying to shut 'em down. *My* contract they were breaching. *My* property they destroyed. Gates, fences, what have you. I honored my end of the deal, I always do. Remember that, son. Marcus Alonzo Hanna is as good as his bond. Always. They may not like the deal they signed; they may cry that I got the better end of it. Well, you're damned right I got the better end of the deal. I always do. Remember that, too, McKinley. Mark Hanna always does."

"I don't take sides in your business matters," McKinley says. "I was representing clients and did them my best. I would do you no worse, Mr. Hanna."

"No," Hanna says, "I am sure you will not. You are running for the Congress I hear?"

"I am," McKinley says. "And I intend to win."

"I have no doubt you do," Hanna says. "I had been wondering what a man in your position, a Republican of reputable credentials, was doing defending strikers. Now the timing makes a touch more sense. I respect the idea, the broadening appeal. Admire it, truly." Hanna pauses, looks the younger man up and down. "Would you care to join me in a cigar, Mr. McKinley? It's a wonderful Cuban." Hanna pulls out a long stogie from his inside pocket and waves it under McKinley's nose. "To the victor and so on. You deserve a good smoke."

"I'm sorry, sir, but I don't smoke."

"Don't—?! You've never tried then, I'll wager?"

"No, Mr. Hanna. Nor drink. And I don't intend to. It is not the Lord's pleasure, so it shall not be mine. And my wife, she cannot stand cigars. The smoke makes her ill."

"Mr. McKinley, I don't intend to debate theological matters with you here and now, or matters of marriage, but the way I see it, the Lord planted the tobacco leaf and the barley as sure as He did roses and carrots." Hanna is smiling as he lights up the cigar and inhales deeply. "Indeed, I might put it a bit stronger. I might say that you are thumbing your nose at the Lord by denying yourself these goodly things He has bestowed for your pleasure. And there is no greater pleasure, Mr. McKinley, than two men ruminating at the end of a long, hard-fought day, over a fine smoke. It's the intoxicating effect of the tobacco; the sight of the smoky clouds is almost dreamy. And there's the scent and the feel. Indescribable is what it is." Hanna waves the lit cigar under McKinley's nose. "You're certain you wouldn't care to try?"

McKinley follows the scent, then shakes his head.

"Thank you, Mr. Hanna. Most kind. But no."

Hanna shrugs his shoulders, then takes another long drag.

"Mr. McKinley," he says, "you will realize one day that nothing remains rigid in this life. Everything succumbs to change. You will learn not to waste strength fighting those winds." Hanna blows a cloud of smoke between them. McKinley inhales, he cannot help it, and coughs.

"We will meet again," Mark Hanna says. Then he swings his gold-tipped cane to the floor and walks out of the courtroom.

30 · LEON · 1894

He walks to the outskirts of the city, then rides the streetcar into Cleveland. The car is empty for the first stops, then a few stragglers grab the handrails and swing themselves on, aimless travelers like himself. Leon glues his forehead to the side glass and watches the people go by. There are gaunt faces, blanched, empty eyes. It is the work that does it, it clears the body of spirit so you can no longer even know what you want, what has been taken from you. There are insights only Leon knows.

From his pants pocket he takes out a bottle he has just received from the mail. Nostrums. He opens the bottle and pours out four tablets and pops them in his mouth and chews them into a powder that burns the insides of his cheeks.

Across the aisle from him sits a mother with her young son, four years old he must be. The boy's eyes are black moons with small white stars inside that wink at him, speak a fierce, soothing poetry of revolution. Transfixed by the eyes Leon does not notice at first that the boy's arms stop at the elbows, he has no hands and his mouth is lopsided, his entire face is malformed. His mother is young and beautiful with a sadness that will never leave her.

What is the nostrum he has ordered this time? He forgets even the advertisement or the magazine he saw it in. Cocaine? Penicillin? Doctor Watson's Magic Elixir? There is a dull, gnawing pain he is becoming convinced the pills cannot relieve. The pain is now a part of him.

A newspaper has been left on the seat beside him and he picks it up. John D. Rockefeller, Cleveland's own, is establishing a new plant, hiring workers. The suggestion is that Rockefeller should be applauded for good works, that by hiring workers he is delivering bread to the tables of their families. Leon can picture the crooked pinch of Rockefeller's razor-sharp nose; there is not a picture in this paper but he has seen it. He knows them all, Rockefeller, Morgan, Frick, Carnegie. Gould, Vanderbilt. He clenches the paper in his fists and tosses the crumpled mass on the floor of the streetcar.

. . .

He gets off at the stop he heard about at work, walks down a few blocks until he hears the music and sees the saloon with the men and women visible through the windows and the red light outside. Then he opens the door and walks inside.

The men told him about a room in the back. He walks toward the music, finds a curtain disguising a doorway and peeks in. A tinny piano is playing fast and loud, a Negro at the far end of the room at an upright. This is the ragtime he has heard only snatches of before, passing saloons on the street. A woman sits on top of the piano, wearing only petticoats and a corset and an elaborate brassiere, kicking her bare, exposed legs in the piano player's face. There are women everywhere, uplifted cleavage, bare thighs. Lips painted bright red against pale white skin. There are men, some in suits, one in a policeman's uniform, some holding the women about the hips, some kissing them, patting them on the rear, giving a squeeze. Bottles are poured, glasses raised, clinked, drunk. The music plays, the fast ragtime.

There is a bitterness deep beneath their eyes; Leon senses it—it's hollow, an emptiness behind the false smiles.

He closes the curtain and walks back toward the door, then spots an empty table in a far corner and decides to sit down.

He scans the room and sees a girl in front of him, just entered from what must be the kitchen. Holding a silver tray with glasses and a bottle with both hands. She is so small, so slight, so weak, the bottle and the glasses might fall, Leon thinks, it all might come crashing down. The girl holds the tray with two small delicate hands as if she is holding a butterfly, her delicate life, what is really air.

He wonders if he has seen her before, on a trolley, on the streets, another bar. There's this sense he has.

Just then things go quiet, the piano, the back room. Everything goes still—moments like this happen. The men at the bar freeze, the girls serving drinks. An old man Leon has seen in the factory stands and begins to sing, his voice deep and rich, a warbling baritone, what's left of it. Workers, brotherhood; impossible love, and then, suddenly, death. Leon can't place the song but he's heard it somewhere; one day he fell asleep at the farm under a tree while a storm rolled in and when he awoke a bird was calling. The music floods over him, seeps in.

Since the strike, he could not keep work.

Since the strike, he lives at home still.

His father's new wife. Her shrill snarl.

A lethargy that sets in when there's nothing to do.

He finds work, another factory. He uses the name Nieman.

There's this grating in his head, a sharp metallic shriek that doesn't stop.

Then people move again and it strikes him: *no one hears the song but me.*

The girl is walking toward the curtain, but Leon steps in front of her.

"Miss," he says. "I wanted, if I could, something to drink."

She looks up at him with dark, swelling eyes.

"I'm sorry—"

"Leon."

"—there is no service. This," she points her head down at the champagne on her tray, "is for a man in the back."

"I didn't expect any service," Leon says. Maybe his smile is too slight for her to notice. "There is no service for the workingman."

She looks at him puzzled. She is just a girl, fifteen, sixteen years old, what can she know?

Leon laughs. "I was joking," he says.

And the girl walks away.

31 · McKINLEY · 1888

His belly is now round, his hair thinning, leaving the temples bare. He stands with his hand in his pants pocket, the stomach jutting out from his parted robe as if it were gasping for air. He walks to the

French doors and opens them, breathes in deep. It is summer, but at this early hour the air is brisk. He gazes at the dark, quiet city for a moment. Twelve years in Washington, and still he expects to see Canton when he looks outside.

He sits down and rings the bell that brings in the Negro with breakfast. Three eggs, two thick slices of bacon, a slab of bread, tea. He reads the newspaper as he eats, skimming his eye for news of the tariff, price reports on clothes, household goods, other affected industries, profit reports, commentaries, letters to the editor. He is drawing the connections in his head, constructing arguments. The other day he saw an advertisement for men's suits that gave him an idea: in Congress, when the Democrats were mocking his tariff as a device to raise prices for the ordinary man and profits for the bosses, McKinley would unwrap a paper satchel and extract a man's suit, the ten dollar price tag still intact. "This was purchased," he would intone, suppressing all hint of a smile, "at the store of my distinguished adversary from across the aisle, Leopold Morse."

A rare instant of theatrics for McKinley, but that is not what he loves so much about the political life. There is the camaraderie of his fellows. The give-and-take of debate, the mental jousting and strategy.

And there's the art of the deal, of facilitation, resolution. Some of his colleagues on the Hill scorn the daily onslaught of the lobbyists, the way they line up outside your office door and camp on floors, on chairs, on the corner of a desk of a fetching secretary. Even strangers will soil the shoulders of your suit with a stinging slap on the back with hands oily and slick from anxiety and fear and last night's scotch still exuding from their pores. They are salesmen, really, pitching the wares of their employers for congressional purchase. And the barter is two-way. Thomas Reed tells of a congressman of an earlier day who would simply post a sheet of paper on his office door on which industry's hired hands would write down, precisely, what position they wished the representative to take on pending legislation, and how much they were willing to provide him in return. "After all," Reed would say, "we are more capable of providing both sides of an argument than these palm-greasers can of either."

Which is not quite how McKinley sees things. Legislation is a cooperative business; the lawyers for Carnegie and Frick, Morgan and Gould, are partners in the national enterprise. They deserve our ears and, if not respect, something less than disdain. You sit down and hear them out and roll up your sleeves, and together you make a bill. One need not be ashamed that the Tariff Act is of varied and uncertain parentage.

McKinley knows he is not the man to share a drink with after a long night's session. There have been enough occasions when he has been on the street outside their apartment house exchanging a word with a man—a senator, congressman, or lobbyist—and Ida has emerged out of the window waving a handkerchief, shouting farewells as they walked away. Or when a winded messenger has charged to his desk on the House floor with an urgent message, and McKinley has had to cede his time on the floor to a less able colleague while he rushed outside, waved down a carriage and, once home, raced up the stairs to find Ida lying on the floor of her room, sobbing and shaking. There is a pattern to his days. The House chamber is a sanctuary, though even there he is not safe.

His colleagues have learned to keep their distance from McKinley, and Tom Reed, certainly, has had his fun with him (behind his back, of course). But still, in twelve years in the Congress McKinley has earned their respect. He is a listener, not a shouter. Not one to rock the boat. Even his more difficult colleagues know that McKinley will not make trouble. He can be counted on.

When he is finished eating, he walks to the bathroom, moistens his mug of shaving soap with water from the sink, lathers his face, and picks up a straightedge razor. Lesser men might nick themselves bloody with the sharp, heavy blade, even while standing still before a mirror, but McKinley shaves as he walks about the room reading letters he holds in his other hand. His mother has written from Canton. The local Republican clubs send well wishes. There are newspaper articles his secretary has clipped for him, on the tariff, the benefits it brings to American business; the currency issue, gold and silver.

It is 1888, but it could be 1877, 1880, 1885. It is the same morning ritual, only slight differences with the years. In 1876, when he was first elected to Congress, he set up Grant Clubs around Ohio, bringing in voters to the Republican Party. In 1880 they were Garfield Clubs. There were Hayes Clubs.

There is never a moment to spare. He walks to the Capitol, or rides, and works there until the evening, then is home tending to Ida.

In Washington issues come and go, but for McKinley they remain constant. The tariff is the bulwark, his signature issue. The tariffs must be kept high. We must protect American business, and the tariff is what our businessmen demand for protection. "The tariff is not an issue of politics for me," McKinley likes to say. "It is an issue of principle."

America for Americans.

His secretary has clipped an editorial from the *Chicago Tribune*. *About two thousand millionaires run the politics of the Republican Party and make its tariffs*, it says. McKinley has read it all before. He knows how it will conclude, its mocking tone. *Whatever duties protect the two thousand plutocrats is protection to American industry. Whatever don't is free trade.*

McKinley would like to sit the editors down and reason with them for an evening. Yes, the high tariffs protect the Rockefellers, the Carnegies, the Vanderbilts. Yes, they are millionaires. And yes, they support William McKinley and the rest of the Republican Party. Yes, those successful men have been known to drop a contribution into the Republican Party coffers. But what you do not understand is that the businessmen the tariffs protect in turn protect the American working-man. Bigger business means expansion, more jobs. Higher profits mean higher wages. The benefits shower down on all.

A shrill sound from down the hall disturbs him, and McKinley walks to the door to hear.

"William, precious? Where have you gone, my William?"

McKinley strikes the last patch of whiskers from his chin, then walks to the bathroom and rinses off. He is still handsome, though not pretty; age has given him a solidity, security in bulk. The chances are good he could be the next Speaker, should the Republicans gain control of the House in next term's elections, as they almost certainly will.

The sound from the hall is louder now, more shrill. Every morning before he leaves to go to the Capitol he hears it. Every morning when he walks outside there she is, Ida, waving at him from the upstairs window.

"Don't leave me, William. I'm all alone."

A messenger knocks on the door and hands McKinley a letter. It is from his friend Mark Hanna. Hanna is preparing for this summer's national party convention, and he wants all Ohio Republicans solid behind John Sherman for the nomination. He is certain that McKinley understands the importance of having a Republican and an Ohioan in the Executive Mansion in 1889. An Ohioan first, a Republican second, Hanna jokes. American third. The letter follows up on conversations McKinley and Hanna have had in Washington over the year. The Ohio Republican Party is preparing for a civil war, and McKinley has received solicitations from both sides. The battle lines are being drawn: Governor Foraker favors Blaine, Hanna will lead the Sherman effort. As is his custom, McKinley has listened carefully and said little. He has even heard talk of a third scenario in which the party feud destroys all in its wake, both Sherman and Blaine, leaving an opening for a bright young alternative, a fresh face unmuddied by the internecine strife. Some star from Washington, perhaps. Congressman William McKinley is a name that has been mentioned.

He has listened carefully, said little.

"Mr. Hanna requests the pleasure of your company, Congressman McKinley."

He had forgotten the messenger was still there in the room as he read the note.

"And Mr. Hanna wanted you to have this, sir."

The boy hands McKinley a cigar. There is something enticing about the smell, something strong and rich, but he hears Ida down the hall and resists.

He gazes outside. A ray of sun is just beginning to illuminate the streets outside. The clap of horse hooves is heard. Streetlights are lit. Soon the capital will be abuzz.

"William!"

"Tell Mr. Hanna not today," McKinley says, and hands the cigar back to the boy. "But I have something for you to deliver to the Capitol, if you could." McKinley walks to his desk and picks up a letter, tucks it in an envelope, and addresses it: To the Honorable Thomas Reed, and underneath: PERSONAL. CONFIDENTIAL. And finally: URGENT.

McKinley hands the messenger several coins.

"Congressman," the boy says, "you'll be wanting how much change from this?" smiling down at the good fortune that has dropped into his palm.

"Keep it," McKinley says. "Have a hearty breakfast. And tell the driver that this morning Mrs. McKinley and I will be taking the carriage ourselves for a bit."

William rushes into Ida's bedroom.

"Get dressed, Ida," he says. She stares at him from the window, stunned that he has returned, that he is not on his way to work, to the Capitol. "Nothing too fancy," he says, "but dress. Let us dress like we were young."

And then the two of them are outside, on the carriage, up on the driver's bench, McKinley at the reins, trotting through the city. A bright day in Washington, the few men on the streets this early morning step back at the unusual sight of a congressman driving himself, but know enough to tip a hat as he passes by.

At first Ida keeps her distance, wary that they are on their way to another doctor, but when the breeze catches her, she grabs William by the arm and soon they are holding each other close.

"Where are we going, William? I've seen so little of Washington."

"I haven't seen much myself, Ida. But there is a place I've heard about. It is a sight we should see before—"

He stops himself and clenches Ida tightly around the wrist.

They drive on until the buildings recede, and there are open spaces along the roads. They trot past two Negro boys with fishing poles over their shoulders, a wild horse grazing, the sound of cattle bells. Just up ahead a man has hitched an ox and is plowing a field.

"There," William says, pointing ahead. "Listen. The water."

And there it is, the Anacostia River. William steps down from the horse, ties it to a tree, and lifts Ida down from her perch. Together they walk to the river. As the banks turn marshy Ida takes off her shoes and so, too, does William.

Around them cattle are lolling in the waters, grazing in the thick marshes. A bird flies off between them. A frog leaps, then plops in the mud.

"A bit of Ohio here in the city," Ida says. "Who would have imagined?"

"They say there is a hippopotamus who lives in the water," William says. "But she hides in the mud when visitors come near. That's what I've heard."

"How wonderful!"

"We can be happy here," William says. It's a statement he can't keep from becoming a question.

Ida feels herself sinking into the mud, ankle-deep, so she high-steps, finds a tree jutting out from the bank that hangs over the water, and perches herself on its gnarled trunk, on dry ground.

William watches her. Still graceful as a dancer. Her eyes light up as she gazes at the water and giggles as a calf slips trying to follow its mother up the bank of the river. There was a summer's day in Canton soon after they'd met when he had been told he could find Ida by the lake and when he got there she was looking out just as she is now, but then, before he could make his presence known, she slipped off her dress and petticoat and dove, naked, into the water. There was no lust in his heart, he was just lapping up the beauty of the image, her nakedness natural as a bird in her feathers, preening herself on a limb.

"You can swim," William shouts, all of the sudden. He jumps onto the tree trunk beside Ida and sits down, peels off his socks. "We can both swim. There is no one here but the cattle and the birds."

He is taken with the idea and is unbuckling his pants when suddenly he hears Ida snuffling above him. She has sat down in the mud on the bank and is slapping the water violently with her hands.

"Katie," she is saying. "Ida. My girls would love it here so."

Across the city, in his lavish office in the Capitol building, the Honorable Thomas Reed is handed an envelope. Reed is the titular head of the Republican Party, at least its contingent in the House, and is sure he will be its next Speaker when the Republicans wrest control of Congress. Reed tells his boy to place the envelope on the stack at the edge of his desk, but when he is told it is marked URGENT he resignedly takes it and, with a pearl-handled knife, slices it open and reads.

I had looked forward so to continue our legislative battles in the months ahead, so it is with heaviness of heart that I must request a leave of absence from the Congress.

It is a matter of personal business that I do not care to make public, and I would request your confidentiality with the reasons. It is my wife. She is not well.

32 · LEON · 1894

The next day after work Leon returns to the saloon. The man behind the bar yells, "What'll ya have?" but Leon ignores him and moves to a table farther away from the bar, near the curtain leading to the back room. He hears a girl's voice but isn't certain who it is when she pulls aside the cloth and stops just short of him.

"I have got no service," he says. She looks at him, not understanding. "Remember? I expect no service. It is right?"

He smiles and stares until she nods her head and remembers.

"What is your name?" he says. "Last night you didn't say."

"Megan. Megan Wisemki."

"Leon." He offers his hand. "I said that before, didn't I? Chawl—gash. Leon Czolgasz. When do you get off work, Megan Wisemki?"

"Whenever I'm not needed. Or can get away. That's my father." She points again with her head, this time to the burly man serving beer from a tap behind the bar.

"I'll wait for you," Leon says. "I'll wait for you here, Megan Wisemki."

And she disappears behind the curtain.

Leon watches Megan's father behind the bar. His life is a routine of pouring beer and whiskey, doling out nuts from a barrel, slicing hunks of bread and meat. His customers suckle on their glasses like calves on their mothers' teats, all with a violent urgency. You listen to sad stories and say nothing because there is nothing to say but, "Here's a beer, salami on a roll. Two bits, thank you much." Leon orders a beer and takes it to a table in the back.

"You the one waiting for Megan?"

It's an older girl who taps Leon on the shoulder and whispers to him. Her lips are bright red and her face a pasty white. It's makeup, Leon can see now, a disguise to add years to her, and she looks half-dressed, her breasts lunging at him from a half-cut brassiere, a silky skirt. One of the girls from the back room.

He nods.

"I'm her sister." She leans over and whispers into his ear. "Take a right out the door to the alley in the back."

She vanishes back behind the curtain.

Leon drops a few coins on the bar and heads out the door.

It's a cold night and he finds Megan in the alley, warming her hands by a fire in a metal can.

"I only have a few minutes," she says. "My father will notice."

Megan is shivering, so Leon takes off his jacket and wraps it around her shoulders. She holds his hands there and rubs them, encouraging him to massage her warm. The moon is bright in the sky, and they can hear the ragtime piano from the back room and a woman is singing with it, a deep-throated bluesy tune, and the stars are sparkling to the music.

"Your sister—"

"Emily."

"Emily. Your father must know she works there, behind the curtain."

"Knows?" Megan laughs. From somewhere she has found a cigarette and lit it, and now she is blowing smoke up at the night sky. There is a forwardness to her and a toughness that Leon didn't notice at first. "He demands it," Megan says. " 'She's eighteen,' " now parodying her father's gruff voice " 'she can earn her own keep.' "

"Will he demand it of you?" Leon says.

"We all have to work," Megan says. She shrugs her shoulders, puffs on her cigarette. "We all have jobs to do."

33 · RATIONALES, EXPLANATIONS,
POSSIBILITIES (Ida)

Because, though she and her family did not know it at the time—no one did—she was genetically predisposed.

It was from something her mother ingested when she was carrying her.

Because she had it all mapped out in her mind, the way things would be—Katie, little Ida, little William to follow her; they would be a team, a childhood gang. They would chase the rabbits out back and follow their cats up a tree chasing squirrels, and Ida would point out a nest they would find on the limb—this is how you build a home, this is how you make a life—and they'd watch the chicks grab at a worm from their mother's beak.

The neighbors would mutter from behind their picket fences that Ida Saxton always was a little off; there was the day when she worked at the bank and—*Why did a girl from Brooke Hall work at a bank?*—*What sort of father*—*When she came back from Europe she wasn't . . . pure; I have it on good authority*—. And she wouldn't care because the neighbors would just see the piling of twigs and she, Ida, would see the nest, the warm wonder of their home.

Because if it wasn't hard enough to deal with, her mother's death, then Katie's, then little Ida's, there was something her doctor said about the world.

Because when she was at Katie's bedside she was dreaming, and then this vision flashed in her head where everything went black and fiery, and when she woke up her little girl wasn't warm anymore; the fire had taken that, too.

Because when she was at Ida's bedside she traveled to the same hellish vision, it wasn't a dream but a real place she had always feared—*Death hounds me*—and once you knew it was real, you could never live in this world again the same way.

Because she gave up.

Because William wasn't really there for her.

Because life was easier this way.

What were her options?

Because some things are unexplainable.

34 · IDA · 1888

"Do you recall, my dear, when we were last here?" William says. Ida feels her husband's arm tight around her shoulders as the carriage races down the street. "The city has grown so!" William goes on. "Buildings to the sky! And the people."

Ida can hear the traffic, the clatter of hooves, the rattling of wheels. A pace and pitch that is not Canton, and is not Washington either. The scents, too. Roasting chestnuts, sausages, breads.

She knows by the smells that she is snapping out of her spell, regaining consciousness, reentering the world. Her head is shaking just a bit now, the flutter of her hand is less violent.

The cab has stopped.

"Congressman, sir," the driver speaks quietly, nervously. "Mrs. McKinley can go out now, can she?"

This is how they speak around her now. *We are here. We can help.*

William lifts his hand from her eyes, removes the fingers of his other hand from her mouth. Her teeth chatter at first, but after he rubs her shoulders, they settle down.

"Now," McKinley says, and he and the driver grab Ida's arms and carry her out of the cab.

For an instant, when they are suddenly outside in the street, the world converges on her. Babies cry, mothers scream, little boys punch one another, hurl icy snowballs, lovers promenade under umbrellas, carriages clatter and rush. There are Christmas carols and bells, street urchins hawk newspaper extras, beggars mutter, "Alms for the poor, alms for the poor." She hears a piercing scream and looks up to see it is a train above them, bouncing on rickety tracks in the air. This living and dying, this loving and hate, devils and saints—it is too much, this world. The pace spins everything off its axis, all out of control. What she wants now is quiet, to go back into the cab and go home. Not to Washington parties with other congressmen's wives who stare and stab with covetous eyes, cabinet secretaries, committee chairmen, judges, ambassadors, presidents, strutting their job titles about like a peacock's plumage. Armies of them on parade, though they are not armies, they have not the bravery of soldiers. Politics is the battle of image and voice; the arrow is the personal slight, the pistol is scandal. Strut, strut. Preen, preen. The streets of Washington are coated with garish feathers, the aftermath of peacocks cockfighting. She wants to return to Canton, to their home on Market Street. Settle into her girlhood chair and rock by the window upstairs.

The next she knows she is in the doctor's office. She has lost the name of this doctor. There are so many.

The doctor congratulates William on his good work in Congress, promises he would vote for him were he an Ohioan. There is talk of committees, upcoming elections. The gold standard, free silver. These strikes, the tariff.

"President Hayes spoke of you in the highest," William says. "He sends his regards from Ohio."

Ida waits while the two men speak, now in hushed tones. Her husband is telling the doctor her story. The life of Ida Saxton McKinley in posed photographs, dramatic tableaux, operatic arias. It is so simple, her legacy of death: Mother, Ida, Katie. There are those who shed the wages of death gracefully as silk Italian bed clothes, and those who cannot. Ida is of the weak, the infirm. The doctor will cast about for diagnoses, but those fish will squirm out of the holes of his tattered nets and, eventually, leave him to search vainly on his knees on the riverbank.

"What is your diet?"

"What are your stressors?"

"How often do you walk? A constitutional is suggested twice a day: morning and night. Other exercise? A bicycle ride is suggested. . . .

"What medications have been prescribed by your previous doctors? Potions, salves? Medicines of any variety? Anheuser-Busch has a salve that cures headaches, you might want to try.

"Baths? Hot baths can steam the toxins right off. Towel off quickly afterwards though, or catch your death of—."

The doctor, if he has the nerve, will come around to ask her about children. About what happens immediately before her spells, what she is thinking of, what she is doing. What does she feel during and after.

He will not ask her what she was like before, and so she will not tell him about that dark night on the gondola crossing the Grand Canal in Venice when the moon struck her in a certain way and Pina had nodded off to sleep and she let the gondolier give her a kiss. Or the long walks with John Wright in the woods, before those European adventures, and they didn't care that the dinner bell was sounding and finally, when they ran back, laughing as she smoothed her skirt, it was too late for Sunday dinner.

The doctor will not ask her what she thinks is the cause of her problems.

If he does ask, though, Ida thinks, still alone in the waiting room while the doctor speaks with her husband, she knows what she will tell him.

She will say, "I am allergic to feathers."

35 · McKINLEY · 1889

"William, my precious?" The noise comes from down the hall. "Are you there?"

Mark Hanna and McKinley are standing in the foyer of McKinley's apartment in the Ebbitt House in Washington, putting on their coats.

"I should stay in tonight, Mark," McKinley says. "We'll go out another time."

"The tickets aren't for another time," Hanna says. "She'll survive."

Then he lights up a cigar so quickly there is nothing McKinley can do.

"Ida will smell the smoke," McKinley whispers. "She hates it so."

"William?" Ida is louder now, almost shrieking. "William, don't leave me!"

"Come on, we'll be late," Hanna says. "The nurse has her under control."

Hanna grabs McKinley around the shoulders, leading him out the door. "Trust me," says Mark Hanna.

The theater is only a few blocks away so they walk. It seems to McKinley that Hanna must be blowing cigar smoke directly into his face, the odor is that strong. But there's a sweetness to it.

"Ida and I saw *Rip Van Winkle* once before," McKinley says as they reach the theater. "It was years ago, and we sat near the back. Ida had to leave in the first act."

"Well, William," Hanna says, following a tuxedoed usher who appears to know him, "we won't be sitting in the back this time. And I don't expect to be taken ill."

The usher escorts them to a private box on a balcony just off the left side of the stage, so close that McKinley is certain the actors must hear Hanna speaking during the show, not that it stops him. He is talking constantly, and smoking his cigars.

"I thought of you when I read the review in the *Post*," Hanna says. "A man wakes up to find himself alive again, in the future."

"I'm not certain if I understand."

"You're coming back to Congress, aren't you? Getting back to work?"

Below them, on stage, an actor playing an old man with a gray beard is wiping the sleepers out of his eyes, then stares out at the new world before him.

"Makes you think," Hanna says. "Second chances, grabbing life by the ears, giving it a shake. What world do you want to wake up in? Create a future. Hell, I'm no poet but you get the drift."

McKinley nods. The view is wonderful this close up; he can see the beads of sweat on the lead actor's forehead, the makeup caked on, lights beaming from backstage and above. He peeks up and gets a glimpse of men crawling on the rafters, holding lights and cables. For the first time the machinery of the theater is revealed to him, what creates the illusion. The seats in Hanna's box are soft, the velvet smooth. It takes him away; up here, his mind is free to wander. Ida is so distant she even disappears for a moment.

He motions for a cigar, but Hanna doesn't see him.

"Know what world I see?" Hanna says.

The bearded man, Rip Van Winkle, had been wandering about on stage, shocked at the new world before him, but now Hanna's voice draws the actor's attention and his head jerks up suddenly to their box.

"I see you in the most important seat in the Congress," Hanna says. "Where does Carnegie go when he wants a special provision in the tariff bill for his iron ore rates? Where does Rockefeller go when oil needs a boost? I know you're a churchgoing fella, William, but don't look up to the heavens. I'm talking about a committee chairmanship. I'm talking about Ways and Means."

36 · EMMA · July 23, 1892

She wakes up on the floor clutching herself. She can longer trust her sense of touch, of hearing. She imagines a man is in bed on top of her, then looks quickly around to discover she is alone.

The gun has been delivered to Alex. The last installments of money she was able to earn have been sent to him. The deed, in all likelihood, has been done. She expected there to be news in yesterday's papers, but nothing. Perhaps something came up, some glitch that caused Alex to delay. Nothing serious. If it were serious, she would have heard. She has friends in Pittsburgh she can count on for news.

She wonders how it will feel after Alex carries out the *attendat*. When Alex and she had discussed it before he left, they had sensed the revolution would sweep the nation like a wave. The workers at Homestead would hear the news that Frick had been conquered and they would storm the mills, take them over. Word would spread to other factories in Pittsburgh, then down state, down the Ohio River Valley, to New York, to the Capitol in Washington. The Homestead mills would give workers throughout the land a steady supply of steel. Other factories would supply clothes, food. Farmers would join in. The message would spread: if Frick was struck down, then Carnegie had been defeated. If Carnegie could not stand, then Rockefeller could be toppled. White flags would appear up and down Fifth Avenue, atop châteaus and office towers. In Washington, President Harrison would broach a settlement to foster a bloodless transition to the new worker's state. Money would be turned over to its rightful possessors. Capital pooled for the good of all. The nonstate would be born. Alex will be the hero, the champion of the people.

She walks to the bathroom, does not look at herself in the glass but steps immediately into the tub, pours a bucket of cold water over her head. She feels that she is covered with mites, impurities, something passed on to her by a man from the street. Or maybe she merely imagines the disease, symptoms tattooed to her conscience. She washes, she scrubs.

It has been days since she has heard word from Alex.

It is when she arrives at Justus's saloon that she gets the news.

Justus greets her from behind the bar. "I am so sorry," he says.

There are nods from the men and women on the bar stools, whispers of condolences. Glances and muttered asides. A feeling of death, unspoken tragedy.

Fedya grabs her elbow and pulls her down in a booth. "The papers, you have read?" he asks.

Emma shakes her head. "You must tell me!" She grabs his arm and shakes him. "Spit it out!"

He wriggles out of her grasp, unfolds a newspaper onto the table between them.

"There!" Fedya jabs a finger at a sketch on the front page. "Alex got into Frick's office. The disguise worked; they thought Alex was some hapless worker. Frick was meeting with someone, and Alex pulls out the gun. Frick is shocked—can you see the look on his face?! I am not invincible! Alex pulls the trigger, fires. The bullet hits! Frick is hit! He bleeds! The great Frick bleeds! But then he smiles, an evil cackling smile. Frick's associate runs at Alex and tackles him. Alex reaches to fire again, he gets a shot off but there is a worker, a carpenter fixing the office door, and he strikes Alex with a hammer. Frick is hit again, but the carpenter has tackled Alex! Alex sees that he is caught now, he is captured. He reaches for the poison he has carried with him, but when the capsule is in his mouth he is surrounded by police and guards and they force the pill out of his mouth."

"Does Frick live?!" Emma shouts.

"He lives," Fedya says quietly. "For now. He lives."

"And Alex?"

"They have captured him."

Emma clenches her fists, digs her fingernails into the back of her hand. Her eyes shut. The shame Alex must feel. They would not allow him the dignity to take his own life. Now they will kill him.

"Emma," Fedya says, "Most is speaking tonight. We both know what he will—"

"I must see him," she says.

That night when Most takes the stage Emma is there, seated in the front row, but off to the side, in the shadows. She has not seen Johann in some time, and it strikes her that he has grown even uglier, his disfigured face more distorted and severe since they first met.

Most immediately launches into Alex, the Frick episode.

"It is likely," Most says to the crowd, "after all Brother Berkman's troubles, that Henry Clay Frick will indeed live. And it was a workingman who saved him! A workingman who attacked Brother Berkman with a hammer, who prevented the fatal blows from being fired. A workingman! Berkman has not only failed, he has made the workingman a defender of the capitalist Frick! Berkman will be seen as the anarchist madman, Berkman who wears the horns! This is what I have been saying for so long." Most howls, his contorted mouth snarling. "These episodic violent attacks will destroy the movement! In one day this Berkman, and all who worked with him," and now he glares at Emma in the front row, "have undone all of the progress we have made. The public watched with horror the battle of Homestead, but now they will see only Berkman—anarchists—as the villain! We had exposed Frick as the devil he is to the workingman. The tide was turning. And now Berkman has transformed this devil into a martyr. Worse, a martyr who lives on, to crush workers like ants under his iron heel. Berkman has done this to all of us! An idiot! An imbecile! Whatever punishment they give him, it will be light compared to what I would dole out, given the chance!"

Most slams his fist on the lectern, then waves his arms up to encourage applause. Then, suddenly, the crowd is quiet.

"You're a spineless, kowtowing puppet!" Emma yells. She has leapt onto the stage, in her hand a horse whip that she snaps to the floor. "You are not worthy to say the name of Alexander Berkman!"

She is crying as she lashes Most across the face with the whip. He turns to shield himself with his hands, but then she lashes him across the back.

"Disobedient horse!" she yells. "Thieving cur! Traitor! Lascivious, lusting betrayer! You are gutless!"

She whips him again, and again. It is a scene she has played out in her mind; she is not certain where it has come from. The whipping repeats itself.

Men rush the stage. Some gather round Most to help him up from the floor, others chase after Emma. She runs, and Fedya pushes the men back to allow her to escape from the building.

37 · CARNEGIE · July 1892

Andrew Carnegie is standing on his expertly manicured golf course, setting up to hit a drive off a tee atop a hill from which he can see all of Castle Dulsinore, the high circular towers topped with medieval turrets, the smoke drifting up from twenty-five chimneys, even in July.

There are, after all, kitchens, furnaces, and stoves to be fired. There are rooms where one may need to warm one's feet after a blustery day on the course. Those rooms may never be visited, but the fires must be kept tended and warm for the off chance that the rooms may be visited. A man twice Carnegie's height could walk into the fireplaces with a beaver pelt top hat and jumping high as he could would have room to spare above him.

Carnegie swings his club back. When the swing is right, he feels at one with the shaft and the shaft is at one with the ball and it is all one fluid motion, a stirring of the air. But not today. He struggles to push the clubhead through a fierce wind that keeps him from the tee. The club hits and the ball sails high into the air, seeming to fly up into the sky, above every turret at Dulsinore, higher than the smoke from the chimneys.

The ball is off course, and Homestead is the cause. The workers at Homestead. The idea that Homestead, those workers, that any thought should force itself into his mind when he is in the midst of his backswing unnerves him. What could be more aggravating? His workers up in arms, arming themselves with rifles and revolvers. To fire on whom? Guards lawfully employed to protect his own property. Employees lawfully employed to do the work that these workers chose of their own volition not to perform. Could anything be more absurd? Andrew Carnegie did not get where he is by refusing to work!

He is not a tyrant, not a selfish man. He has given back so much. Andrew Carnegie is a philanthropist. He is a living testament to the goodness of capitalists, why people like Carnegie *should* have custody of the world's wealth, why evolution has enabled him to rule over lesser men. Andrew Carnegie is a good man. But the workers do not understand this. That is why they need the books, the education. And Andrew Carnegie gives them that, too.

As he watches the ball drift off to the left, hooking into the woods, perhaps even into the marsh off the green, he sees one of his boys running toward him, waving a paper. The ball will be irretrievable. Were he a younger man, Carnegie would hitch up his breeches, or strip them off entirely if the water was that deep, and, club in hand, do battle with the bastard ball. He would hack away at it in the water until it skimmed out of the pond. If it landed submerged in muck, he would hack it until it landed on hard soil. Strokes be damned; it would be an exercise in patience, in determination. The ball was success, victory. The goal: to bring it to daylight. He was no golfer in those days; he did not know what he was doing on the links. But the exercise was not about golf.

Carnegie nods his head at the boy and in a moment a small carriage appears.

"It is a cable, sir," the boy says. Then he escorts Carnegie onto the cushioned seat inside the carriage.

"Damn the blasted ball," Carnegie says. The horses are racing and he can see the sudden drop off the cliff. "Who is it from?"

"From Mr. Frick in Pennsylvania. America."

"Read it to me," Carnegie says. As the carriage races to Castle Dulsinore, Carnegie towels off and listens.

"*Our victory is now complete,*" the boy reads aloud. "*Do not think we will ever have serious labor trouble again. We had to teach our employees a lesson and we have taught them one they will never forget.*"

The carriage stops under a side archway at the castle. A faint rain has begun to whip in from the ocean, but the archway will enable Carnegie to walk directly from the carriage into a den in his castle without being disturbed by a drop.

"Follow me," Carnegie says. He stomps inside, drops into a chair by a fire, and allows a man to pull off his shoes. "Pour me a short one," he shouts, "and you," pointing to a servant on his way down the hall, "take a letter."

Carnegie claps his hands. His mind is clear. After lunch he will return to his golf course. No longer will his backswing be disturbed. He will return to the hill overlooking Dulsinore, and his drive will not hook. The ball will land softly on the green fairway, set up perfectly for a manageable chip, which will earn him a quite makable putt.

The brandy is given to him in a golden goblet. He takes a sip. His secretary is seated behind him, so Carnegie sees only the raging fire before him and the cliffs out the windows on either side.

"A cable to Frick," Carnegie says. "*Life worth living again. Congratulations all around.*"

38 · MORRIS · 1888

The seed of the idea comes to him the evening before, when he joins the other sausage makers at a house with a red light out front. It was a late night and more drink than Morris was used to and some of the guys saw a girl at the bar they said looked like Amelia, but before Morris could check she was gone upstairs with a man and was nowhere to be seen, so who knew. It could not have been Amelia, for even Morris had only heard of such places but had never been.

The next day at work is sluggish. The crew moves in labored half-steps and shuffles. The meat grinders, the cleavers, the slicers: Morris feels the machinery grating in his head, the noise sharp and piercing. A boy wheels a vat of stuffing over and hanging over the edge is an empty tube, a fragment of casing inadvertently strewn on the wrong bin. One end is already tied, and the intestine has been bleached white so it resembles a narrow, cylindrical sock.

Which recalls the night before at the red-light house. There was this jar in the bathroom just before you walked upstairs. The girls told you to go there and reach inside and get one, but when Morris did he didn't know what it was. Morris mentioned it to a friend when they walked home, a man who scraped intestines to make into casing for the sausages. And when his friend explained the device and gave him a sample he had taken from the house, it still took some time, alone, thinking it over, imagining, playing around with it on his finger, for Morris to truly understand the contraption.

Walking to work the next day, Morris toys with the sample some more. With his fingers he tests its construction, the shape and consistency. He meditates on its purpose, the reason for its invention and use, the history and meaning behind it. Which is pure Morris: he cannot help but consider rationales, explanations, possibilities. Every person and object is a mystery, a vortex of random contingencies that might as well have come to an opposite result. One man's immorality is another's sacrament, and each is as false as the other.

Which is what strikes him that morning at work, what leads him to tuck pieces of casing under his shirt, and under his socks and pants, to secrete them home with him. This is what leads him to lay the intestines out on the floor of the bedroom he shares with Amelia, to soak them in water and soap in the bath, then dry them, hanging in the window. This is what leads him, that night, when he is in bed with Amelia, to charge out of the room after he has stripped off her clothes, remove his shorts and measure a casing against himself, then snip it, with a scissors, to a slightly longer length.

39 · McKINLEY AND REED · 1889

"Do you speak in another tongue?" Representative Thomas Reed asks. Reed has an elegant New England brogue that is very England and not at all new.

"French, par example?" Reed says. "Or even Italian, Greek, or Latin?"

McKinley shakes his head.

The two congressmen are sitting in the Speaker of the House's opulent office, facing each other in stuffed leather armchairs by a raging fire that a Negro has just stoked.

"I find," Reed goes on, "that turning the mind over to a foreign tongue works wonders. For an hour every evening I enter my diary as a Frenchman would. No longer the Honorable Thomas Brackett Reed of Maine. No longer of Maine at all and, being French, not honorable. Cleanses the mind and soul I find. Of course, one risks acquiring certain diseases of an earthly variety. My apologies to President Jefferson, bless his soul."

Reed chortles, but McKinley only nods.

"Tough going there about the wife," Reed goes on. "I assure you, we who remained here in the Capitol were working double hard for the party during your, ahem, respite."

"Thank you, Mr. Reed."

"Nothing, really," Reed says. "To the point then. It has been an eternity since our party took control of the House. Sixteen years I have waited for this day. We need an expert hand at the helm of our ship. A parliamentarian to lead us. A man steeped in the time-honored customs of these hallowed halls." Reed leans back in his chair and brushes a speck of dust off the cuff of his monogrammed shirt. "Mr. McKinley, I will be our Speaker. C'est un fait accompli, n'est-ce pas?"

McKinley watches Reed gaze at his polished fingernails, elegantly straighten his bow tie.

"I realize you have Mr. Hanna in your camp," Reed continues. "I know Mark Hanna and his tactics. And his money, of course. I dare not forget his lucre. I know that Mark Hanna thinks the Speakership of the United States House of Representatives can be bought. No, please don't interrupt. Mark Hanna thinks anything can be bought. It is a new country, I realize, and he has a point that, for most things, there is a price in gold. Or silver. By the way," Reed leans over toward McKinley, waves him close for a conspiratorial whisper, "have you decided which side of the currency battle you will fight?"

Reed laughs again. The Honorable Mr. Reed laughs too much, thinks McKinley.

"Mark Hanna," McKinley says, "is an honorable—."

"Yes, yes. And so is my French maid. I don't like it. I don't like what he is doing to our party. To our politics. He tries to sell you, sir, like a bar of soap."

Reed takes a sip of his drink.

"Why did you call me here?" McKinley says. "You have the votes. You will win the Speakership."

"Yes," Reed says. "One more vote than your right honorable gentleself from Ohio. You have quite a knack for losing the close fights, Mr. McKinley. But that is not answering your question. Ah well, I was coming round to it. It is all about Hanna, really, and money and politics. What can be bought was the real question, the dirty little secret festering at the root of our chat. Not the Speakership of the House, I've made that clear." Reed beckons McKinley close again, this time with one of his newly polished fingernails. "But what about the chairmanship of the Committee of Ways and Means?"

40 · HANNA · June 1892

"Choose a candidate like you would a racehorse. His life story, what he has done with his years is his pedigree. Is he a veteran, has he faced death and won? All the better. Study his face, look for soberness and depth. Is there a smile or a darkness, indications of some mental know-how? That's his flanks. Does he have the belly for the fight, the to-and-fro of the political fray? We don't want no quarter horse to take on the chase for the presidency. His convictions, ideas, I couldn't give a goddamn about. But can he convince the money men he's one of them, that he'll do what needs to be done? That's what I'm after. That's how you choose a president.

"There are exceptions, to be sure. Your Lincolns, your Grants. But I don't give a goddamn about Lincolns and Grants. What I care about is William McKinley."

"The man is steadfast.

"He understands the plight of the businessman. The owner, the manager. I know. I am one. For almost a decade and a half he fought to keep the tariffs high, protected our businesses. America for Americans.

"Reliable I tell you. Recall the last Republican convention and if you weren't there I'll tell the story, or even if you were I'll tell you again. We were Sherman men, both McKinley and myself. It doesn't matter if you were a Harrison man, that's not the point, boy! We are Ohioans, me and McKinley and Harrison and Sherman, and the late martyred James Garfield, too, God rest his soul. And on the convention floor there was a rush for Harrison; things looked bleak for our boy Sherman, and it looked that the two giants might split the vote. Emotions were too frayed to patch up for the general campaign, and there was talk that McKinley himself might be the man for the party. But no! William McKinley would have none of that. McKinley says, 'I'm a Sherman man and so I remain a Sherman man! I would rather have my right arm cut off,' with these very ears I heard Bill McKinley utter, 'than desert John Sherman!'

"A man of principle, I tell you.

"A man of Washington, who commanded respect in the Capitol. Reached the heights, chaired the Ways and Means Committee. It was he who crafted the tariffs. Andrew Carnegie should call his dollars McKinleys, or Williams, or some such. The man creates wealth, I tell you.

"Yes, he lost the Speakership to Tom Reed. By a single vote! And that because he refused to dance the Washington tune, the back scratchers' serenade. Yes, he lost his seat in Congress. But that because the Dems gerrymandered his district, and still he came within three hundred votes. And that because our friend Harrison is leading the party down a gangplank. Harrison is no fighter but this William McKinley, yes siree.

"A leader of men. An executive. A governor now, of my home state of Ohio. Much loved. Respected. A true leader I tell you. Capital L.

"A friend of the workingman. Let me tell you how I came to meet this decent fellow. It was in a small courtroom, long ago. . . .

"This veteran, this man of peace. Have you heard of his heroics at Antietam? Sit down, feller. Let me tell you a story."

It is at the Republican convention, and Hanna has launched the McKinley for President campaign. He has had McKinley and his wife over at his home in Cleveland for many days during the spring and early summer. They have talked politics, strategy, policy. There are interests to consider, to cater to, business, labor. Business. All business. There is the currency debate: should our dollars be silver-backed or remain on the gold standard? There are the unionists, the socialists, the populists, anarchists. The tariff, protecting American business. Protect business and you protect the workingman. It is all about business.

Now Hanna has set up shop in Minneapolis, where the convention is being held. He has begun the push for McKinley. He is talking to Negro delegates from the South. He is talking to business friends from the Northeast. There is a sense of inevitability that Harrison will take the nomination, but still Hanna is working, raising interest among the delegates, the politicos, the power brokers. He is trotting his man about. Try a jump here, a gallop there. You become comfortable, then adept. Then professional.

It is all very unofficial.

41 · EMMA · 1893

Emma is alone in her cell, staring at the walls. She has the sense that she has been in prison before. It may be a book she has read, a character she has lived through, some revolutionary. Or maybe it is her visions of Alex's life now, what the rest of his life will be like.

Emma knows she will not be locked up for long, a year at most on this trumped-up disruption/incitement charge. A trifle compared with Alex's punishment.

When she visited Alex a year ago he could not look at her. His skin was painted on the bones, his eyes sunken, caverns dipping beneath his chipped glasses. She did not tell him about Most's reaction to the failed *attendat*, but she sensed he knew; there was shame running through him, it made his body weak. To cheer him up she began to tell him of the movement. The workingmen were listening and learning. She would speak to them—*strength in solidarity, your fellow workers are brethren, unity is the only way to combat the strength of capital, the might of amassed wealth*. The message was getting through, she could see it in the eyes of a young man at a rally, exhausted and hungry and scared but suddenly aware, liberated from his constricted imagination, he could see a better world, that was freedom, she could see it in his eyes. You gave birth to a revolutionary, Alex, she could be a mother

(Would she tell him of her pains? What the doctors told her?), the mother
of a movement that would carry on until the chains of capitalism were
decimated, no more. Looking into the eyes of a believer she would feel
the future all around her, breathe it in.

Alex said little. When he spoke, he referred to himself oddly. He
thought of himself as a caged bird. The guards would toss him seeds
through the bars, and just above him, at the window, he could hear
chirping and the wind rustling through a branch; and that was what
made it unbearable, the world outside taunting him. There's your possibility. *We are sometimes more free in chains. Who said that, Emma? I forget now. I forget so much.*

They were sitting together on the bench, and she placed her hand
on his leg and rubbed him gently, on his thighs and then up to the
crotch. Then she slipped her other hand under his pants and massaged
him there; she knelt on her knees and placed him in her mouth, gently
slapped him with her tongue. He was soft, limp; she wondered if he
even felt her. And then he looked down at her, shook his head, and
pushed her away.

He lifted her up and held her hands and looked into her eyes. *Say
nothing, do nothing.* Just look into each other's eyes: capture an image,
compact it with memory and spirit. Something to return to. It was all
about dreams, imagination. Possibility. It didn't have to be real.

She has decided her turn in prison will allow her to share Alex's experience, to join him in solitude for a moment. She will not have abandoned him like the others. If he gets out, their bonds will not have
been severed. This is what she hopes.

She thinks of criminals and innocents. Frick, stoking a fire in a
Fifth Avenue mansion, as his servants carry a new shipment of art just
off the boat from Europe—paintings of a sunset, a night sky, a girl
standing on a beach. Alex, standing alone in a cell so small he can
barely lie down in it, no one to speak to for months, sunk in a silence
so deep that his thoughts echo; memories of his old freedom torment
him like a baby returned to a womb he can never again escape.

Here in the prison there are women who rented their bodies for a
night to buy supper, women who stole a bolt of cloth, a loaf of bread.

The ones who stole a dime. The ones who stole a million, who steal youth, dreams, freedom—they are stoking a warm fire, returning from Europe with paintings of beautiful women they would spit on if they happened upon them on a street, had they a chance. Justice is the roulette wheel of birth, nothing more.

Governor Altgeld has just declared the Haymarket martyrs innocent. The jurors were biased, the judge was biased, the governor has decided, the entire trial was rigged. There was no evidence, the police fabricated the stories that killed those good men—the governor himself has declared so.

Six years after Parsons, Spies, Engel, and Fischer were murdered by the state in its gallows.

Criminals, innocents.

At her trial the prosecutor asked, "Do you believe in a Supreme Being, Miss Goldman?"

"No," she said, "I do not."

"Is there any government on earth whose laws you approve?"

"No, sir. They are all against the people."

"Why don't you leave this country if you don't like its laws?"

"Where shall I go?" she said. "Everywhere on earth the laws are against the poor, and they tell me I cannot go to heaven, nor do I want to go there."

And so she was convicted. Of what? Telling a crowd: *protect what belongs to you, what you have produced, and in the first place take bread to quench your momentary needs.* Those were the explosive words that were so criminal, words said to incite a riot that never occurred. The good Christians of New York, using the same logic, would jail their beloved Jesus Christ as well, sentence him to a year here in Blackwell's Island.

In prison, time has slowed to a crawl. The hands on the clock are frozen; the calendar is one page that, once it is torn off, keeps replacing itself.

Things are simple here, divisions clear. The guards wear uniforms, and so do the prisoners. The laws of hierarchy are rigid, accepted by all, enforced by the dictates of the warden, the butt of the guard's stick.

It is like the world outside, only no one is pretending. Here we dispense with the illusion of freedom, of classlessness. There are the capitalists, luxuriating in their châteaus. Here are the workers, locked away in their cells.

42 · HANNA AND McKINLEY · Late June 1892

Before the sun rose Hanna and McKinley began working the convention floor, and now it is past midnight. Till the end Hanna was busy striking deals, scrawling promises on a notepad to convey to delegates, messages Hanna preferred not to vocalize out on the floor, bids and counterbids as the state delegations announced their tallies. The crowd was a wave Mark Hanna was riding, McKinley his child, helpless, caught in the surf. Hanna was summoning help from shore, and the roll call of the states was a sand dial too: the Constitution State, the Carnation State, the Empire State. The Buckeye State. Time was vanishing between his fingers. And then the day, and the night, and the convention was over.

Now McKinley joins Hanna in the hotel lobby. They walk silently up the stairs, then down the hall to Hanna's room. It is dark and no one bothers to turn on a light.

The room is as hot as it is outside, as hot as the convention floor. The fan isn't working and their clothes are sopped through with sweat. Hanna strips off his shirt, his pants, his boxer shorts, then drops onto the bed, on his back. McKinley does the same. The two men are stark naked, side by side on adjacent beds, looking up at the ceiling.

"So it is Harrison again," McKinley says.

Hanna lights a cigar, then takes a long drag as McKinley watches, the embers glowing in the dark.

"For god's sake, William," Hanna says, "the time has come." Hanna leans over, showing a stogie to his friend. "If you want to get some place eventually, learn to smoke a goddamned cigar."

McKinley looks around the room first, half expects to find Ida lurking in a corner, then takes the cigar and inhales, releases a tentative puff.

"I have been at this for so damned long," Mark Hanna says. "You remember the last go-round? The fight we made for ole John Sherman? A lot of work and dollars I put behind that man. Called in a number of chits, too, money from the likes of men who do not like to part with the stuff, I tell you what. But Harrison's boys beat us back. I suppose it wasn't so bad in the end. Benjamin's been all right for me and you. He's signed whatever we've placed under his pen and hasn't pride nor interest of authorship. But the best damn thing he's done is sign your tariff bill, William. Heck, I can sign my name to the bottom of a page, if that's what we need presidents for."

"Ida hates the smell," McKinley says, watching the ash build up on his cigar. "It disgusts her. She simply can't stand it."

"You lose a fight and they forget all your victories," Hanna says. "So you get up and fight again. That's why we have elections so goddamned often in this country. Beats baseball games."

"Mark, can he defeat Cleveland again, do you think?"

Hanna blows out more smoke, turns to McKinley and smiles. "The first time I see you, you're refusing a legal fee you earned. Last convention, you won't let your name be introduced from the floor. Now this. I admit, it was brilliant, letting the Ohio delegation cast their votes for you, then leaving the podium and refuse to accept them, demand that they be given to Harrison. You're a sharp one, William."

McKinley watches Hanna puff more smoke up toward the ceiling. There was a night in Canton when he and Ida lay on their backs on a hill behind her father's house, watching the clouds race by. Ida laughed as William tried to explain the stars to her. Then there was a night after one of the girls died when he tried to get her to join him outside on the lawn again and gaze up at the night sky but of course she would have none of it, she wouldn't dare.

"I fight battles to win," McKinley says. "Those are the only ones worth fighting."

"I suppose you're right," Hanna says. "But Lord, we could have given 'em a fight, couldn't we? That was a damned close squeak!"

Hanna blows a smoke ring up at the ceiling. McKinley watches the smoke, then rounds his lips in a circle and does as Mark Hanna does. A small ring floats up toward Hanna's. In the air above them their boundaries blur, and the two rings merge to form a unified cloud.

43 · LEON · 1895

Every few weeks he goes into the city to see Megan. At first they meet in the alley when her father thinks she is taking a cigarette break. Then they time their visits for when her father leaves to go upstairs. Leon is not sure what her father does when he leaves the bar, but Megan says when he goes he will be gone for an hour or more.

They walk around the neighborhood, talk in the alley. One time a circus is parading through town, and they march behind the elephant and the men dressed as harlequins walking on their hands down the street. Another time there is a rally with posters pasted on the building walls and socialists speaking about the workingman and a better life than this.

They find a stoop and talk.

Leon tells her about life in the factory, the strike, the boys who couldn't move fast enough to get out of the way.

Megan cuts him off. "We all have stories to tell," she says. "Take me away, Leon. Take me away from here."

And so they tell each other their dreams. Megan cannot read, and so Leon tells her what he has read, of remarkable worlds to come.

He tells her stories of Jules Verne, the boat that travels through the earth, into its dark center. The balloon voyage around the globe, the voyage deep beneath the sea. "There are worlds everywhere, Megan, worlds you cannot even imagine. But they are here, all about us."

He tells her of H. G. Wells, the machine that takes you back in time, or forward into the future. Imagine a carriage, or one of the new horseless types with engines, but instead of traveling through physical space, it travels through time. The signposts point to years, not towns and cities. Ahead in one direction is the future, behind is the past.

. . .

One day Megan tells Leon, "My father is out. When he left he brought with him another shirt, a razor and bag." She brings Leon up the stairs and into a bedroom. "Don't think about time."

She pulls out a suitcase from under the bed, takes out a small guitar, its back patched with miscolored panels, but it has been cared for; Leon can tell by the way she cradles it in her arms.

She plays Leon music. It is sad, soulful. "This was written over one hundred years ago," she says. "This is something I heard my mother sing when I was a girl. This is something I dreamed." Leon closes his eyes and lets the music carry him away.

"I do not have music for you," he says. "My music is ideas. My music is stories."

Leon and Megan lie together on top of the covers on the bed. She puts down her guitar and holds him tight as she can, clutching him as if he is a bird carrying her through the air.

Leon places his hand over her eyes and speaks. "*Looking Backward*," he says. "You close your eyes in 1887 and wake up in the year 2000. Imagine. Look around! Beautiful music in the houses, some magical invention pipes concerts into every room. In the morning you set a fantastic clock and music wakes you up. There are no smoke-stacks. Turn a screw and your house lights up. The streets are lined with flowers and trees, the cities full of parks. There is no money. You have a card with credits and buy all you need."

Leon watches Megan. Her eyes open up and brighten into sparkling stars. She is lost in the future, the utopia his words create for her, as if Leon has transported her on his own time machine.

"But that is not the best of it," he says, "not nearly. Let me tell you what has happened in the world since now, in the 1900s. It is considered ridiculous that an owner should reap profits off the labor of others. Capitalism is like slavery, no more. Everyone pools together, everything is provided for: doctors, school, food, shelter. You have these things because you are a man; you are not denied them simply because you are too ill to work, or your father is not a factory owner. And because there are no profits, people only need to work enough so that everyone can be supported, no more. There is no war. There is little crime, for what reason is there to commit crime? Children do not work. They play and go to school. Their parents work shorter days, eight hours or less, and everyone retires after twenty-four years. Then they spend the rest of their lives doing as they please. People are happy, content."

Leon drifts off into silence and there's the way his mouth twitches, his eyes flutter, and Megan hears him mutter words only he can hear. It happens like that with Leon; sometimes he just leaves her, but still, there's enough for her, more than enough. It will do.

Megan is looking up at the ceiling as if it displayed the future Leon is describing, Bellamy's utopian vision. She is smiling and Leon has created this, this happy girl, a veil that shields her from the cold winds shrieking outside the bedroom, downstairs and outside in the streets of Cleveland. He looks up with her; they watch the fan's blades whip the air into spiraling gusts; Leon's head spins. He smoothes Megan's shoulders, her hair, the way her spine dips into a culvert down her back. He leans over and kisses her on the forehead.

"The way you tell it, Leon, I can see it. I can almost believe it."

"It will be true one day, Megan. I will remake the world for you."

44 · McKINLEY · 1893

H e is on a train to New York when he is given the news.

Ida's latest round of treatments is complete; he will meet her at the doctor, who will tell him of her latest ups and downs, the latest medications and treatments, medical science's latest miracle cure-alls. When to expect the next relapse. He is not even certain what this latest doctor believes in: potions, salves, exercise, diet, or perhaps some bizarre theory of the mind that is all the rage in Europe, dream studies or hypnosis. The doctors are horses on a merry-go-round that Ida and William ride like children, up and down, round and round.

Gazing at the window of the train, he imagines Ida's face reflected against the trees outside. She will be so happy to see him. My love, she will say. My sweet. Her eyes will light up and for a moment she will be James Saxton's beautiful, blushing daughter, all of twenty-two once more, vibrant and happy. But she will be in a patient's robe on a doctor's couch and nothing will be right.

He will take her home.

"Governor!"

McKinley is gazing out the window of his cabin and does not hear at first.

"Governor McKinley!" A blue-uniformed porter, young and fresh-faced, knocks on the door of the cabin and rushes in. "Your office wired at the last stop," the porter says, waving an envelope in his hand. "They said it was rather urgent, Governor."

McKinley grabs the envelope and looks for a quill pen to open it, then hands it to the porter who slices open the top and hands back the telegram.

When McKinley reads it, his legs go limp and he must grab the porter's shoulders for support. He searches for glasses in his vest. He reads the letter again.

"My God!" McKinley screams. "Stop the train! Stop the train and turn around!"

He has the porter send a telegram immediately and telephone Mark Hanna—*yes: Marcus Alonzo Hanna! In Cleveland! That's where the telegram goes too!*—and when he arrives back home in Canton he telephones Hanna but the telegram he sent has already arrived or the telephone call must have gone through for the secretary assures him Hanna is on his way. And when he calls his top advisers, Herrick and Kohlsaat, he is told Hanna already sent for them and they have left for Market Street, too. He racks his brain to think of who else can save him. Who else has the money. The money.

The money.

When Hanna arrives, he finds McKinley slumped on a stool in the center of the living room, his head in his hands.

"William, William," Hanna says, reaching in his jacket for a cigar. "What the hell did you do?"

"He went bankrupt," McKinley whimpers. "How could I know he would go bankrupt."

"Everyone's gone bankrupt, William." Hanna lights his cigar and puffs to get it going. "There's a goddamned depression on out there. You read the papers. Farms are folding up, factories closing. Every poor bastard that couldn't afford anything before sure as hell can't now. A damn good thing we didn't get you the nomination last year. Good thing we had you perched pretty in the governor's mansion, out of blame's way. Damn good thing I knew this panic was coming."

Hanna drapes an arm around McKinley. "Now tell me, William," Hanna says, exhaling smoke into McKinley's eyes as he speaks. "Who's this poor bastard's lost his shirt? And why the bejesus are *you* sobbing about it?"

"His name was Walker," McKinley moans. "Robert Walker. It was just a note I signed for him. It was a modest sum as I recall. Walker had his reasons he needed the loan, a stake, some investment. He didn't ask me to lend him anything, just sign the note with him, give my backing. I didn't think I could be on the hook for whatever happened. But now. They say I owe one hundred and thirty thousand dollars because of it! Mark, I can't pay that! I don't have that kind of money! I'm ruined! Bankrupt."

Hanna stands up and finds an ash stand in the corner of the room. "Good Lord, William," he says. At first McKinley thinks Hanna is laughing, but then he sees his friend's cheeks have turned red.

"The American people can forgive a great many things," Hanna says. "You can mess around with just about anything and live to tell about it. But they'll never forgive someone who doesn't understand the sanctity of the dollar. Lord, William. Never trifle with a thing as sacred as money."

Herrick walks in the room, then Kohlsaat. Hanna fills them in on the note, Robert Walker's bankruptcy, the whole sorry mess. Then, for a few moments, the room is silent but for McKinley sniffling, Hanna puffing his cigar.

"We have to nip this thing in the bud," Hanna says finally. "I have sold one hundred and thirty thousand dollars' worth and more in my day. It can be done. True, that was shares of stock, something with documented financial return, but still. A politician should be no different. We cannot ask for handouts. We are seeking *investors*. The men with the money to bail us out of this will not trifle with charity. These men, Carnegie, Morgan, Frick—they will only put money into machinery that will bring them a return on the dollar. Iron ore at five brings you fifty in processed steel. A dollar in a day's wages brings you one hundred dollars of product. That's investment. That's how money is spent. Now. These men know our William. When you were in Washington, William, when you chaired the Ways and Means, they came to trust you. The tariff was their issue. You protected them. But you cannot expect them to return favors. You must have a future, William, you must be able to produce. You cannot present yourself to them like some union hack begging for table scraps. This is not a dollar a day we are asking for. Five thousand dollars, ten thousand dollars each I will ask of them. With all due respect to you and our beloved state of Ohio, there is not a governor in this nation worth that kind of money. Even when you were in Congress you never got that kind of money."

"Then how can I survive?" McKinley cries. "Mark, how can I if I am not worth it?"

"I must make them believe," Hanna exclaims. "You are down now, William, but you must rise up. You must be strong! For me to sell you to these men you must believe! *I* believe, William. You know I believe. Myron," Hanna turns to Herrick, "do you believe? Do you believe in our William? Kohl," Hanna turns to Kohlsaat, "you believe, don'tcha?" Hanna raises his hand, looks up to the ceiling and pledges: "I, Marcus Alonzo Hanna, do believe."

Hanna has slid off his chair and fallen to his knees. He motions for the others to join him on the floor. When they do, he grabs the hands on either side of him, McKinley's and Herrick's, and they all kneel together on the floor, holding hands in a circle. They watch Hanna. When he closes his eyes and bends his head down, the other men do the same.

"Oh Lord," Mark Hanna says. "We are rich men, most of us, though perhaps not as much so as we'd like. No matter. We are not the worst apples in the bunch. Lord, William here has served his country in battle. Not quite as a soldier, not a fighting one anyway, but hell, he was in the front lines, you know the story, the food wagon at Antietam. He's served his party well and true. Served his state as congressman, now governor. He has not taken the path of wealth, oh Lord, but don't hold that against him. Our William knows the value of a dollar. He just done a stupid ass thing is what he did."

Hanna pauses, lowers his voice. When he speaks next, he bellows.

"Bail him out, oh Lord! Make him believe, as I do, as You do, that he will indeed lead this great land! There are infidels amongst us, oh Great One! Those who preach of false utopias and errant ideologies, who demonize Your Chosen People simply because they cherish what You have bestowed upon them, because they hold Your gold in due reverence and awe. False words, I say unto you! False dreams, without an adequate grounding in economics, or human nature! Your servant William McKinley knows otherwise.

"And so I beseech thee, oh Lord. Make Your Chosen People believe that our William will rise to that exalted seat in Washington. Oh Lord, make them do that which even You, in Your infinite power and wisdom, cannot do. Make them give us money. Let the rains come! Oh yes! Oh yes, William! Can you feel the rains?"

Hanna clenches William's hand as he leans his head back up to the heavens, beaming. Eyes still closed, Hanna can see the rain falling on them, a torrent of gold coins, falling, falling, cleansing them all in their lustrous glow. Andrew Carnegie dumps out his wallet and fills Mark Hanna's pockets with ten thousand dollars. John D. Rockefeller drops in five thousand. Henry Frick, good for another five. Gods who make the rains fall, the sun shine. Two thousand, three thousand, four thousand, five. A phone call here and there, a telegram, a dinner at Delmonico's, a meeting at a private club on Fifth Avenue, a quiet word over whiskey in a back room. Hanna sees himself leaping home with pockets full. One hundred and thirty thousand dollars, free and clear. The rain washes away all debt, all recollection of ne'er-do-well Robert Walker, that unfortunate victim of the Harrison Panic of '93. And when the storm clears, Hanna can see, William McKinley will be back in the stable and primed, a horse ready at the paddock, but with a host of owners now, each with a parent's pride and dedication. Mark Hanna is not prone to visions or poetry, but this he knows is true.

"William," Hanna says, caressing his friend's hand. "We shall be all right."

45 · EMMA · 1895–96

On the stage before her is a towering form, a young man carrying a torch that illuminates his blond hair and a muscular chest that appears ready to burst through his skintight black shirt. The young man is holding hands with a girl just as blond, leading her through the woods. Emma is transfixed, seated near the back of the theater, watching. The young man and woman are brother and sister, they are lovers, they are bound inextricably, two halves of a single soul. This is nature, its pure essence, innocent of society's arbitrary delineations, the crude, ad hoc lines that purport to distinguish right from wrong, what is lawful from what is taboo.

The man sings with a rich tenor voice, the woman a soaring soprano: a lion, a lark. The voices are one with the instruments of the orchestra, the music is one with the images painted on the set, the opera is one with a truth Emma senses she has always known. Misshapen dwarfs lust for gold; deformed giants and fire-breathing dragons guard the treasure. There are gods and kings, heroic battles, timeless quests in search of gold and magic elixirs that have nothing to do with magic or gold. The golden hair is youth, is beauty. It is the lust for gold that is dark, that is awful. In this world even the gods are petty, tempted, greedy, brought down by the smallest of emotions.

Everyone has a leitmotif. That is life, Emma thinks. We all carry a music that defines us.

The music and images take her away, carry her soul in flight, far from this opera house in Vienna, back to New York—she can't help it—to Most. Is he the disfigured dwarf lusting for gold? Or does the beauty of Wagner's music disguise a lie: is it the golden boy who is truly disfigured? She knows the anti-Semitism some see in Wagner's *Ring,* she knows how cruelly Wagner was mocked by Nietzsche at the end, but she is defenseless to its majesty, the power of the music and images.

She has been living with Edward Brady for a year now, but she has left him back in the States and now she has forgotten him, for a moment anyway, even though she is traveling under his name: Mrs. E. G. Brady. As if she could ever become Mrs. E. G. Brady.

In Europe she has communed with history, with great minds.

In London she visits Westminster Abbey. She walks through crypts housing dead kings and priests. She rubs her fingers in the crevices of stone, words that some peasant, four hundred years ago, chiseled out to honor his master. How the old order was maintained; someone had to document it.

Kropotkin, the great anarchist teacher, her idol, one day invites her to tea. He is a gentle, quiet man, far from the fire-breathing radical the American press depicts. He pours from a teapot made of delicate china. A simple rose floats in a glass vase between them. The table settings match the flower.

He engages Emma in dialogue, teacher and pupil.

"What are laws?"

"That which the powerful impose on the powerless. That which protects property."

"Why are they bad of necessity?"

"The powerful will never enforce laws to punish themselves."

"What is government?"

"That which enforces the laws. That which protects the inequitable distribution of property, of wealth."

"What of the socialist vision, of a people's government?"

"That is only possible as an interim phase. But power itself corrupts. The ability to rule, to dominate, creates a will to rule, to dominate. We must do away with the means to dominate."

"What of necessary laws? Those which prohibit murder or other harm to our fellow man?"

"True laws are not necessary. There is no need to empower a court to enforce laws that we all know. Laws are only needed to prohibit that which is of uncertain morality. Which is to say, to prohibit that which may be right. Should that which is right be prohibited simply because its adherents are powerless?"

"What of democratic solutions?"

"Democracy offers no real solutions. The powerful offer people the illusion of freedom, of choice, but the candidates will only do the bidding of the powerful. The powerful would never allow a true agent of change, a true man of the people, to take over their government."

She has flung herself into the writings of Nietzsche.

A friend tells her that Nietzsche is incapacitated, that six years ago he collapsed on the street in tears as he embraced a horse being whipped by its master. It was the senseless violence that struck him: the beauty of the beast, the beastliness of man. He has not been coherent since. His body could not contain his mind, her friend says. His brain could not contain his ideas. And so he has discarded his earthly being. His thoughts live on without him. His journey is not complete, though his life is over.

As she walks the streets of London and Paris Emma senses the presence of Nietzsche's mind like a lover speaking to her from the next room.

In Vienna she hears lectures by the great young scientist-philosopher of the mind, Sigmund Freud. He has small intense eyes that beam out from the podium, casting rays of light throughout the crowded lecture hall, at nothing, at everything. Freud says the mind is a fountain bursting up from below the earth's crust. It is too powerful for society to suppress. The water, man's urges, will find a way to vent. Trap them in society's false boxes and they will only intensify in force and explode.

Sex is not a matter of immorality. It is human. It cannot be denied.

Here at the opera, viewing the Ring Cycle in four consecutive nights, the ideas to which she has been exposed merge together with the music. Travel has freed her mind from its moorings, from context that clouded her vision and made no alternatives seem possible. Powered by

Wagner's music she floats like a Valkyrie, views herself and America as if she were a spectator, a critic, analyzing the players beneath her. Watching *Götterdämmerung*, feeling on her face the singe of the dragon's fiery breath, it all comes together.

It seems far more than a year since she was released from prison in New York.

The mind must be liberated before the body can hope to be free. That is the foundation of a free state, of anarchy, true liberty.

The critics have it all wrong about Nietzsche. His belief in the *Übermensch*, the superman, does not make him an aristocrat; he does not side with the rich over the poor, the strong over the weak. His philosophy is poetry, is music. The power of the superman is spirit, not physical power wielded over man; the superman cannot be contained by laws, by society's petty judgments and definitions. Nietzsche's superman is an anarchist.

Freud speaks the same music. The young professor spoke of the power of sexual urges, that if those urges are suppressed, the energies, needing to find expression are released in unhealthy ways. Hence insanity. Hence violence. Hence crime. There is a solution Freud does not say, a solution beyond his science: free love. Free thought. The end of laws, of government.

The minds all say the same thing. Thoughts in a circle Emma wears round her neck like a garland of roses.

She writes a letter to Alex and tries to get it all down, the interconnected thoughts racing round her brain, the garland of roses. She is a part of him, she is Alex's free self, his body roaming the world outside the prison walls. She must write him letters to report back to him, the senses reporting back to the mind.

All the voices say the same thing, Alex, my love. Freud and Kropotkin and Nietzsche and Wagner. One word captures it all, the freedom of thought and of body, of society and spirit.

Anarchy.

She returns to America in the fall of 1896. Her friends tell her there is an election to take place of some importance.

PART THREE

THE
EXECUTIVE
MANSION

I · SUMMER–FALL · 1896

There are flags everywhere, and bunting—red, white, and blue. Hanging from every awning, draped from every balcony. Above the signs that promote the hardware store, the dairy, the bakery, the butcher. Flags, bunting, banners, streamers—all red, white, and blue— waving in the wind, battered in the summer rain, drooping in the storm's misty aftermath.

The sun is just peeking over the horizon, only its slowly rising glow visible beyond the city streets of Canton, through the outer circle of woods past the edge of town. The birds are chirping outside, but McKinley does not hear them. A cool, predawn breeze is blowing through the open windows of his wife's bedroom, but he cannot feel it. Inches from him the mother bird carries twigs to her nest, feeds worms to chicks who sit precariously on a tree limb, a single misstep from death, but here in Ida's room McKinley is oblivious to all that is outside.

He has a thick cigar in his mouth and is puffing, surrounded by smoke.

He knows better, but on this early morning he cannot stop himself. Mark Hanna gave him the cigar in St. Louis, a box of them toward the end of the national convention, when his nomination was all but certain.

"The first day of the next stage," Hanna said, "you light the first stogie. Breathe it in. Blow out the smoke, make a wall out of it that separates you from the riffraff, those who will never make the grade. There are worse ways to begin your day, William; enjoy it for God's sake. Start every day with a good smoke. End every day with another. Smoke in between. When you finish the box you'll be president. Then I'll buy you another."

Hanna has taught him to smoke a cigar as long as he can without tapping the ash; you wait patiently as the fire marches inexorably toward you, but stand firm, inhale, let the ash grow. Watch the embers illuminate and glow.

At his feet are woolen slippers Ida has crocheted. He had not noticed Ida's pile recently, has not visited her room to see what she has been up to, but there they are. Mounds of slippers on either side of Ida's rocking chair. Fifty, sixty, maybe even a hundred pairs, or more. At first he is taken aback by the amount. He had thought her crocheting was an idle hobby, something to calm her between spells. He recalls there was a doctor who approved, may even have recommended the practice, though he is not certain now.

He kneels down on the floor to get a closer look.

Each slipper appears to have been dropped from the chair haphazardly, yet there is an order to the chaos. The Lord has His plans. Even the apparent madness of his wife's life is part of God's plan. Not ours to understand.

Yes, there are well over one hundred pairs of slippers, two towering piles on either side of Ida's chair. And he had noticed the maid remove several bags full of them just earlier in the week.

He begins to calculate the hours his wife must spend crocheting them but cannot concentrate enough to run the numbers out. Another time.

He exhales his cigar. A chunk of ash drops into a slipper and he picks it up but most of it crumbles between his fingers or rubs into the wool.

"William?! My God, the stench."

McKinley looks up and there is Ida standing in the doorway, glaring down at him crouched amid the slippers. Still in her nightgown, white lace drapes loosely to form pools on the floor where her feet should be.

Has she always been so thin, so light, so ethereal? The wind from the open window might blow her away.

"I can't breathe from the awful smoke!" Ida yells, then makes herself cough. "It's so vile, disgusting—. You know it, William! You know it—you know I—God, it's hell, William!"

Her long delicate fingers are clenched, transforming her hands into small red balls that vibrate with slight, restricted motions. Her face is red, too, about the temples, round her eyes. This is the way it goes: she will close her eyes, then drop to the floor and writhe uncontrollably, lost to whatever it is that takes her during her dark spells. He should not have smoked inside, he knows, he should not have set her off.

"Why must I be tortured so?" Ida's voice is cracking and she begins to cry. "Never in my house, William. Never in my house. Never in my house!"

On the streets children are waving little flags, parents roll out large flags, flags are posted in windows, shutters are painted red, white, and blue. Canton is an ocean of stars and stripes. The people are unified. They walk the streets together, the city a wave of humanity, an exuberant, chanting, laughing, singing wave that rolls down Main Street, from the railway station where they pick up today's visiting entourage, and then escort them, singing, chanting, their exuberance infectious, up and down with their flags, awash in red, white, and blue. Everyone knows one another, grew up together. The wave rolls through the center of town, then turns off Main Street onto Market, roars through a high archway adorned at its zenith with a crest, plumed with more flags, painted with stars and stripes that surround the small portrait of the plain, noble face of the town's hero and favorite son, William McKinley.

McKinley holds Ida's head in his hands until she is through with her spell, then escorts her to her bed and leaves her with a nurse. Then he walks to his den to await the visitors of the day. His secretary has jotted down a few notes about the group who will come today, and Hanna has described them already on the telephone line that links the McKinley home on Market Street directly to Hanna's in Cleveland. Today it will be a band of veterans from Missouri.

There will be great ceremony to the event. The delegation will be met at the train station by a messenger, an emissary of McKinley. The impression will be that the nominee is already a head of state, that his house is already one that is visited by those who seek access to power.

The group will then be led to the house on Market Street by the red, white, and blue wave. A parade every day. Canton is not New York City, visitors from afar are not a usual occurrence, and so the out-of-state entourage sparks an enthusiasm that could only spring from the heart of isolated middle America, an innocent excitement that could not be found along the nation's jaded edges.

When the wave washes ashore on his front lawn on Market Street, McKinley will leave his chair on the porch to greet the visitors. There will be a podium set up in the yard and he will offer a few kind words. He will lavish the crowd with details about their guests. The leader of the entourage lost a brother in the war, at Antietam, McKinley will tell the crowd, and then warmly embrace him, thank him and his family for their service to the nation. McKinley will tell the crowd that another man here today—he will provide a name—has a grandfather who fought in the Revolutionary War, a man who knew General Washington, once met Benedict Arnold. The themes will go unstated, echoes of our history, our creation, our betrayals, near destruction. Washington and Lincoln were veterans, too. *Thank you all for your loyal service. Let us give thanks to those who were left behind on the battlefield, and those who your grandfathers left.*

There will be great spontaneity to the event. The crowd will be awed by McKinley's painstaking attention to detail, his concern for the trifling turns in the lives of his guests. What breadth of knowledge! What care for the common man! What quickness of mind, what fleetness of tongue!

The leader of the visiting delegation might then remind the crowd that William Jennings Bryan was a babe of five when Major McKinley served nobly at the battle of Antietam, wearing a uniform under the martyred Lincoln, sacrificing his life to help repair the breach.

The man might then regale the crowd with a tale of political bravery of young District Attorney McKinley, Congressman McKinley, or Governor McKinley. The McKinley tariff and how it has protected

American business and secured a prosperity that is lavished on all Americans, the high and the low.

McKinley is certain that the leader of the group will say all this. For McKinley is reviewing his guest's speech at this moment, revising and editing the text where appropriate.

"How many more trips are you asking for?! Perhaps you are under some delusions, Mr. Hanna. If you are, allow me to dispel them. We are not a charity house! Mr. Hanna, the Chesapeake and Ohio Railroad is not a charity house!"

Hanna pulls the earpiece of the telephone away from him to muffle the bark on the other end.

"As its general counsel I can assure you, Mr. Hanna. The C&O is a profit-making enterprise! We are not accustomed to giving for free that for which we can obtain a fee!"

Hanna puffs his cigar and lets the lawyer go on.

"Last week it was the New York Suffragette Sisters Committee, fifty-eight round-trip tickets from Manhattan to Canton. Before that there was some veterans' group from Boston, ninety-six fares, scot-free! Managers of coal and steel from Pittsburgh. Newspaper men from Washington, Saint Louie, California even! Workingmen! Negroes! The scot-free Canton express, every day! Do you manufacture some of these groups, Mr. Hanna? I haven't imagined such organizations could exist! And don't a one of them have money to buy fares to Canton and back to wherever it is they lower their heads at night?! Half these trains wouldn't even be venturing to Ohio if it wasn't for these folks! There's paying routes in the summertime, a trifle more so than to Canton, Ohio! And we give them all to you gratis, free, no cost! I can't understand it, never have. Decrees made over my head is all I know, but the line must be drawn, mustn't it?"

On the other end of the line the lawyer catches his breath.

"Fine points," Hanna says, finally. "And you are right, 'course you are. It's all about the bottom line. But let me explain a few things. First, speaking on behalf of Governor McKinley, which I believe I've got cause to do, he is much appreciative of the C&O's cooperation in this great venture of which he is proud to be a part. It is a noble quest to seek the presidential reins of this blessed land. You read reports of the Republican convention? My boy McKinley beat dainty ole Tom Reed like a kettle drum! We—he—Governor McKinley—intends to take this quest all the way to Washington and when that blessed day arrives—March of next year, Lord willing—*President* McKinley will not forget his friends. Prosperity will trickle down to help the poor and lowly. But to our true friends, the C&O and the rest? Let the rains shower down upon ye! William McKinley is a man who remembers his friends, take my word."

"I don't need to be sold on your man, Hanna," the lawyer barks. "We know McKinley. He was a good man for us long before we were giving out free rides to anyone who wished to visit his house. That's my point."

"But wait one minute there," Hanna yells. For the first time Mark Hanna is as loud as the company lawyer. "It's not McKinley you should be worried about. Do you have any idea about his opponent? Do you have any idea who has joined up with the Democrats? Do you have any concept—an inkling! a notion!—what our opponent has in mind should he, perchance, win this election? Son, sit down a minute. Let me tell you about William Jennings Bryan."

The election is the talk everywhere. In the factories, the beer halls. At Justus Schwab's saloon in New York City.

"The stakes are high."

"This election can make the difference."

"The battle is joined, workers versus capitalists. Just look at the sides. Morgan and Rockefeller and Carnegie and the railroads and the steel trust and the banks lining the Republicans' pockets. Mark Hanna maneuvering McKinley's arms like a marionette. On Bryan's side there's Eugene Debs and Sam Gompers and the unions and the socialists and the anarchists and free thinkers."

"When you hear the gold buggers say we musn't mint silver, that they want to keep the dollars sound, only half is true: they want to keep the dollars to 'emselves is all. They're clenchin' that gold in their fists and won't let go. Mint silver at sixteen to one of gold, I say, and give the workin' man his share!"

"I've a name for 'em that fits. Gold buggerers!"

"Don't forget the Silverites. The Silver Democrats and Silver Republicans and the silver mine owners out West are with Bryan. Sixteen to one ain't just a pretty slogan. More silver coins don't just mean more money for thee and thine. With silver minted at sixteen to one, that's sixteen times the business for the silver mines."

"And there's Big Bill Hearst. There's money there, too."

"That's not real money, not McKinley-type money. It's the little man versus the wealthy. The immigrant versus the man who's become rich enough off greenhorns to forget that he too came on the boat. There's right and there's wrong. William Jennings Bryan will grab J. P. Morgan by the suspenders and flip him over on his head, shake out his dollars, and the money that falls out he'll spread throughout the land. Bryan sees the hungry babe and says, 'Give the girl some food, give her some milk.' McKinley says, 'Let the millionaire rut about the countryside, gnawing on workingmen as he romps. Let the largesse trickle down like rain. Let the workingman fill his dinner pail with what falls from the sky.' "

"We are on the verge, here in America. On the verge of the great change. The revolution will not come with guillotines and blood in the streets, but come November with the ballot returns. There will be a fairness here in America."

"Bryan will bring the change."

"This is not like other elections. This is not Harrison or Hayes or Tilden or Jefferson or Adams or even Lincoln. Bryan feels the pain of the workingman. He will rein in the corporate powers; he will tax the wealthy man, give to the workers, give to the poor."

"Bryan will lead the change."

"Bryan will bring the change."

William Jennings Bryan is in Chicago now. Yesterday he was in Rockford, Illinois, Peoria, Bloomington, Indiana, Evansville. Days earlier he was before raucous true believers in Muscatine, Iowa. Before that it was St. Louis, Kansas City, San Francisco, Dallas, New Orleans, Savannah, and Washington, then back again to Chicago.

He is standing on a balcony on the back of a train that never stops moving. His long hair is waving in the wind, his hands chopping the air with firm, strong strokes, as if the air was some bloated eastern financier splayed out on a golden throne plotting the continued suppression of the farmer class. These are the sinners who are fronting McKinley, those who have traded their souls for the gold of this world, pleasures of the spirit for the path of the Lord. The sun is somehow shining through the trees, hordes of men and women are lining the tracks cheering, and Bryan is hot, he is sweating, water is rolling down his forehead. Even when the sun is not shining he is hot. His words generate their own heat.

He is tuning up his voice with thank-yous, gentle self-deprecating jokes to put his audience at ease, to create the illusion of entertainment: *nothing dangerous here.* The *newspapers are wrong* is the message; their strings are pulled by Morgan and Vanderbilt and Rockefeller and Carnegie, men with their own agendas: *trust them not.* The flag is not owned by William McKinley, Mark Hanna, and the Republican Party. Don't listen to them. I, Bill Bryan, the boy orator of the plattes, am American, homespun. My speeches are music. The words are notes of a John Philip Sousa brass band. Listen to my fife and drum, tuba, and church choir. The Founding Fathers were revolutionaries too, but Jefferson was no fiery anarchist, Washington was no socialist. Listen to the brass band.

The train has stopped and Bryan can see the men and women lining the tracks look up at him in rapt attention. The women are waving fans over their babies, men are waving their hats over their wives' faces. These are working people who cannot afford to sacrifice an hour's wage, and there is always another body to replace them should they miss a day. But still they have come. There are things they need more than food and that is what Bryan gives them. There are truths that even the preacher will not share with them on Sunday. There are visions of a future they can see nowhere else. There is Bryan's music.

Bryan clears his throat and the crowd goes quiet.

"An idea," Bryan says, beginning his speech in earnest after the pleasantries, "is the most important thing that a person can get into his head, and we gather our ideas from every source. I was passing through Iowa some months ago and got an idea from some hogs. I noticed a number of hogs rooting in a field and tearing up the ground. The first thought that came to me was that they were destroying property, and that carried me back to the time when I lived on a farm, and I remembered that we put rings in the noses of our hogs. Why? Not to keep the hogs from getting fat—we were more interested in their getting fat than they were."

The crowd laughs. Bryan dabs his forehead with a handkerchief he retrieves from his shirt pocket. Lord but it's hot.

"We put the rings in the noses of the hogs so that while they were getting fat they would not destroy more property than they were worth." Bryan pauses. The crowd begins to titter in anticipation even before he delivers the punch line. "And then it occurred to me," says William Jennings Bryan, "that one of the most important duties of government is to put rings in the noses of hogs."

"Are the buttons ready?"

"How many?"

"Fifty thousand! And pamphlets—three hundred thousand! I want them in Italian, Polish, Hebrew, Russian, and every other god-awful language they speak in the cities. Simple stuff, mind you. Make 'em read: *McKinley! McKinley and Hobart. The advance agent of Prosperity. A full dinner pail. McKinley!*"

Hanna is surrounded by proofs, mock-ups of campaign merchandise. Boys run in with a new poster—McKinley holding a pail, inside a spark of shining gold.

"Thirty thousand! I want 'em papering every city in the East, and California, too. Have Bryan looking like the baby in the corner there. Oh, and for the foreigners throw in that *The People Against the Bosses* pamphlet. That'll work."

There are miniature dinner pails with McKinley signs pasted on their sides, *To Be Filled When McKinley Is President.* Pipes with bowls the face of McKinley, beer steins with the face of McKinley, children's stuffed bears, dish towels. Porcelain dinner plates with McKinley and his mustachioed running mate, Garrett Hobart. Spoons with McKinley's profile on the top of the handle. McKinley mugs, wearing a three-cornered cap with Napoleon britches. A bar of soap in the shape of a

baby with a face the likeness of McKinley. Anything the woman of the
house might need, the child might want, the father might pick up after
a day's work: slap McKinley on it and give it away. Sheet music, a two-
step march for piano, entitled "McKinley Victory," by P. Cortese, dedicated to Mr. Mark Hanna. "That Man From Ohio," by Kate
Vanderpoel. A souvenir brush. Miniature gold bugs. He is *The Advance
Agent of Prosperity. The Napoleon of Protection. Good As Gold.*

Boys run into the room with cables, a telegraph operator is busy at
a table in the corner, and one of the boys hands Hanna a telephone.

"We need speakers on the stump! When Bryan swings through a
town, I want one of our boys there within a day, telling the people
what's what, what that madman would do if he ran this country! Get
me Roosevelt, get me Reed! Of course I know Tom Reed hates our
guts, but tell him we'll pay good money! Train fare and more for his
time; don't bother where we'll get it! Just get them on the road!

"You say we need more money? Get me J. P. Morgan on the
phone! Get me Carnegie! Get me on the next train to New York and
I'll root about Wall Street with my snout in the dust till my belly's full
with gold coins and paper dollars!" Mark Hanna collapses at a desk, a
cigar in his mouth, a telephone in each hand. "Let me remind them
what we're up against!"

"I'm telling you, Creelman, Biercey, we can turn this race around for
Bryan! Tell me what the Dems have going for 'em. Spell it out."

The publisher circles around his office in frenetic stomps, like an old
Indian ghost dance performed by a gangly-legged society boy, a Harvard
dropout, an heir to fortunes, a newspaper man, a troublemaker, a millionaire Democrat, a shameless self-promoter, the man New York society
would just as soon do without, thank-you very much, here's your return
passage back to California where custom and tradition, apparently,
never quite caught on: William Randolph Hearst.

"Biercey," Hearst says, "lay it out, lay it out."

Hearst is smoking a cigar with his top reporters, Ambrose Bierce
and Jim Creelman. It is three in the morning, and Hearst has just
returned from an evening out on the town, then shook Bierce and
Creelman awake from their couches here in the New York offices and
ordered up sandwiches and coffee.

"Come on, let me hear it."

"Bryan was still suckling when Big Mac was fighting the big bad rebels," Bierce says. "Wasn't he, boss?"

"That's what they say," Creelman says.

"Some of us are still suckling," Hearst says. "Try again, Biercey."

"Boss, wouldn't this a been a more interesting place if the rebs had won? Passports across the mighty Mississippi. Two nations, under sops, incomprehensible, with intoxicating libations for all."

"You're drunk, Bierce."

"That's what you pay me for, boss." Bierce is lying on his back on Hearst's couch, his eyes closed. "I'm funny when I'm drunk. I'm witty and urbane. My humor gets at the dark center of the American nightmare. I see through the shit and make 'em laugh."

"Creelman," Hearst says, "you tell me what Bryan's got. Bierce here is drunk."

"I'm drunk, too, boss," Creelman says.

Hearst stuffs a sandwich in his mouth with one steady drive of his hand. "When Bierce is stone sober he's drunker than you'll ever be. Speak, Creelman."

"Bryan's got no money, for one thing. As Roosevelt said, Hanna's selling McKinley like you sell soap. Teddy Roosevelt might be one dandy bastard but he's got it right there. Morgan and Carnegie and company are handing cash over to Dollar Mark Hanna in buckets for his baby Bill."

"In dinner pails," Bierce corrects him. "That's the full pail McKinley's promising. 'Cept I believe he plans to keep it all. Or Dollar Mark Hanna will."

"That's good, Bierce. You *are* funny drunk. Go on, Creelman."

"McKinley's got the bosses, Platt and Quay, and so goes New York and Pennsylvania. The East is his, where the money is. And they say he's against the bosses, when he needed to be, when it didn't count. Hanna's fucking brilliant, the way he engineered the convention. Launches a few idle parries against Speaker Reed, a gentle rattle of Boss Platt's cage, just enough to start a tussle, knowing all the while they'd come round to McKinley's camp once the battle lines were drawn. But he gets a catch slogan out of the sham tiff: *McKinley Against the Bosses.* Then he tinkers with it, makes it *The People Against the Bosses.* Then the bosses get their ballot barrels ready for election day. Behind the scenes Hanna spread the money around, purchased the delegates he could get on the cheap, a few Southern Negroes. You've got to love Mark Hanna."

"Creelman, you're almost as bad as Bierce. The two of you'd love the devil if he made for a good story."

"And you'd print it, boss, page one."

"So I would. But I wouldn't support the bastard. I'd battle for the ordinary working stiff. Someone has to take care of 'em."

"Bully for you, boss," Bierce says. "Millionaire hero of the workingman."

"Shut up, Bierce. You're drunk. The question was Bryan. What has he got?"

"The Silverites. But there's no legs there. No votes. So Bryan'll carry the West, the farm country. But that's not where you win elections nowadays. It's here in New York. It's the East. And the man who represents the money is the man who gets the money and that ain't William Jennings Bryan. We've never seen money the type that Hanna's raised. No one's seen anything like it. Bryan's got a drop in the bucket. Nothing."

"He's got something."

"Well, boss," Creelman says, "Bryan's got Gompers and Debs and Darrow all making speeches for him. The labor folks are for him. The radicals, socialists, what have you. The ones that ain't voting for parties of their own. Bellamy's traveling the rails as much as Bryan himself, making speeches for him, selling loose copies of *Looking Backward* on the side. And Bryan's got Bryan."

"That's something," Bierce says from the couch. "He's got himself one vote."

"Make it two," Hearst says. He is gazing out of the window, out at the city. "I'm voting for the bastard."

"He is a good man, this McKinley. Just look at that forehead, so high. Look, the soft cheeks."

While Leon's stepmother is stirring the soup she's reading a pamphlet laid out on a table beside the stove, her pinched nose peeking out from the rising steam.

"And he prints these papers for the people, in Polish," she says. "In Russian. Latvian, Swedish. This man, he cares for working people. Not every president. In the old country, hah!" She slaps for emphasis or perhaps at the fly diving into the pot.

Leon walks in from outside to hear this; the woman is so loud she drowns out the cackle of the geese, the moos of the cattle on the farm.

"Look who's in for dinner," she says, her eyes still fixed on the pamphlet. "Any work today, Leon? Any money for your poor father and his hardworking wife?"

Leon does not look at her. "I don't care what language he prints his lies," Leon says.

"He believes in hard work. Leon, what do you know about such things? You eat your fill, then leave for two, three days at a time without saying where or why. You may not care but your father, he worries."

"He is a thief, your McKinley." Leon tears a hunk of bread from a loaf, tosses the rest back in the bread box. "I read where Mark Hanna bribed the Negro delegates to win the nomination. It was the millionaires' money he used."

"Where did you hear that? It sounds like Hearst's lies."

"Hearst speaks for the workingman."

"He is one of the millionaires, your Hearst, one of the rich you hate so. You say the rich lie, but how come not your Hearst?" Laughs spit out of her beak of a nose, the lips rigid.

Outside Leon has the newspaper that tells the truth about Hanna and the thievery of McKinley. It's there in black and white. He has left it under a tree.

Leon shouts, "Hearst owns money, but the money does not own him."

Then he grabs the McKinley pamphlet; the streets of Cleveland are cluttered with them—McKinley, Hobart, the full dinner pail, prosperity, gold not silver, the People Against the Bosses.

"Garbage and lies!" Leon screams. "Garbage and lies!"

He crumples the pamphlet in his fist and tosses it on the floor. Then he walks outside, slamming the screen door behind him.

· · ·

"Mr. Hanna, Governor McKinley says he stands by the gold standard with all his heart and soul. Says it's reckless for Bryan to come out for silver coinage."

"Of course, young pup." Hanna is walking down the street and the press boys are after him, dogs nipping at his heels. "Not much older than baby Bill Bryan now, are you?"

"But Mr. Hanna, then how come he voted for the free coinage of silver when he was in the House? How come free silver was okay with him until he ran for president against a fellow who felt the same way?"

"What paper you from, boy? The element'ry school times?"

"And how come McKinley voted to override the president's veto of the same bill?"

"I never said Will McKinley was a financial genius, young lad." Hanna pats his vest pockets, there's a cigar somewhere. "He never did neither."

"Mr. Hanna, sir, how much money's your man McKinley getting from the millionaires? They wouldn't want to see all that new silver money come out, so as some of the less fortunate types might get a few coins, too, would they?"

"Less fortunates? Let me tell you, boys, I was in the newspaper biz a time ago. Did I ever tell you—what was the question again?"

"Money, Mr. Hanna. They say there's never been a campaign like this, the thousands of dollars that's pouring in for the Republicans. What the millionaires gettin' for all that dough?"

"What they *gittin'*? What you think? Those gents didn't make a mint by being dumb. They're gittin' 'zactly what they're payin' for." Hanna stops suddenly and the reporters stumble into one another behind him. He lights his cigar and draws deep, then blows the smoke down into their gap-toothed, open-eyed faces. "They're gittin' the best damned president money can buy."

Emma is back from Europe and the talk here is Bryan, William Jennings Bryan. Bryan and that bastard McKinley.

"We are uniting," Justus Schwab says to her. He is behind the bar drawing Emma a beer. "Eugene Debs, Sam Gompers, and the other union men. Bellamy. We're putting aside our differences. We're all decided we must stand behind Bryan."

"We're joining with socialists?!" Emma shouts. "Who was right, after all, Bakunin or Marx? We do not want another state. I thought all this was settled. Yet I go to Europe and return and now socialists and anarchists are one."

"We are together on this election," Justus says. "Like the eight-hour workday, it is an issue on which we must unite. And Bryan is the man. He is not perfect but the battle lines are clear."

"He is not perfect?!" Emma says. "He is a capitalist!"

"The capitalists are against him, Emma, with every fiber and dollar."

"But he believes in their system! And what is all this nonsense about silver coinage? Since when, Justus, did we think that the proletariat would be freed when they are paid in silver rather than gold?" She laughs, gulps the beer.

"It is not *the* answer but it is *an* answer," Justus says. "Mint more money means more for those who don't have."

"And how do they get that new silver money, Justus? We are still at the mercy of the capitalist, whatever he wishes to give us. It makes no difference whether the pay is in silver or gold."

"I said Bryan was not perfect, Emma. Besides, they say that if you support Bryan, the Democrats can help Alex get released when they get in power. They can pardon him. He can have his life back."

"For that he shot Frick? To be indebted to the liberal capitalists? And you trust Bryan? He will forget about us once he gets elected."

"Emma, we must walk before we can run."

"Bryan is not walking," Emma says. "He is crawling on his knees."

"What is the latest, Dawes?" Hanna says.

Hanna is in Chicago, at McKinley's campaign headquarters. They are based here because this is where the election will be decided, in the nation's middle: Illinois, the Middle West. The campaign is a battle in which territory is fought, then conceded, the remainder is contested. Bryan will control the farm states, thanks to the poor ploughmen deluded by visions of silver coinage raining upon their fields like manna from the heavens. McKinley owns the East. The moneyed men have brains, which is why they have the money, why God entrusted them with the stuff. The Midwest is the battleground that remains.

"We have ten million pamphlets on the streets, two hundred thousand buttons last month—"

"That's not what I want to hear, boy! Give me the real numbers, the buckets of blood. How much is coursing through our veins?"

"Mr. Hanna, I'm not sure what you mean."

"Money. Contributions. Politics is money, Mr. Dawes. From the dollar all else flows. That may not be Shakespeare, but it's truth. Not something Baby Bill Bryan understands, but there you have it. Out with it."

"New York Life brought in fifty thousand."

"Nice."

"A bunch of the Western railroads gave us one hundred seventy-four thousand."

"Mighty fine."

"A man from one of the railroads brought in this." Dawes hands Hanna a canvas bag. Hanna reaches inside and pulls out a handful of dollar bills.

"Good lord! How much is here?"

"Fifty thousand."

"Rich. And how about Rockefeller? John D. promised he'd be chipping in his due. Said I wouldn't be disappointed."

"I was saving that for last, Mr. Hanna. Standard Oil gave us a quarter of a million dollars. Two hundred and fifty thou."

Hanna leans on his cane and is silent for a moment. He places his cigar down on the table, walks to the window, and looks down on the city. There are the meatpacking plants, the slaughterhouses. In the late summer heat Dawes has the windows open so you can smell the stench, hear the cries of the cattle and the workmen, the sharp piercing scrape of the cleavers and grinders. The churn and coughs of the engines. Dawes thinks Mark Hanna might cry.

"Our boy McKinley is right," Hanna says, finally. "God's in his heaven. All's right with the world."

Bryan continues to trek across the country, making speeches. He has no money, and so no trinkets to give away. The gospel of free silver is not published in five hundred thousand copies, enough to paper the cities; Bryan's words are not translated into every language an immigrant can read. There are no courtly visits by dignitaries to the Bryan family home in Nebraska, no lavishing of praise in the great newspapers of the East. There is only Bryan, the song sung from his baritone as he travels from town to town.

He is a man used to the hard fight. Longs, some would say, for the hard fight.

"The presidents of the insurance companies oppose free silver," Bryan says, "because they are more concerned about their own salaries than they are in protecting their policyholders." This he says in Hartford, home of the great insurance companies.

"You cannot trust the financial wisdom," he says, "of those who manipulate your stock market." This he says in New York, home of the Wall Street manipulators.

His enemies know where to find him.

His train stops every hour, every half hour. He tries to keep his speeches short, to conserve his voice, save his energy, stay on schedule. But he cannot restrain himself. He cannot give a crowd of working people less than the previous crowd received from him, or the crowd of the previous week, or the crowds of July, August, or September. The people are hungry and Bryan is feeding them with speech. They are thirsty and he gives them words to drink. He is bathing them with dreams. Belly for the fight ahead.

The businessmen are pressuring their workers to vote for McKinley. The moneylenders are pressuring the borrowers. Bryan is certain of it.

The Democratic Party chairman says, "If this conspiracy succeeds, if the people do not stand firm against the corporate pressure, government by corporation will have succeeded government by the people."

The *New York Times* prints a letter from, supposedly, an esteemed alienist, who says he has analyzed Bryan's speeches and discovered that the mind of William Jennings Bryan is not sound, he is a man of abnormal egotism. His father was a religious fanatic and a crank. Bryan's election may bring a madman in the White House.

The *Times* concurs with the letter writer. They too have found, in Bryan, signs of a deteriorating mind. One may call it unsoundness in English, or insanity in Latin, says the *Times*. His procedures are not adaptations of intelligent means to intelligible ends.

This election is not a matter of political differences, says the *Times*. It is a question of sanity.

Bryan is an anarchist, the papers are saying.

Bryan is a socialist, the papers are saying.

Bryan will destroy the economy. Morgan, Carnegie, Rockefeller, they know of what they speak. What is bad for them is bad for all.

Bryan does not have the money to print the truth in pamphlets and soap bars, and so the truth is whispered in union halls and factory floors.

He is not an anarchist.

He is not a socialist.

He is not insane, unstable, or unsound.

"We care not upon what lines the battle is fought," Bryan is saying.

His wife tells him he is in New York again and so he must be. He no longer has the energy to gather new insights, or even tinker with his words to make them just right for the audience of the hour. He has traveled so far, so fast, that his body feels it is still in motion even after the train has come to a stop; the sounds of the engines chugging down the tracks never leave him. He clenches the rail of the train car balcony to brace himself, tries to hold his body still before the crowd. It is the motion and the travel and he is so tired; his voice is worn and ragged. He can only go through the motions of words he knows too well.

"If they say that bimetallism is good," Bryan recites, "but that we cannot have it until other nations help us, we reply that, instead of having a gold standard because England has, we will restore bimetallism, and then let England have bimetallism because the United States has it. If they dare to come out in the open field and defend the gold standard as a good thing, we will fight them to the uttermost."

He pauses, allows the crowd to yell, to cheer. They all know the words of his speech, the song he is singing. It is the song he sang months ago, in June, when he won the Democratic nomination. There was such optimism then, such hope. The coalitions were forming an army of workingmen and -women behind him; all sensed that the time had come to take back the nation that was rightfully theirs. They had built it, they had fought for it. When Morgan was selling the government defective guns, who was killed by the defects? Whose blood did the moneyed men transform into gold? Good working people. Yes, the moneyed men were Goliaths, but Bryan was a David, his lyrical words a slingshot, simple but undefeatable.

That was June, before the moneyed men banded together. David did not have to face such wealth, and what such wealth could buy. The lies Hanna spread through the nation, the fears he fomented. The newspapers painted a halo around McKinley on his front porch in Canton. A man who will not leave his home when he is running for the presidency—who, like British royalty, will not go out to see the people even when he needs their vote—such a man cannot know the people. Only Hearst would print the truth about the campaign, that Hanna and McKinley were buying the election, that the capitalists were purchasing the government from the people. (And only Hearst would give Bryan money, matching contributions dollar for dollar. But that could not compare to even a single railroad's offering to McKinley.) The people had heard so much propaganda, so many lies. So much to fear. Whose faith could survive such a barrage?

"Having behind us the producing masses of this nation," Bryan continues, "and the world, supported by the commercial interests" (*a lie, he knew even in June*), "the laboring interests" (*a truth, but now they are confused by Hanna's words, the spellbinding delusions of the moneyed salesmen*), "and the toilers everywhere, we will answer their demand for a gold standard by saying to them—"

Bryan pauses, gives the crowd a chance to gather themselves before he delivers his last triumphant notes. Bryan knows: The issue of bimetallism, the policy of free coinage of silver, is not a simple matter of economics, of monetary policy. It is an issue of ethics, morality, and faith. The gold bugs are men of greed, those who care not for the least of these. Men who listen not to the words of Our Savior. Christ would not have been wedded to the inhumane gold standard, certainly not in these dire economic times. He'd have counseled for the coinage of silver.

Bryan's speech is no longer a call to arms but a farewell tour, a nostalgic look back at what will become known, a few short weeks from now, as the failed campaign of 1896. The last stand of the workingman against the onslaught of the corporations. The workingman's Wounded Knee.

Bryan gathers himself for a last dramatic fling, a fiery, simmering solo of his baritone.

"We will answer their demand for a gold standard by saying to them: You shall not press down upon the brow of labor this crown of thorns. You shall not crucify mankind upon a cross of gold."

The newspapers say, "No man who drags into the dust the most sacred symbols of the Christian world is fit to be president of the United States."

"The bosses are worried," Waldek says. "They sense the momentum, the excitement of the people."

"It cannot be the silver issue that scares them," Frank says.

"Silver or gold," Leon says, "it is still the wealthy man's money."

They are in the kitchen, sipping coffee in chipped, tarnished mugs. Leon and Waldek's stepmother has gone to town so they can drink in peace with Frank, talk, and smoke.

"Leon is right," Frank says. "The problem is not a question of currency. It is not even a question of producing more money. Bryan does not understand this, and so I do not understand Bryan. The problem is distribution."

"The bosses fear what Bryan represents," Waldek says. "I tell you, I see it at work in the factory. Bryan may not think like us, but he has become a leader of an army. Anarchists, socialists, communists, unionists, so many rallying behind the Democrats. It is a rare opportunity."

"I have never seen such unity," Frank says, "I will give you that. We are used to fighting each other more fiercely than we do the capitalists. Bryan has changed that."

"Yes, yes," Waldek says. "And when Bryan is elected, the tail may become the dog."

"The tail becomes the dog," Leon says. He lights up a cigarette. "I like that."

"That is what the bosses understand," Waldek says. "They have told us, if Bryan wins the election, we need not come to work the next morning."

"I am not surprised," Bryan says, "at the means that have been employed."

He is in Iowa now and the election is just days away. The reports of businessmen threatening workers to vote Republican are so widespread that he feels compelled to address it himself, to convince the people that their ballots are indeed secret, that the bosses cannot control their votes.

"I am not surprised because when a party starts out with the proposition that we must submit to such a financial system as money-lenders demand, they go further and say that any man who borrows money must submit to dictation from the man who loans him, and that any man who works for wages must submit to dictation from the man who employs him."

He looks at the crowd and there are knowing nods, wry smiles that say silently: But what can we do?

Give the people all you can give them. Finish the speech.

"This doctrine of submission," Bryan goes on, "will be carried all the way down the line until the right of the citizen is lost. And the corporation becomes all powerful."

EIGHT READY TO INDICT MARK HANNA

A telegram from the Republican National Committee has been found that authorizes an offer of $40,000 to pay for the electoral votes of Texas. The indictment of Mark Hanna this week, Democrats claim, is all but a certainty.

"Are the people reading our papers?" Hearst says.

"Yes, boss," Creelman says. "Our circulation is nearing Pulitzer's; the other week we even beat out the *World*. Not that it didn't cut into our losses. We dropped over one hundred and fifty thou last month."

"Maybe we're not writing clear enough then? Perhaps we're being too subtle for the masses?"

"No one's ever accused you of subtlety, boss. If they did, they couldn't prove it. You wrote that Mark Hanna purchased the nomination in hard cash, point blank, and he's doing the same with the presidency. You've called McKinley a two-faced hypocrite, a spineless tool of Hanna and the bosses. I don't think these points have been lost amongst the loyal readership. Sir."

"Well, why in hell don't the people understand then? They are going to be taken by these Republican bastards. The bosses are going to tighten the screws. I've explained all this in the editorials and I know everyone reads that page at least. So tell me, Creelman. Why the hell's that gutless rat going to win?"

"You know as well as I do, boss. There's only one vote counts in this country. What can you do?"

"Ah hell, Creelman." Hearst stands up and looks out of his office window. Creelman grips the arms of his chair tight, awaiting what will come next. A desk-clearing-papers-on-the-floor-books-flying-out-the-office-door tirade? An invitation to an all-night escapade to clubs, bars, and restaurants, with two ladies of choice—or three, or four—an evening violently joyous, spare no expense? A pitched scream? A prolonged sob?

"Last Saturday I went to the Columbia football game," Hearst says quietly. "Have you seen this sport, Creelman? A spectacle of violence. Young men, the largest you have ever seen, crouch down on either side of a line, and when play begins they smash into each other with as much speed and force as they can muster. A disfigured ball is carried, and whatever poor lad has the ill fortune to be given it is the main object of attack. His teammates do their best to keep the opposition away from the ball carrier. They kick, they gouge, they punch. The man with the ball is mauled, piled on by a mass of bodies. It is not unusual for a poor bastard to be carried off the field senseless after a play. This is the game that is all the rage, Creelman. This is the latest thing. Mark Hanna understands this. He understands football."

Behind Hearst is a painting of Napoleon, on his desk are busts of Lincoln, Jefferson, Franklin. From his office he can look down and see a man hit by a carriage that has run amok when the horse got a sudden inexplicable fright. There are hoboes in the alleys and girls accompanying their fathers to sell rags on the streets, neither understanding, because they have not learned to speak American, the policeman's insistence on a fee for a license that does not exist.

An epiphany strikes Hearst. He cannot believe he has not thought of it before. Such a damned young country; money was the glue, the quest for it what held us all together. Bryan did not understand that, he couldn't. McKinley might not have either, but Hanna taught him, or Hanna really did pull his strings like a marionette—either way, the knowledge was there. You need to have money—or to have held it once, to have showered in it, to have lathered your body in gold coins like French soap: at least to have longed for it—or you could never understand America. That was the core of William Jennings Bryan's problem. That was why he would never be elected.

"There is a beauty to it, this football," Hearst says. "There's chivalry there. There's honor. At the end of the game, just moments after the competitors have been locked in mortal strife, the teams will shake hands on the field, congratulate the winners, console the losers."

Hearst turns around, sits down in his chair. "Take a note," he says. "I want you to send something to Mrs. Bryan. She must be taking this campaign hard."

"Boss," Creelman says, "I told you we lost a truckload of money last month. It's better than it was, but still. One hundred and fifty-eight thousand dollars in the red, and that was in a good month."

"I don't give a goddamn," Hearst says. "Spend a thousand. Hell, spend five thousand! Send Bill Bryan's wife orchids, a room full of 'em. A goddamned house full. Enough to take away the stench that'll come from Washington when William McKinley and the fat ass of Mark Hanna get there for good."

Bryan arrives home on November 1 to rest his ragged voice and exhausted body and await the election returns, but he cannot stay still. The next day he and his wife and their daughter, Grace, travel across Nebraska. He makes twenty-seven speeches. His last campaign speech ends minutes before midnight on election eve.

· · ·

The flags are still flying in Canton, the bunting still coats the walls and fences, flags hang from homes and storefronts. It is November 3. Election night.

Dawes is in the back of the house on Market Street, an ear to the telephone, an eye to the telegraph, listening to the returns. When he hears new numbers, he runs outside to give them to McKinley. McKinley is on the phone too, mostly to Hanna. Now he is alone on the front porch, smoking a cigar.

Throughout the day crowds have filled the front yard, cheering, singing, waving flags. As cold air blows in with the evening, bottles are tipped. The Canton faithful turn a blind eye to the sin, almost forgivable on such an occasion.

Past midnight now, and the crowds have thinned only a bit. To Ida, alone in her room upstairs, the sound is still thunderous, unbearable. The man with the kettle drum outside in the yard may as well be beating on her skull, clashing cymbals on her ears. This room is her own private space. She is not bothered here; she is alone with her memories, visions of Katie and little Ida. That is what happens when she rocks in her chair, when the crocheting needles begin to move in her hands of their own volition. All quiet but for the creak of the rocker, back and forth, back and forth. The moon powers the ocean's waves, and so the steady vacillation of the rocker guides the days and nights in Ida's room. The visits are what she lives for, the visits from her girls.

But the campaign has kept the visions away, all summer and fall. It's the parades, the entourages, her husband's speeches on the front lawn. She has kept her distance for the most part, though on certain days, such as when J. P. Morgan and Mr. John Rockefeller came to dine downstairs, she had to entertain, play the hostess. It was all she could do to keep her eyes and mouth open, to keep seated in her chair throughout the meal. She felt the urge to slide onto the floor and allow her body to take over, give herself over to its mad impulses.

Even on the quiet days, when she could remain upstairs in her room, the commotion outside was invasive, the noise of the crowds, the speeches and glad-handing piped in to her skull as if by some new Edisonian invention. Even her rocker and crocheting could not lull her. Ida and Katie stayed away.

But now, at least, it was November. The campaign, the election, would all be over. Her quiet days upstairs at Market Street would return. And so too the visions. So too her cherished girls.

She hears a cheer rise up from the crowd outside. There is a bang and she shudders. Then another bang, loud as cannon fire. Out the window across the sky is a silver flash, a golden shower of stars. Fireworks, cheers, applause and hollers. A bottle smashes on the street in front of the house on Market Street, glass shatters.

"Speech! Speech! A speech, Mr. President!"

More cheers. Her husband's words drowned out by drunken revelry, by the deadly explosions of the gunpowder.

Ida closes the window. Closes, then, the shades. Drops to her knees beside the bed.

She clasps her hands, covers her tearing eyes. She has not prayed for some time, since when she cannot remember. Not when Ida left her, nor little Katie. But now she prays.

She believes that if she speaks out loud it will bring her words to God's attention.

2 · BERKMAN · 1897

A dark figure is hunched in the corner of a small cell, his back against the wall, his knees bent. Alex has found a volume of Tolstoy in the library, and when he sits a certain way there is just enough light from the bars for him to read. The prisoner in the cell above him is rattling his bars in a code Alex does not understand; it is a code intended for the prisoner in the next cell. Every few minutes a guard walks by to glance in, knock an outstretched hand off the bars with his nightstick, chat up one of the cell block snitches.

Alex has just returned from a three-month stint in solitary. He knows that any day he may be brought back to the isolation cell, so now he tries to soak in the chatter of the prisoners and guards, the skitter of rats' claws on the prison's stone floor, books he can read when he is allowed access to them. You store sensations and recollections so you can recall this world best you can, though, inevitably, the details will be lost. He is familiar with the process, the inflow and outflow of the prison's social tides. When he returns to the other prisoners, he will have to teach himself to speak again, to interact. To convince himself that he is no longer alone. His memories make echoes in his brain that do not stop.

Alex is cradling a bird he found in his cell when he was last brought back from isolation. The bird first visited him many months ago, and Alex befriended the creature. He named the bird Dick. At nights he would lie in his cell with Dick resting in his cupped hands and stroke his feathers, whisper to him like a lover. Alex would joke with him; together they would plan the revolution. When the guards came, Dick would hide in the straw of the mattress.

One night the guards grabbed the bird from Alex's hands and tossed him out the window. They said he was carrying messages in and out of the prison.

And now here was Dick, returned to him, resting in his cupped hands, nestling his head against Alex's fingers. It was magic, it was destiny.

This time it is the snitch down the hall who hears Alex speaking to Dick. Two days after they are reunited, the guards storm into Alex's cell in the middle of the night. One grabs the bird from his bed, another pulls Alex up by his collar.

"Watch!" they yell, holding Dick just under Alex's nose.

Then, slowly so Alex cannot help but see, a guard clasps both hands around the bird.

"Listen to the bones crack," says the guard. Alex can hear a whistling shriek and a whimper as the guard's fingers close tightly, then flatten the bird. Then the guard opens his hands, picks Dick up by one of his mangled feet, and tosses him. The limp corpse hits Alex in the face.

"Now you can keep him," the guard says. "He can teach you what happens to reds."

3 · LEON · 1897

Leon gets up early to walk to town where he catches the streetcar to Cleveland. It is the day he will see Megan. When he is about to walk into the saloon, someone grabs him from behind and pulls him away from the door.

It is Megan.

"Come here," she whispers, grabbing his hand. "Follow me."

They run down the street and turn the corner, then duck down an alley. When they stop, Megan is laughing, pulling down on his shoulders from the back.

"My Leon!" she yells, half-laughing with excitement. "How long has it been?"

"Five weeks. Just a little longer than usual. There were things."

She has grown more and more at ease, but Leon notices a greater change than usual this time. There's a hint of a smile.

"They have been a long five weeks," she says.

They find a run-down hotel with a man in the vestibule with a fistful of money.

"How long do you need the room for?" the man says.

"An hour," Megan says, and hands him some coins. Then she pulls Leon up the stairs, into a room at the end of the hallway.

When they are in bed, Megan kisses Leon on the cheek, then grabs his chin with one hand and turns his face toward her. She looks at him deep in the eyes, kisses him full on the lips.

"Megan, what is it?"

"There is nothing to worry about, my Leon," she says. "It's just, I have been thinking since we saw each other last. I turned seventeen years old two weeks ago, did you know that? I never could have imagined I would be so old."

They kiss again and hold each other close. Megan slips off her blouse, then slides under the sheets of the bed quickly. Then she tugs Leon under with her.

Megan pulls the sheets over their heads, making a dark cave for them under the covers, just enough light to illuminate the outlines of their bodies. She shimmies down and unbuttons his shirt, kissing his chest as she makes her way to his belt. She unbuckles it, then begins unbuttoning his pants. Leon shakes and begins to roll away from her—he has never experienced anything like this—but she holds him tight around the hips. She slides his pants off, then his underwear, kissing him everywhere. Her tongue is massaging him and tickling him; he can't help but squirm and laugh. She rolls him over to his side, and he feels the nipples of her small breasts against his back as she rubs her hands up and down his body and sucks the side of his neck. Her mouth is everywhere, her hands are everywhere. He closes his eyes and lets the feelings take him away. Under the sheets they are fish in dark waters: all sensation, no mind.

"It is time, Leon," Megan says. "I am ready to give myself to you."

4 · INAUGURATION · March 4, 1897

The servants dress Ida in her gown. Her rocker has remained in Canton, upstairs in the Market Street house, so here in Washington she sits in a rigid straightback chair. The girls grasp her pasty shins and struggle to pull up stockings that are even whiter. They slip on her petticoats, strap around her corset. It is like dressing the dead, one girl thinks, or a wax statue. No one speaks.

A doctor stands behind the servant girls, observing it all. President McKinley has instructed him to make certain Ida is fit before she attempts to appear at the ball.

Ida stares straight ahead without seeing, though she can feel the girls strapping her in a dress, adorning her chest and neck with jewelry Ida had laid out earlier in the week.

When the girls have finished, Ida finds herself standing before full-length mirrors in her changing room. The drooping jeweled earrings and necklace create the illusion that her face is sparkling, the train of her gown gives her weight, a solidity not really there. Her hair is bobbed behind, but the bangs are not teased in curls like she wore as a girl, or at her wedding; her hair is pulled back severely to each side. The girls set atop her head a golden tiara resembling a crown bedecked with feathers.

Ida sees herself, suddenly in focus. It is not Ida, she thinks, but it befits her present position.

She coughs to clear her throat. The doctor turns toward her: her first sounds of the morning.

"I can make it to the ball," Ida says weakly. "You will need to carry me down the stairs. My husband must put his arms around my waist when we are standing. When I receive the guests, he must hold me up. But I will be there, with him, at the ball."

Mark Hanna is marching down Pennsylvania Avenue, stomping his feet in outlandishly high and heavy steps. He is in a carnival parade, he feels like. He should be carrying a baton with an elephant behind him and a brass band out front. It's godawful cold out and silly as hell.

The crowds lining the sidewalks on either side of him are cheering, they are hooting and laughing, and Hanna allows himself, for a moment, to imagine that the cheers are for him. He knows the president and his wife are in the carriage just ahead of him. Knows too that Mark Hanna is not a name one has ever seen on a ballot, much less voted for. He is known more by the bloated caricatures of him in Big Bill Hearst's tabloid rags than by any serious depictions in legitimate news outlets. But there are politically savvy folks out there, too, those who know how the election of 1896 was won. There are those who know Mark Hanna more than they will ever know William McKinley. And for good reason.

It has not been an easy four months since the election. The moment had been so long in coming, so many election cycles, so many years focused on the next maneuver in a constant campaign. It was not until the morning after the election, after the initial euphoria of victory

had passed, that it struck him, how he was feeling. It was he, Marcus
Alonzo Hanna, who had ventured to Wall Street, to Newport, to
Pittsburgh, and squeezed out of the vicelike grips of J. Pierpont Morgan, John Rockefeller, Andrew Carnegie, and others like them—men
not in a habit of opening for anyone, or anything—twenty million dollars (twenty million dollars! Twenty Million Dollars! TWENTY MILLION
DOLLARS!). No one had ever raised a fraction of that sum for any campaign in all human history! He, Mark Hanna, had, like the greatest
military mind, marshaled that money to engineer the campaign against
Bryan, matching Bryan's fiery speeches with the Republicans' meagerly
equipped rhetorical troops—that madman Theodore Roosevelt, the
caustic Tom Reed, fourteen hundred more orators even less able,
assigned to lecterns throughout the land (what was lacking in quality
was made up with sheer volume: a constant flow of foot soldiers tossed
into the first bloody wave of battle). It was Hanna, all Hanna—from
the first opening gambit of his pawn, to the master counterstrokes of
his bishops and knights, to the final brilliant pincer move, using the
whole arsenal, including the king and the queen. Mark Hanna who
had gotten the votes.

It was Mark Hanna who had won the election.

Yet now, after the initial euphoric balloon had burst, it was
McKinley who won the election.

When Hanna called McKinley the next morning to offer congratulations he expected some mutuality at least, but received only . . .
after some delay . . . a pause . . . some prodding . . . a . . . thank-you.
As if Mark Hanna were a mere notch above some grubby office-
seeking well-wisher. Finally William came around to asking what cabinet post he might be interested in, should such a post become
available. A cabinet post! A post that *might become available* could as
easily, the next day, *become unavailable.* In the cabinet he would serve at
the president's beck and call, at McKinley's whim. Public pressure, the
onslaught of Hearst's daily demagoguery, could force Hanna out in an
instant.

A cabinet post was out of the question. Hanna needed a position
with some independence, a position of dignity, befitting his stature.
The Millionaire's Club would suit Mark Hanna. The United States
Senate.

Which would only be possible were there an opening in the Ohio delegation . . . which would have to be created . . . and that would have to be achieved through a carefully choreographed series of masterfully executed maneuvers that navigated through the Byzantine rivalries of Ohio politics, by which old John Sherman would be convinced to give up his Senate seat and join the cabinet—and hopefully could then maintain a sufficiently acceptable impression of a mentally facile and breathing presence while his functions needed attending—and Governor Bushnell, who was historically aligned with Hanna's old foe, now Senator-elect, Foraker, would be convinced to appoint his archenemy, Hanna, to replace the departed Sherman. It was a plan that seemed doomed from birth, a far more difficult venture than winning the presidency, but Hanna convinced McKinley that a Senate seat was his singular, final demand. And Hanna knew that McKinley knew that William McKinley could not risk embarking on his presidency having renounced the mother who birthed him into the political world.

McKinley came to see things Hanna's way, eventually, but the tone of the conversation was upsetting. It was no longer a friendship; it was a business spat, a squabble of unspoken threats, bluffs, and parries.

But now the battle with Bushnell and Foraker was over. Hanna would be appointed his seat. He would be the Honorable Senator Marcus Alonzo Hanna from the great state of Ohio. He would have the ear of the president; they were friends again, allies at least, but Hanna would have his own base of power, a podium from which he could speak his own views. Not that they differed on *views;* it was a matter of tone. Hanna's voice would have none of McKinley's willy-wallying, shilly-shallying, mamby-pamby. People understood straight talk; didn't matter if you were rich or poor or even colored. From his perch in the Senate, the sky was the limit for Mark Hanna.

Someone is laughing—a girl, and another girl . . . everyone on the left side of the street . . . and Hanna now realizes that his cigar is in his hand and he is raising it up and down as he marches, pumping it like the baton of P. T. Barnum when the circus hits town.

"Who is *he?*" somebody has the gall to say.

"Who are *you?*" shouts another in the laughing mob.

Hanna stops to look at them for a moment, stuffs his cigar-baton into his mouth and puffs. The girls are gawking at him, jabbing their fingers like lances at the town fool. The *real* president, he should say. The man who *made* the president: shit into gold and so forth.

"Big Injun!" Hanna yells. The words just tumble out of his mouth, who knows from where. He thrusts his chest out, and stomps his feet again, marching. "Me Big Injun!"

Back in New York, Hearst has taken a lady friend to the theater, for drinks, and then, back in the suite that adjoins the *Journal* offices, has allowed her to undress him. Now that he is finished with her and left her sleeping in his bed, he doesn't bother to put back on his bow tie or jacket. At the *Journal* there is no need for formalities. There is a newspaper to run—more than a paper, really—what will become the people's voice and will capture the public mind and spirit, its very soul. What is needed—the recent election has proven it once and for all—is a paper that will render campaigns meaningless, that will insulate public desires from the money thrown at them from those who seek their enslavement, that will dictate what the people want, what they demand of their government. It will entertain and enrage, will raise and lower the public's temperature like something Thomas Edison might invent or H. G. Wells might imagine.

It will make William McKinley, and his goddamned, underhanded, bought-and-paid-for election of 1896 powerless. All power will be dictated by the people, who will be dictated by William Randolph Hearst.

Hearst picks up a phone in his office. The sky outside is dark and the streets are quiet but what the hell, the stakes are high.

"Creelman!" he shouts. "Get to work!"

McKinley stands just inside of the ballroom door, welcoming the crowd. Pina is there too, holding her sister around the waist to keep her steady, but Ida is slumping, the occasion is too much for her. McKinley nods to a nurse who hurries over, then leads Ida up the stairs and places her in a seat on the balcony, at the presidential table, to wait for dinner.

From there Ida watches Pina take her place on the receiving line beside William. The line moves slowly, a series of still pictures. President Hayes bows, offers congratulations and advice. President Cleveland bows, offers congratulations, advice. Ida's husband nods, returns the kindnesses with thanks. There are cabinet secretaries and ambassadors and senators and congressmen and business owners all in a line, all bowing in courtly fashion.

Does he see her wave to him from the balcony? Does he realize how much she yearns to return to their house on Market Street?

Even now, when he has reached the peak, his destination, only the faintest hint of a smile can be detected on William's—her husband's—the president's—face. And even that hint is not joy, is not happiness; he will not permit such frivolity. It is a smile of begrudging recognition, of accomplishment and station. What is expected. Nothing more.

At dinner President Cleveland sits to McKinley's right, Ida is to his left. A military band is playing "Stars and Stripes Forever." All around is bunting, flags—red, white, and blue.

"There is the question of the Spanish," Cleveland says. The outgoing president says this with the relish of a man suddenly unburdened of responsibility. "The Cuban matter will not go away, Mr. President, or—may I call you William?"

McKinley nods, slices his beef.

"Have you thought out your position?"

"As I said in the campaign," McKinley says, "I follow your position, Mr. President. We must resist the call to fight Spain over Cuba. We will not give in to the pleas for expansionism. Safe at home, I say."

"Hearst and his newspapers may have something else to say on that," Cleveland says. "He is no great fan of yours, or your dear friend." Cleveland points his nose toward the far end of the long table, where Mark Hanna is arguing a point to an enraptured audience of tuxedoed men and long-gowned ladies. Cleveland and McKinley and everyone else can hear him.

"All questions of government," Hanna is saying, as he blows smoke in the air, "are questions of money."

"They'll tie Mark Hanna round your neck like a cinder block," Cleveland says. "Then toss you in the Potomac together for a night swim." Cleveland gnaws a piece of rare beef as he speaks. There's gristle caught in his teeth that the point of his knife won't get out.

"The papers will say what they will," McKinley says. "They have their point, I grant you. We have obligations for the darker regions. We must bring some light into their world. But it will not be up to William Hearst or Joe Pulitzer. The Lord will have the final say."

Cleveland laughs mildly and swallows a large forkful of beans.

"And then there's the Negro question," Cleveland goes on, "and the matter of the women." The former president can hardly contain himself with joy; it is a room filled with trash—that's the image—that he is leaving for the next tenant to clean, or live in, or—what's the difference anyway, anymore? "A delicate balance, if I may be so bold, Mr. President."

McKinley nods.

"Many in the South were none too happy that I vetoed that literacy bill the other day," Cleveland says. "To hell with them, I say."

"As you say, Mr. President," McKinley says. "A delicate balance."

Ida is not hearing their words. A woman is speaking to her, but she hears only a rumble of sounds emitting indiscernibly from a sea of mouths up and down the long dining table. From her seat on the balcony she can see the whirl of dancers down below, tuxedoed couples who seem so young. The Negro waiters seem to spin as well, the large potted plants beside the marble pillars, the vines below the bunting.

The dancers turn like screws into the floor and down the rabbit holes created by their circular motion. The girls scurry down the hall, their long curls bobbing behind, and Ida sees herself young, and scurries after them.

Why does her husband refuse to smile, even now? Because this path of their life was inevitable. He willed this path to be. There was an exchange made—Ida is convinced her husband made an exchange—through his prayers and his dreams and his letters to President Rutherford B. Hayes when they were just married, starting out in this life. A horrible exchange.

Her husband the president is speaking now with powerful men, slicing his beef as if he were slicing up the world—here a piece for you, there a piece for me.

A horrible exchange.

The rumble of the dancing crowd is the laughter of children. Little Ida and little Katie. Ida follows them down the hole, down the hole. *There, there they are. Ida! Katie!*

Cleveland nudges McKinley with an elbow, lets out a horrified gasp. McKinley turns slightly. With only a glimpse out of the corner of his eye he knows it is Ida, another of her spells. Her head is shaking in short rapid rotations, her eyes roll back. Soon her face may land on her plate, she may spit up her food in front of everyone, she may collapse on the floor.

Without looking at her, the president shakes out his linen napkin and places it over Ida's head, covering her from sight.

5 · *THE HEROIC SAGA OF THE CUBAN JOAN OF ARC · 1898 · (Part One)*

Does our flag protect women? We know who the government of Mark Hanna, and his puppet-in-chief, President William McKinley, protects. The Steel trust, the Railroad trust, the Sugar trust. But does it shield women, on foreign shores, in desperate straits, in danger of being robbed of their womanhood? Does this government even protect the innocence of an eighteen-year-old girl, who is valiantly fighting to save her beloved father from a tyrant's prison? Sadly, dear readers, the answer is no.

But happily, someone does fight for our values. There is heroism left in America. There is chivalry. There is William Randolph Hearst's *New York Journal*. It is more than a newspaper. Far more.

We have told you, noble readers, of the doings of Baby Bill McKinley and his nursemaid, Dollar Mark Hanna. How Hanna bribed convention delegates to give his baby boy Bill, that tool of the trusts, the Republican nomination. How Hanna shook

down the heartless, ravenous owners of those trusts to bail out
Governor Baby Bill when he went bankrupt in '93. How he
shook them down three years later to stockpile unprecedented
sums to sell Baby Bill to the people like bars of soap made of
snake oil. Those millionaires—Rockefeller, Carnegie, and the
like—they do not hand over their bills unless they are buying
something worth far more than what they are paying. It was the
Journal that told you long before Inauguration Day that this
president was bought and paid for.

It was the *Journal* that told you how Mark Hanna got his
president to appoint the senile stooge Sherman to the high office of secretary of state, a man who didn't realize or didn't care
or didn't understand *(which is worse, I ask you?)* that Spanish
goons were raping the poor, good people of Cuba like sheep by a
lonely herder, and that the poor decent Filipinos weren't faring
much better under the Spaniards' cruel yoke. Why would the
president appoint such a feckless imbecile to such a key post, at
such a crucial moment, when all of history counseled for a
strong steward willing to use our American forces? When our
nation yearned for brave American fighting men to liberate the
Cubans from their shackles? Why? Because Mark Hanna
wanted to play senator from Ohio, and Sherman was sitting in
his playpen. Yes, readers, our government is but a plaything for
the rich in the land of William McKinley and Dollar Mark
Hanna.

Dollar Mark Hanna himself let the truth slip out in a rare
moment of honesty: "No man in public office owes the public
anything," he said. It was the *Journal* who reported that nugget
for you.

It was the *Journal* that told you how Dollar Mark Hanna,
to hold on to his seat, paid off a fellow Republican, a man who
threatened to bring the cause of free silver coinage to the people
of Ohio and thus threatened Dollar Mark's continued member-
ship in his millionaires' club. Yes, dearest readers: bribery
again.

And what was our good President William McKinley doing
for the people, for you and me, while his loyal colleague in corporate crime was mortgaging high elected office in our government? What was he doing to help the poor immigrants trapped
in their dank, rat-infested tenements, too hot to sleep in summer, yet freezing in the winter?

Nothing.

What did our president care about childhoods sacrificed to scratch for a few loose dimes to pay the family rent?

Nothing.

What was our cherished leader doing about the hardworking farmers in danger of losing all to the greedy moneylenders who trapped them into usurious loans that foreclosed the poor families out onto the streets to live like stray dogs?

Nothing.

What was our great chief doing about those innocents caught in the merciless maw of the depression?

If you haven't bailed him out with large quantities of funds from your personal account, when he was trying to save his personal neck from his own debtor's noose, or when he was trying to buy his way into the presidency, nothing.

And now . . . let us tell you about the saga of the beautiful Evangelina Cosio y Cisneros. Hear her wail away in a cold Spanish cell, see her clutch her full, heaving breasts, near naked in tattered garb, imprisoned for the crime of loving her dear father too well. For the sin of not wishing to see him languish in a cell colder and more dank than that in which she herself now wastes away. Let us tell you about the Cuban Joan of Arc.

Tomorrow.

6 · LEON · October 1897

The rust-colored sun is low in the sky, somewhere out beyond Cleveland. Leon recognizes the other men at the bar: regulars who are always here, suckling desperately from their beer mugs and whiskey tumblers. He is sitting on a stool at Megan's father's saloon. He knows that Megan does not expect him just now; he has come early to speak to her father.

"Mr. Wisemki," Leon says when there's a pause between customers. "I would like a minute. It's about your daughter Megan."

The older man tugs at a tap, looks down at a beer, and Leon thinks he is smirking at him.

"I am a workingman, Mr. Wisemki. A man of simple means. But honest."

Her father is grinning fiercely now, as he pockets some change that rattles on the counter.

"We have nothing to say to each other."

Mr. Wisemki begins to wash a glass, wipe the counter. Busywork, keeping his eyes down.

Leon has rehearsed his lines on the streetcar ride and as he walked round the block before he steeled himself to enter the saloon.

"I love her," Leon says. "I love your daughter. Megan."

Her father looks up from his rag.

"We love each other," Leon says. "I would like her hand."

"And what could you do for her?" her father says. "You are nothing."

"I work in the factory. I live with my family on their farm and put money away. I have saved. I have always saved."

"We are not like you," her father says. "We are service people. Emily here," her father motions to the curtain leading to the back room, "every night she meets men who own the factories you sweat in. Men who will spend in a night all the money you can make in a year. One of them will take an interest in her, one day. Megan could have had the same. Maybe she still will. Who knows for sure?"

This is not the conversation Leon imagined; all he can do is repeat the little he remembers from what he rehearsed. "We love each other."

Megan's father looks at Leon. Their eyes lock; time freezes, words are spoken in silence.

Leon does not say: *Do you grow children to harvest them like corn and sell at the market? Are they cattle to you, or sows?*

"This is a woman I love," Leon says.

The words in Mr. Wisemki's eyes are not angry. What's there is disappointment, lost opportunities: a realization that the glimmer of rock in the pan is not gold.

"You have ruined her," the old man says, finally. "You will never see her again."

7 · RATIONALES, EXPLANATIONS, POSSIBILITIES (William)

Because William McKinley was born with an innate desire to smoke, though, due in large part to the strict Methodist teachings instilled in him in his youth, that craving had been suppressed.

Because he knew Ida hated cigars especially; she couldn't stand them, wouldn't tolerate them in her house.

Because, when puffed for long periods, he was able to form clouds, foglike and thick, that shielded him from view and from the world, closed doors, inward and outward, leaving him to his own thoughts, and at heart he was a shy and introspective man, though his chosen profession did not reward those traits.

There was something about the aroma.

And the sensation your mouth and head and body get; almost intoxicating.

Because Mark Hanna told him to.

It's not that he wanted to irritate Ida, but, now and again, he needed a brief respite from the day-to-day, the hustle and bustle; to take him away, you don't have to think, no comfort like the familiar. Lord, didn't he deserve one?

Because of the memories; Katie and Ida, so young, so weak, so helpless.

Because, in a sense, he fell in love with Mark Hanna. Or maybe— rather—what Hanna represented: the world apart from his travails.

Because of the pleasures of incessantly puffing, in his office, on the floor of the House, mapping strategy with colleagues, chatting with his assistants, supporters, reporters, delegates, petitioners, strolling about the Executive Mansion, the grounds, Washington, Canton, the nation at large. Twenty or so a day.

There was the whole ritual of selecting one from the humidor, snipping off one end, wetting the other, extracting a match and striking the blue tip against the edge of his desk or the sole of his shoe, lighting up and working up a fine, long ash.

Because, unbeknownst to him, tobacco was addictive; he was hooked.

Because some things are unexplainable.

8 · LEON · November 1897

He has taken the streetcar but noticed no people on the streets. No images strike him, no insights. He only sees Megan.

It is two weeks since her father sent him away.

Last night he woke with a start and found himself outside, at the base of the willow tree on his father's farm. There were no stars in the sky, no moon. He was in some nether region between dawn and dusk, night and day. In the pitch darkness not even the grass was visible. He was utterly alone. At similar times in the past the bull would visit him. At other times one of the Haymarket martyrs, August Spies, would appear before him and recite his courtroom speech, but it would be a conversation with Leon and Leon alone. "Go with me to the half-starved miners of the Hocking Valley," the ghost would shake his fist and shout. "Look at the pariahs in the Monongahela Valley, and many other mining districts in this country, or pass along the railroads of that most orderly and law-abiding citizen, Jay Gould. And then tell me whether this order has in it any moral principle for which it should be preserved!"

At those times the Haymarket ghosts would linger with Leon, but not this morning-night. The sense he had was orbiting in space. This must be death.

And then: no. Loneliness. Solitude.

A future.

It was then he woke with a start and walked quickly beyond the edge of town to where he could catch the streetcar to Cleveland.

Once Leon arrives at the saloon, he walks straight past the bar, past Megan's father, and opens the curtain to the back room.

"Where is Megan?" he says.

There are painted women on the pianos, bare legs draped down and crossed and kicking, and men sipping champagne and laughing and the Negro at the piano is playing ragtime fast and loud.

"I need to see her! Where is she?"

Nobody says anything. He rushes down a hallway and begins opening up doors, looking in. There is a bed with two of the large-breasted ladies stripping the jacket off of some politician or business-man. Leon thinks he's seen him before, in the newspapers, billboards, somewhere.

"Where's Megan?!"

One of the ladies on the bed, Leon now sees, is Emily.

"She's gone."

"Where did she go? I need to know! I must know!"

"He sent her away. She's—"

Then Leon feels a pull at the back of his collar and he is yanked off his feet. He lands on his back, then tumbles headfirst down the stairs, twisting as he goes, trying to right himself. On the landing someone grabs him again and tosses him out the door. His face lands just under the rear of a lavish carriage parked outside, in a pile of manure.

Leon does not move. He remains, facedown in the shit, sobbing.

9 · *THE HEROIC SAGA OF THE CUBAN JOAN OF ARC* · *1898* · *(Part Two)*

Our heroine, Evangelina Cosio y Cisneros, remains as we left her, clutching her full, heaving breasts. At the tender age of eighteen, this girl, delicate, refined, sensitive, unused to hard-ship, absolutely ignorant of vice, oblivious to the existence of such beings as crowd the cells of the Casa de Rocojidas, where the Spaniards have imprisoned her, was seized, then thrust into a prison maintained for the vilest class of abandoned women of

Havana. There, among the most depraved Negresses of Havana, she faces the next twenty years in a servitude that will kill her in a year. Her crime? She attempted to save her noble father from the Spaniards' notorious African prison colony in Cueta. *His* crime? He attempted to save his countrymen from the heartless shackles of those selfsame Spaniards.

Months ago these facts were laid out for all to see on the pages of this chronicle, complete with drawings of the languid beauty, Evangelina. The president knew all this and far more of our heroine's tragic circumstances. Yet President McKinley, with America's vast armies and navies at his disposal . . . did . . . nothing.

So what happened to our Cuban Joan of Arc? Was she roasted at the stake like her historical predecessor? Or was she left to wither away in her cell?

If it were left up to our president she might have, and the news would not have interrupted his midday cigar. But the *Journal* would not allow it. Our publisher, William Randolph Hearst, would not allow it. We at the *Journal* were forced to take matters into our hands.

We sent our man, Decker was his name, across the ocean to dark Havana. His mission? Liberate the beautiful Cuban damsel. Decker secured the rental of an apartment across the alley from the infamous prison, on the top floor, from which he could gaze at the dreaded towers. By means of artifice that dare not be divulged to our enemies in these pages, he was able to arrange that a gift be brought to Evangelina, what appeared for all the world to be a basket of chocolate bon-bons, irresistible to the brutish Spanish guards. By means of secret communications and codes that, too, dare not be divulged here, our heroine was instructed that these sweets were infused with sleep-inducing potions, toxins, and drugs. By means of her feminine wiles (at this juncture her tattered garb, which admirably exposed her voluptuous curves, certainly aided her), our heroine enticed the guards to her cell and fed them the luscious desserts, employing her willowy seductive fingers to pop the doctored bon-bons into their gaping mouths. The men soon fell fast asleep. A white handkerchief was then tied upon the outer bars of the damsel's window (another prearranged code), and our man Decker was ready. He and his trusted accomplices climbed out of their apartment window, scaled a ladder to her cell, cut off the bars by means of a hacksaw, and absconded with the shrieking, smiling, laughing, crying, breast-heaving, palpitating, hugging, ingratiating, disbelieving, kissing, hugging again, weeping some more, laughing more too, young beauty.

Evangelina was free!

She and Decker returned by boat to America. And it was not the president who met her with a hero's welcome at the dock. It was the man who had made the cause of Evangelina his own, then the nation's, who had entreated President McKinley to show a modicum of compassion for her tragic plight but, when his pleas fell on callous ears, seized the day, planned the entire escape, paid for Decker, his accomplices, and his far from customary and usual expenses . . . William Randolph Hearst!

10 · MORRIS · 1891

There are workmen everywhere—painters, stonemasons, brick masons, an army of tradesmen—trailing behind Morris as he traipses up the winding, marble staircase of the Fifth Avenue mansion he purchased three weeks ago from Mr. Nils Vandeveer. Vandeveer was Morris's most reliant client over the past year and a half and had spread the word throughout New York society that the quality of Morris's product was rivaled only by his discretion. But then his friend informed him—mopping his brow, panting, hurried to say the least—that he had to leave the country immediately; the details could not be shared. As Morris told his good friend when, with a goblet raised, they closed the deal on Château Vandeveer, Nils Vandeveer's continued purchases and reference were personally responsible for the financial explosion of Morris's Freedom Rings Corporation. Nils muttered something about the pair serving as each other's salvation and damnation. (Morris, exuberant over the prospect of purchasing such a grand palace, did not comprehend the meaning until weeks later.)

The hammers and chisels are banging incessantly, but to Morris the noise is music, the sound of beauty, architectural resurrection.

"Mr. Steinglitz, this shade of pink we had found for the master bath—"

"Too floral."

"Mr. Steinglitz, is this the proper shape for the central chandelier in the foyer—"

"Too many teardrops."

"The marble for the top of the main dining room buffet?"

"Too marbled."

"The table?"

"Too tabular."

No one joins Morris in laughter except for Amelia, who realizes her husband has been pestered long enough and, besides, there are visitors waiting for him. She leads the workmen down the west wing of the second floor as Morris retreats to his office.

"In two weeks all of New York society will be here to inaugurate this place," Morris exclaims as he walks through the door, "and it is chaos. Pure, unrefined madness."

Morris brushes the tail of his silk robe under him and sinks down, with a mock-exasperated flourish, into a chair at the head of the long table.

He is silent for a moment, his head down in his chest, and then he lifts his gaze and surveys the men and women seated at his sides. A ragged bunch, motley, multicolored, and wild. As if the cacophonous noise of the hammers and chisels and saws outside had taken form in a band of people. Morris has acquired a reputation as a philanthropist for causes not favored by Andrew Carnegie and his ilk. Some months ago he provided the woman heading this group with a sizeable check, for legal costs of a friend if he recalls correctly. But now he laughs to himself. *This,* Morris thinks, *is who will transform America into some communal utopia?*

"You people want more money, I suppose," he says. "Tell me why."

"The answer is simple, Mr. Steinglitz," the woman leading the group says, and now Morris recollects who she is. "To make more of your unrefined madness."

11 · COMSTOCK · 1898

A shadowy form scurries through the dark street, thundering on heavy tiptoes. His cheeks, forehead, and neck are coated with coal, as are his muttonchop sideburns, mustache, and beard. Under his cloak, his belly is strapped tight with a woman's girdle—to disguise his girth, he will say, if he has the ill fortune to be asked. He reaches the newsstand and glances around surreptitiously.

He locates a bundle of *New York Journals* that have been left on the sidewalk. Then Anthony Comstock casually lights a cigar and, as he walks away, drops the lit match and the smoldering stogie on the papers and, even before they ignite, breaks into a run down the street.

12 · *THE HEROIC SAGA OF THE CUBAN JOAN OF ARC* · *1898* · *(Part Three)*

DATELINE—CUBA

And yet the near-tragic saga of our Cuban Joan of Arc is not the worst of it. The beautiful Evangelina is but one of thousands who each day fall prey to the brutish Spaniards! Even the *Journal* and its ever-enterprising publisher have not the means to save them all. The Spaniards hold this entire idyllic isle tight in their tyrannical fists, maiming, ravishing . . . killing the poor Joses, Juanitas, little Miguels, and little Conchitas of Cuba. Our intrepid reporters have witnessed a child being ripped from the anchor of his young mother's loving embrace, at which point the mother is promptly dragged (after she is ravished and despoiled) to a hastily constructed garrot and guillotine where her beautiful head is displaced from its rightful place atop her neck while her loving children are forced to watch the gruesome sight. . . .

And might we mention the two hundred and sixty valiant American fighting men blown up on the *Maine* by the sinister Spaniards? Our battleship is our soil, wherever it travels! Ergo, the underhanded explosive that destroyed *our ship* was set on *American* land! The ship floated in Havana Harbor, but it carried with it American waters under its mighty hull! Remember the *Maine*!

Does our president have a heart? What sort of president does nothing in the wake of such carnage? What sort of man is this William McKinley?

President McKinley, the American people are in a frenzy; they have caught the war fever and caught it bad. The good voters are of a single mind. The nation demands justice! The nation demands war!

13 · McKINLEY · February–March 1898

McKinley is in his office, surrounded by his top political advisers, diplomats from State, military men from War. They have discussed the Cuban matter so often in the past months that their conversation has become a ritual. They all know what the others will say. They wait for their turn to speak but do not listen.

"Hearst claims a Spanish diplomat insulted you, Mr. President. Questioned our nation's honor."

"Hearst claims you are allowing the Spanish to run roughshod over Cuban womanhood under our noses."

"Hearst claims the evidence is clear that the Spaniards blew up the *Maine,* but you refuse to recognize the truth."

"Hearst claims there is no alternative: we must stand up and protect Cuba. We must declare war on Spain."

The voices fire at the president from all sides, but McKinley stands firm, then waits a moment for the sounds to subside before he speaks.

"I have seen enough of war," he says quietly. "That is something that Hearst does not understand. He knows only the lies he sells in his vile rags. I have picked up the corpses of men I knew well and carted them off the battlefield. There is nothing simple about this Cuban matter."

Mark Hanna is leaning back in a chair, puffing on a cigar. "Mr. President, sir," he says, "I have agreed with you all the way." He hands a stogie to McKinley and lights it for him. "While you have hung tough against Hearst's barrage of bluster, while he and Pulitzer fomented the riffraff, I have been there with you. I've preached patience on the Hill. Sometimes the best action is to stand pat. The business folks have hung with you, too. In war anything can happen. Business does not want instability. The risks are not worth the most that victory could bring. People may have been frustrated, seen you as a bit too cautious perhaps, but it was prudent, responsible. But this *Maine* business has changed all that. The Spaniards blew up our goddamned boat!"

"We do not know that the Spanish did it," McKinley says. "The investigation was inconclusive. It could have been an internal explosive, a faulty engine. It may well have been—"

"It doesn't matter anymore," Hanna says. "It's too late for such details."

"I won't allow Hearst to bully me into war."

McKinley buries his head in his hands. His eyes are ringed with wide red swatches. It is partly the weight of things, his indecision, and part exhaustion. He has not slept more than an hour or two any night in the past months.

"If I may, Mr. President, sir." It is one of the military brass speaking now, an admiral perhaps; McKinley cannot be certain peeking at him through a crack in his fingers. "Mr. President, our forces stand ready. The navy can take out the Spanish fleet. The island of Cuba will be captured. If I may be so bold, sir, we will destroy the Spaniards in a fortnight. Their boats will join the *Maine* at the bottom of Havana Harbor."

"We will make the world take notice," says another. "We will teach the world a lesson about what America is made of."

"Spain is dying," says the first uniformed man. "Britain will be next. Europe's old colonial powers are taking their last gasps. This will be our time. You can be the first president of the American century."

"There is another matter," Hanna says, "of some importance." Hanna is smiling now as he puffs his cigar. "Mr. President, the public loves nothing like a war."

14 · THE SPANISH-AMERICAN WAR · 1898

"Do you feel uncomfortable, Creelman?"

Hearst's gangly body is standing upright, though the soldiers marching around him are all crouched or crawling on their knees and elbows, hugging the hillside.

"Lord, Cuba's hot," Hearst says. He stops to mop his sweating brow with his straw hat. "We never reported how damned hot it is, did we, Creelman? Creelman?"

Only then Hearst realizes that Creelman is hunched on the grass below him, in the fetal position, cowering.

"That's gunfire, boss," Creelman says.

Hearst, grinning ear to ear, cups his hand to his ear dramatically.

"No," he says, "I think you've got it all wrong, Creelman. There's cannon fire, too." Hearst leans down and whispers into his reporter's ear. "That's war for you, Creelman. That's what they do in war." Then Hearst laughs, louder than the explosions, which are now half a mile off. "Now get up!"

"I can't, boss," Creelman says. "I don't think I can move."

"Good God," Hearst sighs. With his teeth he rips off the linen band of his hat. Then he kneels down and begins to wrap it around Creelman's head, but when it strikes him that there might be blood Hearst feels his stomach wretch and quickly turns his head away while he secures the bandage.

"I haven't been hit, boss," Creelman says. "I'm sick. It must be dysentery."

Hearst stands up again. Soldiers are shouting for him to get down, he's drawing fire, but Hearst remains standing.

Hearst and Creelman are on a hill in Cuba, God knows where, and there are cows still grazing below them, lazily chomping clumps of grass while all around them lie the bodies of men, dead or dying. Hearst can hear the groans. He can hear the pained mutterings of death; in Spanish or English, it is the same sound. He reaches down and takes Creelman's pad and a pencil.

It strikes him that the way to go about telling this story is by detailing the life of an ordinary Cuban, Jesus Caban, say—good a name as any. Jesus tends a small cattle farm outside of Santiago with his young wife, Evangelina, and their four—five—children (names to be determined). This morning Jesus milked his cows, carried the buckets to market, bought treats in town for his kids, said a prayer at church before he left for home. He returned for breakfast with his beloved family. He did not tell his wife where he was going; to tend the herd, she must have thought. But then, by afternoon, Jesus was fighting for the liberty of his country.

And now he lies on a hillside overlooking his farm, moaning, muttering prayers and well wishes to his God and his wife and his children *(make names biblical)*, a Spanish shell deep within his chest. He draws his last breaths as his cattle graze, oblivious to their master's fate. . . .

Suddenly Hearst hears a sound and reaches for the revolver in his side holster, but it is only a bird next to Creelman, desperately flapping its wings in the mud. It must have been hit by gunfire, a fluke shot.

"Creelman," Hearst says. "Get up. I got us into this war. Now we've got to beat every paper in the world with the story."

15 · VOICES FROM THE UPPER CHAMBER · 1898

John T. Morgan, the esteemed senator from the great state of Alabama, is recognized to state his opinion on whether the United States, after its resounding military victory over Spain, should annex the formerly

Spanish territories of Cuba and the Philippines: "After long and considered reflection, my colleagues, I rise in favor of annexing the territories, justly acquired through hard and heroic labors of our fighting
men. The president's well-stated opinions on America's moral obligation to Christianize the heathen natives, with all due respect, misses
the point. Being as said territories may serve as a final resolution to
this great nation's nigger problem. Being that is where we can put
them."

Whereupon the esteemed Senator Ben "Pitchfork" Tillman, from
the equally great state of South Carolina, rises and is recognized by his
esteemed colleague from Alabama to respond: "While I see wisdom in
my esteemed colleague's proposal, I must, after equally studied reflection, voice my dissent, for two principal reasons. The first: being that
the Cubans and Filipinos would come to our shores in droves full, once
they were invited, and thereupon would commence to mix their
already mongrel blood with the white race here at home, and thus forever taint and despoil us. The second: being that after sending some of
our niggers to the islands, we'd never hear the end of it from those left
behind. It'd all be, 'You should hear how well we've got it in the Philip-
pine territory, or Cuba.' And that'd be the last honest day's work you'd
see out of these here niggers. That's God's honest truth."

16 · McKINLEY · October 10, 1898

McKinley is on a train riding through the Middle West—Illinois,
Iowa, Wisconsin, Nebraska. The key states in the last election,
what will hold the key to the next, in 1900. At every stop there is bunting, flags, brass bands, an ocean of red, white, and blue. The crowds fill
the railway stations, hurray like a convention. They wave, they scream.
Ladies cry, thrust small babies at him to kiss, to acknowledge them
with a wave, a smile, a nod of the head. There are no Silverites, no socialists, no anarchists. The newspapers who say the people oppose him

have been telling lies. It took a trip out here, to the heartland of America, for McKinley to find the truth. America is a wave of adoring citizens, good-hearted Christians all. McKinley is not simply their president. He is a conquering hero. Even now, when he has finished his speech and the train is pulling off and they can no longer even see him waving at them out the window, they cheer ecstatically.

"You learn things about a people when you become president," McKinley says, "things you never thought about them before."

His secretary, George Cortelyou, is nodding but not responding. He is too busy chatting with another secretary who is summarizing a report he has just handed over.

"People like nothing like a war," the president says. "Except winning a war. Sad as it is, it's true. God bless Admiral Dewey."

McKinley pulls out a cigar from his vest pocket and lights it, leans back in his cabin and inhales.

"The report is complete, Mr. President," Cortelyou says as the other secretary scuttles to the next cabin. "If now is appropriate. . . . We'll be in Omaha in three hours."

"Fine, Mr. Cortelyou. Let's hear it."

"The analysis of your speech was done line by line, Mr. President," Cortelyou says. The secretary has the habit of tugging an edge of his handlebar mustache as he speaks. It's nerves, McKinley thinks, youth and awe.

"The stenographer annotated the text with notations signifying the applause registered in response to each phrase or line, noting intensity, length, and loudness. He's very good, really. He was able to mark particular words the crowd liked. By comparing responses from the crowds in similar venues, he even can tell which intonations were effective."

"Does Bryan go through this sort of thing, do you think?" McKinley is smiling as he says it, teasing his officious secretary.

Cortelyou hesitates, then continues.

"Well then, to the report." Cortelyou looks down at the stack of papers in his hand. "The idea of foreign markets. There was some uncertainty when you first broached the issue; scattered, sporadic claps, and even, truth be told, a few hoots. That's the X's he has down there in the margin. But once you explained the concept a bit, that we needed to open up new markets to keep the economy strong, the crowd seemed to come round."

"It's an important point." McKinley takes a deep puff from his cigar. "Selling our products abroad. Complex, but key."

"Next. Obligation and duty are fine words, Mr. President."

"Yes, Mr. Cortelyou?"

"I mean—well, of course—Mr. President. What it says is, when you spoke of our duty to Christianize the heathens, that it was our obligation to bring light into the dark corners of the world, our man noted: 'Prolonged, enthusiastic response.' The highest ratings. Top-notch."

"Thank you, Mr. Cortelyou. Does that mean they want me to take over the Philippines or not?"

Cortelyou searches his papers.

"I wouldn't draw any—that's not my—"

"That's the point of all this, isn't it? The main point anyway." McKinley smiles as he watches his secretary squirm, study the papers for answers that are not there. "Go on, Mr. Cortelyou. Finish up."

"Well, there's a list of other words and intonations that we think you should work into the next speech. And then here, on the next page are some that, well, to be blunt, sir, it might be better to drop from the text."

"You know, Mr. Cortelyou, I was just reading this magazine. And I found this piece quite interesting." McKinley stands, holds up a magazine, and points to a picture of Admiral Dewey, the white-mustached hero standing before a mirror in a bathroom. "Let me read you what it says here beneath the admiral. It says, 'The first step toward lightening the White Man's Burden is through teaching the virtues of cleanliness.' It goes on to talk of brightening the dark corners of the earth as civilization advances, and so on."

"That sounds like your speech, sir. The admiral's taking some liberties, if I could be so bold."

"You may, Mr. Cortelyou. But it's not the admiral's words, or ours. It's not an article either." McKinley places the magazine down on the table and puffs out a series of smoke rings. Cortelyou does not know if the president will laugh or cry at the moment, only that he seems in an odd mood, a rare divergence from his customary even keel.

"Take a close look," McKinley says, and Cortelyou takes the magazine from him and holds it near his face. "It's an advertisement," the president says. "For Pear's soap."

17 · PARKER · 1898

James Parker is standing in the back of a small room that serves as a school for all Negroes in the community whose parents can afford to allow their children the time off from work. His tall frame peers over the crowd. There are only Negroes here. Some are teachers, some ministers, some children and their parents.

A young man is seated at the table in the front of the room, pen in hand. His eyeglasses and starched white shirt speak of education from the North, perhaps college. He is listening, writing what he is told.

The others are lined up to tell the young man what they have seen so he can write it all down. It will all become a petition, a plea to be sent to the president in Washington. Their stories will be sent to President McKinley to request that action be taken. That attention, finally, be paid.

There are personal stories, accounts of the life they have fled in the South. A woman tells of how the Ku Klux Klan raided the Negro part of town in the night. A man tells of how, when the colored men tried to vote, they were moved to a separate line to where they were asked questions about the Constitution that made no sense and then they were directed to go home. Others were shoved away from the polls before a question was ever asked. A child tells of how the colored children are only permitted to go to schools that have no books to read; children of all ages are cramped together in a room in which nothing is learned.

As he waits for his chance to speak James Parker thinks about what he should say. He wonders if he should tell of the odd fellow he befriended on the farm he worked in Ohio. Of how James lived with his mother in a shanty in New York City as the great buildings were being built. How they had come from the South to find a pasture in the city where they leaned together a few planks of wood and with a few nails banged together a one-room shack with space enough for him and his two sisters and mother. There were goats they kept outside the shanties and chickens for the eggs. Then they were all chased out by the workmen, the bricklayers, and they watched from afar as wondrous castles emerged out of the dirt where their animals had grazed. So they moved again and banged together another shack, but the space was always too precious for them to stay long. The pastures vanished. A roadway was built and up went more castles, cluttering up the sky. Parker and his family lived in the shadows of the castles, always scurrying to keep ahead of the next construction plans. Soon there were no open spaces. The city had spread its wings uptown.

He wonders if he should tell what became of his beautiful young sisters in the wilds of the great city. What became of his mother.

Of his father he does not know; his mother will not share her sadness.

He wonders if he should tell of his life as a fighting man. Of what he witnessed after the battle of Wounded Knee. Of what he saw in Cuba. Of how his battalion of Negro soldiers stormed San Juan Hill, then were given warm congratulations by Teddy Roosevelt himself.

Thinking back on his life he feels the rage burn inside him; the vision of his mother and sisters are embers that spark. There are nights when his practiced veneer of serenity vanishes, and he lashes out at those responsible, bosses and foremen and presidents and judges and lawyers and businessmen whose names he does not know. He allows himself to bathe in an orgy of violence, those nights, and when he awakes he is refreshed and his calm takes over.

Parker is facing the young man at the table now. It is his turn to speak.

He decides he will tell of the time just recently when he almost met William McKinley.

The president was in Georgia, touring the South to gather public support for taking over the Philippines. It was in all the papers. The South was not where the president could expect folks to support him, but he figured the Southerners would appreciate taking over another nation of darkies, America ruling over the Filipinos.

Parker had left New York to visit his mother, who had gone back home to Atlanta.

There were five black men who had been arrested and were in the local jail in the town next to where the president was scheduled to speak the next day. Parker never heard what their offenses were. But one night it so happened that the jailhouse door was left unlocked, and a posse of white folks from town rode in carrying torches and guns and rope. When the Negroes were found the next morning, their faces were unrecognizable. There was little skin left on their backs. Muscle and bone were seared by the flames as each hung from a tree in the woods.

When it is his turn to speak, to have his words transcribed by the educated young man at the front of the room, Parker recounts what happened in Georgia. "Mr. President," James Parker says as the man writes down his words, "those men who were lynched in Georgia next to your door, they were your brothers, they were God's children, for them Jesus fought and died. But almost before your eyes they were cut down. Did you speak, sir? What did you say of the crime that was done them, and of the sheriffs and lawyers and businessfolk that played their parts in the act? Why did you stay silent, sir?

"Mr. President," Parker says, "they say you are a good Christian man. But then, sir, Mr. President sir, Mr. President. Will you do justice?"

18 · McKINLEY · October 13, 1898

McKinley senses that the applause in Omaha is louder than in any city, more prolonged and enthusiastic. He says the words they want to hear; his intonations are as they should be. He wonders if here in the hometown of William Jennings Bryan he has won these people over from the boy orator. Yes: with Bryan it was merely words, the deceptive allure of his music. With McKinley, he tells himself, it is the man and his deeds. He hates himself for his joy at the petty victory over another man's defeat, but he cannot help himself.

As president you learn aspects of man you never knew before. Or ever cared to know.

"One of the great laws of life is progress," the president says to the crowd, "and nowhere have the principles of this law been so strikingly illustrated as in the United States."

The crowd is hesitant, waits for clarification. He hears Hanna in his ear: *red meat to the lions!*

"Shall we deny ourselves what the rest of the world so freely and so justly accords to us?!"

"No!" yells a man in front, his body almost pushed against the railroad car where McKinley is standing, setting off hoots and wild applause throughout the crowd.

"No! No! Let us take what's been given us!"

"The war with Spain was no more invited by us than were the questions which are laid at our door by its results," McKinley shouts. "Now as then we will do our duty!"

The crowd is one voice, man, woman, child, all in a single, unified yell, arms waving upward, clapping over their heads. McKinley watches the mass, pauses to let them express themselves for a time. "Take what is ours! Philippines for America! To the victor go the spoils!"

The people deserve a moment to speak, too.

Before McKinley began his speech the mayor and the leaders of the Nebraska Republican Party had taken him to an exposition where they showed the president exhibits of all manner of animals and men. As he watches the crowd, the one that sticks in his mind is the Indian Congress. The mayor had led McKinley to a podium where they sat and watched the tribes in full war gear, feathers and face paint, enter the corral before him. Some were on horseback, others on foot. There were Americans in the corral too, dressed as soldiers. Together they acted out the old Indian wars—not so old, really, but past nonetheless. The soldiers fired blank shots at the Indians; the Indians threw dull spears at the soldiers.

At one point a red man on horseback charged out of formation toward the podium, spear in hand. His expression was menacing, and he screeched as he rode straight toward the president. The soldiers and Indians who were fighting the fake battle were confused, uncertain whether the charge was part of their play-killing and play-dying. Some of the soldiers rode toward McKinley and drew their prop guns to protect him.

McKinley could tell, with one look in the Indian's eyes, that this rogue must be the great Geronimo. He had been told the old Indian general would be there at the expo. The charge was so fast, there was no time to panic, no time for McKinley's entourage (there was no security) to step in front to guard him. In that moment time slowed to a standstill, his mind floated out of his body and looked on, from a distance; gathered perspective. In the war McKinley had spoken with fellow soldiers who, faced with death, had experienced such sensations.

McKinley's eyes locked on Geronimo.

A noble savage, the president thought. But a savage nonetheless, a man whom even the truth of Christ could not save. President Cleveland had no choice but to imprison him, the nation had no choice but to defeat all the Indian heathens. War was not something McKinley welcomed, but again, some modicum of civilization and decency is needed before you can sit down at the bargaining table in good faith and work out differences peaceably. In the dark corners of the globe the Christian message could not be understood. Hence, war. Hence, Cuba, Puerto Rico, the Philippines. Havana, San Juan, Luzon—dark places all. True, the Spanish were a Christian people, but they were of the Old World, and perhaps darkness had eclipsed the light in the backward colonies. Yes, war was necessary. And America had been forced to conquer its own dark forces: the Indians, Wounded Knee, and all that. This was not something that one questioned. The world is a dark place, and America so bright with Christian light. It was duty, it was obligation.

As soon as Geronimo reached the edge of the podium he stopped, reared up his horse. McKinley knew there was no need for protection. Perhaps Geronimo had been a wild animal, but now he was defanged. A general, defeated, deposed of his army, his power, his people. The Indian nodded his head at the president, ever so slightly, as if in submission. McKinley stood up and tipped his hat. The crowd's shocked gasp gave way to an awed applause. . . .

And now, standing in the balcony at the rear of the railway car, McKinley looks out at the crowd, bathes in its cheers. He does not mention Cuba, does not mention the Philippines, because they do not need to be mentioned. The message is understood: duty, obligation.

"Right action," McKinley concludes his speech, "follows right purpose."

19 · LEON · 1898

He has spent weeks looking for Megan. He waits outside the saloon to talk to Emily and other girls who work in the back room; he grabs them when they walk out the door, then interrogates them. "Where has Megan gone? Is there anyone else who might know?" He tracks down rumors, takes the train to farms outside the city, to Columbus, to Cincinnati.

Nothing.

There are days when his temples throb, and he feels the veins in his head expand and pinch against his skull; when the sharp pain recedes there's a dull numbness and he feels weak in the joints of his legs and his wrists.

He does not work. He has vowed to never enter a factory again.

"It is the illness," he says.

"Go to the doctor if you are ill," Waldek says.

Leon laughs. "You know better," he says. "In this country you must have money or the doctors do not care."

A benevolent workers' association sends him sick benefits.

20 · EMMA · 1899

Emma is on a train, gazing at her face reflected back at her in the window. Drifting off to sleep . . . drifting . . . the drama of her past plays out. She is a girl in Russia, wandering the streets, dancing; she cannot feel her feet hit the roadway. She is lost in her own thoughts, a child's world of play, when she hears a human wail. A young man in ragged peasant clothes is being whipped by his master, a stocky, bearded landowner in a black fur hat. The lashes of the whip slice the back of the poor man's jacket and shirt, streaks of blood form dark stripes that soak through. The beating has no context. It is not punishment but rage; it is ritual, something demanded by forces the master is not even aware of. Men and women continue to walk along the street without stopping, mothers and fathers with children in carriages, peasants whose beatings will be meted out another day, policemen and Cossacks. They glance at the disturbance as if it were a midwinter's snowfall. The man's scream is absorbed by the clatter of horse hooves, coaches' wheels, a policeman's whistle.

The beating repeats itself.

Alex sits in his cell, too tired to weep; those emotions are no more.

She is on a stage, lashing Most with a whip.

The beating repeats itself. In Kovno. In Cleveland. In New York City.

21 · LEON · 1898

Leon is sitting under a tree, smoking a cigar. His eyes are transfixed by a bull that is yoked to a plow, its thick neck chafing against the tight rope and leather bridle that ties him to the harness. The animal's eyes a fiery red, Leon reads them easily, understands.

The bull's muscles are so powerful that were he simply to lift his mighty head he could snap the wooden brace of the harness in two, shake off the shackles, and escape from the farm. Free, he would loll in the meadows, eating his fill of grass and wildflowers. He would mount the cow who happens to stroll before him and ride her. His horns would needle her head, pry bleeding holes in her temples, his hooves kick her sides, crack ribs; his penis so engorged it would become another weapon. Then the bull would dismount and leave the cow in a heap on the grass and wander on, eating the intoxicating grass and wildflowers. A free being; wholly free.

Leon is transfixed by the bull's red eyes.

The bull lifts his head and tries to needle with a horn his master standing above him, riding the plough.

Then the master slashes his hindquarters with a whip and the bull kicks up his rear hoof, but the man only whips him again.

The master is a farmhand, the child of a freed slave named, like his father, Jimmy Parker.

The bull is subdued, but Parker whips him again anyway, then once more. Parker turns to Leon and stares hard in a way that unnerves him.

The bull's eyes have lost their fury. He pulls his heavy plow. He rends the field with the sharp blade affixed to him. He no longer dreams of snapping the harness with his neck.

Leon's father and stepmother have bought this farm, and Leon has put four hundred dollars of his own money he saved from work to help them pay for it, though that does not make it his. It is only where he sleeps.

Leon has been sitting under the tree since early morning. Before the sun came up he was able, somehow, to drag himself out of bed, to fire the woodstove, fry an egg and a chunk of bacon. His father's wife found him in the kitchen, so Leon took his plate with him outside without saying a word to her. He watched the sun rise to its peak, then vanish amid dark clouds. Thunder crashed, lightning struck across the fields, and the rabbits ran, the lightning bolts thrown from the heavens, chasing the small creatures out of the woods. If God is above us, he is toying with spikes he hurls at the animals. The horses kicked, the cows trotted toward the barn, but the bull and Leon stood firm. The bull pulled its plow, steadily, defiantly, and Leon remained under his tree. The skies opened and dumped pails of rain onto the fields, and the chickens in their wire-walled prisons pecked and squawked. The rain soaked Leon's clothing straight through—his hair, his shoes—but still he sat, watching the bull.

Leon hears the dinner bell.

It is dark. The field is empty. *When did Parker take the bull away? When were the animals locked back up in the barn?*

Time to return to his room.

Perhaps he will sleep outside under the overhanging tree limbs and the stars, let the dew shower him awake in the morning.

It strikes Leon suddenly that the field has been empty for some time, perhaps all day. Yes, perhaps it has rained all day. He has imagined the bull behind the plow. Or perhaps it has not rained at all and it is the wetness on his head and clothes that he imagines. Or the bull is before him still.

Leon knows not whether the bull is or ever has been before him, what is real. Knows only that the image is in his head.

22 · EMMA · 1899

Edward Brady has been her lover for seven years now. Before she left on the train he asked that she delay her trip. Demanded, more accurately.

"There are things more important than your lectures and rallies," Edward said.

They were in their apartment in New York, lying in bed. Emma's head nestled in her lover's chest as he stroked her hair.

"You love me, Emma, do you not?" Edward said.

She nodded.

"Then I must have you."

"I am here, aren't I?" she said.

"This is not enough," he said. "You just spent a year in Europe away from me. You are back for a few months and now you are off to California with your speeches, your organizing. Have you asked yourself why you must move away all the time?"

"How can you ask that?"

"I think you are afraid."

"Afraid?" Emma laughed. She pulled away from him, sat up in bed. "If I was afraid I should think I would be rallying for Carnegie and Morgan, or working for McKinley. Or be silent."

"That is not what I am talking about." Edward lit a cigarette, stood up from the bed. The light from across the street danced on his naked body like on a mountain lake, his chest, hard and smooth.

"You are afraid of falling in love too deeply, Emma. Of loving something more than your cause. You think you will lose yourself, or lose your freedom, I'm not certain which."

"You have always been so jealous, Edward, so possessive," Emma said. "Love is not enough. I must become property. Well, I am no man's property."

"You know that is not what I mean," Edward said. He stepped into his pants, then hurriedly threw on a shirt and began to button it. "What I want is to spend my life with a woman I love. If that is too much for you, well. . . ." He was dressed now, and he turned to face Emma a final time. Edward knelt down and held her shoulders, looked into her eyes. "You are a free person, Emma. I would never take your liberty. I love you too much. But as a free woman you have the power to make choices. And now you have a choice. Do you want a life with me?"

She looked back at him, bit down on the inside of her mouth. She had known Edward's tendencies. The world could remain on its axis, the poor in their shackles, and Edward would be content to lie in bed with her, stroking her hair. With him, in time, she would be happy, but she would no longer be Emma Goldman.

"Emma, you only love what you cannot have," Brady said. "If there is any man you love it is still Berkman, but that is only because Berkman is no longer a man to you. He is a symbol. To have your heart you must give your life to the great cause. But there is one problem with such a man. He is dead to you."

She said nothing. She could have told him that she could not bear children, that that is not something her body could do anymore. That there was this operation, the doctor recommended it, that could make her able to give birth, but that she had decided against it. She should try to explain this all to Edward, why it seemed like a kind of fate to her—it was all very complicated—she did not believe in a god; she was not one for mysticism or spiritualism; she was no Victoria Woodhull—but still, her body was a message. There was a life that she was meant to live and the nature of her body, untampered by surgery, made that clear, undeniable. Other women would be mothers. She would make a better world for their children.

But she told him nothing.

Edward slammed the door behind him and was gone.

She has not heard from him since.

23 · LEON · 1898

His brother-in-law Frank insists that he get his mind off of Megan. "She is not coming back," he says. "And besides, it is all for the best." Frank says that during the strike Leon showed promise, a dedication to the cause. There are insights Leon understands.

And so in the evenings Leon takes the streetcar into Cleveland and goes to meetings. A Polish educational circle, it is called. Frank introduces him to the other men. They hand Leon a paper and a pencil. There are socialists, anarchists, unionists. They meet in the outskirts of the city, near where he used to meet Megan. They meet in basements, by candlelight.

The men pass around books with Jacob Riis photographs of

ragged children in New York tenements. The men wonder what is the idea behind the photographs—they could be portraits of their own families—and then someone says the idea is that the photographs are intended for the wealthy who would otherwise never see a tenement. Riis's idea is that good Christians, when they are exposed to the sight of such suffering, will question the system that has bestowed upon them such wealth. Changed men, they will then work for reform. That is the idea.

On the table is Karl Marx in Russian, Polish, English, Italian, and German. *Das Kapital, The Communist Manifesto.* There is Henry George's *Progress and Poverty.* There is Bellamy's *Looking Backward.*

There are magazines and newspapers, each the voice of a breathing soul who does battle with the world and visits Leon in the basement room. *Lucifer* is Moses Harman; the old prophet of free love and free speech, Moses has spent a lifetime being chased into jails by the self-anointed morality policeman, Anthony Comstock. There is the story that Harman printed passages of the Bible alongside texts that Comstock has declared illegal and obscene, so that the similarities are unavoidable. *Woodhull and Claflin's Weekly* is Victoria Woodhull and her sister, Tennessee: more free love, women's emancipation. Marriage is a shackle of the state is the point. Woman is not property.

The books and magazines are kindling to fuel the heated talk of the men.

Words are dynamite.

Ideas are dynamite.

And there in the pile of pamphlets is a speech by Emma Goldman and a picture of her alongside: small circular glasses shielding eyes that burn, a tangle of hair that is compelled to spring out in mad curls. There's such strength, but a softness there too. If Leon's mother had lived, imagine her strong enough to fight off the sickness, holding it off until Leon returned, and there she is: *Leon, you will make me proud; you are not like the others, you will make us all proud.*

Leon listens, takes note of what is said. The anarchists and socialists fight each other more intensely than their common enemy, and Leon does not want to get caught up in these factional wars. You keep your eye on the true enemy: the foe of my enemy is my friend. He listens.

The talk now is imperialism, the recently completed war with

Spain, McKinley's conquests of Cuba, Puerto Rico. His inevitable conquest of the islands in the Pacific, the Philippines.

"The president swore he would not lead America on imperialist ventures," one says.

"And you expected McKinley to speak the truth?"

"It is enough for the millionaires to take over America," says another. "But no, they must conquer the globe."

"Cuba was one thing," someone says, "but the Philippines are something else. Two hundred thousand Filipinos have died. Tens of thousands of Americans have met their end in the jungles. It is the sickness, the disease. All for what? New American markets? A show of force? These peasants are stage props for a play written by William McKinley and Mark Hanna."

"McKinley always protected American business with his tariffs. Now he's extending the wall across the ocean. His talk of Christian enlightenment, of saving the darkies—that is bunk. They're trying to hoodwink us again."

"Justice is in the next world, we are told, so don't seek it here and now. But there is no next world."

"Capitalism is a disease, greed a symptom."

"Nietzsche is right."

"Marx too."

"This all shall pass, come the revolution."

"But how do we hasten the inevitable? How do we trigger the revolution?"

Leon is silent. He listens.

24 · HANNA · 1899

"Tell me what you know, Mr. Wilkie."

Hanna is in his office in the Senate chamber, puffing a cigar.

"Mr. Hanna, this information should go only to the president. The Secret Service, after all, is not the Senate's business."

"And Mark Hanna is not any senator, Mr. Wilkie," Hanna says.

"Without me, you're working for President William Jennings Bryan, there's anarchy in the streets, Red Emma Goldman and her band of hooligans are running roughshod o'er us all and Will McKinley is trying penny-ante lawsuits in a musty Canton courthouse and, come to think of it, you're not working. I'm the president's right hand."

It is no longer true, Hanna knows as he says it. It has been six months at least since he has been invited to the White House, and then only for a formal dinner along with Tom Reed, Boss Platt, and a few other party leaders. Hanna suspects that Wilkie himself must know that he and McKinley are no longer so close. Should anyway, if the Secret Service is worth its keep.

"Let me hear it, Mr. Wilkie. It must be important if Mr. Cortelyou wouldn't even share it with the president. Let's have it."

Wilkie stands up. His belly slumps comfortably over his belt, and when he speaks his mouth is hidden by a bushy red mustache that hangs down over his lips. Blown-out veins line his face with smeared blotches of color, and his nose is red as a boiled beet.

"The mouth is dry, Mr. Hanna," Wilkie says. "I'd fancy to wet the whistle, don't you know."

"Irish is your pleasure, I'll bet," Hanna says. Wilkie nods and Hanna snaps his fingers and a tuxedoed Negro appears with a decanter and a tumbler on a silver tray. The Negro begins to pour, but Wilkie grabs the decanter from him.

"Leave us alone, boy," Wilkie says. "Git."

The waiter looks at Hanna, who nods, and the men are left alone.

Wilkie takes a long sip of the whiskey, finishes the glass, then pours himself another.

"This is confidential information, Mr. Hanna," Wilkie says.

"Understood," Hanna says.

"Well then." Wilkie takes another sip. "Don't ask me how Ahern and Griffin got in a coal chute, but there they are." Wilkie downs the glass, pours another. "It's a long ride from the White House and the throat gets dry, don't you know."

"Who the hell are Ahern and Griffin?" Hanna says. "And what were they doing in a coal chute?"

"Two intrepid agents of mine, Senator Hanna. The fellows secured a tip that there was to be a meeting near the mines, some rather nasty business to be plotted. So they hid in the dark, then shimmied up a chute when they heard conspirators approach. It wasn't easy to hear the men talk; they were whispering nefarious like, so the words were a bit sketchy and I can't repeat the verbatim. But the gist? Ah."

Wilkie finishes his glass and begins to pour himself another when he feels a heavy hand grab his wrist and Hanna snatches away the decanter.

"Of course." Wilkie longingly eyes the decanter as the Negro, who has appeared from somewhere, walks it away to a cabinet, beyond his reach.

"You were about to tell me the gist, Mr. Wilkie."

"Yes, of course, Senator Hanna. The gist, this is Ahern and Griffin telling me, was the president. These conspirators were plotting to kill the president."

"McKinley? William?"

Wilkie nods.

"What did the bastards say?"

"That was, as I say, the gist. The gist is all that was gotten by Ahern and Griffin. As I say, much of the words were missed. These were anarchists, my boys could tell, and they were prattling off a list of leaders like notches on a cane." Wilkie holds out a scrap of paper, but before he can read from it Hanna snatches it from his hand.

"Empress Elizabeth of Austria," Hanna mutters. "Wasn't she—?"

"Yes," Wilkie says. "Killed."

"King Umberto of Italy."

Wilkie nods again. "The anarchist Bresci shot him down."

"The Czar of Russia. Queen Victoria, or her son Edward. Dead." Hanna pauses, looks over at Wilkie who is still nodding.

"Good Lord," Hanna says. "It's right here at the bottom. The president of the United States."

"A plot, Senator Hanna. Most certainly."

"And these bastards, who were they?"

"Well," Wilkie twirls the end of his mustache between his fingers, "I told you Ahern and Griffin were top-notch, didn't I? And that's why, once they heard the message, they decided it was time to grab the conspirat—"

"The bastards."

"Yes. The conspirator bastards. Ahern and Griffin were readying themselves to get out and grab 'em when someone released a load and coal dumped onto their heads. Damned if the rocks didn't land on them and push 'em on through the chute. When they slid out, their rears landed in the bin at the bottom and they were covered in coal dust and rocks. They wiped the dust off their eyes—" Wilkie acts out the motions as he describes it—"to see where the bastards were, don't you know, where had they gone."

"And where the hell had they gone?"

"Nowhere. To be seen that is. But does that stop Ahern and Griffin? Not my men. Ahern runs this way, Griffin runs that, and they see some branches snap in the woods up ahead. Ahern—or Griffin—I forget which—sees the bastards in the trees when the other—Griffin, Ahern—screams to his partner. The two are a team. Pinkerton's got nothing on my fellows."

Hanna stands up. "And then?"

"Well, there's the rub, Senator. Now I'm not one to prattle on about the rights of the Negro, but here's the thing. As soon as Ahern and Griffin begin to run toward the woods they hear screaming. 'It's them!' 'Get 'em!' That sort of thing, the sort of thing Ahern and Griffin themselves might say when engaged in hot pursuit. Except then what they hear is, 'Grab the nigger bastards!' 'Why you runnin', boys, if there's nothin' you done?!' And then it struck Ahern and Griffin at once: the coal. Covered them, so for all intents and purposes, they were Negroes. And there wasn't a darn thing they could do about it."

Wilkie now sees that the Negro waiter is standing behind Hanna's chair; he detects a smile.

"Should he just be standing there and—" Wilkie points at the waiter.

"Finish up, Mr. Wilkie. I've got a vote on the Senate floor. What happens to your prize men?"

"Well, Senator Hanna, they're fast but my men couldn't outrun that mob. They tried to explain, but the folks what chased them weren't listening. The posse gave Ahern and Griffin a good whumping, first rate don't you know. Wrestled them, boxed 'em, kicked 'em like a football. And they may be tough but Griffin—and Ahern—they've got a soft side too. And it was that soft side that saved their hides. For it wasn't 'til they were crying, after the mob had roped them up on a tree and their tears were dripping down like Niagara Falls, that the folks could see that underneath it all they was really white."

25 · McKINLEY · 1900

McKinley is in his office, gazing out the window, shaving, George Cortelyou and his aide, Charles Dawes, are standing in front of his desk, paging through newspapers, discussing today's agenda.

"There are new tariffs, Mr. President," Dawes says. "I have the bill from Congress."

"A few amendments," Cortelyou says. "Requests from steel, coal, sugar, and the railroads. Carnegie put a special word in for a provision he demands."

McKinley nods. Pro forma matters; his men know what to do. The president is focusing on the big picture, the grand scheme, and he keeps his thoughts to himself. Business is the engine of America; government, the oil that keeps the engine running smoothly, steadily down the tracks. McKinley carries out the image, plays with it—the engine carries a man to his dream, what his hard work entitles him to: the castle. The tariff is a wall of brick and mortar that keeps foreign invaders outside of the castle. What a man does inside his castle walls is his own business.

And sometimes the castle walls must be extended. Nature is not static. Things must change to exist.

McKinley smiles, the purity of his logic amusing. He imagines himself a giant setting down pieces of a cosmic jigsaw puzzle.

The Spaniards have been fought back.

The Philippines is an annex to the castle grounds. Sanford Dole sends his regards from his thriving, now secure pineapple company. So shall it exist for all time.

"It is all but official now," Cortelyou says. "The Democrats will nominate Bryan again. No great surprise. Do they think he will fare any better this time round?"

"It will be a very different election," Dawes says. "Even Bryan knows that silver is a dead issue. He will try to beat us on Spain. 'Imperialism!' he'll cry. 'The president conquered the poor innocent Filipinos.' "

"Cry is right," Cortelyou says. " 'Defeated again!' is what he'll cry."

McKinley laughs with them, then opens the door and pokes his head into the hallway. He is listening for noise from the next room, to hear if Ida has woken up. The last days have been difficult for her. Last night especially. A state dinner for various foreign dignitaries, a tribute to Admiral Dewey to celebrate the victory over Spain. Ida tried to greet the guests. Her maids and Pina were able to help her out of bed and dress her. She looked beautiful in her flowing gown, her lace, her feathered headdress. She so wished to show it off. But when McKinley went to check on her, to escort her downstairs to greet the guests, her mouth began to twitch. Then she collapsed on the floor, contorting in a frenzy. Once she recovered, she broke into tears. "I have let you down," she said. "I have let you down so."

He hears a rumble from the next room, the tap of feet lightly touching the floor.

"I must go," he says. "Is that all?"

"Just one thing, hardly worth mentioning," Cortelyou says. "There is another of these letters from the Negroes. This calls itself a petition for redress of grievances. The usual complaints: lynchings, voter intimidation, the Klan. This one—"

McKinley wipes the shaving cream off his cheeks and neck, then hands the towel to Dawes.

"Mr. Dawes," he says, "write: The Negro has made progress. Say: We admire the Negro for the progress he has made."

26 · MORRIS · 1895

Morris Steinglitz changed his name for two reasons. First, shortly after his condom business had achieved considerable notoriety, and earned him a fortune beyond his wildest dreams, he received a knock on the door of the Fifth Avenue mansion he was having renovated. His servant pulled open the imposing oak front door and let in a man who professed to be a customer. Ordinarily, Morris would send one of his salespeople to handle the account, but it so happened that the old man stepped inside just as Morris was walking out on the way out to Delmonico's; Morris's coach, in fact, was waiting outside. And there was something about the man, crouched over a cane, jowls shaking up and down, head staring at his feet. He seemed so pathetic, he was irresistible.

"It's my daughter," the old man said. "I know it's wrong to use such devices, but I can't stop her from cavorting about, so it's this or the streets, I'm afraid."

"I understand," Morris said, placing his arm around the old man. Morris snapped to his servant, "Charles will bring you a package of my finest, the smoothest and cleanest in all New York. On the house."

"No! No!" the old man yelped, tugging on Morris's arm. "I must pay you! I simply *must*."

At which point the old man thrust a wad of bills into Morris's pocket, then tossed back his head, tore off the wool cap, gray wig, and glasses that, it only then became obvious, had been joined with a fake, bulbous nose to disguise his true appearance.

"Have you not heard, vile man, of the Comstock Act?! " the until-recently old man yelled, flourishing, with some difficulty, a set of handcuffs from his coat pocket. "The law condemns your—products" (he spat out the word) "for what they are: an obscenity! An illegality! An affront to morality and Christian virtue!"

Morris was too stunned to struggle. He just stood there in the foyer and watched. His servant was frozen too, hovering Morris's mink coat about his shoulders. The old man snapped his fingers and a young boy appeared from the street, grabbed the handcuffs from his employer, tugged Morris's arms behind his back and buckled his wrists. The boy looked up apologetically as he shepherded the arrestee toward the street.

"If you need an introduction to me," the old man shouted as they reached the sidewalk, "let me tell you who I am! I am your conscience, your better half. You may curse me when you lie in shackles in the Tombs, contemplating the moral error of your ways, but I am the force that may redeem you." The old man (and he did appear aged, even without his disguise) shoved Morris into the back of a wagon. "My name, sir, is Anthony Comstock!"

27 · FROM THE NEWSPAPERS OF WILLIAM RANDOLPH HEARST · 1900

After Kentucky governor Goebel is assassinated, the Hearst papers print a poem by Ambrose Bierce:

> *The bullet that pierced Goebel's breast*
> *Cannot be found in all the West;*
> *Good reason, it is speeding here*
> *To stretch McKinley on his bier.*

On another occasion, an editorial in the *Journal* writes of the president:

> William McKinley is the most hated creature on the American continent.

And yet another *Journal* offering on McKinley:

> If bad institutions and bad men can be got rid of only by killing, then killing must be done.

28 · McKINLEY · 1900

"Mr. President," Charles Dawes says, "if you have a moment, I wanted to pass on some news from the party."

McKinley is in his office in the Executive Mansion. There are telephone cables draped from the ceiling, tables and desks line the far wall, one cuspidor is placed near the door and another beside the president's desk, and standing ash cans are all around. McKinley is standing behind his desk, before a set of open French doors. As he blows his cigar smoke out, the spring air blows in, and there's a slight whirlwind that results, a swirl that sends rose petals circling on the lawn outside; dust and smoke and ash form an image in the room, an uncertain shape, papers rustle that send Dawes after them, wielding, like a spear, a bronze paperweight (McKinley's bust on one side, Garrett Hobart's on the other: leftover from the '96 campaign). McKinley stands there, watching ghosts of dust dance on the walkway, pussy willows and dandelions and whispered asides from cabinet secretaries and party leaders who left the office moments ago. He allows himself to imagine he has summoned it all from his lungs, the whirlwind outside.

"Wind's picking up," McKinley says.

"Must be a rain storm blowing in, Mr. President," Dawes says.

"That must be it, Mr. Dawes."

McKinley shuts the doors, turns his back to the now silent fury, and sits down.

"Mr. President," Dawes says. "Some business?" Dawes rattles a small stack of papers before him.

"The sense is," Dawes goes on, "and I have heard it expressed rather forcefully from Messrs. Reed, Platt and others, that your handling of the war has placed you on a new level with the public. Even Reed is quite complimentary, I should add. Fawning, one might say, given his norm. They all have noted that your stature has been heightened, your shadow has been lengthened along with the nation's—that's how Reed put it—and is now cast around the globe. If the phrases sound familiar, they should; many were born in this very office."

McKinley chuckles and grinds the stump of his cigar into the nearest ash stand. "My guess, Mr. Dawes, is that Tom Reed did not ask you to simply report his affections and good wishes."

"I will get to the gist," Dawes says. "There's some concern in the party. About Mr. Hanna. His visibility, that's what is being said, in relation to yourself."

"Mark has never been a difficult man to see," McKinley says, smiling. "Nor an easy man to hide."

"Mr. Reed's point, Mr. President, is that Mr. Hanna is no longer quite as necessary as he once was. There has been considerable talk about Mr. Hanna's less-than-flattering reputation and there has been some weighing of that, in relation to—"

"I don't need to be taught politics by Tom Reed," McKinley says. "He should know how I've kept Mark at a distance, best I could. It has not been a simple thing, or a pleasant one. It's distasteful, and painful, if you must know." He pauses. "I know his faults, more than anyone I do. But there's more to it. We often acquire parents after birth."

Dawes puts down his papers and looks across the desk. The president has been exhausted through the war but still, Dawes has never seen him in such a state: his head in his hands, running his fingers through his thinning hair.

"What is asked of me?" McKinley says.

Dawes wonders if he could have broached the subject with more delicacy; he should have known Mark Hanna was a sensitive issue for the president. But it had to be done. Dawes had delayed bringing the matter up for months now, but as the reelection campaign neared, Reed and Platt and Quay and their emissaries buttonholed him with more and more frequency, insisting that the Hanna matter be dealt with. *We* are the custodians of the Republican Party, was the message. *We* will be here through 1900 and well into the next century, when the president and his wife are retired back in Canton. "We cannot afford the luxury of friendship," said Thomas Reed, "or of loyalties that, if quaint, were ill-advised from the start. Get on with it, Dawes." There was a vague threat lurking behind Reed's words; Dawes could not envision the punishment to which he would be subjected for his negligence, but he attributed that to his own lack of imagination, not Reed's will. Dawes had no choice but to broach the issue.

"Mr. President," Dawes goes on, "no one is suggesting that Hanna be banished or ostracized. It's just a matter of perceptions. And degree."

McKinley has stood up and turned back around to face the glass, the latched French doors. The trees are being lashed about in the wind; leaves, petals, and twigs are lining the walkways and cluttering the lawn. There is no whirlwind out there, just a hard spring rain, and the droplets are pelting the windows, coming full steam *at* the office, not *from* it.

Ida is resting now but soon she will be awake, wailing for Katie, for little Ida, for her William. He will have a nurse deal with her at first, complete this meeting if he can, some correspondence and memoranda, a speech on foreign trade. He had not been certain, until this moment, whether he would even run again in the fall, but suddenly it strikes him that he will.

"Do what we must, Mr. Dawes," McKinley says. "Do what we must."

29 · LEON · 1900

Leon has purchased a revolver, and he takes it out in the woods with him and shoots at trees, a leaf, a stone he tosses up in the air. He will not shoot at an animal; he is even careful not to aim where the mosquitoes are swarming, or near flowers where bees gather. What he enjoys is the feeling of the gun gripped tightly in his hand, the blowback when it fires. You gird yourself to keep the arm steady. Eye on the target. You are alone, one with the weapon; your eyes are beams of light that merge at the nub on the end of the barrel; your sight is the sight of the gun. The world is silent. There is no motion. You enter a universe of stone and dust and dried hay, a place without wind or rain. The finger pulls the trigger in motion so slow it is imperceptible. You create no sound, no wind. You are the metal of the gun.

The revolutionary is a musician, the revolver is his instrument.

There is a painting somewhere of Leon Czolgosz alone with his gun, his finger on the trigger; it is hanging in the den of the workers' hall in some Bellamy utopia in the future, over a raging fire. This is the moment. Time has stopped. He can see the image in the painting, the moment in history.

History is a road, and this moment marks the beginning.

He has not seen Megan for months now, and his image of her is vague. Sometimes he does not even think of her; there is just the acid gnawing in his stomach and the grating in his head and a blurred sense of her father, the dull face, lips sloppy with rage, drooling, McKinley, the hard eyes of a foreman at a factory Leon used to work in: Emma Goldman, some pictures he saw in a newspaper, books and magazines passed about at the workers' meetings.

Then there is wind, a rustle; the bullet leaves the chamber and races through the barrel, and the oak leaf on the end of the branch just ahead is pierced through the center, precisely where Leon's sights were, where he pointed the beams of light. He wants to race after the bullet, capture it like a butterfly as it flies. He should make a necklace of his bullets and wear it like a Filipino peasant lying dead in a trench outside his village, a peaceful place that is no more, thanks to President William McKinley.

He should crouch hidden like some backstreet urchin and lie in wait.

He should rise up, one day, and Megan, Waldek, his stepmother, everyone would be silenced and in awe.

Leon bought the gun a day after he read of the anarchist, Gaetano Bresci, leaving his home in Paterson, New Jersey, to return to his native Italy where he tracked down the King, Umberto I, and in broad daylight was able to get close enough so that with a squeeze of the trigger finger the silence of the world was broken, the stillness of the air was disturbed by a racing bullet. There is a painting of the moment captured in Leon's head, hanging in the raging fire that is his skull, in a utopian den in the future world, after the revolution. The king is dead.

There is talk in the papers now of an anarchist ring in Paterson, of plans for attacks on one leader after another, like dominoes the rulers will fall, a global revolution. The world's shackles will be smashed.

Freedom shall lap the shores of the world like a tidal wave reaching the desert. All begins with a bullet.

The music of the moment is ruined by the dinner bell, the screech of his stepmother calling his father and brothers in to eat. Waldek calls for Leon to join them, but he ignores him.

There is another Leon who will live one day in a better world, who will raise a glass by the fire in a utopian workers' hall, gaze up at the painting of the moment the world was remade. The painting will be entitled, *The Last Voyage of a Bullet*.

PART FOUR

THE ROAD TO BUFFALO

I · HANNA · 1900

Mark Hanna is sitting behind his desk in his office. At this moment he is writing a letter, though he is not certain to whom he will send it. He is still in the habit of corresponding with McKinley, though that is something he has tried to wean himself away from during the past four years—particularly since the president's secretary, George Cortelyou, had insinuated, then made clear, that the relationship between Senator Hanna and President McKinley could not have the same . . . closeness . . . as that between Campaign Manager Hanna and Nominee/Candidate/Governor McKinley in years past. Some distance was now in order.

That was what was said. The meaning was something else again. The meaning was: we're damned tired of Hearst's cartoons showing McKinley suckling at Marcus Hanna's trust-infused, money-flowing teats. Of William McKinley mocked as a marionette pulled hither and yon by the master puppeteer, Marcus Hanna. The meaning was: Hanna, you're embarrassing us. Thank you for giving us the presidency, much appreciated and all, and yes we were the closest of buddies, good times and good counsel and good money . . . *oh, damn it if the money wasn't nectar itself—stuff of the gods, so forth*—and in such overflowing buckets . . . thanks for picking young William McKinley of Niles from your stable of prize Ohio Republican studs to ride to the White House . . . but to hell with you now. We're done. We'll see you again in 1900, when the next election rolls round.

How many cigars had they smoked together over the years?

There are habits you can break in this life. A good friendship ain't one of them.

Suddenly Hanna clutches his throat and realizes he cannot breathe. His chest is clenched up, as if someone had reached beneath his skin and grabbed his heart tight in a fist. He reaches for the papers on his desk, the half-written letter to no one, but they provide no support. He collapses. His wife hears the thud and rushes in. She finds him on the floor.

At the theater that night he tells the men sharing his box—a coal mine owner, a newspaper owner: his old businesses—that he has had a heart attack that afternoon, or so his doctor tells him. He has gone to the theater, he says, because he has reached that point in life when his heart needs nothing so much as entertaining diversions.

2 · HANNA · June 1900

Two months later Hanna is back in Washington. He is in the Capitol when an aide rushes into his office and tells him, "It is Pettigrew, Senator Hanna. Senator Pettigrew has taken the floor and raised your name."

"Again?" Hanna says. "You may as well tell me that Senator Pettigrew is taking a shit. Cursing Mark Hanna is how the senator releases bile."

The aide—Hanna cannot recall his name—does not laugh with him. "No, Senator Hanna, this is more serious than the usual. I suggest you come now and take the floor. You can do so out of order in such circumstances. It's called a matter of personal privilege."

"I have better things to do than listen to Petty Ass Pettigrew. His voice grates in my ears. Bad for my heart. Tell me what it is this time and tell me straight."

The aide pauses. The two are now walking down the corridor toward the Senate Chamber. "Senator, Pettigrew says there is a manufacturer of warships who gave you a four hundred thousand dollar contribution to the party in '92. He says the gift was on condition that the administration would send a naval contract his way. What the Senator's accusing you of is, not putting too fine a point on it, Senator, is graft."

Hanna stops walking. The two of them have reached the door to the Senate Chamber and Hanna looks at his companion. His face turns red, but the rage quickly converts into something else: iron, steel, something hard and strong.

"It ain't the first time," says Mark Hanna. "Won't be the last."

3 · HANNA · Late June 1900

Hanna is in Philadelphia for the national party convention. For months he has waited for a telegram, a hand-delivered message, an intimation dropped at a dinner party that McKinley wished him to head the reelection effort in the fall. Perhaps Pettigrew's scurrilous charges bollixed up the plans, put things behind schedule. Hanna could imagine the machinations laid by suitors for his throne. Now in Philadelphia, he waits again. Once the formality of renomination is done, the campaign will be front and center. Then, surely, the president and his fellows will come to Marcus Alonzo Hanna on bended knee.

Nothing.

Philadelphia is not St. Louis in '96; it is not Hanna's convention. Choose your analogy: he may have hired the orchestra, he may have trained them and rehearsed them each night, but someone has taken his baton. The wife has remarried and his children no longer recognize him. His dog's left him.

The sole contested issue of the convention is the vice presidency: who shall replace poor Garrett Hobart, who left this blessed party—and this life—in the midst of the first term. Hanna hears the reports that the New York bosses are maneuvering to put on the ticket that dandy radical, that insane poseur, that grandstanding scourge, Teddy Roosevelt. Boss Platt would like nothing better than to kick young Teddy and his wild business-bashing reform ideas upstairs and out of New York for good, to some place where he can't hurt the trusts, the party machines, Tammany Hall and Boss Platt and . . . anyone. The vice presidency of this godawful beautiful nation is as safe a place as any.

For months Roosevelt has vowed that he would never take the vice presidency, but there's always an impish wink behind his thick round eyeglasses. Some say he has vowed this even as he has lobbied for the nomination.

But the pressure has mounted. The rationales for the pick have become more compelling. Teddy brings young blood, a man to rival Bryan on the campaign trail. (The Democrats have not yet convened, but who else could they choose but their beloved boy orator?) Teddy is no stooge of the trusts, no puppet of the big money men, and so can answer Hearst and the other liberal critics (government of corporation, by corporation, so help me . . .).

He is a man who is no Mark Hanna.

Who else *could* McKinley pick to share the ticket?

Hanna has heard all this, time and again. And still he cannot believe that the Republican Party, *his* Republican Party, will nominate such a man.

Hanna calls, but McKinley will not speak to him. The president is busy, he is working on his acceptance speech, before him are matters of state, the world does not rest for political events, there are staffing matters . . . yes, William McKinley is too busy for a minute with Mark Hanna.

Hanna cannot actually believe it until it happens.

He is standing on the convention floor when the vote is cast that puts Roosevelt over the top, onto the ticket. Hanna grabs the arm closest to him and pulls the man attached to it toward him.

"Can you believe it?!" Hanna says. "There's just one life between that madman and the presidency!"

4 · HANNA · Fall 1900

Hanna enlists himself as a speaker on the stump. He decides he will go to South Dakota to speak, where it so happens that Senator Pettigrew is up for reelection. Before he leaves, a messenger from the White House comes to his hotel room in Washington.

Hanna's bags are packed and he has the workings of one hell of a speech in his vest pocket, giving Petty Ass Pettigrew something he won't forget. The campaign is rolling along, stronger than '96, better than ever, and damn it if the Democrats won't be crushed godawful. Mark Hanna's work. And here it comes, finally: thanks, from your old dear friend the president.

"Senator Hanna," the messenger—Cortelyou, Dawes, somebody— says, "there is a sense in the administration that perhaps going on the road is not wise for you. Your skills may be better served in Washington. And then there's your medical condition; travel won't do you any good. And perhaps South Dakota, in particular, might dredge up some old dirt. Open some not-so-old wounds, as it were. It is a concern, Senator Hanna."

Hanna pauses for an instant before he speaks: a boxer loading up before delivering a roundhouse right.

"Tell the president," Mark Hanna says, "God hates a coward."

He goes to South Dakota. He likes the stump, in doses anyways. Relishes doing battle in the belly of the beast. He knows Mark Hanna irritates the hell out of the Dems, especially where they live. Which is why he goes from Pettigrew's stomping grounds to Nebraska, home of Bryan, the boy orator.

Hanna arrives in Nebraska soon after Bryan declares that Hanna has formed a vast fund for the purpose of bribing election judges, buying votes, and intimidating working men. The telegraph poles are lined with posters:

POPULIST FARMERS, BEWARE!!!
Chain Your Children To Yourselves
Or
Put Them Under The Bed.
MARK HANNA IS IN TOWN

The joke that only Hanna knows is that he has had his own advance men post the warnings.

5 · HANNA · Late November 1900

When the campaign is over, and McKinley has defeated Bryan handily, by greater margins than he did four years earlier, Hanna returns to John Rockefeller and Standard Oil, $50,000, a fifth of their total contribution, with a note. "You gave more than your fair share," writes Mark Hanna.

6 · EMMA · 1900

During the past year Emma was in Europe; she felt death close by. Nietzsche died, his body having carried on for more than a decade after his mind left him. She wonders what became of his spirit, the power of his will. It seems illogical that it would cease with the last beating of his heart.

She thinks of Alex alone in his cell. She has raised money for him from supporters, and her own speeches and writings. She has not heard from Alex but that could be the prison guards. He must have received the money she sent.

She thinks of Edward Brady, that rugged face, his chest, their passionate nights together.

Outside a boy is tearing down posters from the wall of a building before a man wallpapers advertisements on top of them. November has come and gone, and so, too, the political season.

She sees now that the boy is carefully tearing off the billboard to preserve it. There is a picture of William Jennings Bryan and the boy is crying as he looks at it, watching his hero's picture being covered by the ad.

Emma has never heard Bryan speak, but she has heard that his voice is powerful yet melodious, wise yet funny, with a people's touch.

The boy runs off with his keepsake and the man finishes covering the space with a new advertisement and now Emma can see it unfurled.

The circus is in town.

7 · BERKMAN · 1900

Alex stands still in his cell, trying to listen to a guard talking to a prisoner at the end of the hall. Alex is fairly certain that neither of them knows that his friend and former cellmate, Tony, has rented the house across the street from the main gate of the prison and has begun excavating the cellar, that Tony is digging a tunnel beneath their very feet. That Alex lured an old-time prisoner, a man whose several terms had provided him intimate knowledge of Western Penitentiary, into revealing the layout of piping under the prison, and the best escape route. That before Tony was released he and Alex had decided on their escape plans. Alex is fairly certain that the plans have remained secret. But still, he is listening carefully.

The money Emma sends him pays for the rent of the house across the street and to hire workmen. The tunnel will begin with a hole in the cellar of the house that eventually will connect up with the prison's pipes, then travel a course to a secluded spot in the yard, behind a tree, little watched by guards. Alex and Tony have agreed to go over details, in letters that use a code: Tony will update Alex on progress, they will decide on a day for the escape.

With each letter from Tony, Alex's vision of the tunnel becomes more real. The pencil sketch in his mind becomes a painting that becomes a photograph. When he sleeps at night he enters a dream world in which the tunnel is a bustling city. When he emerges, Emma is greeting him at Justus's saloon, the eight years since he was jailed for his shooting of Frick never happened.

Then there are gaps in time when Tony's letters do not come and Alex senses disaster, dreads what the news will be when the letters return. Tony has been arrested, Alex imagines. He is a turncoat, a double agent in league with the warden, with the Parole Board, with henchmen of Henry Clay Frick bent on revenge. Alex has nightmares of being taken in the night, secreted across the ocean to Carnegie's Scottish castle where he is subjected to all manner of torture. His skin is coated with tar and feathers. An American flag is rammed into his asshole and Frick forces him to sing the national anthem.

A letter from Tony arrives. The language of the code is second nature to Alex now; he deciphers it almost instantaneously. *There is a delay with the plans*, Tony writes. The tunnel somehow hooked up with the wrong prison pipes and became filled with noxious fumes. The workmen collapsed underground while they were digging. When they did not emerge as scheduled, others came down to rescue them, then dragged them up to safety.

Alex writes back that he cannot tolerate such delays, it is unbearable. Tony must appreciate what the silences are like. Even if it is bad news, Tony must keep the letters coming.

But then there is another gap, more silence. The nightmares return. Perhaps the story about the fumes in the tunnel was just a story. Tony *is* a double agent. After all, Alex did not know him well in prison. He is relying on references and faith. His sense of the man cannot be separated from the man Alex wishes him to be.

Then the next letter arrives, Tony writes that the money Emma has raised has been spent. He needs more, much more, to continue the job. It is not Tony, it is the diggers and the landlord who need it. The delay from the fumes in the pipes means more time, and time is money.

How could more money be needed!? Alex writes back that night. Already he has raised more than could be expected, more than Tony had thought was needed. The diggers could be trusted, Tony had said; only workers who were sympathetic to the cause would be hired. But Tony's letter suggests the workers are blackmailing them, demanding money for silence. *Can these men be trusted? Reply immediately.*

Alex does not write what he thinks: can Tony be trusted?

Tony does not write back that week, or the next or the next. Alex writes Emma to ask her to raise more money. Tell their supporters that funds are needed for his legal defense team, appeals, attempts at parole.

A friend writes back that Emma is in Europe but he will try to contact her.

When Tony next writes he does not mention the need for money, which only worries Alex the more. Maybe more money was not truly necessary, and Tony is simply extorting all that he can get. Tony writes that he has decided it is best to alter the plans. The tunnel will now emerge nearer to the center of the prison yard, not in the remote location Alex had decided earlier. This is for the best, Tony assures him, though given the openness of the spot, Alex will only have a limited time to enter the tunnel when it is completed. They will have to discuss that later, nearer to the completion date. *Be patient, Alex. Things are progressing.*

The change in plans is unacceptable! Alex writes back. It is madness to think that he could enter a tunnel in the middle of the yard! Besides, as Alex told Tony when they first drew up the plans, there is construction going on there; they are extending the prison, and the center of the yard is crowded with workers and supplies. By the time the tunnel is ready there may be a floor constructed over the hole! Tony must stick to the original plans! They had a deal, and Alex stuck to his end of it. *Reply immediately.*

Alex sends his letter two hours after he receives Tony's. The next morning, when he is allowed in the yard for exercise, guards study him; they are always studying him, suspecting him, so he acts as if he has lost a screw from his eyeglasses. Crawling on his knees on the dirt he finds the location Tony has decided on for the entrance hole of the tunnel. It is already piled over with bricks and stones, huge immovable stacks that cover the area.

The next letter Alex receives from Tony is the last. Some children were playing in the house and crawled into the cellar. They found the tunnel. One of the children told his father, who happened to be a guard at the prison. The diggers and Tony were able to escape in time and leave town, but the house has been seized by police. The tunnel is being filled up. The plan is over.

For two days Alex is not given food or drink. Then he is called in by the warden.

"Have a seat in my office," the warden says. "Care to smoke? Would you like a glass of milk? I respect you, Berkman," he says. "You Jews are a smart, crafty bunch. Much smarter than your average felon." The warden lights a cigarette and hands it to Alex who draws the smoke in so he can taste the tobacco. "Too smart not to understand what a friend in high places can do for you. Your next parole hearing I could make things happen for you. All we need to know is who was behind this tunnel. It was Goldman wasn't it? Red Emma was behind this."

The milk is so thick and rich Alex feels he could eat it with a spoon. The white gel coats the aching emptiness of his insides; it lubricates his head, his joints, his stomach. Only one small sip and he feels rejuvenated, better than he has felt in eight years.

"You stinking Jew bastard!" the warden says, and snatches the glass from Alex, then knocks the cigarette out from his other hand. "We know it was your tunnel! Admit it! Admit it!"

Alex says nothing. The warden presses a button on his desk and guards storm into the office and grab Alex by the arms. They drag him down the long hallway, then kick him down the stairs. Alex knows the route; he is certain where he is being carried.

He can still call up images in his mind, of the sun shining through the completed tunnel, poking his head out in Justus Schwab's saloon.

There is Emma—*drinks all around! Steak for the returning hero!* And there is Tolstoy telling stories in vivid detail, Bakunin and Kropotkin and Nietzsche holding court, their books come alive. *Cold, fresh milk all around! Cigarettes!* Dick, the beautiful bird, has returned and is resting on Alex's shoulder, pecking food from his hand and chirping a song. There are beautiful girls. *Now comes the revolution!*

Alex's eyes are closed but he is crying. The images get smaller and smaller until, as the guards toss him into the solitary cell, they vanish entirely, and again he is alone.

8 · LEON · February 1901

He finds a map in a bookstore and buys it. In his room he spreads it out. There it is, America; up close, he takes it all in. His stepmother has a box with pins he takes from the hall closet.

He plots points, working backward.

Cleveland.

Detroit.

The ocean.

There must be an arc if he could see it.

Chicago.

California.

Buffalo.

New York.

He plots points, working forward.

He plots points, trying to find an arc.

There are magazines Frank brings him when he is finished reading them, newspapers and pamphlets. There are stories of factories and workingmen and millionaires he does not need to read. There is a picture of Emma Goldman.

There is a speech by Emma Goldman.

There are the Haymarket martyrs.

Alexander Berkman. A golden glow emanates out of his prison cell, streaming through the bars.

The pin in Alpena, Michigan, is a tombstone: bless you, mother. To a better world than this.

The pin in Chicago is a tombstone. Bless you, August Spies. A better world.

The picture of Emma; there is a date below it, a place. With a pen he draws cross-hatching for railroads, double lines for roads, blue for barge canals. America is a tapestry he is wearing. He cuts pictures from the magazines and glues them to the sky. He cuts stories out and glues them to the ocean.

America is a corridor he has spent his life walking down, guards holding either arm as they escort him.

9 · MORRIS · 1896

At his trial, Morris Steinglitz was advised by his attorney that legal precedent was clear. Products relating to sexual matters were, without doubt, obscenities under the Comstock Act; there was little hope of a defense.

Once the judge delivered his sentence, Morris is led away in leg irons. Guards walk him down a series of stairs and tunnels and a walkway that links buildings, then back down farther until he smells the moistness of the brick and the dirt of a deep basement, and then the aroma is overtaken by urine and excrement. The guards apologize. One of them says he is a customer, that Morris's wares have saved his marriage. Morris isn't certain what that means but thanks him anyway. Morris is about to ask the guard how far his sense of gratitude would take him when he finds himself locked away in a cell. The guard's heavy boots echo down the corridor, then up the metal stairs.

Soon Morris falls asleep. When he awakes, there is a face staring at him through the bars: fatty and round like a baby's, but with a mustache that curls out past his nose and meets up with a thicket of muttonchop sideburns. Morris recognizes the man from the trial: the government's star witness against him, the old man without the disguise.

"Mr. Steinglitz," says Anthony Comstock, "you may wonder why I have chosen to spend additional time from my rather demanding schedule to visit one such as yourself."

Morris says nothing. He isn't even certain if he is awake.

"Well," Comstock says, "I will tell you. I am in the soul-saving business. My foe is not you, good sir, just as my foe is not Moses Harman or Victoria Woodhull or Emma Goldman or name your propagator of vice. No, my adversary is the devil. And if you know me, you know one thing: I will not shy away from a battle. Let me tell you a story, sir. A true tale from some years back. In the course of my work, engaging in espionage on occasion as I do, I became familiar with a young family, the sort with whom I have had the ill fortune to become all too familiar. I first met the daughter, a beautiful young girl who had been sent to the streets to earn money for the family weal. Thirteen years old, though the way she was dressed and her face painted, one could hardly imagine it. When she refused to take the streets at night to consort with strange men, her father beat her; I would see the bruises on her face, much as she would try to powder them up. Any money she received would be seized by her father, and he would spend every dime on pornography and drink. The man was addicted to evil, the sins were imbued in him. One evening the girl was sent out to the dark streets and she never returned. I searched for her but was never able to find her. To this day I know not what happened to her, whether one of her clients became sickened with his deeds and did away with her, a reflex of conscience; or perhaps she ran away, though I tend to doubt that. A happy ending I find inconceivable, given what I've seen, Mr. Steinglitz, the cross of experience it's been my lot to bear.

"A few weeks later I woke early, Mr. Steinglitz. I knew where I could find what was left of the family. Without the girl's income, the father had nothing. The wife had left him after their daughter met her end. All the man had left was a son, twelve years old. While the old fiend tried to find a debauched trade for the youngster who remained, the two slept on the streets, close to a newsstand, as if the elder man would find nourishment in the sap from that decadent tree. When I happened by, I found the man covered with newspapers, as his boy stood by. The boy still had hope, there was a chance there for some good in his life. And I do not say that his father was born evil, but he had become so and there was no turning back. And so I saved that boy. I took him away and gave him Christ's love and the hope that only the Gospel, truly told and understood, can bring. I left the father alone on the streets, and I tell you I continue to do battle with that which destroyed him and his family, what made him destroy his family. The devil has many henchmen, many soldiers in his war. Is not America today a devil's playground? Is it not Sodom and Gomorrah and Babel all in one? Was I not right to save that boy? Am I not right, sir? In your cell of redemption, Mr. Morris Steinglitz, can you not see the truth?"

While Morris is in prison, Amelia is visited by a number of other victims of Anthony Comstock. Some had also sold contraceptives of one sort or another, others had published magazines or newspapers that the mighty Comstock had deemed off-color.

"You must be strong," they tell Amelia. "Carry on. You cannot let this ogre win by persistence and intimidation. But for God's sake," they say. "Change your name."

And so, when Morris was released from imprisonment, Amelia became Lily. And they both became Vandeveers.

10 · LEON · April 1901

"The money I gave you for the farm."

Leon corners his father in the kitchen. His stepmother is out in the fields, milking the cows, and so the two of them will be alone.

"What money?" His father is sitting at the table staring at the smoke drifting up from the woodstove, the steam from the simmering soup pot, the empty space between them. He is a quiet man who prefers silence.

Their eyes avoid each other. "When you bought the farm how many years ago, I gave you my earnings for the payment. All I had saved."

"For details you will have to ask your mother—"

"She is not my mother. It was four hundred dollars. I remember."

"Was it so much?"

"It was."

"And so, this is our farm. We all live here, we share—"

"I never wanted this. I cannot live with her. This is not my home."

"You should work more, Leon. She is right about that."

"This is not about that, Father. It is my money. I want all of it back."

"That will be difficult, Leon. You must know, the money is in the land, in the animals—"

"There is money."

"But why, Leon? My boy, you have no family. What you need for a home? Why all a sudden you want this money?"

Leon looks up at his father. Finally their eyes meet, above the steam of the soup pot, the fire of the stove. The old man's thick muscled body is slumped, worn like an old rusted plow out back, its blades dull, wheels warped and busted. A good worker on its last legs. Even his eyes are tired and glassy.

There is a lifetime Leon has spent under the willow tree out back and now there is not much time left; he must live it all fast, what remains.

"I need it, Father. This is America you brought us to. I must have the money."

II · LEON · May 6, 1901

"Men under the present state of society are mere products of circumstances," Emma Goldman says. She is looking down at Leon when she says this; that's the way he sees it, no others in the crowded room, the two of them alone.

"Anarchism aims at a new and complete freedom," she is singing. It's the warble of a bird; wisps of music fill the air all around him.

"It strives to bring about the freedom that is not only the freedom from within but a freedom from without.

"It will prevent any man from having a desire to interfere in any way with the liberty of his neighbor."

Emma pauses, looks up to recognize the others in the hall, but still Leon senses there are secrets passed between them no one else can hear.

The picture he had seen of her in a magazine at the workers' hall, her eyes, they looked only at him. Red Emma they called her. He had to see her.

"Vanderbilt says I am a free man within myself, but the others be damned. This is not a freedom we are striving for." Emma allows the audience to laugh, then continues.

"We merely desire complete individual liberty, and this can never be obtained as long as there is an existing government. We do not favor the socialistic idea of converting men and women into mere producing machines under the eye of a paternal government. We go to the opposite extreme and demand the fullest and most complete liberty for each and every person to work out his own salvation upon any line that he pleases. The degrading notion of men and women as machines is far from our ideals of life."

Leon is not really listening. He is letting the words form pictures in his head, compacted with meaning like a dream.

"Anarchism has nothing to do with future government or economic arrangements," Emma says. "We do not favor any particular settlement in this line, but merely ask to do away with the present evils."

At this the crowd rises in heated applause and hoots. The police up near the stage point to a few of the loudest, and other uniformed men quickly step toward them. The sense is that suddenly things have come unhinged, the secret is out. "This will all be over soon," Emma says with a silent smile that Leon understands.

"The future will provide these arrangements," she says over the commotion. "After our work has been done."

Leon watches Emma, mesmerized. Her eyes cast beams of light through her small round glasses, her face serious, but not stern.

What can I do? What must I do?

"The pain inflicted by society's cruelty is all around us," she goes on. "Most of us come to accept it; we forget that it is there, and that it does not have to be. But there are some men and women who always feel the pain of others. The cries of the poor and mistreated echo in their skulls." *It is me.* "They become the will of the masses, their body becomes our greater selves, our desires." *Me, Leon.* "They are not individuals, these sensitive souls, they are truly social beings." *You, Leon.* "It is among these sensitive souls that come the acts that change the nature of things, *attendats* or propaganda by deed. So revolutions are ignited. So history is made."

Leon hears cheering, hooting all around him; it wakes him up. Sees the painting where history took a turn, and Megan, somewhere, sees it too, in a magazine, a newspaper. It is as if he is emerging from a trance.

A handful of policemen have approached the stage, slapping nightsticks in their open palms. The crowd turns toward the doors in the back of the room, a wave cresting toward the exits, but Leon stands firm. Above him Emma hovers, still standing on the stage. Her speech is over. She is shaking hands. Leon walks against the wave, toward her.

When he finally gets to the stage, he does not know what to say. Emma has just autographed a pamphlet. Up close she is a broad woman with a soft, round face. Her Jewishness brings him back to a day when he ran through the streets of the Jewish ghetto, looking for a woman. In his pocket he clenches the nipple from the baby bottle he held that day. Emma could be Leon's mother, or his lover.

She steps down from the stage; a man helps her down, her escort apparently, the man who introduced her to the crowd before she spoke.

"I heard you speak," Leon says. Emma turns and looks at him. "I had never heard anything like that before."

Her escort tries to guide her down the aisle, toward the door, but Emma stops.

"I could see it all," Leon says. "I had seen it all before and I know it is real. It will be real."

"We must go, Emma," her escort says. "Your train will be leaving."

Emma's face breaks out in a wide smile as the sea of people flows in between them, pushing her away. Her back is turned; only a few loose strands of wiry hair are visible waving above the crowd. Boots clatter and horses; voices shout. It is pure noise, pure sound, but somewhere Leon can hear Emma Goldman say, "What an extraordinary young man."

12 · LEON · Later that Day

Emma walks past him on her way out of the building. Leon catches up to her, but another man shoves him aside and runs past, then taps Emma on the back.

"My dear Emil," Emma says as she embraces the small, mousy man, his back hunched, lips pursed. His small hands clasp to his chest a magazine Leon has seen before: *Free Society*. They kiss each other's cheeks.

Leon follows a few steps behind them, listening.

"My dear, you were inspired tonight," Emil gushes.

"You are kind," Emma says. "But I was tired. Some nights the music will not flow."

They cross the street and Leon follows. Then a carriage races past and he loses them for a moment. When he can see them again, Emma is hopping into a carriage that Emil has flagged down.

"Keep up the fight," she says, smiling. And as Leon runs to catch up, she is gone.

13 · LEON · May 7, 1901

Leon follows Emil through the streets, notes down the address of the house he enters. The next day Leon comes back and rings a bell.

The door opens a crack.

"What is it?" Emil's nose snivels as he speaks, as if he were allergic to words.

"Do you print *Free Society* here?" Leon says.

Emil's eyes dart about Leon, around him, behind him out on the street. "Who are you?"

"A friend. An admirer of Emma Goldman. I saw her last night. But you are right to check, you cannot be too careful. The capitalists have their spies everywhere."

"What did you say your name was?"

"I didn't," Leon says. "It is Nieman. Fred Nieman."

14 · LEON · May 8, 1901

The next day Leon returns and Emil invites him inside. They walk upstairs to a crowded room on the top floor, hot and stifling with smoke from the cigarettes. Men are banging fists and glass mugs on the roughly hewn tables. Leon stands in the back and listens.

These are not socialists like Frank; these are anarchists. In words they turn history on its axis: implement a utopia, then dismantle it, form a totally free state. Leon hears Emma's words recited: "We do not intend to replace tyranny by the owners with tyranny by the workers. It is all tyranny."

"It is all theory," Leon says finally.

The others look at him.

"What we need is action."

After the meeting Emil gives Leon books to read. There are anarchist texts, issues of *Free Society*, pamphlets with articles by Emma, Kropotkin, Proudhon, and Bakunin, a book about Haymarket called *Chicago Martyrs*.

"Bring them to our meeting next week," Emil says. "We will see what you have learned."

15 · LEON · May 28, 1901

It is several weeks later when Leon finally returns. He is dressed in a suit and tie. He seems different than before, not taking things seriously.

"Why did you miss the meeting?" Emil says, opening the door. "Where have you been?"

"I was working."

"Where?"

"In a cheese factory." Leon laughs. "I was making cheese."

"The books," Emil says. "What did you think of Proudhon? You understand the anarchist/socialist distinction? Tell me."

"I understand it," Leon says, and he laughs again. He has walked past Emil into the room and is busy poking around in the bookshelves, paging through the pamphlets on the table.

"You didn't read any of them."

"I read it. It is all theory."

"I don't understand you, Nieman. You have no interest in who we are."

"Oh, but I do. I know about Bresci. The Paterson cabal, the plot to take out the leaders, one by one. I know there are secret societies."

"You don't know what you're talking about. Secret societies? That's the talk of the capitalist press."

"You don't have to say anything," Leon says. He turns to face Emil and for a moment his eyes lose their distant look, his mouth its smirk. "But know this," he says. "I am ready."

16 · LEON · June 4, 1901

Leon returns the next week. This time he is dressed in a black suit, white shirt, black string tie.

"Are you coming from church?" Emil says. "Perhaps that is where you have been all these days."

"If I was there it would not have been to worship," Leon says. "The priests do not deserve to live."

Emil eyes Leon closely. There's a way his emotions shift all of the sudden; violent weather you can never know.

"When my mother was killed, the priest may as well have plunged in the knife himself."

Emil tries to size him up again. Leon's eyes are staring out at something, a vision lost somewhere in space.

"My brother Waldek and I got a Polish Bible in the mail and it was then we discovered it was all lies what the priest was telling us. Jesus was for the workingman, not the bosses like they have you believe."

Emil smiles. "You have a directness to you, Nieman."

"And so I will get to the point," Leon says. "I am here for one reason. The books are meaningless. I must meet her. You must give me letters of introduction. I must meet Emma Goldman."

17 · LEON · June 23, 1901

And then everything turns upside down again. Yesterday he received news from Emily. Waldek gave him the letter when he came back to the farm. Megan was in West Virginia. She told him the town.

His father gives him back some of his money, Waldek gives him some money, Leon had saved some from work, the wire factory, odd jobs. This is what you get from hard work, living at home, when you don't spend but save.

He takes a train, he walks, he hitches rides on carriages, he walks more. At night he sleeps by the roadside or finds a place in the woods. There is silence in the darkness and animals all around.

I always said I would take you away, he imagines himself saying to Megan, *to bring you to a better world. Now I am here. Wells imagined a Time Machine but this will be real; there is no place we cannot travel together. This I know: I will never set foot in a factory again.*

Her father, his father: there are traps he will not fall into. He will tell her about the words of Emma Goldman, the visions she stirred up in his head. They shall have freedom, on the road and in love, Megan and Leon, but it will be a romance of liberty; they will lead the world around a corner of history. *Megan, that world I spoke to you about? That utopia? I have seen it. Let us go there.*

He jumps off the back of a wagon when the driver tells him this is Kanawha, West Virginia. The streets are empty. On the far end of town is a smokestack, and you can look straight down the roads and see the coal mines. It is too far to see the furnace, but Leon can see it, a raging, fiery face that snarls and cackles at him from the edge of town. That is where the men are, that is where the boys are. The mine is a monster that sucks in the townspeople, that devours them in the day, then spits them out at night, returns them home, disembodied.

When he sees Megan she is wringing out sheets and hanging them on a line, clothes for ten families. A job, a living. Her blouse is loose fitting but still he can see there is weight she has taken on, a heft to her hips, and her breasts are fuller, too. But her face still has that soft glow.

He hears the child before he sees it, the high-pitched wail. It has been sleeping but now something has woken it up. A shock of black hair, a scrawny chest that looks concave and hollow; he thinks he hears Megan call it Leon. Leon steps onto a front porch of a house, ducks behind a pillar.

"Leon. Leon, my love." He is across the street, behind a pillar; her back was turned away and the wind blowing out. But he heard her call the baby Leon.

Everything closes in on him all of the sudden, thick metal doors shutting all around him and somebody turns a key. *You can't run in chains.* His breath catches in his chest and his throat clenches tight.

He cannot bring himself to cross the street to speak to Megan just now, to meet his son. He remains behind the pillar, then walks away, outside of town, back to the woods.

18 · LEON · June 24, 1901

The next morning, when he walks to Megan, at first she runs from him.

"How could you have taken so long? You must have known about the boy. I had thought you were different, Leon."

He does not say anything. She is so much larger than she was; it is even clearer now when he is up close. No longer the thin wisp of a girl. Stretched across her hips is a dress that is just a bolt of burlap sewed together with holes above to poke her arms through. The room she lives in is little more than a closet. A door opens into a dark window-less alcove with a wood box for a crib in front and straw and blankets on the floor for a bed, and in the corner a pipe runs from the ceiling to a grimy black box that passes for a woodstove. You can hear babies crying and men and women screaming at each other next door, bodies thrown into walls—the rooms down the hallway are that close. He wants to turn around and leave, but the baby screams and the time is not right.

The child is sullen and frightened. He is a boy; Leon cannot imagine it is his. There was no baby, just this little boy emerged out into his life, listening and intent. Megan spoons porridge into his mouth, then he slips into sleep in a corner.

Megan is doing what she can to get by, she says, sewing patches on the miners' pants and shirts, laundering clothes, looking after some older children while their mothers feed cattle and pigs and chickens and butcher them.

"My father, he sent me away," Megan says. "There was nothing I could do. But I thought you would surely find me, Leon. I waited. I thought you would come."

They look at each other from across the small room, the boy's small crib behind her. He thinks to say *I am here* but he doesn't.

"What will you do, Leon? There is work in the mines. There's a nail factory in town."

"I have money," Leon says. "My father will send more. I will send him an address, a box at the post office."

"But you must work."

"Does the boy look like me?" he says.

"He *is* you, Leon," she says. "God help him."

19 · LEON · June 25–30, 1901

The next days Leon spends wandering around the town. He goes to the mines first. He watches the men stagger out of the tunnel after their shift, the lanterns on their helmets forming a third eye, the lights a parade. Slowly they emerge out, the earth vomiting a new race.

Every face is his father's, every slumping, broken body.

When he returns Megan lights into him about did he find work and did more money come from his father.

"It will come," he says.

"Did you take a job?"

"I saw the mines."

"There was work there."

"Is the baby awake? I want to see him."

Megan stomps outside, leaving Leon alone in front of little Leon's crib.

The boy's huge eyes look up at him. He has heard everything and gives Leon a knowing stare.

A healthy boy. His mother takes good care of him.

20 · LEON · Early July 1901

Leon takes a job at the nail mill. There are tongs you hold to grab the vat of molten metal, but even then the steam singes your face and arms. When you pour the liquid, you turn your face away from the heat again and there's a pool of cold water that sizzles and smokes, and then there is both the heat and the cold; you shiver and you sweat and the cold is when you feel the burnt skin.

The foreman keeps everyone in line, everyone working smoothly, no delays, no breaks. The nails are for the houses, to hang pictures on the wall, to make sofas, chairs, bookcases. "Keep it moving, keep it moving. We're in back order. The economy's booming, business is booming, tomorrow's output is already sold. Keep it moving."

A man's tongs snap from the cold and the molten metal drops to the floor, splashes into his eye; he slips and lands in a pool that glows red, and Leon can smell the skin burn and his clothes, too.

"Business is booming," the foreman says. "We can't sell things fast enough. It's the houses, new towns. Keep it moving. Keep it moving."

21 · LEON · The Next Day

The next day Leon goes to a store one of the workers at the factory tells him about where he buys a copy of *Free Society*. He reads it as he walks back from work. There is news of lockouts, rallies. And there, on the third page, a drawing of her. She is speaking. In just a few days, she is speaking in Chicago.

In bed that night Leon waits for Megan to fall asleep. Then he slips out of bed, careful not to wake her. He has kept his clothes on and now he puts on his shoes.

The child's crib is beside her. Little Leon.

"I wanted to speak to you," he whispers. "Megan, my dear, I will not enter the fires again. I am not a piece of metal. I will not be broken."

He leans over and kisses her on the cheek.

"Now Leon, my son. We were not meant to live this way. Your mother was meant for a better place. What they do to a person. You never met your grandfather, my father. Or my mother. She was a long time ago. It is good you did not see her at the end. The things one must do. The things they make us do."

He kisses the boy on one cheek, then the other.

On a wall in a lodge in the future there is a picture of a moment in time when history took a turn. Leon wants to paint it for his son, something to remember him by.

He counts out ten dollars and leaves it on the table beside Megan's bed.

"Your mother will take care of you."

22 · LEON · July 10, 1901

Leon takes a train to Chicago and arrives a day early. He has no place to stay and there is no hotel near the auditorium, the room where she will speak, so he stays on the streets near the hall to remain close.

At night a different world takes over the streets. The streets are left to those hoboes and stragglers who emerge out of the darkness, whose homes are the alleys; the streets, their front lawns. An old man with a gray beard and tattered pants lays out on the sidewalk a newspaper as if it were a satin tablecloth, then places down a half-eaten apple, chunks of hard bread that he appears to have robbed from the pigeons. As he gazes at the feast for a moment a boy races out from the alley and grabs the apple, and as the old man feebly gives chase, a rat scurries out and disappears with the bread down the sewers.

Watching the scene from across the road, Leon sees himself everywhere: he is the young boy, the old man, the rat scurrying down the sewer grate. He is clever, he is quick. Is pained, is evil. He is good. Nodding off now, it comes to him that he has witnessed this scene before; it is a play, an improvisation he has requested, all to prove a point.

He wakes up when a policeman's boot kicks him in the back and, nudging, flips him over. Leon gets up and sees that there is a line of bodies sleeping in the alley. The police are stomping on them like daisies, a fire that must be extinguished before it spreads. There is the old man, there is the boy. It is all part of the play that repeats itself.

Emma's speech is not until the afternoon, so he walks about the city. He buys a coffee, a newspaper. He wanders past the tall buildings, watches the white-shirted businessmen elbow one another to enter the offices first. Move fast, notice nothing. From the office buildings the smell draws him to the slaughterhouses, the metallic shriek of the cleaver, the grind of the machinery, the screams of cattle. The bull from his father's farm, Parker whipping his proud hide. A death house seems fitting in the midst of the city.

Leon returns to the auditorium, still early, and finds a seat up near the front. A man asks him what he is doing there, who he is.

"My name is Nieman. I am here for Emma."

The man crosses his arms and grins mean.

"Emma Goldman. The speech."

The man pats him down, turns out his pockets, then allows him to remain.

The other rows fill up. These are workers, men from the stock-yards and factories, the men who built the tall buildings. The crowd chatters with nervous excitement that reaches a climax when the lights go down and a man walks to the lectern. Some in the crowd boo, but the man greets them with a smile. *Yes, she's coming. Somebody has to introduce her.*

And then there she is. Leon's eyes lock onto Emma's; they are continuing a conversation that began when he saw her in May. There is the tyranny of the state, the tyranny of business, the millionaires who control the apparatus of government. The answer to tyranny is not a new tyranny. The answer is freedom. The shackles of the state must be cast off. The shackles of economic slavery must be destroyed. "I am not talking violence," she says. "Anarchists do not advocate the violence of the present corrupt state." (At this she seems to glance at the policemen who are standing just off the stage and at the back of the room.) "The mind must be freed too, and the body. Marriage is a shackle. Free thought is the answer. Free love is the answer. The answer is anarchy."

"This is theory," Leon says. The crowd has vanished, suddenly, and he is alone in the room with her; he sees it so clearly. "What of action? What of my role? Who am I?"

"Listen," Emma whispers. Then the lights go on and the crowd reappears. They are no longer alone and the speech continues.

"The man who flings his whole life into the attempt," Emma says, now loud again, "to protest against the wrongs of his fellow men, is a saint compared to the active and passive upholders of cruelty and injustice. Compared with the wholesale violence of capital and government, such acts of violence are but a drop in the ocean. High strung, like a violin string, they weep and moan for life, so relentless, so cruel, so terribly inhuman. In a desperate moment the string breaks. Untuned ears hear nothing but discord. But those who feel the agonized cry understand its harmony."

23 · LEON · Later that Day

When the speech is over Leon is close enough to the stage that he does not need to battle the crowd to get to her. He knows that Emma recognizes him, she remembers.

"I saw you in May," he says.

"Yes, yes." Emma is signing autographs, answering questions from a reporter. "Thank you."

"They call me Nieman. A friend of Emil. There is much to talk about."

"My dear Emil," Emma says, "of course. Come with me—Nieman? I must leave but we can speak on the way to the station."

Leon follows Emma out of the auditorium. She is speaking to the man who introduced her, then she is hidden within a crowd; an older man embraces her, tall and round, and a bearded man her age kisses her on the lips. A carriage meets them outside and they all get in.

Emma and the bearded man sit down on one side of the carriage, Leon and the others across from them.

Emma says, "Did I not tell you, Isaak, this Bryan business was going nowhere."

"That does not make him wrong," the older man says.

"Pssshhht." Emma dismisses him with a wave. "The Democrats are unionists at best. Incrementalists. They give workers palliatives, nothing more."

"Palliatives!" says the bearded man who kissed her. "Only a European would use words no workingman would understand."

"What would you prefer, Hippolyte?" Emma says, smiling. "Nostrums? Opiates?"

"Religion," Hippolyte—the bearded lover—says as he laughs.

"Were we to say nothing about McKinley's imperialism?" Isaak says. "Conquering foreign markets for the millionaires? We were right to join Bryan."

"What he did in the Philippines."

Isaak and Emma look at Leon; these are the first words he has spoken since entering the cab.

Leon continues, "It does not harmonize with the teaching in the schools about the flag."

"Sounds like one of Emil's editorials." Isaak laughs.

"It did sound familiar," Emma says. "Maybe I have said it myself."

Emma looks at Leon.

"Nieman you said your name was?"

Leon nods his head.

"No man." She laughs. "No man is no man."

"No man is every man," says Leon.

"Every man is no man," Hippolyte laughs, and Isaak and Emma join in.

Isaak and Emma return to discussing her plans, where she is speaking next, what she is writing, where they should organize, when they will meet. Emma is to go to St. Louis, Chicago, Buffalo. Leon sees her as a spirit who will whirl out of the window of the carriage and travel like a sirocco; she will fly through the nation like a ghost, fast as a locomotive.

"Can I come with you?" Leon says.

Emma laughs. "You are very young, Nieman."

"I want to—I am not certain—be involved. There is much I can do."

"We're late already, Emma," Isaak says. "Your train will be leaving."

Emma stands up, and Leon gently holds her arm steady as she steps down to the platform.

"There are others you can see," she says. "This is a movement, remember."

Leon covers his face with his hand, wonders if his look has revealed too much. *Is his mouth gaping, are his eyes wet?*

Emma smiles at him, then takes the high step up from the platform and vanishes inside the train.

24 · LEON · July 16, 1901

Leon takes a train east. He gets off at a station, he isn't sure where, crosses the platform, and gets on another train going the other direction. He gets off again at another stop and crosses another platform and hops the next train. At some point he will get off and his life will gather its own logic.

Emma is riding the rails somewhere, and the baby's cries rise up from the steamy tracks, the coal smoke blankets the sky, the piercing scrape of the train's wheels.

Megan's face, her father between them, T-shirted and muscled, biting down on his lower lip, rips blood. He is alone.

Leon ends up in West Seneca, New York. There is a house with a Room to Rent sign in the window. He knocks and an old woman opens the door. She is holding her dog by the collar, a small ball of yapping fur.

"Who are you?" she says, her face pointed, oddly, away from him. Her skin sags with age, under her eyes, her chin, her throat. "Are you here for the room? I am sorry about the dog; he is hungry."

Leon sees that the old woman's eyes are deep wells with empty sockets.

"Yes," Leon says. "I am here for the room."

She shows him a room, and when Leon wakes up the old lady is asleep. He walks about the house, into her room, around her bed. He is invisible, a spirit among the living, between worlds.

In her night table he finds a Sears Roebuck catalogue. He leafs through, glancing at the products, the prices, so many things to buy, the economy's booming. He takes it with him out of the room.

The hallway walls are lined with photographs: a young girl on her mother's lap, a young man in uniform, the Civil War it must be. The old lady's daughter, her husband.

No one smiles in pictures; a fear takes over when the camera stares you down. God's eye. When you see the flash of the light, He asks a question you cannot answer.

The woman's life flashes before his eyes: Leon knows her story, senses the truth, how people live. She was married young, after the man in the picture came home from the war. Then her husband left her, for drink, for other women, for work. He traveled west and laid rail, tried his hand in the mines. For a moment, kneeling by a mountain creek, the man was certain he had struck gold. He was in the Yukon now and cold and out of money. He sloshed the water about in his dented copper pan and saw the sparkle inside, the shimmering glow. What he could do with money in towering piles like Carnegie's. He had heard of homes that covered entire city blocks in Manhattan, drivers waited for you outside with a team of horses as you sat down for a shave, a drink, a bite of lunch. Then the man poured the water out of the copper pan and looked closely at what remained. There in the frigid wilderness, squatting on a snowy bank off a creek that trickled down the mountainside, there was nothing. It was only the sun reflecting off the bottom of the pan. He now remembered that before he had left home his daughter, the young girl he had photographed in his wife's lap, had been taken with scarlet fever and had passed on to a better world and his wife was taken ill, too, and her eyes were going and there was no money for the doctors. The man laid his pan down by the creek, took out his Iver Johnson revolver, placed it to his temple, and pulled the trigger. His brains landed in the pan and there they sloshed about: fool's gold. The real nuggets were just above him on the mountain, beyond the next turn of the creek.

In the kitchen Leon finds a newspaper, a year old. On the front page is a sketch of fighting men returning from the Philippines with medals and stories of conquest. It's a parade—flags, red, white, and blue, brass bands. In the newspaper there is no dysentery, no Filipino peasants scraping by a living, no death. President McKinley is beaming, the economy is booming. There are no tenements. In the world of the newspaper exists some capitalist utopia. Leon wonders if his mother is alive there. If the church lies there, too.

He hears the old blind lady rustle in her bed, so he stuffs the newspaper inside the woodstove and watches the flames devour it.

25 · EMIL SCHILLING · August 1901

Emil Schilling is sitting at the desk in his study, reading a letter he has just received from his friend Abe Isaak. Isaak tells of an unusual young man he met at Emma's last speech in Chicago. He called him—

self Nieman: No Man. "Nieman tried to attach himself to Emma," Isaak writes. "He wanted to follow her. After she left we spoke a bit and I treated him to dinner. He was well dressed but it seemed that he had not eaten in a long time, and he seemed unused to human company. Something very odd about him; unsettling. He was obsessed with secret societies and plots. He wanted to know if we anarchists had any plans, any secret cabals. He showed me a newspaper clipping reporting Bresci's shooting of King Umberto and it was clear he had heard about the Paterson group. He wanted to know who was the next leader on the list. I had to assure him that it was all lies from the capitalist papers, nothing more. I would not be surprised to find out he is a plant, an agent provocateur. He is the sort we must watch out for."

Emil hears a knock on the door.

"Who is it?"

"Your friend. Nieman."

Emil quickly folds up the letter as Leon opens the door and walks in.

"Where have you been?" Emil says, holding the letter behind him. "You have missed our meetings."

"Working."

"Where?"

"Akron." Leon's face breaks out in a wide grin. "In a cheese factory, I tell you," he says and bends over in laughter.

"Why did you go?"

"Didn't you hear me? I had to"—Leon cannot stop laughing—"make cheese!"

Emil lifts the top of his desk and hides the letter inside. "And why did you return to us?"

"I couldn't stay. But I cannot stay here either."

"Where are you going now?"

"Maybe Detroit. Buffalo, San Francisco. I'm not certain."

Emil has the sense Nieman's plans are not so uncertain. There is a look in the young man's eyes.

26 · EMIL · Late August 1901

Emil places an advertisement in the next issue of *Free Society*:

ATTENTION

> The attention of the comrades is called to another spy. He is
> well dressed, of medium height, rather narrow shouldered,
> and about twenty-five years of age. Up to the present he has
> made his appearance in Chicago and Cleveland. His de-
> meanor is of the usual sort, pretending to be greatly inter-
> ested in the cause, asking for names, or soliciting aid for
> acts of contemplated violence. If this same individual
> makes his appearance elsewhere, the comrades are warned
> in advance and can act accordingly.

27 · McKINLEY · April–September 1901

The idea is that he will begin his second term with a triumphant
sweep across the nation, a train ride across its entire breadth, from
Washington, D.C., to California. As president, McKinley has never
traveled all the way to the West Coast before. During the campaigns,
while young Bryan chased votes like a puppy after a bird, McKinley
stood pat. Now the president and his wife will offer all of their citizens
an opportunity to embrace them, to welcome them, to thank them for
their service. From California he and Ida wil return east, to the Pan-
American Exposition in Buffalo for President's Day on June 13.

A second term. The courtship and honeymoon between electorate
and elected is long over; the initial high hopes and grave fears have sub-
sided. There is a worn comfortableness to the relationship. A sense that
the couple is bound together now. Perhaps we are happiest in chains.

There are new themes McKinley would like to introduce on this trip. It is the start of a new century and American business needs new markets. There is a logic to the foreign wars of the last term, the Philippines and Cuba, that Bryan could never understand. Not a man of business, a man scornful of the economic engines that drive the nation, and so William Jennings Bryan could never appreciate what American business needs. The inventor, the mass producer—yes, the capitalist. New markets. *The days of exclusivity are past.*

The railroad cars are fitted resplendently for the journey with red velvet curtains, upholstered leather chairs and chaise lounges, canopied beds and chandeliers—a traveling White House worthy more of J. P. Morgan than Abe Lincoln or William McKinley.

In Pennsylvania their train passes a sky filled with fireworks and a band led by John Philip Sousa.

In Ohio the tracks are lined with veterans in uniform, from the War Between the States, the Philippines, and Cuba.

In Nebraska there is a cornfield that has been cut to spell WELCOME PRESIDENT AND MRS. MCKINLEY.

In Dallas a Mexican band serenades them with mariachi music, ladies spinning round in black skirts studded with rhinestones that sparkle in the sun.

28 · IDA · April–September 1901

In Los Angeles the people have adorned the streets with flowers on the lampposts, and the president's carriage is pulled by six white horses garbed in yellow satin.

Ida has decided to forgo her husband's regal chariot. She is wearing a new dress that billows all around her as she sits, around her hair a garland of flowers that was given to her by two girls when she arrived in Los Angeles. She is caught up in the spirit of the parade; William is the major again, she feels young. It is the California sun, it must be; it reminds her of Italy when she was just a girl out of Brooke Hall. She will run ahead of William, not on foot in a field of wheat but in a carriage led by a solitary black horse, its lustrous coat shimmering, its muscles rippling. She will hide in plain sight and laugh, wave at the little girls on the sidewalks and laugh. For the first time since she cannot remember she will lead the way.

A jolt of pain strikes through her. Not her usual dizziness and confusion, this is sharp and piercing, a wire rod sliced through the left forefinger it feels like—the pain is that localized and focused. She is waving at the little girls, but now the pain is so intense that she realizes she is not smiling; she cannot laugh. She closes her eyes, winces. Someone is thrusting the wire rod into the bones of her finger, into the marrow, then down the arm into the elbow, winding like a snake through her body. The wire is infected with toxins it injects into her bloodstream, a black oil that floats into the whites of her eyes and blinds her.

She looks at her hand. No wire there. Only her white gloves, but still the pain is sharp.

She stands up, tries to wave to the crowd, but she feels something drip down her leg and sits down quickly.

Somewhere behind her is her husband, but she cannot see him.

There are two little girls on the sidewalk waving.

She is sliding, falling down the rabbit hole.

29 · IDA · The Next She Remembers

She is in the hotel room, lying on a couch; the doctors are standing over her, speaking to her husband.

"What is it this time?" her husband says.

"We believe we have localized the problem," one of the doctors says. "It emanates from the finger."

"And that caused it all," her husband says. "Even the—"

"The diarrhea, yes. The infection has spread through the blood. We can operate—"

"And that will resolve it." McKinley's question becomes a statement; certainty makes things true.

"It is all we can do. But what is in the blood already—"

"There is only so much we understand," another doctor jumps in.

"God's will," says McKinley. "Do what you can."

30 · IDA · The Next Day

When Ida wakes up, she is lying down in a hospital. William is huddling over her, speaking to a doctor at the foot of the bed. There are tubes and canisters and syringes, nurses in white hats. She wants to say hello; she wants to be welcomed back to the world.

"When can we expect her to awake?" William says.

"I am awake, dear!" Ida yells, but no one hears her, not even William who is close enough to feel her breath but does not even turn his head.

The doctor is shaking his head. There are words leaving his mouth but she cannot make them out.

"Are you saying she may never—"

The doctor nods, and William's head falls into his hands.

It comes to Ida now that she is looking down at William and the doctor; she is floating above them. "That is why you cannot hear me," she says. "Look at me! Up here! So high!"

She feels heat she imagines to be light, but it is only heat. She floats.

The girls waving on the sidewalk, they are here. Little Ida. Katie. Floating up in the steamy air with their mother. Together.

We will miss your Daddy, but the three of us will be so happy now.

In the sky the three hold hands and dance, in the air, in a circle round and round.

The pain is gone. The hospital bed is gone. She cannot recall when she was ever without her beloved girls.

31 · IDA · Thirteen Hours Later, 1:38 A.M.

When she opens her eyes next she has lifted herself out of her body and she is her shadow self, a montage of fractured points of light. With her solid form she has stripped away her years. She is in the fog, she is in the clouds, she is air.

A man waltzes toward her. He is dapper and suave, a shock of black hair lacquered across his head and glasses just as dark and a suit the color of a white sand beach she saw on an island off Italy when she was with her sister Pina after they finished Brooke Hall.

Music is playing; from somewhere there are violins and an organ and a girls' choir—it might be Bach—and Ida and the man are dancing. On the street around them are beggars and street urchins. All of them are clapping and crying and cheering—there is something desperate about it all—and they are swirling in circles, holding one another as their shadow selves, those fractured points, vanish in the light.

32 · WILLIAM · That Morning

A funeral train is readied. William has given his assent. The doctors say the infection may pass through her body without taking her, but it is not likely.

The coffin will be in the rear car, and the rear doors to the train will be open off the balcony so onlookers can see it. An American flag will be draped over the casket; red, white, and blue bunting will line the outside of the car, and there will be a flag on the ceiling. Had God spared her this last illness and were the casket open, Ida could gaze up at the Stars and Stripes like the canopy of her bed back on Market Street.

William will sit in the car next to his Ida. His back will be turned to the waving, grieving masses who will line the railroad tracks from California to Washington, where Ida will lie in state, to Canton, where she will be buried in a grave between her two girls.

How will he complete his term in office without her? Perhaps he will resign, leave the White House to young Roosevelt. He imagines Mark Hanna's blood boiling at the news, the shocked, angry phone calls he will receive from Morgan and Rockefeller and Frick, and even here, gazing down at Ida, comatose in her hospital bed, her face so pale, her slight limbs utterly still, his imaginings overtake him. He laughs at the vision—he can't help it—then cries again.

33 · IDA · 4:32 A.M.

"How long was I asleep?" Ida says.

There is only a nurse beside her. The windows are open, letting in a cool night breeze. The only light is a candle burning on the small table beside the woman's chair. The nurse is snoring.

Ida feels that she has been away a long time.

"Am I awake?"

No one responds so Ida tries to drift back to sleep, but she hears the patter of footsteps out in the hall and the voice of her husband carrying on his business.

She decides that she is happy she has died. It is for the best. Is, in fact, what she has looked forward to. It comes to her that it was the two girls who gave her the flowers at the parade. The flowers must have infected her blood; it was the thorns on the stems of the roses. They were her girls, Ida and Katie, calling her home. *We will be together again. Finally.*

34 · IDA · 8:58 A.M.

When she wakes again it is morning and William is beside her bed. He clasps her hand and kisses it. Still she is not certain where she is.

In a day Ida is well enough that William can leave her bedside to travel to celebrate the embarkation of a new battleship, the *Ohio*.

It is decided. They will return to Canton to allow Ida to recuperate. Their visit to the Pan-American Expo is rescheduled. In early August it is announced that the President will visit Buffalo on September 5 and 6.

35 · MORRIS · 1901

Morris is sitting alone in the abandoned upstairs ballroom of Château Vandeveer when the inspiration strikes him. It is dark, which could mean day's end, evening's start, or most any time between, for there has been no gas since he was released from incarceration. Even the candlestick holders are empty. He and Lily sold the curtains, along with the tablecloths, tapestries, and rugs (besides, there were never windows in the room; it was especially designed for a lavish party he held he cannot remember when, to muffle the sound of gunfire). A week before the silverware brought in a few needed dollars, two weeks before the furniture, a month before the master bed, two months before they loaded the contents of the wine cellar onto a cart and hauled it door to door to neighbors on Fifth Avenue. They soon learned only the servant's door was open to them now. It brought a few dollars.

The floor of the cavernous room is smooth and serene as a mountain lake. On it a single item shimmers from light that could only be the product of Morris's imagination. Morris has been staring at the object for hours now; his thoughts flutter around it, half-wondering what it is, where it came from, how it came to enter his house, his life, what sort of life could bring him to such a barren end, where to go from here. There were days, in his prime, when condoms were shipped from his factory in bulk, business was booming, when Morris held court in this room, granting audiences to would-be investors. One man visited with an idea for a new horseless carriage that could float, a disposable safety razor, a contraceptive for women, moving pictures. Morris would strut about the chamber trailing his silk robe like royalty, his gold-tipped cigarette holder aloft, letting the smoke trail up to form whirlwinds in the fan above. "Let me tell you how an idea is born, young fellow. Let me tell you how money is made in America. You must first understand the American soul, something deep and rich, the subterranean yearnings, the lava of our being. We businessmen are prospectors, truly, searching for clues. Liberty, lust. Altruism, anarchism, communism, capitalism, socialism, and jism. Questioning, questioning, always questioning. Conquering and caring. It's a stew, my young man. Smell the spices. Think what's to be added to the mix."

"Why did you leave Germany?" someone asked once, he vaguely recalls.

"I didn't smell the stew, young man," Morris would have answered. "I was young and followed my own nose."

Over his hours of contemplation Morris has edged his way across the floor and has finally found himself inches away from the object that inspired his reflection, the wellspring, the root. He is lying on his stomach, leaning up on his elbows, and there it is, unmistakable. He has never seen it before, yet he knows precisely where it came from, the moment it was separated from its rightful owner. And once he recognizes what it is, and its origins, a rush of thoughts flood in a sequence of explosions, fuses tied together between stashes of gunpowder: fireworks or ammunition, who can be certain.

It was the party, the hunt, years ago. Which detonates, in his mind: Mark Hanna, William McKinley, the war, war, America, man. Lava, the stew. Anthony Comstock taught him something—these are ideas that festered in Morris's mind during his long nights in jail. Though it was Morris who had realized that condoms held a place in the stew, the lava, the soul, Comstock had reminded Morris of the puritanical strain, the contradictory American undercurrent that sought to repress that which was primal. Mark Hanna and William McKinley taught Morris something else, that and this ear—what he is staring at, the wellspring and root, is, after all of those years since the party that inaugurated Château Vandeveer, it is still unmistakably the ear of a Negro servant, a piece of one anyway—and what this holy American trinity (Hanna, McKinley, the ear) teaches Morris will, he is certain, inspire his second fortune, his return—a financial phoenix—to the moneyed American heavens. The key isn't freedom, isn't liberty, isn't simply lust.

It's state-sanctioned savagery.

36 · LEON · August 1901

The white satin lashes that are his mother's fingers, they caress his cheek.

The white heat of the factory, how the fire burns liquid into glass. It's the seamlessness of things, how lines blur, the falsity of divisions. The hypocrisy of science.

The smell of fresh pine in the forest when the men were striking. Frank's words, Emma's words, a vision of the world.

Reading *Looking Backward;* traveling to Bellamy's utopia.

His father shrinking before his stepmother's scowl.

Megan's eyes, watery and staring through him, the dip in her back, the sadness beneath her laugh. And then her father suffocates the sun.

Emma's eyes.

Little Leon's eyes.

The realization—an insight that flashes in his mind, then takes hold—that he can transcend history.

37 · MEGAN · August 1901

She is in bed but awake the night Leon returns. How long has he been away? Ten days, three weeks? A month? Leon is a bird who flies in and out of her window from the garden, migrating in seasonal patterns all his own. *What worms have you brought for my baby?* she wants to say. *Where are the twigs for our nest?*

She remains still in bed, feigning sleep. Watches, with an eye half open, Leon.

He enters slowly, quietly, jiggling a key she was not aware he had. Before he can close the door the wind wrestles it open and the cold wind rushes in, harsh rains sharp as razors across her face.

Everything is a struggle with you, she wants to say. Life; opening a door. The idea comes to her: *It will always be so. Poor Leon. Best that you stay away.*

He is finally able to close the door and latch it shut. The boy has rustled awake. He lets out a small cry and Leon picks him up, gripping him so roughly Megan jerks from the bed to protect him, their son, but then Leon gently rests him against his chest.

Megan watches as Leon gazes down at the boy, rocking him quiet. Little Leon's eyes are open, gazing up at his father's. The two are speaking, the boy silent, his father muttering, but they are speaking. That is why Leon has come back. It is just for this moment, this dialogue, this speech. A message to deliver. There are words that Leon must pass on to his son, words only he can tell, only now; there will be no other moment.

Still in bed, tears stream down Megan's cheeks. It will be her role to tell her son what his father had to say, when he is gone, who he was, but all she can hear is the rain pelting the thin walls and windows, the wind blowing so the ceiling buckles; it exhales timbers toward them all as if they are passengers together in a tiny, fragile ship and a storm is raging at sea.

PART FIVE

THE TEMPLE OF MUSIC

I · PREPARATIONS · Late August–September 1901

Take me to Dreamland. Take me to the House Upside Down. Take me on a Trip to the Moon. To Futureland. To Darkness and Dawn.

Leon is standing on the deck of a boat, thumbing through a program advertising the Pan-American Exposition in Buffalo. The waves are spraying onto the pages, so the images on the backside can be seen through the front, merging the pictures and words.

There are Negroes dancing before a campfire, singing as they pull a plow tied to their muscular shoulders. *A veritable old plantation with genuine darkey families and their pickaninnies.*

There is a space ship and the smiling face on the moon. *The journey is made on the airship* Luna.

There are spirits leaving a body, still and silent on a bed. *A realistic representation of a departed spirit, whose life on earth has not been exemplary.* Eskimos huddle round an igloo, Indians whoop war chants, a house is filled with aisles of babies in incubators. Cleopatra's Temple. The Beautiful Orient, Fair Japan. Venice in America, Nuremberg. The Expo is America; it is the world.

Since he has received the last of his money from his father, the sense Leon has had is that his money is a fuse that has been lit, a line of dollar bills that burns steadily and the flame is chasing him.

In Chicago he wrote his family to tell them he received the money and that he would be traveling west, to Fort Wayne, perhaps farther. Then he took a train back to Cleveland, then switched trains again.

Though he now had the money to buy a ticket he waited beside the rails with the hoboes and stragglers and hopped a cargo freight filled with corn and in the next car there were cattle, there were sheep. Dozed off and dreamed he was on a ship, and Megan and baby Leon were back at shore, their images vanishing as he rocked away from them in the waves; there was a force he could not control that kept them apart. When he awoke a cow was licking his face and he jumped off and rolled away from the rails, he didn't know where.

He picked up the program to the Pan-American Expo. The pamphlets were everywhere. Tiny boys were handing them out in packs; when you walked past, they stuffed them in your hands, in your pockets if you had any.

He hired a boy to carry his bags and caught a trolley car to Buffalo. He was rich, his lifetime earnings in his coat pocket. He gave the boy ten cents.

He did not read the program he was handed until now, after he had left Buffalo and got on a boat back to Cleveland.

President's Day Rescheduled, the program reads. *The president and Mrs. McKinley Will Visit the Exposition on September 5, 1901.*

"Why in hell must you send me to Buffalo of all places?" Creelman says. "The air is wretched cold off the lake. Too blasted cold to stay outside and not a damned thing to do in."

Hearst laughs. He is looking out the window at a building so tall it pokes the sky with the silver pole on its tip.

"It can't be all that bad," Hearst says, imagining himself in the top suite of the new building that has sprouted up across the street from the *Journal* offices. Hearst thinks he might buy it.

"Creelman, the president will be there. When McKinley blathers on about civilizing heathens and tariffs and trade, when he lies prostrate before Messrs. Morgan and Carnegie and lets them ride him like a two-bit whore, the *Journal* must be there to cover it. Who knows, perhaps he'll announce he's running for a third term."

"You need to know your opponent so early, boss?" The words must have come from Bierce, though Hearst and Creelman had thought he was still sleeping on the chaise in the corner of the office. "Election's not till '04."

Hearst takes something out of his vest pocket and tosses it at Bierce's head: a pen, a cigar, something.

"There will be other reporters there, boss. The *Times*. And someone from your friend Pulitzer's *World*. I'll tell you what: I'll get McKinley's speech off the wire and write the story like I was there."

"You lazy bastards miss the point," Hearst says. "There must be someone there to tell the truth."

James Parker is stuffing clothes into a tattered suitcase on his bed.

"It is work," he says to his wife.

"But a dancing slave, James?"

"The money is good." Parker is so tall and the room is so small that when he stands he must bend his neck at the ceiling. "A few weeks' work at the Expo will earn us more than I could make in a few months here, even if someone would hire me."

Parker puts his weight down on his clothes and is just able to latch the suitcase shut.

"So we can tell our son his father was a volunteer slave." His wife leans on top of the suitcase and cackles at him. "But at least he got good money."

Parker slaps her across the jaw with the back of his hand, landing her on the hard floor. Their boy has opened the door just now and seen it all and Parker wants to explain but decides it isn't possible.

Morris has set up a tent on the midway, across from the Infant Incubator, catty-corner to Darkness and Dawn. He has cordoned off this spot to draw the president's attention.

The canopy is a fine silk, sleek and slick. Stars, stripes—red, white, and blue. Lily stitched it herself, along with the name of Morris's new enterprise—what the tent is promoting, what will be revealed at the Expo—emblazoned above the entrance, on all sides, on a flag waving from the post on top.

This is it, the idea that struck him.

The road to his recovery, his rehabilitation, his rebirth.

Mannequins stand on either side of the tent opening, rigid, at attention. Wearing pristine white, royal blue, regal red. Epaulettes with medals of all variety and color are strewn about their shoulders, dollops of sherbet. Caps, helmets, and plumed hats. Everything has a military air but not quite. There's an overriding sense of a dress ball. Panache is the word that springs to mind. Not state-sanctioned savagery.

Yet the flags and the signs read: *Triple S Military Supplies.*

Emma Goldman is in St. Louis. There is a strike going on, workers of all trades have joined forces to fight the railroad. Porters, line men, stokers. Two days and already they have been replaced by others eager to get a dollar for a day's work. The workers are losing hope and Emma is here to inspire them, to tell them that they are part of a grander movement, that even if they lose the battle it is but a small skirmish in a long war; they are foot soldiers in an army fighting for a just state.

"Who among you has children?" Emma shouts. "Who wants them to live a better life than you were given? Who believes that can happen unless we change this system, where owners tell us what we are worth, where we take what we are given? Who among you?"

She looks out at her audience, the exhausted, haunted faces, the fear masking a false courage as they gather the strength to raise their arms. There is an old man she recalls seeing years ago whose questions she could not answer. For an instant she is separated from her audience: no connection. She is alone in an empty room looking at herself in a mirror, trying to answer her own questions.

Ida is back in her room in the old house on Market Street, crocheting in her rocking chair. She removes her hook and drops another slipper onto the pile next to her chair. She is in Canton to recuperate, to rest up. *For what?* To return to Washington, that land of preening, false hugs, and backstabbers.

She hears her husband speaking in his den. *Must be on the telephone.*

"William," she says. He cannot hear her, and she does not have the strength or will to yell. She smells his cigar smoke, and she does not even have the energy to tell him again that it is not permitted. The smoke chokes her, it suffocates her. When they first met he would not think to smoke.

Mark Hanna. Politics, this life.

"William," Ida says, though she knows he cannot hear her. "Why can't we stay here? William, my dear, this is home."

2 · LEON · August 31, 1901

As soon as Leon gets off the boat from Cleveland he walks to Walbridge's hardware store. Every day he returns to Buffalo to see if his package has arrived.

"It will be coming from the Sears Roebuck," he says.

"We know," says the clerk. "You ordered it from the catalogue. You are No Man."

"Nieman," Leon says. "Fred Nieman."

The clerk's smile suggests the package is there, just behind his desk, it has always been there.

"Try tomorrow."

Leon wanders the streets until it is dark and the people vanish, the married couples walking arm-in-arm on the sidewalks, the children playing on the lawns, in the fields. He finds a saloon called John Nowak's near the hardware store. At the front desk he asks for a room.

"Your name?" the clerk says.

The man at the store, this one here, the smirking men on the sidewalk, they are all the same man.

"Doe," Leon says. "John Doe."

After he registers and is given the key, he pulls out a coin and waves it to the boy behind the desk. A man with money does not carry his own bag. It is not the weight of the bag but the feeling of the thing, the sense of power. *Class is a game you play with money.*

His money is a wick that is burning.

As they walk up the stairs to his room the boy asks him, "Why did you give that name?" The boy must be eleven or twelve. Leon saw him in Alpena scurrying about on factory floors with loose bits of wire; he carried vats of molten metal in Cleveland. He is the boy who was not crushed, who escaped the flames of the factory furnace.

"You see," Leon whispers, leaning over, "I'm a Polish Jew and I wanted to be let a room."

The boy nods. Jews are from a land far away, where Jules Verne writes of, where H. G. Wells.

"What is your real name, then?"

"Nieman," Leon says. "Fred Nieman."

3 · LEON · September 1, 1901

In the morning Leon walks to Walbridge's hardware store again. He stands up in front of the clerk and glares at him. As the clerk begins to shrug his shoulders, *come back tomorrow*, Leon steps behind the counter and sweeps his arms along the shelves beside the cash register. He finds a package, pulls it out, and sees it is from Sears Roebuck; he can hold it in one hand. He takes out a roll of bills from his pocket, peels off a few dollars, and slaps them down on the counter.

That night he goes to church, a midnight mass. Leon has lost track of the days and so is not certain if it is a holiday but there it is, the candles, the music in the night. He has not been to church in a very long time.

He finds a seat in a back pew. The priest forces the sacraments down hungry throats. He is the priest from home, the priest who killed his mother.

Leon opens his package. The packing paper he stuffs under the seat. What is inside he tucks under his belt and covers with his shirt.

4 · LEON · September 2, 1901

There gets to be a ritual to his days, a repetition, a pattern that passes for faith.

He walks the streets at night. He may return to Nowak's saloon to wash his face upstairs, then go back downstairs for a drink. "Whiskey, and none of the cheap stuff." He flashes the roll of bills to show he means it. He lights a cigar, reads a newspaper. The president coming to Buffalo and the Expo is all the talk and, yes, he has seen the Midway; when he has a chance he wanders the grounds, pokes his head in a tent, checks out the sights.

The impression is of a man who has come to Buffalo for business.

5 · LEON · September 3, 1901

"I went to church the other night."

"Oh?"

At some point in the evening, several drinks ago, Leon has realized that another man has sat down across from him at the small round table in the back of the saloon. He must have seen the roll of bills when Leon paid for the last round. Rats, scraps of food. He is old and unshaven with gray wiry hairs growing down his nose into the empty whiskey tumbler he shakes in his hand. The man is shaking the glass to get Leon's attention, to indicate his glass is empty, or simply because his hand shakes. Leon does not know.

"I went to the Midway this evening," the old man says. "That Electric Tower, it's a miracle a nature it is. The height of the thing. The light."

"Have you read the Bible?" Leon says. "Not have you sat down and had the priest tell you what he says it says. I mean, have you read it for yourself?"

The man shakes his head.

"Lies," Leon says, "what you hear the priests tell." Leon puffs from a slim cigar, sips his whiskey. He has never lived so rich as since he left the farm, his life now. "The money isn't supposed to go to them," Leon says. "What they tell you, the priests? It's not the way it's meant to be."

The old man nods, gazes longingly at Leon's glass.

"That's good whiskey," he says. "None of that cheap rotgut."

"I wanted to kill him," Leon says. "Right there. The damned priest and his lies. Shoot him in the church."

The old man looks at his companion for an instant and, not sure whether he is joking, decides to laugh. Leon does not join him.

"What's the point?" the old man says. "They're like ants. More where he comes from."

6 · LEON · September 4, 1901

3 A.M.

A burst of noise and light, whiteness, then suddenly a fire so close he can feel the flames on his face. Then nothing.

Leon opens his eyes. The image has awoken him, but he cannot remember what it is, only that it has stirred him so deeply he knows he cannot return to sleep.

That is how the nights are now; he naps when he can, then stares up at the ceiling and lets the thoughts rush in and trample through till morning. The days a walking trance, exhausted and jittery.

His room has the narrow dimensions of a jail cell, a tomb; walls contain him, a ceiling low enough to suffocate for lack of air. No fan and it's oddly hot this autumn night.

Earlier tonight he went to the Expo again, this time to Cleopatra's Temple, the House Upside Down, and the African Village. He saw the

Edison kinetoscope, the moving images, photographs come to life. They showed a man exercising: bending down at the knees, his hands held out straight before him as he squats, then standing up. Then again. Someone explained how it is done: one picture taken after another, each a fraction of a second after the last, then shown in quick succession. You can thumb through the photographs in a stack and watch the pictures move, but there is something very different about sitting in the dark tent and watching the scratchy images on the big screen. Then it is not simply time divided into separate moments but re-created life, a parallel world. *Men are marionettes pulled by strings held by Thomas Alva Edison.*

His mouth and throat are parched dry and there is no water here. He knows there is a sink in the room of the old man across the hall. Leon strikes a match, lights a candle next to his bed, and crosses the hall.

When he opens the door Leon sees the old man spread out on the floor, his chest heaving upward toward the ceiling with each labored breath. A bottle is clenched in one hand as if the glass itself exudes the alcohol that sustains him. Scientists place the corpses of frogs in jars; Leon has seen the pictures in magazines. They scoop out human brains, hang skeletons on hooks to examine. *There are parts of the body that vanish when they become no longer necessary.* A tail, fur covering the skin, a sixth finger.

Leon steps over the old man to get to the sink and pumps a pitcher full of water.

In ten years his stepmother will have sucked whatever spirit remains in his father, a witch casting spells. This is what work does, the factories, the fields. *We become no longer necessary.*

His father will become the old man, chest heaving in his sleep, clutching an empty bottle for strength that is not there for him.

Leon sips the water, then spits out a shard of metal from it, dislodged pipe it must be, looks down and it's brown, liquid mud in the pitcher. Darwin says this is what we crawled out of and perhaps one day we will return.

He looks down at the old man sleeping on the floor and tosses the putrid liquid in his face.

6 P.M.

Leon is there at the train station with the rest of Buffalo and the visitors to the Expo, thirty thousand, forty thousand, it could be one hundred thousand bodies and faces—a sea of humanity crowded on the platform, as if a river of men, women, and children had raced down the tracks and formed a tidal wave of bodies that picked up the flotsam from the streets, then crashed onto the platform and flowed thick and deep and raged *(can smiling faces rage?* Leon thinks so), flooding the area. There are McKinley posters, McKinley buttons, McKinley-Roosevelt buttons, pipes with bowls the shape of the president's stern face, words screaming at Leon from billboards like an angry priest: *The Full Dinner Pail, Welcome the Advance Agent of Prosperity, Thank You Mr. President.* An ugliness in their satisfaction with the tyrant, Leon senses it, a reveling in their own ignorance. Let the master place his hand up your spine and manipulate you like a puppet: no need to think, it is the easy thing to do. There are ladies Leon swears are his stepmother, but multiplied out in replicas. Leon is gagging; the people must be sucking up all the air like cattle overgrazing, crowding him with their words and thoughts.

"Any minute now."

"Saw him in Canton in '96. There's a lightness and warmth you only see up close."

"Bryan never had it."

"The papers say he doesn't care about the little man but they don't know."

"A good Christian soul, praise be."

"That Ida McKinley's a doll, yes she is."

The words from the smiling faces never stop, the subterranean rage.

Leon has been at the station for an hour at least. He knew there would be crowds, though not this much; he has never seen so much humanity. To remain standing he must elbow those who elbow him and shove back and listen to the lies.

He hears the crowd that lines the tracks whoop and yell, then the locomotive whistles and then he can hear the train as it chugs toward the station. He senses the crowd surging, so he braces his legs apart to form an immovable base. A rock amid the floodwaters, the rising wave of people. There is no way of knowing where along the platform the president's car will stop, where he will get off the train. But Leon is certain the two of them will meet.

The train is a moving stream of red, white, and blue, bunting and flags powered by bare-chested men in the engine room shoveling coal into the furnace while the president—Leon sees him, *sees him!*—waving in the window, not even bothering to stand up but waving in a steady, monotonous motion like a mannequin, a wooden Jesus his step-mother still prays to in church, though Leon focuses on the others aboard, not the passengers but the workers, those bare-chested men in the engine room, Negroes or dark as Negroes from the dust and the chunks of coal the young boys carry to them when their cheap shovels break, the heat they feel from the furnace, Leon has felt it, a heat that sears the skin, saps the liquid out of your eyes so the lids stick together when you close them, saps the spirit from the soul; it burns, not the flame but the heat alone, all for eighty cents, a dollar a day, and you have no home to sleep in; you shovel and the train moves down the tracks and at night time you return with your train, while the president sits in a car upholstered with velvet and silk and gilded with gold foil, a moving White House, Leon has read of these luxurious moving palaces, Carnegie has one, and Morgan too; the president's slight smile is steady and motionless, so still he could be a wooden image; the people on either side of Leon are screaming, women are crying at the sight of the president, they thrust babies at him for absolution, for baptism, for blessings—*this is religion*—McKinley is a savior who lives for the blinded, mindless masses, and the train moves on taking the president to the far end of the platform and there is no way that Leon can get to him, the masses make a mad rush that immediately fills the empty space between Leon and McKinley, water over the banks splashing into the neighboring canyon; Leon stands firm, lets them pass and watches the cars go past while the bare-chested men in the engine room scream in a pitch that cannot be heard over the roaring, adoring crowd, and it comes to Leon that this train, this moving engine of streaming red, white and blue, this parade of illusion and lies, is America.

7 · **LEON** · September 5, 1901

"Expositions are the timekeepers of progress," McKinley says.

The phrase came to him months ago in the midst of his West Coast swing, when he was initially invited to speak at the Exposition. Immediately he rang for Cortelyou to write the words down. *When the muse strikes, its message must be captured.* After all, William McKinley is no William Jennings Bryan. He knew then the phrase would form the centerpiece of his President's Day speech. The rest of it he and his staff would have to fill in as responses to questions he would give his audience: *Where have we come from? Where are we going?* McKinley is straddling two centuries, a bridge over which the nation will travel to the twentieth—the American—century.

Standing behind the podium, at the dais, he glances over the crowd, the largest he has seen since the inaugural, but he cannot see a single face, he cannot hear one distinct voice, not a word. It is all a blur of dots, a buzz of sound. There are only the words Cortelyou has written on the pages in front of him, the sound of his own voice echoing back in his head. He will read the speech, and the papers will run with the story that the man of the high tariff has welcomed a new age of foreign trade, that McKinley is courageously leading the nation forward, riding the new technology that will fuel the engine of business that is America. *If the man at our helm is not afraid of competition out there in the world, then why should we be?*

And so the speech will be a success, but still, why must he be here? His message is to the business leaders, the captains of industry, those who are not here. There is something undignified about yelling messages that an unlearned audience cannot even comprehend. Were it not for what is expected of him, he would hand his speech to the reporters and have them simply reprint the text in the newspapers. Deliver it themselves, so to speak.

To help himself endure the speech, he must assume a role. And so he becomes a minister, the faceless mass before him his flock. He must instruct them in the way the world is and how it should be, here and in the next. In his mind, McKinley organizes his thoughts with headings for a sermon:

On the Sanctity of Struggle
"Business life," he says, "whether among ourselves or with other peoples, is ever a sharp struggle for success. It will be none the less so in the future."

On Modernity and Progress
"Without competition we should be clinging to the clumsy and antiquated processes of farming and manufacture and the methods of business of long ago, and the twentieth would be no further advanced than the eighteenth century."

On the Effect of Technology on Proximity
"How near one to the other is every part of the world. Modern inventions have brought into close relations widely separated peoples and made them better acquainted. Geographic and political divisions will continue to exist, but distances have been effaced."

On God's All-Powerful Invisible Hand
"Prices are fixed with mathematical precision by supply and demand. The world's selling prices are regulated by market and crop reports."

More on God's Technological Advancements and Its Beneficent Effects
"At the beginning of the nineteenth century there was not a mile of steam railroad on the globe. Now there are enough miles to make its circuit many times. Then there was not a line of electric telegraph; now we have a vast mileage traversing all lands and all seas. God and man have linked the nations together. No nation can longer be indifferent to any other."

On the Prosperity That God (and My Administration) Has Bestowed
"Trade statistics indicate that this country is in a state of unexampled prosperity. The figures show that we are utilizing our fields and forests

and mines and that we are furnishing profitable employment to the millions of workingmen throughout the United States, bringing comfort and happiness to their homes and making it possible to lay by savings for old age and disability. That all the people are participating in this great prosperity is seen in every American community and shown by the enormous and unprecedented deposits in our savings banks."

On How to Protect the Aforementioned Prosperity
"The greatest skill and wisdom on the part of manufacturers and producers will be required to hold and increase it."

On Connectedness Through Commerce
"A system which provides a mutual exchange of commodities is manifestly essential to the continued and healthful growth of our export trade. We must not repose in the fancied security that we can forever sell everything and buy little or nothing.

"What we produce beyond our domestic consumption must have a vent abroad. The excess must be relieved through a foreign outlet, and we should sell anywhere we can and buy wherever the buying will enlarge our sales and productions and thereby make a greater demand for home labor."

On the Gist of the Matter, for Those Who Haven't Gotten the Point Yet, and for the Headline Makers
"The period of exclusiveness is past."

He knows that is the greatest applause line, and he lets the audience revel in it while he takes a sip of water to clear his throat. He pats his vest and feels a cigar in his pocket that he must smoke; it has been an hour since he took a puff.

He glances over the crowd again before returning to finish delivering his text. Is it his eyes or something he has learned that makes the people a single-headed beast, their hair a blur, their eyes, their voices one? The people are an ocean, not drops but a vast pool of water spread out in front of him as far as he can see. His words are cast stones. *Prosperity!* and there is a plop and a ripple of applause. *The business of*

America! Plop. *The wise and wondrous bounties our businessmen bestow:* ripple, plop.

Is this how Bryan sees the people? Probably not. Which is why Bryan is Bryan and not McKinley. And not president. A leader needs some distance, so the greater good is always in the forefront instead of the discrete cry: petty tragedies, not a nation's business.

McKinley places his reading glasses back on and looks down at the paper before him.

Beyond the crowd, past the water's edge, lies the Midway, the heart of the Exposition. Out of respect for the president each exhibit is taking a brief recess during his speech.

This is the thing: there are two worlds turning simultaneously, parallel, each invisible to the other. There is the world out there, of James Parker's young wife scrubbing the outhouse floor of the white children's school in midtown Manhattan; of young Megan Wisemki rocking her child to sleep in Kanawha City; of Emma Goldman, after a heated speech to a local anarchist club, making love to a man ten years her junior in St. Louis; of Anthony Comstock seizing and desisting a vile, degenerate young woman he has surreptitiously stalked for weeks and now catches red-handed in the streets of New Haven handing out pamphlets advocating, of all things, birth control; of J. Pierpont Morgan dictating million-dollar buyout proposals to an aide on his yacht, now just offshore of Newport; of Mark Hanna in his Senate office on Capitol Hill puffing on a cigar while checking off those campaign contributors who have not pitched in their share of late; of Vice President Teddy Roosevelt camping out in the Adirondack Mountains in New York, armed with five shotguns and three rifles his staff carries for him, while his secretary jots down insights that come to him as he strolls through the woods; of Henry Clay Frick in an art gallery in Paris, bargaining for crates full of paintings that his advisers assure him are beautiful and of lasting value; of Alexander Berkman crouched on the floor in a dark cell, talking to an imaginary bird about a tunnel that will bring him out to freedom in Schwab's saloon in Manhattan; of William Randolph Hearst in the *Journal* offices in New York, penciling through entire paragraphs of Creelman's latest article and writing over it in block letters: MAKE THE READERS KNOW THAT THIS MAN McKINLEY IS LETTING THE MILLIONAIRES WHIP THEM LIKE A DOG! LET YOUR WORDS CONVEY TO THEM THE FEELING OF THE KICK OF HIS BOOT!; of Jacob Riis opening a door to a tenement and waving in a photographer to rush into the dark, crowded room and record for all eternity the reality inside—a mother, a father, six boys and girls with faces so muddied they might have burrowed into this small space from deep within the earth's core; of Victoria Woodhull sipping tea in her English estate, fed up with America; of Ida McKinley, resting in a bedroom not her own, hoping that by shutting her eyes the images in her head will become real, and this suffocating dread will vanish; of young Negro men swinging on the ends of ropes and children tossing loose sticks of wire into vats of molten metal; of inventors and speculators and more dollars than you can imagine and jewel-studded dog collars and families that will not eat in a week; and of President William McKinley speaking before the tens of thousands of men and women gathered at the Pan-American Exposition in Buffalo, New York, on September 5, 1901.

And there is the other world, reformulated and displayed, of the Expo, the fabricated history of the exhibits, now frozen in time. The spaceship is not traveling to the moon; the African Village is quiet; the Eskimos have stripped off their fur coats and, wearing T-shirts and denim pants, toss a ball among themselves; the nurses in the Infant Incubator sleep next to their fake babies; the spirits in Darkness and Dawn have peeled off their makeup and masks and are having a smoke; the man who stands on his head just inside the entrance to the House Upside Down has somersaulted to the floor and, on his back, rests; behind the closed doors to the Old Plantation James Parker, not smiling now, not dancing, is writing a letter to his wife.

Across the way, deerskin blankets are tied together over the entrances to the tepees of the Indian Congress. Inside, Geronimo has washed the war paint off his face, and Red Cloud has removed his feather headdress, something he never wore when he ruled over a nation that no longer exists. They sit alone near a fire, eyes closed, palms raised up to the sky.

. . .

Leon stands near the back of the crowd.

The woman to his left is his stepmother. The woman behind him is his stepmother. An old man seeks sustenance from an empty bottle, a baby wails for milk that is not there.

There are words the president speaks, a constant drone, dull and inane. The president is a dot in the distance, a rock on a distant shore.

Leon cannot listen to it anymore. He is so tired and the words pound in his head; there must be ants in his stomach, gnawing as they march.

He is far enough away from the podium that he can walk out the back and leave. As he does, the president's voice for an instant becomes louder, more clear.

This is what the President says: "Who can tell the new thoughts that have been awakened, the ambitions fired, and the high achievements that will be wrought through this Exposition?"

8 · ON THE MIDWAY · Evening, September 5, 1901

Men and women are crowding the Midway, pulling their hats down over their ears as the wind rushes at them. The Electric Tower looms over the Expo grounds, casts shadows that obscure the small patches of vanishing light left in the sky. A cold snap in early September. The breeze off the lake in the early evening. God blows out the daylight like a birthday candle. It's the breeze off the lake.

There are exhibits to see, the House Upside Down, Darkness and Dawn, all opened again after the president's inspiring speech this afternoon, but for a moment the people do not move here or there but stand motionless, gazing at the man under the black curtain that drapes down from the moving camera.

"Don't look at the camera; act natural. Mr. Edison wants to capture life, the way it is, the way it was." *True history.*

The moviemaker stands in the center of the Midway and turns slowly around in a circle, so though the men and women stand still the film will create the illusion of motion, an inexorable orbit, a circle of people that meets itself like a snake devouring its tail: the man with the muttonchop sideburns, bushy mustache, top hat, and string tie is the man at the beginning and the end. It makes you wonder if humanity is made up of a limited number of models, like Mr. Olds's moving vehicles, a handful of plaster casts into which is poured molten matter from God's furnace. Things repeat themselves: people, life, death. But here God is the cameraman's boss, Thomas Alva Edison, he who has done the old biblical Lord one better: made sound that outlasts the life of the voice, light that knows no darkness, and now has made people who do not die, whose images shall remain forever on the earth in celluloid. And, from that which he has created, the light and the phonograph and the moving pictures and so much else, he has made what any true God must make here in America. Money. Piles of the stuff.

And so the man behind the camera gazes out through the lens of the motion picture box, turning in a circle, each revolution faster than the next, turning, so the illusion takes hold that men and women are walking, then running, then are whipped into a frenzy of motion— there is change; there is progress—they merge with the wind off the lake, a tornado, a twister; it's the breeze off the lake and time is a jumble, past and present and future, their bodies decompose into a molten circular band of matter where body and spirit are one.

Leon is riding the elevator up the Electric Tower. The Midway below is lined with miracles; the tower looms over them all, sparkling with luminous lights in a world in which you can remember that in your youth a solitary flickering light was miracle enough, and a rotating spotlight on top that casts its searing glance on all ends of the Midway. The towering creature must be God; the all-seeing eye must be God's eye, though it has become a world in which gods reveal themselves and multiply so fast that the concept has begun to lose its meaning.

Earlier in the afternoon Leon found the tent where he had watched Mr. Edison's movies and he sat in the dark and watched some more, the men and women moving jerkily; a waving arm transported itself instantly from forehead level to waist high with no stations in between *(a king in a carriage was waving; it was Europe but might as well be here)*, moving life-sized marionettes. Leon stayed so long the movies began to repeat themselves, and soon he was caught up in the time loop of the puppet world, everything merged, the series of static images and the spectators, *who was real? who was not? who pulled the strings?* And then there was the circularity of time, that Ferris wheel of moments. When Leon stepped out of the dark tent, molten needles of light pierced his eyes, but he quickly found a bar that served him three shots of good whiskey lined up in a row, and then he returned to the tent and this time he truly could not tell who were the spectators, when the events on the screen were occurring.

And then, when he left, on the Midway there was the moviemaker spinning round, and Leon watched him and the men and women he filmed and everything ran askew: artist and subject; creator and created; God, man. Leon has a vague sense of the future now, what the next days will hold for him, and he has the vague sense he has lived these days before.

He grabs the railing of the open elevator car and sees people down below and he closes his eyes. It is not the fear of falling. It is the fear that he will jump.

Below, on the Midway, a man is being shown the exhibits: *here is the Infant Incubator, here is the African Village, there the Old Plantation.* The man's wife wants to remain at the Infant Incubator, she is drawn to it, babies in heated bins as far as the eye can see. The babies are not real but it makes no difference. She wants to enter the land of children; the fakeness is part of the thrill—it adds to the magic, the wondrous illusion of it all. Reality could not hold out the same prospect of possibility.

The man down below, escorted through the Midway, knows this is not good for his wife; it is not what the doctors would want. But then again there is nothing he can do. And besides, John Milburn, his host, has a box of fine cigars he looks forward to.

From the top of the tower, Leon gazes down, follows the spotlight; he rides its rotation around the Expo. The trick is to become the spotlight; *your gaze is its gaze, your eye is all-seeing, you cast the searching light.*

Float down from the top of the tower, circle like a bird coasting with wings spread. No need to flap from that height, just let gravity and the night breeze gently ease you down, here, then there.

The Midway is crowded with people, but time moves quickly and the families peel off, some to the right, others to the left. They walk home, automobiles pick them up to bring them to hotels in town, or to trains to the outlying areas—West Seneca, Niagara, a ferry across the lake. Hands of a clock spin quickly, signifying a rapid passage of time. Soon the Midway is empty; it must be one in the morning and the Exposition is supposed to close at midnight. Thinks: *this may be an exposition of the mind.*

Leon sees a small procession of dignitaries wend through the tents. The center of attention is the man and woman from the Infant Incubator, and others fawning over the couple—*Have you noticed this washboard, Mr. President, sir? The Negroes would hit it like a drum after a day's work and they would sing; Might I carry your umbrella, Mrs. McKinley, you look pale, if I may say so; May I give you my wrap?*—all captured in a cloud of smoke that grows (the men are smoking cigars) and seems to carry them through the grounds. The face Leon recognizes from the train and the newspapers and Homer Davenport's cartoons in the Hearst papers (though here he is without swaddling clothes and his nursemaid, Mark Hanna): the president, William McKinley and his wife, Ida.

God's eye, God's plan.

A carnival barker appears out of nowhere, in minstrel makeup, whiteface with a body painted blue with red stripes and white stars on his chest, leaps out in front of the presidential entourage like a demon in the night, jumping and shouting, "Ride the Aerio-Cycle! See real live Injuns! See Geronimo! Fly to the Moon! Travel back to the old South, a plantation of yore! Visit the spirits damned for all eternity!"

McKinley, shocked, steps back from the intruder, drops the cigar he had just lit after leaving Ida with her sister, Pina, at the Infant Incubator. He had not noticed the barker before. Wonders: *How could he have emerged so suddenly, out of the air?* Looking round it seems to McKinley that no one else even notices this bizarrely painted fellow, as if he were invisible to John Milburn, Ida, and the bodyguards. The voice of the barker is extraordinary too; every word he speaks ignites a wildfire of images in McKinley's head.

"We can put off seeing the Indians, Mr. President," says John Milburn, the president's host. "They're to visit you tomorrow, after the reception at the Temple of Music. They want to give you something; what it is, I haven't the slightest." Milburn bends down to pick up the president's cigar, then hands McKinley a fresh one. "Who knows with Injuns? They keep to themselves so."

The barker walks toward the Darkness and Dawn exhibit. McKinley and Milburn follow. Wilkie, who is in charge of the president's security here in Buffalo, directs four Secret Service men to form a human box around the presidential party: two in front, two behind. To Leon, gazing at them from the Tower, the men are a constellation of stars creeping through the night.

McKinley is puffing his cigar, and the smoke clouds that surround him create an image of Mark Hanna. Leon blinks his eyes and the next he sees McKinley is beside his wife, Ida; they stand together in the Infant Incubator tent. Around them babies are screaming, the place is dark—he has seen it all in a photograph by Jacob Riis—and there's another cry from inside, a deeper wail that won't stop, and Leon sees it is Ida.

"Step right up!" shouts the barker. "On we go! Darkness and Dawn!" The barker reads from a poster tacked in front of the entrance to the tent before them. *"A realistic representation of a departed spirit, whose life on earth has not been exemplary."*

McKinley and his entourage follow into another tent, and Leon, gazing down, senses he has entered the president's mind.

Music, an organ, a thunderous Bach fugue, booms throughout the tent, sound so deafening it consumes all the space around them, like someone sucking out the air. McKinley thinks, *there was a night in the fields outside Canton with Ida when we were courting and we were still young.*

A face, disembodied, appears before him: *he was on the battlefield at Antietam bringing the soldier coffee and bread when a cannonball hit and he had to drag the body onto the back of his wagon.*

Someone sings, "Nearer, My God to Thee," and McKinley wonders when he was last in church—it seems a long time.

Then another face appears. These are images on a screen, on the curtain wall of the tent, flashing at him. McKinley searches his memory and thumbs through volumes of photos that he now recognizes are of political supporters from over the years, the delegations that visited him at his front porch in Canton in the '96 and '00 campaigns, hands he has shaken. The faces have no names; they are only votes and dollar bills.

Leon silently implants messages in the president's mind. August Spies, Louis Lingg, Albert Parsons. *Remember the names, remember the faces, remember their words and ideas. These are the Haymarket martyrs. Your hands are bloody with them too.*

Leon is a puppet master pulling the strings. He sees all: *God's eye.*

The president is crying now; the scene is biblical—he is Job, Abraham at the mountaintop with Isaac except the knife in his hand is dripping with the blood of the Haymarket martyrs and bodies who are rolled before him in some modern-day factory with the president the plant manager, and the factory floor is packed with babies, young girls from the sweatshops, Leon's mother. The president makes the priest's sign of the cross that slashes them each with his knife, which makes sense since hymns are intoned; the church is here, too, everything is rolled into the maw of the furnace; everyone dies.

McKinley is on his knees, hands clasped; a desert wind whips sand in his face.

Suddenly the carnival barker yells, his mouth so wide all Leon sees are his red painted lips and the white backdrop of his painted skin.

"Old Plantation! *Reproducing a veritable old plantation in its minutest detail, and giving the visitor an interesting glimpse of the sunny South! The slave quarters and log cabins were brought from the South and are occupied by genuine darkey families and their pickaninnies! Dancing and other pastimes dear to the old Negro are given at the theater, included in the attraction.*"

In front of the tent is a wooden porch, on which two shoes tap-dance. The movement is lively and skilled, but you sense a heaviness to the feet, a sadness there. The dancer is James Parker, a handsome, well-muscled Negro who must be six foot five.

An old Negro woman suckles her master's baby and sings.

We are
climbing
Jacob's
Ladder,
We are
climbing
Jacob's
Ladder,
We are
climbing
Jacob's
Ladder,
Shelter
from the
storm.

And it is James Parker—Leon recognizes him now: the farm-hand—who sings "Nearer, My God to Thee."

McKinley is on his knees, weeping.

The barker emits another shout, timely as a railroad whistle. "INDIAN CONGRESS! *The different tribes of Indians appear before the visitor, presenting their different styles of war and ghost dances, with their songs and weird musical accompaniments!*"

And things move fast. Leon watches the entourage pass a tepee, the Indians doff their headdresses at the president; then the barker, now on stilts, shouting loud as a train conductor, yells, "DREAMLAND!"

And things speed up even more, the jerky images accelerate, and the barker peals again: "TRIP TO THE MOON! *The journey is made on the airship* Luna *and is of thrilling interest to everyone who gets aboard. After a stroll among the streets and shops of the earth's satellite, the visitor returns to earth, safe and sound.*"

Leon loses sight of McKinley as he tries to imagine the spaceship *Luna*, the moon's shiny silver surface, what he imagines to be a Martian. He rushes down to an elevator, but when he reaches the ground the Midway appears empty.

Where is the president and his wife? Their fellow travelers, the barker, the exhibits in the tents? The Midway is empty, and Leon has the sense that he has always been alone. The dream is not there for him.

The moon is as real as the rest of the Exposition, as real as history, the truth that will survive.

9 · RATIONALES, EXPLANATIONS, POSSIBILITIES · (Leon)

Because he was crazy.

Because he wished to avenge his mother's death.

Because the light struck him a certain way one morning, months before, when he was walking the streets of Cleveland and there was a billboard that cast shadows from the trolley car as it screeched by with its ragged razor howl.

Because somewhere, always, a baby is crying, a young woman shrieks in ill-fated childbirth.

Because the shadow was cast from a billboard portrait of the serene, almost smiling William McKinley and the line below him read something about *Prosperity*.

Because everyone has an urge to kill another man. It is just a question of acting on impulse and faith.

Because Emma Goldman told him to do it.

Because Emma Goldman intimated that it would be best if he do it.

Because he loved Emma Goldman.

Somehow, in his mind, it was all mixed up: Emma, his mother, his father, his stepmother. Society, America; this life.

Because only Leon Czolgosz is true to his spirit. Because only Leon Czolgosz has the courage to do what needs to be done.

To free the lovely Ida Saxton from her shackles.

Because the social structure, the economic structure, the governmental structure of America and the world is interconnected in an oh-so-elaborate interplay, a jigsaw puzzle of insatiable corporate desires; it all seems so fixed, immutable and sturdy: it will last forever, except that there is something only Leon can see: the structure is but a house of cards; there is a false door, a piece that, if removed, will cause the whole thing to crumble.

Because it is time for revolution here in America. It is past time.

Because there will be something Megan will remember him by. Because everything is for his son, little Leon.

The devil made him do it.

Because God, the Great Spirit, the forces that rule the universe, ordained that it be so and there is no way that Leon, McKinley, or anyone else can alter that.

Because millennia ago a form of being that no longer exists (evidence of it would be invisible to the human eye, as presently constituted) killed, for no reason, another being of the same species.

Because the chemical composition of his brain, when combined with the food and drink he consumed during his life, compelled him to.

It might have been a disease.

Or something in his blood. An infection, a burst vessel, something.

Because some things are unexplainable.

Because everything, in fact, is unexplainable.

10 · THE TEMPLE OF MUSIC · September 6, 1901

5:15 A.M.

The sun is still hiding below the horizon on the outskirts of Buffalo, but John Milburn's servants are busy at work. They scrub the president's white shirt, boil it and starch it, then dry it with steam heat and fans. The gemstone studs are polished with a fine silk wrapped around a smooth, rounded stone. When the president awakes, his bath is already drawn for him. After he is toweled dry he raises his arms and the sleeves of his shirt are slid on; a black satin necktie, pin-striped trousers. McKinley tucks his admirable belly into a vest that matches his suit, then allows his jacket to be placed on. He snaps onto his vest a chain for his eyeglasses, another chain for his pocket watch, slips a heart-shaped ring on his finger.

All while shaving, he needs no mirror. A servant is reading him the newspapers. His speech at the Exposition has been well received. A bold stroke for the customarily cautious McKinley, they say. *A true leader, a man cognizant of history's turns, not wedded irrevocably to his past views.* The president recognizes that the high tariffs that brought him such renown can no longer be relied upon to guarantee prosperity. *Our shores shackle the liberty of our commercial geniuses like dinosaurs in zoo cells. We have quelled the Indian threats, we have lined our continent with rails so the vast landmass can be traversed in the snap of a finger—less than a week—we can create more wonders than our citizenry can envision or afford, our ingenuity outstrips our imagination.* Of course President McKinley is right: *the nation must seek new markets.* In the new century American business will conquer the world. McKinley will be the field general strategizing our mercantile battle plans.

"What will the temperature be?" McKinley says, handing a servant his straightedge as another man pats the soap and blood off with a towel, then taps the worst spots with a styptic pencil that stings for an instant, then closes the wounds. "More of this interminable heat?"

"Yes, Mr. President. But there's always a breeze coming off the falls."

"Make certain a wrap is brought for Mrs. McKinley. Tell the girls."

He snaps his fingers and is handed three ironed handkerchiefs, which he tucks into his vest pocket.

From John Milburn's house . . . down the elm-lined street . . . through the sleeping city of Buffalo . . . the gates to the Pan-American Exposition . . . past the vendors readying their wagons . . . a fire to roast chestnuts, a suckling pig and corn . . . old campaign posters of the president: McKinley with Roosevelt, McKinley with Ida, a full dinner pail, *16 to 1*, McKinley surrounded by American flags, *Prosperity and Civilization* . . . onto the Midway where Negroes and Chinamen impale trash with long spikes, remnants of a particularly raucous evening, a blustery night in which garbage was tossed about in a clutter; their children scurry to pick up scraps of newspapers, pamphlets advertising the exhibits, cigarette butts, cigar stubs from the dirt paths that line the tents; it all goes into the metal cans that are hauled onto the mule-driven garbage wagons . . . there is the Eskimo Village, the Aerio-Cycle, the Infant Incubator, and Fair Japan . . . an odd-looking man dressed in stars and stripes, every inch of his face and lips painted so it is impossible to tell whether beneath the paint he is Negro, white, Indian, or Oriental: *perhaps Uncle Sam is a mongrel* . . . whatever . . . he sleeps, oblivious to the strewn garbage around him, on the dirt floor of the Midway, his head resting just inside the Darkness and Dawn tent . . . and beside him. . . .

Leon feels the boot on his back and wonders at first whether he is still dreaming.

"You."

He opens his eyes, rolls over on his back, and looks up. The sky is still dark but the sun must be out there somewhere, beyond the lake maybe, past the elegant tree-lined avenues of Buffalo's gentry.

The man with the steel-tipped boot on Leon's shoulder glowers down at him.

"We're cleaning up the trash."

Leon gets up and walks quickly across town in the dying darkness, the slowly rising sun chasing him through the empty streets. At Nowak's saloon the old man has nodded off at the bar and there is no clerk, only shadows and the old man's heaving breaths ticking like a grandfather clock. Leon reaches across the front desk and snatches his key.

Upstairs he finds a metal pail in a janitor's closet and fills it with water in the old man's room, then brings it across the hall to his own. Quickly he strips off his clothes, lays them out on the narrow bed. The few possessions he has brought with him from his father's farm in Ohio he places carefully on a small table beside the tall mirror.

The water is cold; he cups it with his hands and pours it over his head so it drips down his neck and dribbles down his back and he shivers. There's a film of grime on his face from last night; he scrubs hard with the rag and a bar of soap he carried from across the hall.

He stands straight in front of the mirror, his hair even blacker from its wetness, his chest caved in at the stomach. You see the ribs protruding against the skin, his collarbone, the bones of his wrists. There are men with ample bellies, layers of unnecessary fat, and then there are the lean, the workingmen. You lose the twinkle in your eye, your strength, your will.

On the bed he has laid out his Sunday suit: black pants and jacket, white cuffed shirt and string tie. With the dry end of the rag he dusts his clothes, wipes off a smudge and a stain. It strikes him as important that today he must be clean and well dressed.

His belongings, what he has carried with him from home, what he always keeps near him—the worn rubber nipple, the newspaper clipping of Gaetamo Bresci's *attendat,* a few strands of a woman's hair—he wraps in a handkerchief and places in a front pocket of his jacket.

9:00 A.M.

Thousands of people are walking quickly behind John Milburn's new automobile; they are a makeshift parade, and McKinley is the drum major—P. T. Barnum leading his circus through town, to the train station. The ocean of humanity surrounds the vehicle, then parts in ripples as the auto slowly creeps forward. There are people hanging onto the side of the car, stepping on the running boards to get close. McKinley waves, smiling, though the jerking of the automobile throws off his ritualistic gestures; the auto is so less reliable than the horse's steady trot. He cannot recall when such pageantry was not a part of his life. *You smile; you wave.*

Ida sits beside him. She smiles a bit, leans her head on her husband's shoulder.

"Perhaps you should stay at the house, dear," McKinley whispers.

When Milburn sees the president reach for a handkerchief, he looks away. He has heard of Mrs. McKinley's fits.

"No," she says. "I've always wanted to see the falls."

The car stops with a sudden jerk, knocking Leon down to the platform beside the train. As he jogged beside the car, he had been looking through the rear window at Mrs. McKinley, her head nestled on her husband's shoulder, McKinley turned the other way. They say she had once been beautiful and hints of it do remain, but the pain casts a pall like storm clouds over a blue sky.

The door of the car opens and Leon sees, above him, legs, then he is kicked to the side; it's a guard, a policeman, somebody. He scurries up to his feet but still his perspective is skewed as he sees the president tip his hat, step up and onto the train. Leon is able to elbow his way through the crowd to get nearer to the train, but there is a mob of outstretched hands that he cannot get through, men and women yearning to touch the president.

Leon walks quickly ahead to find an open car, a door that will permit him entry.

10:20 A.M.

The water drops down from a sheer cliff in a fury of motion that seems to change its matter, transform the liquid into a solid sheet that pounds into the rock below. The noise is overwhelming, nature's machinery, a steady woosh and patter. Leon is standing on the bridge below, looking up at the falls, transfixed. You can look through—like ice, like glass—and see that where the falls land the rock has been worn away to form a hollowed-out pool, a quiet place where the water turns still, refracts the sparkling light of the quartz on the bottom.

Watching the falls, Leon loses track of all that is around him, why he has come here, who he has followed, and it all strikes him so clearly, the insights rush at him all at once.

You pour a droplet of water on stone and it bounces back at you, slides meekly off. Pour a cup and you achieve the same result. But banded together the droplets become a wall that pulverizes stone. And so rock becomes water, water rock. You will never see the result in your lifetime, Leon realizes; this is the process of time. *This is history.*

"Niagara Falls, Mr. President," the mayor says, displaying the sight with an outstretched hand as if it had been constructed for McKinley's visit, an exhibit for the Expo.

"A wonder," McKinley says, smiling.

They are walking through the woods, the falls only slightly visible. McKinley is smoking a Garcia cigar, which the reporters understand they are not to mention in the papers.

The talk among the press is where the president is stepping. The planned route of his walk will place him dangerously close to the Canadian border. An innocent misstep could place him on foreign soil, without formal invitation or anticipatory diplomatic maneuvers between the two sovereigns. On the train up to Niagara reporters were placing bets on an American invasion—albeit one man, one step—and what will happen should that occur.

McKinley looks behind him for reassurance and there is Cortelyou, map in one hand, compass in the other, closely monitoring the president's feet.

"We can still cancel the Temple of Music reception," Cortelyou says.

They are now on the suspension bridge, gazing down at the falls in midflight. Earlier in the week Cortelyou became convinced that a public reception exposed the president to too much danger; there was no way to safely cordon off the crowd. Wilkie and Foster and the rest of the security team could not cover so much ground to protect him. But the president demanded that the event be placed back on his schedule.

McKinley feels Ida stagger and he catches her arm. She had been looking up at the falls—they both were—when she must have lost her balance. The heights, the fast-moving water, the illusion of falling.

Ida clutches her husband's hand.

"You are tired, my dear." McKinley glances behind him and a servant appears. "Take Mrs. McKinley back to the hotel. She is not feeling well."

He kisses Ida on the forehead. "We shall meet for lunch," he says.

The servant takes Ida by the arm and walks her back toward the carriage.

"As I was saying, Mr. President," Cortelyou says, stepping forward to McKinley's side, "we believe the Temple reception is too dangerous. The crowds will be huge. There simply is no way you can be protected."

McKinley turns to face his secretary. "Mr. Cortelyou," he says, "do you think the people do not love me?"

4:05 P.M.

Leon has wrapped a handkerchief around his right hand.

The idea comes to him when he is on the trolley from Niagara, back to Buffalo. It is so hot that handkerchiefs are everywhere at the Expo, and the Midway is crowded with men and women mopping their foreheads of sweat. Inside the Temple of Music it is sure to be hotter still. There will be nothing unusual about a bulky handkerchief wrapped around a visitor's right hand.

He arrives at the Temple early so there is space for him to elbow his way to the front of the large reception room. When he decides he is close enough to the front he stops, braces his legs apart from each other, stakes his ground, then withdraws within himself, hands in his pockets, arms held tight against his sides.

The podium is right in front of him—he could spit on it—and there are bouquets of flowers in pots hanging from the pillars, a fountain gurgling, a cuspidor, a standing ashtray, American flags draped down from the high ceiling, like advertising billboards, a red carpet, a lectern, leather chairs, a red velvet rope. Only visitors are here so far, waiting for a handshake or even a glimpse, but the trappings are laid out. *Place president here.* There must be a cross on the carpet where McKinley is told to stand, a spot for his guards, for his wife, for his aides, dignitaries, the mayor. *It is all prepared for him,* everything so precise. Leon can see the whole social order charted out like an elaborate family tree, lines and arrows connecting the industrialists, the millionaires, the senators, McKinley. The lines on the chart are placeholders to be filled in with names, then erased and replaced with other names; but the chart, the structure, is set. What he is looking at now, this tableau, is the empty line in the chart. *Who constructs the system, this puppet show? Where is Morgan, where is Carnegie, where is Frick?* The image of Emma Goldman comes to him, pounding her fist; take away her small round eyeglasses and there is his mother. *You will help the people.* The thing to do is to snip the cords held by the puppeteers, reveal the rulers for what they are: marionettes.

A red carpet. Oversized Stars and Stripes billowing in the breeze. Flowers in a pot hanging from a pillar.

Suddenly noise begins to rumble through the crowd, heads turn: *a herd of sheep sensing a storm fast approaching; no time to graze; head home.* The heads are looking to the front door, directly behind Leon. Mutterings, yelps, nervous laughter. Leon tries to resist the urge to turn around. He fixes his gaze on the tableau, the empty set awaiting the actors. He tries to imagine the stage remaining empty, what happens when there are no leaders and the people rule.

In a small room off the entryway to the Temple reception hall, Creelman is holding the earpiece of a telephone, waiting for his trunk call to Chicago to be patched through to his boss. Through the open door he sees the president walk in. As many times as Creelman has seen cartoons of McKinley in the *Journal*, this is the first time he has seen the man himself. He realizes then that he has expected the caricature—a baby suckling nursemaid Mark Hanna's teats; a small dog being stroked on the lap of Daddy Coal Trust, the Sugar Trust, Oil, the railroads—but here he is, hesitating for a moment before he enters the hall to mop the sweat off his brow, straighten his tie, hand his cigar stub to his secretary, George Cortelyou. William McKinley is, Creelman knows, a man dedicated to the pure image of himself. A man at the top of his game: reelected and loved, victorious in war, the country emerged out of its depression, the financial panic of his first term a distant memory, and now he has brought his people victory, valiantly conquered foreign markets, peace, prosperity—the full dinner pail at home, civilization abroad. . . .

"There he is!"

Leon doesn't see him; it is a fat Polish woman behind him who yells, wife of a factory foreman by her looks, gaudy dress and feathered headdress covering a greasy tangle of unwashed hair.

He turns around to see the door open and the light stream in. The crowd is herded back from the president's entourage; there are batons, riot sticks, and a path is paved to the podium, the crowd parts like the Red Sea, Secret Service and police with clubs play Moses, the red carpet lines the way. *This is when the actors take their places.*

Leon's mind is removing itself from the present scene: he is floating back to the top of the Electric Tower, looking down on it all. Little Leon lies crying and Megan holds him as she hangs up the laundry—Leon closes his eyes as if that would block out the vision—in a union hall in St. Louis Emma Goldman pounds the lectern: *Poor Leon Czol-*

gosz, she says, *your crime consisted of too sensitive a social consciousness! Your ideals soared above the belly and the bank account* . . . Emma reaches out with his mother's delicate fingers; removes her glasses so the resemblance is frightening. The images flash into his head, sunlight bouncing off a wave in a turbulent sea.

Leon sees it all, the pictures in his brain flash one after each other, increments of time that give the illusion of motion.

Smile at the citizen, make eye contact ever so briefly as you shake the hand before you, grab the far shoulder gently with the other hand to guide him away, smile at the next man, shake the hand. *Keep the line moving*. Say a kind word. That's a pleasant shirt, a pretty wife, a charming child. *Keep the line moving*.

McKinley has never enjoyed the glad-handing side of the political game. No dignity in it, and a bore, truth be told, but there it is. Shake the hand, *keep the line moving*. Smile. A kind word.

There is a rumble to the crowd, but it's joyous, celebratory, and an organ is playing in the background. A Bach sonata, if he had to guess. A wondrous thunderstorm of sound.

Lord, but it's hot.

Leon slips his hand out of his pocket, wraps the handkerchief tight around. It is all done behind the backs of the men and women standing about him; the cramped crowd gives him cover. Besides, all eyes are on the president, ten feet in front of him. He is taller than Leon, and larger all around, a heavyset man of success; money and power spill over his belt. A starched white collar, raised stiffly at the back; black suit coat with, it seems, tails; black silk string necktie with each side tucked under the lapels of his suit coat. His hair is thin, sandy, and gray; his forehead dominates his large face. A sternness to his gaze, hard and emotionless. His skin sags in loose red bags under his eyes. A recent victim of time's ravages.

There are guards, but they are off to the president's far side and slightly behind him.

It is so hot the urge Leon has is to wipe his face with the handkerchief wrapped around his hand. He almost laughs at the vision.

Then he feels a hand on his shoulder. There is a gap of space between Leon and the man in front of him on the line to shake the president's hand and air and space are not permitted, *move along, move along*, and buildings pierce the sky and houses cover every inch, *keep moving*, somebody is shoving him forward. The president is shaking one man's hand and is guiding him past and he is onto the next; *people are hands to shake, nothing more*, and the images in Leon's head are an Edison moving picture, racing faster than ever before: Emma pounds her fist on a lectern, Morgan rocks gently at sea, Hanna barks into his telephone, the cigar smoke blurs the pictures, Comstock and Bryan and the ghosts of the Haymarket martyrs; there is Megan, little Leon, a boy at the nail factory in West Virginia who could not run fast enough and so the rolling bin carried him into the furnace and that was that—Leon was close enough to hear the boy's screams; his mother writhing in bed—Lord, but it's hot; she is sweating through the sheets—Waldek kneels beside him in church and points out the priest who demanded she have the child that would kill her; Leon is a boy running through the streets, a half-full baby's bottle in his hands; he struggles to cover it with the rubber nipple; he is being chased and his father is weeping at his mother's bedside and Emma Goldman is banging truth into a lectern and when she takes her glasses off the resemblance gives him chills.

Then it all stops, the motion, the visions disappear—you awake from a dream, that fast and stark. The president is so close Leon could reach his hand out and touch him. Time no longer moves. The president's hand is in the process of shaking the hand of the man immediately in front of Leon but the movement is so slow it is imperceptible.

There is a slight upward turn to the president's lips that might be a smile or perhaps he is about to say something when Leon pulls the trigger.

FRAME 1: Leon is stepping toward the president, his handkerchief-wrapped right hand thrust toward the older man's belly. The sound of the blast is so loud and shocking that it silences all else, the organ playing the Bach sonata, the rumble of the crowd. The blast echoes, resounds throughout the hall. No motion, except that the gunpowder ignites the handkerchief and a flame leaps up from it though the gun is not exposed. The onlookers, security guards and dignitaries, recede from view as the images of the two primary players elongate into giants, tall shadows fleshed out against the cavernous walls of the Temple. It is as if the right hand of Leon Czolgosz itself can fire bullets and ignite. It is as if he were some avenging angel. As if he were not human.

FRAME 2: The president has raised his arms like a victim of some cheap holdup, and a guard has grabbed his side for support. There is fear in McKinley's eyes, that and shock. The flame has risen and fallen on Leon's handkerchief, leaving a black char that exposes the end of his gun's barrel. There is the smoke from the fire and the smoke from the first shot and the smoke from the second shot, and the echoing blast from the discharge of the first bullet has merged into the blast of the second, carrying it out longer and louder so it thunders through the crowd and down the Midway, into the tents of Dreamworld, the Infant Incubator, the House Upside Down. The bullet has wormed its way through the president's layers of skin, fat and muscle, his pancreas, a kidney, the walls of his stomach, and lodged somewhere between the rear wall and the muscles of his back, the bullet's casing battered, dented, shorn of metallic shards it has left behind in his organs, veins, and arteries, shards that will be picked up like rebel castaways in his bloodstream on a revolutionary escapade to the heart. The large Negro behind Leon has stepped toward him, grabbed his shoulder, and lifted the arm with the gun up toward the ceiling. A woman with a hat covered with fresh flowers on the brim faints. The blood is not yet visible through the president's white starched shirt.

FRAME 3: Leon is facedown on the floor. There is a knee in his back, a boot kicking his ribs on one side, someone is stepping on his spine, someone is kicking his face, stepping on his head, his arm is twisted out of joint, his wrist is wrenched out of its socket it feels like. He has just been able to turn his head to the side to avoid another kick and there he sees the president, lying on his back. McKinley's aides have gently placed him down on the floor and they are unbuttoning his shirt and wiping his face and there is blood somewhere though Leon cannot be sure if it is the president's or his own, it is the same blood. The president's face is at ease, no anger there, no longer the shock, no fear, and his mouth is open. The two men are lying there, Leon on his stomach, the president on his back, and McKinley is saying something. He is speaking to Leon.

11 · AFTER 4:07 P.M. · September 6, 1901

"Get me back to that Negro," Hearst says. He is pacing his office in Chicago, holding the telephone.

"The Negro?" Creelman yells to be heard over the frantic cacophony of clacking typewriters and telegraphs, reporters yelling their stories into telephones in an Exposition Tent that has become a newsroom for those unlucky enough to be stranded in Buffalo on what was supposed to be a two-day gig to cover the president's speech.

"I'm trying to construct the front page in my head," Hearst says. "He was behind the shooter, you say? What was his—"

"Czolgosz. Chawl—gallsh. Leon. Early twenties, parents Polish they say—"

"Visuals, Creelman. What does he look like? And shout it—I'll hold the phone out for the picture folks."

"Young, slender. Clean-shaven, well-dressed. Handsome. A shock of black hair tossed over one side, a bit stern in the face but with eyes that pierce through you and a sensitivity there, too. Or do you mean how did he look after they beat the bejesus out of him?"

"When did that happen?"

"As soon as he shot. The Negro, James Parker's his name, six foot if he's an inch, was standing behind and he grabbed Czolgosz's right arm quick as a cat before he could get another shot off, second or third, then tackled him. The guards around McKinley just standing there saying, 'Aw Christ.'"

"How the hell did he get so close with a gun?"

"He had it wrapped in a handkerchief. Security says they usually won't let anyone near McKinley unless your hands are exposed, but it was so damned hot they let folks hold their hankies today. Others say the guards figured his hand was bandaged 'cause it was hurt. Did I tell you how hot it is here?"

"You know, Creelman, that's a hoot."

"Well, boss, I think we better play down the humorous side. For a while anyway."

"Sure, sure. I'm just talking. Go on."

"So Parker tackles Czolgosz and then the guards jump into action and everyone piles on, kicking and stomping on the bastard, his head, body, everything. They wanted to rip him to pieces right there in the Temple of Music. You've got the whole crowd rushing to wreak holy havoc on the poor fool. A lynch mob. He's not a pretty sight."

"Lord, that's a picture, too! I see two columns on page one: the president is shot on the left, and on the right, the brutalization of Coalgus—"

"Chawlgallsh."

"Make it Leon; keep it personal. Bottom right, six lines on a body found on Mulberry Row. Bottom left: family of three found starving after father thrown out of work. More on Page 2. Thirty-point headline: TRAGEDY. Or VIOLENCE. Leave it vague; let the reader connect the dots."

"I don't think so, boss. We've got to be real careful about this one. I've already heard the talk. People are looking for scapegoats and Big Bill Hearst has a bright red bull's-eye on his chest."

"Awwww hell. Somebody light me a smoke."

" 'Killer inflamed by Hearst's scathing attacks on the President.' They're trotting out the worst of Ambrose Bierce and Arthur Brisbane on William McKinley. 'When there are bad institutions or bad men, then killing must be done.' That sort of thing."

"Where's that smoke I wanted?! A cigar, a cigarette. Something."

"Those bullets are being melted down into a halo over McKinley's head."

"I thought the bastard's going to live."

"Who knows? He's conscious; he's got a fighting chance. But still, I hear the stories the other papers are going with. 'As the president lay with two bullets in his side, fighting gallantly with death, he told those who were apprehending his would-be killer, 'Go easy with him, boys.' 'Don't let them hurt him.' And 'Take care how you tell my wife.'"

"Christ."

Somebody finally hands Hearst a cigarette and he drags on it hard. A secretary is still holding the earpiece of the telephone in the center of the room as reporters and sketch artists crowd around it. The door is closed so Hearst can see, through the glass, typewriters busy outside in his pressroom, but all he can hear is the frantic etching of charcoal and scribbling of notes on pads in his office.

Then the sketch artist holds out two large pieces of paper. In one, the president, pale and bloated, outlines of dollar signs coating his body, staggers from the assassin's gun, and the light hits in such a way that there is the hint of a rainbow that tracks red stripes from the exposed tip of the barrel to the flag in the background. In the next sketch poor Leon Czolgosz lies on the floor, his beautiful face pummeled and bloodied, surrounded by a rabid, angry crowd near out of control. One of the men kicking him is, as any reader of the Hearst papers will recognize, Mark Hanna. Leon's arms are spread out on the floor that appears tilted up so his body is raised like on a crucifix.

Hearst can see, in his mind, the entire front page of the Extra edition plotted out. The sketches will be refined to look like photographs, there will be stories of Leon's life and the president's, and that Negro, James Parker, and the ordinary lives and deaths of the day in the streets of New York and Chicago and San Francisco, September 6, 1901: all aspects. News does not need to be tied up with simple morals, lessons learned. Just lay it out there, rich and poor alike; if it is fiction, then it is Tolstoy not Aesop, complex and layered. *True history*. The lessons will be learned, they are so obvious how could they not be.

"My front page, Creelman," Hearst says. "It would have been so damned beautiful."

"I don't believe in the republican form of government and I don't believe we should have any rulers. It is right to kill them."

It is the day after the shooting and Leon is in his cell. A bare bunk, a narrow shaft of light streaming through the bars above and behind him. Directly beneath the window bricks are chipped away to form a hole that is the toilet. Leon's blood is still on the floor where he slept, and it is caked on his face, too. Someone must have shackled his legs with irons and cuffed his hands but he cannot remember.

The policeman grabs the metal links of his handcuffs and lifts him up to a chair. The room was dark, but now there is a bright light spraying in his eyes so close he can feel the heat.

"Why did you want to kill the president" was the question but now the policeman wants to know if he is an anarchist, who else was involved, who put him up to the job. The questions are coming from everywhere though he cannot see faces in the blinding light.

"McKinley was going around the country shouting prosperity. But there was no prosperity for the poor man."

"What are you? A socialist?"

"I am an anarchist. I don't believe in marriage. I believe in free love. I don't believe in rulers."

"Someone put you up to it, Leon? Your name's Leon, right? Leon."

"Others were involved," says another cop.

"You hang around with other crazy reds, I'd wager."

"I know other people who believe what I do, that it would be a good thing to kill the president and have no rulers."

"Who, Leon?"

"Tell us and we can help you."

"We can't help unless you tell us."

"The anarchists, who were they?"

"Who believes like you do? Who doesn't believe in rulers?"

"You heard it somewhere."

"I have heard it at meetings and in public halls. I heard a lot of people talk like that."

"Who?"

"Who talked like that?"

"Who?"

"Emma Goldman was the one I heard."

Instantly the light before him swings and somebody gets up and the door opens and people are rushing out the door. There are just a couple of policemen left, Leon can see them now from the light through the open door, and Leon has more to say. He is not finished with his statement.

"What I want to say I want to be published," Leon says. "I killed President McKinley because I done my duty." Leon looks around to see if anyone is writing this down. It is important, his words. "I don't believe in one man having so much service," he says, "and another man having none."

EXTRA!
PRESIDENT McKINLEY SHOT BY ANARCHIST!
———————
Emma Goldman Involved in Anarchist Plot
to Kill the President!

Emma is in St. Louis when she hears the boy hawking newspapers. She fishes out a coin and grabs a copy.

A streetcar passes and she jumps in, takes a seat and holds the paper up to cover her face. Where is Emma? is the story. The manhunt for the likely ringleader of the anarchist plot is spread out across the country. Close associates of the notorious anarchist are being rounded up in Chicago.

Police Vow They Will Find Emma Goldman and
Bring Her to Justice.

Abe Isaak, arrested on charges of conspiracy to kill the president. Three friends are rounded up as well. The police are searching for Isaak's son. *Gather up the anarchists, anyone who knew the devil Goldman, anyone you can find.*

On the front page is a sketch of the shooter. Emma looks closely at him, fleshes out the details in her mind. The youth and intensity of Alex as a younger man, when he attempted the *attendat* on Frick. The same sensitive eyes, the seriousness of purpose. *There are souls in whom injustice appears like boils, something inside them that must burst through.*

The face looks familiar. She searches her memory and then it strikes her: *Nieman*, the boy she met in Cleveland, who followed her to the train station.

She thinks of Alex in his three-foot cell, alone for months, a rat for company.

Abe Isaak and his son: in jail cells for the crime of befriending Emma Goldman.

The next morning she dresses herself in a sailor's hat and a blue veil and takes a train to Chicago.

The veterans of the Grand Army of the Republic pass a resolution commanding every member to exclude from his household Hearst's *Journal* newspaper, it being a teacher of anarchism and a vile sheet.

There is talk in Congress that all believers in anarchism be excluded from the country.

"I felt it here," McKinley says, touching his stomach. "The bullet hit me here. The other fell off my shirt."

Ida tries to smile.

"All will be well, my darling," she says. It is something she thinks he might say. "God's will. Not ours."

"Oh, my love," McKinley says, "the doctors will have me up and smoking a cigar in a fortnight. I even drank some soup today."

"So I heard."

"In a fortnight, my love." He has no more energy to speak. He closes his eyes. "In a fortnight."

When Emma arrives in Chicago she finds the apartment of a friend, a wealthy minister.

The police are everywhere looking for her; the papers are filled with talk of the manhunt. The newspapers reconstruct her life, how she might have engineered the shooting, who else was involved. The police find out she was in Buffalo in July, then interrogate who she stayed with there, anyone who may know something, who may have seen her, seen her with the assassin Czolgosz.

The *Tribune* offers $5,000 for an exclusive interview with her. She decides she will need the money for lawyers and calls to accept the offer.

Later that day Emma is taking a bath when she hears a crash of broken glass. It is the police, coming through the window. She slips on a kimono.

"We're looking for Emma Goldman," one cop says, stepping into the living room.

"We heard she was here," says the other.

"I the cleaning lady," Emma says. "I Swedish. No speak English."

She can hardly believe it when the police leave her alone; she cannot recall police ever believing her before. But then, it is the first time she has lied to them.

She almost feels sorry for them as they bumble around the apartment, searching through boxes of Bibles and under couches and chairs for the evil mastermind, Emma Goldman. When they are getting ready to leave, one of them picks up a fountain pen that is lying on the bookshelf.

"Hey," the cop says, "this pen's got writing on it. Says, Emma Goldman."

The two men look at each other, knowing there is a conclusion to draw—a deduction, an induction, something—but it just hovers there like smoke in the room.

Emma places her hands out before her. "Officers," she says. "I am Emma Goldman."

Thomas Edison, in Buffalo for the Exposition, offers use of his new x-ray machine to assist the doctors in locating the bullet inside the president's body.

The president's doctors decline the offer.

The doctors operate. McKinley's stomach has been lacerated, both its front and rear walls, and the pancreas and a kidney may have been damaged.

They do not find the bullet.

"You was with Czolgosz in Buffalo!"

Emma is at central booking in Chicago, a policeman's red face in spitting distance, another swinging his fists. She is tossed into a chair and the flash of a camera blinds her.

"Turn to the left."

The police bring her to the jail, all shoving and dragging and cramped paddy wagons. The first night they wake her up with a reflector inches from her face.

"You're burning my eyes."

"We'll burn more before we get through with you."

Every night the interrogation is repeated.

"I saw you myself. I seen you with that son of a bitch at the Expo."

"Don't lie now."

"Your lover's already confessed. He's given you up, Goldman."

"You financed Czolgosz all the way. Your accomplices decided to save their skins. If you were half as smart as they say, you'd do the same."

"You've faked enough. You keep this up you're sure to get the chair."

"You don't confess, you'll go the way of those Haymarket bastards."

"What have you got to say?"

There must be fifty faces staring at her behind the blinding reflector though she only hears the voices. Her memory of the past nights in jails have merged to form a single nightmare.

"Why'd you want to kill the president?"

"You don't understand," Emma says. "If McKinley were here, I would nurse him."

Somebody laughs behind the blinding light.

"And what about Czolgosz?"

"The boy? Blame those who are responsible for the injustice and inhumanity that dominate the world."

"So you did wish the president dead?"

She shrugs.

"And you, Goldman? What about your blame?"

"I have said all I have to say. I know nothing about the act."

"Will he survive?" Hearst pleads into the telephone.

The lights in his office are off and he is looking out of the window, onto the street. Hearst has ordered his staff to reverse his editorial policy overnight. Instead of the usual indictments, the *Journal*'s pages are full of paeans to our heroic leader and vicious attacks on the nation's anarchist foes.

Hearst has offered Emma Goldman $5,000 for an interview, a trap so he can expose her complicity, her duplicity, her guile for all to see . . . but then the police snap her up in Chicago with another offer.

A shout rises up from outside. Someone on the street is holding a lit torch, and others are holding a trio of crude scarecrows, barely recognizable except for the name tags posted to their chests: Emma Goldman, Leon Czolgosz, William Randolph Hearst. There is a noose around the necks of each.

It strikes Hearst as more than a trifle unfair that his competitors insist on continually . . . revisiting . . . a few scattered lines, wrenched mercilessly out of context, from his papers' outdated disagreements with this president. Such as where his editors suggested that McKinley should be killed, for example.

"He isn't in such bad shape, really," Creelman says.

Hearst had forgotten he was holding a telephone and there was someone on the other end of the line.

"What do you say?"

"McKinley. His condition is on the mend. The wounds probably won't kill him."

"He'll survive then?"

"I didn't say that. I said the bullet wounds shouldn't do him in. But the doctors might."

"God help us all," says Hearst.

The matrons at the jail bring Emma letters and she reads them and wonders if they come from her interrogators.

"You damn bitch of an anarchist. If I could get at you I would tear your heart out and feed it to my dog."

"We will cut your tongue out, soak your carcass in oil, and burn you alive."

"Murderous Emma Goldman, you will burn in hell-fire for your treachery to your country."

The letters from her friends are kept from her for days and are then given to her so edited they are unintelligible.

The doctors measure Leon's head, his ears, the slope of his forehead. The shape of the head is normal, the face is symmetrical, though one eyebrow appears askew, as it was reportedly cut some years ago in a fight or a factory. A light is flashed in his eyes and the results noted: *pupils are normal and react to light.* A doctor taps a metal hammer onto his knee and the results are noted: *reflexes are normal.* A doctor opens his mouth: *the tongue is clean.* A doctor brushes his hand against Leon's face: *the skin is moist and in excellent condition.* A history is taken from the suspect and the results are noted: *he does not drink in excess, uses tobacco moderately, eats well, his bowels are regular.* He appears in good health.

The doctors conclude that the suspect Leon Czolgosz has false beliefs, the result of false teaching and not the result of disease. He is not to be classed as a degenerate, because we do not find the stigmata of degeneration. *He is the product of anarchy, sane and responsible.*

Emma is brought to the Cook County jail. A guard comes to her cell at night.

The guard says, "I was here when Parsons and Spies and the rest of the Haymarket anarchists were brought before their hanging."

Emma smiles. She has sensed that Parsons and Spies are with her even before the guard tells her.

"Buffalo wants to extradite you," the guard says. "They want to try you with Czolgosz."

"There's no evidence. There is nothing they can get on me."

"And was there evidence in Haymarket?" the guard says.

"We had some good times, Mr. President," Mark Hanna says. "We will again."

He is sitting at McKinley's bedside, holding his hand.

"I remember when I first spotted you in that courtroom, defending those bastard strikers. If I may say so, Mr. President, you can never truly appreciate the value of property unless you have some substance, a million or so. I am sorry for saying it, and Lord knows you gave it a try, but there you have it, plain as day."

McKinley remains silent in the bed.

"We tried so many times, didn't we?" Hanna goes on. "We fought and fought and we had some hard times, some setbacks, but there were good times too and then we finally made it and how."

Hanna takes a cigar out from his vest pocket.

"I gave you the taste for a good cigar. I'm sorry for that." He bites the end off. "Damn it, I'm not. There are pleasures in this world, too."

A nurse taps him on a shoulder and he puts the cigar away for a moment.

"Ida will be well," Hanna says. "The nation will survive. We will suffer, Lord knows, but we will persevere. Lincoln, Garfield. The damn nation's cursed is all."

McKinley is just lying on his back, eyes open, staring blankly up at the ceiling. There are nurses and doctors and needles, tanks of oxygen.

"I made you the president, Bill," Hanna whispers now. He does not want the others in the room to hear him, he does not want his friend to hear his voice cracking. No one must hear him cry. "I am sorry for that."

Hanna places the cigar on the table next to McKinley.

"I'll leave a box of Garcias for you," he says. "For when you are ready."

"Czolgosz, my name is Titus. I have been appointed by the court to represent you. Let me make clear my position from the outset, as I will tell the jury and judge when the time comes. I detest what you have done. President McKinley was a paragon of virtue, a truly noble man. You struck him down I know not why. What goes on in your mind I cannot fathom. Nor do I intend to try. But this nation is more just than you deserve, and so you are entitled to legal representation. You are not entitled to escape your fate, a fate you must be well aware of. But you will be given lawyers and a trial. And you will then get what you deserve. Have you anything to say?"

Leon says nothing. Through the bars of his cell he can hear the crowd outside.

"String him up! Lynch him with his mistress Emma! Hang him now! Throw the switch! Burn the body!"

The chants are incessant. It is like a factory; it grates, it booms, it consumes the space in his skull, then becomes background noise, the air in the room, wind. Death is no longer a fear.

He does not turn around to look at his lawyer. There are images in his head he does not want to disturb.

"You know they will have to kill you," his lawyer says. "The trial has not even begun and already the applications are coming in to watch your execution. There aren't enough chairs is the problem."

"I am not afraid to die," Leon says. "We all have to die sometime."

The president's temperature is down, his mind is lucid. His doctors are encouraged. He appears out of danger. There is talk of placing him on a train back to Washington to recuperate.

The emergency passed, Vice President Roosevelt leaves Buffalo to rejoin his family on their camping trip in the Adirondacks.

The days have a pattern. Emma is brought letters by the guards. She tears them up and throws the scraps into their faces.

Most days the guards bring her to the court where the prosecutors from Buffalo argue for her extradition, though it has become obvious there is no evidence that Emma played a part in the shooting. The prosecutors now simply plead for her to be delivered to Buffalo without bothering to recite facts or law supporting their position. *We know Mrs. Goldman, we know what she was up to. Let us have her.*

Even the judge has grown weary of the State's empty arguments.

After fifteen days in jail, she is released.

Hearst has Creelman call him immediately whenever there is news of the president's condition. It seems, to Hearst, that the prospects of McKinley track his own fate.

The president is able to drink beef broth, then coffee; today he nibbled on a slice of toast. He even asked for a cigar.

The dummies hung in effigy outside of Hearst's office at the *Chicago American* are removed, the angry crowds go home. Though he still cannot escape the jeers on the street or the boxes of hate mail he receives each day.

Then there appears to be a setback. The press is told that the president is fatigued. Vice President Roosevelt is alerted. Mark Hanna is summoned to Buffalo again.

When will it end?

Hearst feels like a caged tiger, his jaws clamped shut while

McKinley's fate wavers from martyrdom to recovery, and Pulitzer and his other rivals taunt him mercilessly outside the bars. No, Hearst is no longer hung in effigy, he may not have a bullet in his side, but isn't his a deeper pain? A misery of the soul, an agony of the spirit? Each day Hearst must order loyal Creelman and Bierce to dull their incisive wit and write like some *New York Times* lackey for the bankers and trusts, and Hearst must print paeans to the president. He has even taken to following the *Times*'s leads: today the *Journal* printed that the father of the assassin Czolgosz helped lynch a man twenty-five years ago, then turned state's evidence to convict the leader of the mob. The assassin's mother—or stepmother; Hearst isn't sure—says, "I always thought Leon was crazy, he was a coward." His own mother? What humiliation! He prints it all: stories of the anarchist cabal, the Paterson Ring, Emma Goldman plotting the attack. But does that stop his critics from accusing him and his loyal band of journalists of—why beat around the bush? his rivals and critics surely don't!—attempting to kill the president . . . with words! With truths!

Hearst stomps to the typewriter in his office and bangs frantically on the keys.

> From coast to coast this newspaper has been attacked and is being attacked with savage ferocity by the incompetent, the failures of journalism, by the kept organs of plutocracy heading the mob. One of the Hearst papers' offenses is that they have fought for the people, and against privilege and class pride and class greed and class stupidity and class heartlessness with more daring weapons, with more force and talent than any other newspapers in the country.
>
> Note the thrift of the parasitic press! It would draw profit from the terrible deed of the wretch who shot down the president.

Hearst has a date at the theater. As has become his custom, he will sneak out the back door, raise the collar of his overcoat high, and slip his revolver into his jacket pocket, just in case. But before he does, he passes Bierce's desk.

"Mr. Bierce," Hearst says, handing him the screed he has just typed. "Print this as soon as we can come out of hiding."

. . .

Leon's father and Waldek visit him in jail. His father is dressed in a suit, as if for church; his body stooped, hat in hand. His hair is more gray than Leon remembers. He is so thin and bony, withering away. It is not time that has done this, Leon realizes. It is the distance.

"The neighbors, everyone in town," his father says. "They say if it was us." He speaks quietly, staring at his feet. Leon hears his step-mother's words out of his father's mouth: more puppetry. "Murderers, they say. Assassins."

Leon walks away from him to the far corner of the cell and sits down on the cold floor, leaving his father near the door with the guards.

Waldek follows his brother to the corner.

"The girls came too," Waldek says. "They stay outside. You understand. The prison."

Leon nods.

The two sit in silence on the cold floor. They look at their father, the guards, the bars in the window above them with the light shining through. The screams of the crowd outside.

"Lynch the assassin!"

"String him up!"

Waldek squints at his brother. It is the sound of the crowd; it takes some getting used to. Leon wants to say: *It's all right, the crowd out there. I killed their president and now they will kill me. It is all right.*

"Where is Frank?" Leon says.

Waldek shrugs. "It's been years."

They are silent again as their father mutters small talk to the guards; the crowd's yells become a rumble, rhythmic and indecipherable.

"You read the papers about Father? A lynch mob? I never heard before."

Waldek says nothing, but Leon knows from his look he has read the stories and they are true. They sit and listen to the mob some more.

"Do you still have it?" Leon says finally.

"What, Leon?"

"The Bible. The Polish Bible."

"It's somewhere."

"Father," Leon calls out. The cell is so small his father can hear him with little more than a whisper. "Did you ever speak to that priest? Did you ever tell him what he did to our mother?"

His father looks at Leon, puzzled. Then he shakes his head and walks out of the cell.

Morris Vandeveer has taken his entire inventory and loaded it onto a cart and, taking on the role of the plow horse, he pushes it himself down the Midway, out the Expo gates, onto the streets of Buffalo. He thinks, at first, he should stop by John Milburn's house, as Milburn, the night before the shooting, had expressed an interest in purchasing uniforms sufficient to clothe a battalion (government contracts were in the works, Milburn assured him), but then the notion drifts out of his head. The sound of the gunshots he heard at the Temple still reverberate in his skull, chasing out all other passing thoughts. And the idea of it: a pull of a finger, the magical release of blood. Yes, the president may live. Yes, Morris never held a fondness for William McKinley. Yes, the president was little more than a potential customer to him, the foundation of Morris's planned financial resurrection. Yes, yes, yes. But the disturbing principle still nustled, like a hog's snout, the roots of Morris's psyche: the machinery—technological, political, cultural, whathaveyou—that causes a bullet to attack a human heart, be it in Havana, Buffalo, or wherever the next murder or war happens to occur.

Morris feels sick, he feels dirty. His uniforms, piled high on his cart, whence their beauty? Whence the sly humor he had felt, imagining America's fighting forces marching off in sleek silk more fitting in a Paris boudoir than a battlefield? Adornments for corpses in production is what they are. *Another man's stock and trade, not Morris Vandeveer's.*

He reaches the alley, panting—he has raced here, the cart is heavy, the years have taken their toll on Morris and his legs were never of much use—and when he sees the hoboes, the urchins, the ragged creatures of the street, he tosses to them the entire inventory of what was to be the Triple S Military Surplus Corporation, until his cart, full of the most dashing military outfits the nation had ever seen, is empty.

12 · McKINLEY · September 13, 1901, Late Afternoon

"It may have been the broth," says one of the doctors.

They are huddled in the far corner of the president's room in John Milburn's house, whispering.

"Or the coffee."

"His weight."

"His smoking."

"Twenty cigars a day is not good."

"It's contamination of the blood. Metal from the bullet."

"You're suggesting I could have removed it when we had him open and I resent the implication. Besides, this was a heart attack, not gangrene."

"One of my other patients broke her water. I will return as soon as I can."

"Perhaps we can try Mr. Edison's machine. We could find the bullet."

"Gentlemen," McKinley says. His voice is scratchy and dry.

The doctors turn in unison toward the bed.

"He is speaking," one says.

"He is awake," says another.

"We did not mean to disturb you, Mr. President."

"It is useless, gentlemen," McKinley says. His eyes are open in narrow slits, but he can see the doctors, the nurses at his bedside, the syringes on the table, the vials of medications on the bookshelves. In the hallway there is a piano with scored music spread out and in the next room a rocking chair where Ida would like to crochet—he said as much to her when they first came to Buffalo how many nights ago he can't remember.

"I think we ought to have prayer," McKinley says. His voice is so weak the doctors must step closer to hear. "I would like to see my wife."

The doctors consult one another with nods, and McKinley smiles slightly it seems, and you cannot escape the fact that he is not just a patient but the president.

One of the nurses walks out of the room with one of the doctors and there are whispers in the hall, scurrying and telephone calls and messengers sent out the door. An automobile is cranked up and chugs to a start, horses are hitched and somewhere a special train takes off for the Adirondacks where a search party will scale Mount Marcy to find the camp of the vice president, Teddy Roosevelt.

There has been this gnawing pain in his side where McKinley can feel the bullet. In his mind he can see it lodged there smack in the middle of a muscle in between his stomach and the back of his rib cage. That soldier at Antietam, the tin cup in his hand had chipped blue paint and a gold rim, and the rifle shot must have come from the other side of them or McKinley would have felt the whir of the bullet over his supply wagon or perhaps it would have hit him and not the soldier. The cup jerked out of the soldier's hand and the hot coffee splattered on both of their blue coats. McKinley was about to say, *I just brewed it, maybe it's worms in the sugar*, and then the soldier fell forward, facedown in the mud just behind the rear hoof of one of the horses hitched to the supply wagon. McKinley knelt down and found the hole in the side of the soldier's jacket where the blood was leaking out, then felt around for the bullet and there was an instant where he could visualize its path through the young man's midsection, if only he could find it and remove it, like a splinter, a parasite—the metal projectile was the illness—but it was too late; the soldier was dying. Then he stood up and saw the battlefield cluttered with bodies, boys like himself tending to the dying and the dead. An ocean of death.

He wonders what it would be like if he were back in Washington, in his own bed in the Executive Mansion. Would he see himself as part of that official history, with Lincoln, with Garfield? Here in John Milburn's house in Buffalo he belongs only to the broad, vast continuum of death.

"My love."

His hand is lifted up and now he sees Ida's face above him, suspended, her hair done up in braids that cannot contain her vivacious curls; a mind of their own, they spring out all over her forehead. Yes, he is the young soldier again now, and she is young Ida Saxton, just back from Europe, and small Canton cannot contain her. She is running through the wheat fields and he is chasing her and she is holding her skirts up so she can race over the stalks and the wheat is blown by the wind for God is a painter and the elements his palette. Lord, she was pretty. Lord, he was in love with her.

My God, the continuum of death.

He and Ida are standing over little Katie's crib and the little girl's skin is so cold and her eyes are closed and she never had a chance to live.

He and Ida are standing over little Ida's crib and her skin is so cold and her eyes are closed and she never had a chance to live.

My God, the awfulness of it all. My God, the cruelty.

He has spent his life distancing himself from these memories: *press on, work to be done,* but Ida feels it always; she is always standing there, beside their deathly cribs, she has been looking out for them. *Always.* He wants to sit up and hug his wife, if only he could; he wants to clutch Ida to his chest and thank her, though that word is so inadequate. He will embrace her with his soul and bathe her in the tears he should have shed every hour of these past thirty years. He will give his life for her, for that is all he has to give.

"What's that sound?" someone says. A nurse, a doctor, one of the servants.

Ida is the only one close enough to hear him. She is kneeling on the floor at his bedside, her face so close to his they could be kissing full on the lips. She can feel on her mouth the faint hints of what remains of his breath. It would be so like William to say it was God's will, not ours, be done. She never liked church—that was William—but he had a beautiful voice, rich and deep, and there was a Sunday they took a picnic by the river—that was Ida's idea—this was soon after they met, they hadn't married, who could have known about little Katie, little Ida, who could have known there was no future; William was the young soldier, her hero, and for Ida they took a picnic and for William then they went to services and they stood next to each other in the pew so even when the choir sang she could hear him sing, his voice, her William.

Nearer my God to Thee,
Nearer to Thee.

There let the way appear
steps unto heaven;
All that Thou sendest me
in mercy given;
Angels to beckon me
nearer, my God, to Thee,
Nearer, my God, to Thee,
nearer to Thee.

Ida opens her eyes. She has never been so close to William as she is at this moment. She can see the very pores of his skin, the blisters of blood in his eyes, the points of color that make up the pupil, each strand of hair. It all seems oversized and vast, a mountain, not a face, something elemental. He smells odd. It is the medicine and how many days without a cigar, and the nurses, the doctors. He has not been shaved so there are gray hairs sprouting out from his chin and cheeks. She should recognize the details; she could have examined him this closely throughout their lives together, as she had vowed she would watch Ida and Katie had they lived; watched the hairy stubble sprout, then turn from brown to red to gray, watched the skin dry up into papery flakes, the bones thin and arch, the stomach bulge; the body transforms. There is a whisper of strength she feels, a faint wind. *She will endure.*

She looks into his eyes; the graying brows are heavy but his eyes are staring up at her. If there is another message there she does not, cannot, read it. Simply: God's will, not ours. Good-bye. *Good-bye.*

It is only then that she realizes she can no longer feel his breath. She places her fingers on his mouth. The skin is cool, there is no response. She stands up and leans over to kiss her beloved William on the lips.

13 · **DEPARTURES** · October 29, 1901–December 21, 1919

There are stories you hear on death row, from the guards, other men in their cells. A history to the place. There was the man who robbed a stagecoach and had the ill fortune to frighten a woman passenger so that her heart gave out on her, right there on the spot. There was the man who poisoned a stranger with whom he was having a drink. The man who killed his young wife and two daughters with an axe.

Of course there is more to it than that, one learns. It is not simply random violence. There are stories within the stories. The man who robbed the stagecoach had been fired for leading a strike, the woman on the stagecoach was the boss's daughter and his lover, he had broken off the relationship and she had her father fire him in spite. There are stories of justification and excuse, stories of the innocent, the falsely accused. The stranger whom the man poisoned had committed some unpardonable sin that could never be forgot, or remembered clearly. The man who killed his wife and daughters did not kill his wife or daughters. These are the stories you hear, stories we will never know for certain, secrets taken to the graves.

What do you learn on death row? Two things. Nothing is simple. And no one can know the truth.

During the month Leon has lived at Auburn Penitentiary, his cell was only twenty feet from the chair. Had he cared to, he could have looked out through the bars just so and caught a glimpse. But now is the first time he has seen it. The uniformed men, prison guards in their dress blues, grab each arm and walk him down the short hallway to the chamber. When he last walked without leg irons or handcuffs he does not recall. And there it is, the chair: wooden, high-backed, oddly wired with metal plates, cuffs, and straps. Where has he seen it before?

The Time Machine.

Yes. In Cleveland, lying in bed with Megan, telling her stories of books he has read, Bellamy's utopian visions and H. G. Wells, the vehicle that transports you across time, through past and future. The chair is a chariot, *winged history.*

The chair is a throne. Who else can know with certainty the instant of his death, preordained, precise? It is a privilege to partake in this ritualistic death.

Leon grasps the arms of the chair firmly as the men strap him in with belts across the chest and arms and legs and around the neck.

He closes his eyes and this is the vision: Leon is holding hands with Megan, and he is carrying their child, little Leon, on his lap, and the utopias merge: the Time Machine lands them in a world where Bellamy has traveled, a world with no rulers, no rich, no poor, no sickness, no want. He is certain of this vision, this future. *How does one get there from here? Where does one begin?*

Someone has shaved a circle of hair from the top of his head and wrenches a sponge over him so water drips down his face.

In front of him are men and women sitting in chairs that face him. He expects to see someone he recognizes, but no one looks familiar.

He looks around again but, no, his father is not there. His mother is not there. No Waldek. No Megan.

He expects someone to ask him if he has something to say but no one does so he clears his throat and says it.

"I killed the president because he was an enemy of the people, the good working people." He speaks resolutely, a voice without fear that takes the men and women in the crowd aback, unsettles them. "I am not sorry for my crime." He pauses, searches the audience again, then finishes quietly. "I am sorry I could not see my father."

Before he can say more the warden quickly lifts his hand. Leon knows that the signal is an order: when he lowers his hand, someone will throw the switch, triggering the first jolt.

Eighteen hundred volts of electricity. Through the head. The water on the bald patch of his skull conducts the charge like a lightning rod in a storm—that is the theory, that is how it burns the brain first. And that is where the death row wisdom ends; what happens to the brain and body is left to dreams and conjecture in late-night rantings through the bars to formless voices in another cell of the prison while the scent of sizzled skin is fresh and hangs heavy in the air. Leon sees it as a moment when the lights go out and you reemerge in the next world. Where the Time Machine lands. There is a den and a fire and a child, a growing boy, in the future, gazing over the mantel at a painting of a solitary courageous act that made history take a turn.

From where Emma is standing up on the deck of the ship, she is high enough that she can see the whole shipyard. The dock is stuffed with people, as if the ocean has spilled over and left a beach full of shattered shells, men, women, children, bundled up against the cold December breeze, wrapped in scarves, waving at the passengers on the ship that towers over them. Waving, waving.

On the dock a crowd of reporters with pads and photographers stand in a loose circle, listening, laughing, taking down notes. The man in the center is short and squat with a pug face but he is dressed nattily: a blue cashmere coat, matching scarf, a hat that sets it off, a yellow carnation in his lapel, and a perfume that smells like a French lady's.

"Don't call it the *Buford*," the squat man says. J. Edgar Hoover: the Justice Department's young crusading star. "I call it the *Soviet Ark*," Hoover says. "It's not just the Emma and Alex Show. Two-hundred and forty-nine communists, anarchists and ne'er-do-wells. I can give you the details on each and every. Merry Christmas, America!"

Surrounding Hoover in the center of the circle of press are congressmen and senators, posing for photos, smiling with the steamship behind them.

Hoover is waving and laughing at the passengers, and his entourage joins him in hoots and whistles. *Good riddance, Red Emma. Fare thee well, Comrade Berkman.* Fragments of Hoover's oration are audible over the shouting and laughing; words spray here and there like fire from a Gatling gun: *subversion, conspiracy, un-American, perversion, free love, communist, socialist, anarchist, assassin.*

> The True Story of How J. Edgar Hoover, Armed Only With The Slender Evidentiary Reed Offered Him By The Sketchy Citizenship Status of Emma Goldman's First and Since Absconded Husband, Jacob Kersner, Employed His Acute Legal Acumen, Timing, and Indominatable American Spirit and Will, To Eradicate, Via Deportation, The Red Rebels Who Had Tormented The Nation For a Quarter Century & More, And Were Sure To Stop At Nothing Until America Bedded Down With Their Bolshevik Brethren.

The press frantically take notes because it is important to document what Hoover tells them; the stories must be published, transmitted, delivered to the people.

"Were you surprised Emma gave up her appeal, Mr. Hoover?" someone shouts.

"Boys," Hoover says, "the Supreme Court would have upheld the deportation, mark my words. They were toying with her was all."

"But they took her case." The reporter won't quit. "She did it for love, don't you think?"

Hoover snarls at the man, young and slim with a handsome chin and a chest that lunges out at him. *Love?* he almost says. But then Hoover sees something and, his mind clear again, points. The press follow as if their noses were hooked to his hand. It is out there in the harbor, but it is not, as the reporters first think, the Statue of Liberty, fondling her beacon of light.

"There! There they are!"

Now it is obvious what Hoover is pointing at: up there on the deck of the ship, the old couple leaning over the railing.

The photographers rush to the edge of the dock as someone smashes a champagne bottle on the bow of the ship, and the crowd roars; everyone is waving their hats, everyone is laughing, every camera is flashing, every pen is documenting it all as the ship recedes from the dock, retreats from view, and the ocean begins to separate it from America.

"Merry Christmas, Emma!" yells J. Edgar Hoover.

"Frick died two weeks ago," Emma says. "So we outlived him in the end."

Berkman, still leaning over the railing of the ship, looks over at Emma, then back at the ocean.

"You should not have given up your appeal, Emma. They were certain to deport me, but the Supreme Court might have let you remain."

"But without you, Alex. Why would I want to increase my punishment?"

Berkman smiles. Emma isn't sure what he's thinking anymore.

"Johann Most passed, too," Emma says. "And Mark Hanna."

"We should go through everyone that's died?"

The rest of the passengers have gone inside to escape the stiff, frigid wind blowing over the waves, but Alex and Emma remain, standing silently together, leaning on the railing. The ocean sprays their faces in a cold mist and the wind tries to yank them across the deck; they are sails billowing in the wind, the railing they grasp is their mast. Alex is slim and frail now; it is the solitary years that have done it. Prison time ages you double they say, and they are right. Emma is as old, but she is bulky now, sturdy and fiery.

Yes, she thinks. *We should go through everyone who has died.* Johann Most: 1906, the year Alex was released from prison. The Haymarket martyrs: Albert Parsons, August Spies, Samuel Fielden, Oscar Neebe, Louis Lingg: November 1887. William McKinley: September 1901. Leon Czolgosz: October 29, 1901.

The ship seems to linger as they pass the statue of Lady Liberty. It was new when Emma first passed it. That was December, too, just before New Year's, and New York was a place she had visited only in dreams. Sixteen years old, a young girl from Russia, and she stood on the deck of a ship gazing up at the towering stone lady who had emerged, magically, from the ocean, and there was her new home, America, and young Emma Goldman cried at the sight, standing there in the cold breeze, December 29, 1885; she was smiling and laughing as tears streamed down her cheeks.

She can still see Alex as he was, before prison, when he was young, barking out plans as if the future were something you drew out on an architect's desk with rulers and sharp pencils, to scale. The memory merges with another. Nieman—Leon—that boy: his eyes had the same intensity, something indefeatable about them; they looked through you and onto some other world.

Does an idea die when you kill the body that embraces it? Do you silence a voice when you cut a throat, or exile it across the ocean?

Emma puts an arm around Alex and holds him tight, she hugs him. She wraps him with her shawl, anything to shield him from the cold wind.

Afterword

Emma Goldman and **Alexander Berkman** lived the rest of their lives in exile, traveling through Europe mostly. They did go back to Russia but found the Bolsheviks too repressive, too stifling of liberty. They traveled in Sweden, Germany, England, France. Eventually Alex's body failed him, and his attempts to make a living in business failed, too. It was time to clear out, he decided. On June 27, 1936, he had planned to surprise Emma for her sixty-seventh birthday with an excursion by boat to Saint-Tropez, but instead he sent best wishes to her. "I embrace you heartily," he wrote her, "and hope that this birthday may bring you some joy and brighten the days that will follow." He mailed the card. Then it was time; the moment had arrived. He took out a gun, aimed, and fired it at himself.

He missed, hitting himself in the side. It took sixteen hours for his body to pass away.

Emma went on to fight fascists in Spain later that year. She was sixty-seven years old at the time. After suffering a stroke, she died on May 14, 1940. Four days later the Immigration and Naturalization Service granted her reentry to the United States, and she was buried in Waldheim Cemetery in Chicago, near Albert Parsons, August Spies, and the rest of the Haymarket martyrs.

Ida McKinley returned to live in her home on Market Street in Canton. She reportedly visited her husband's grave almost daily. She died on May 26, 1907, and remains entombed beside her husband, near Katie and little Ida, in the McKinley Memorial Mausoleum in Canton.

Mark Hanna continued to serve as a United States senator until February 15, 1904, when he died of typhoid fever.

Anthony Comstock crusaded against indecency, immorality, and vice through five decades. A week after arresting his last victim—a seventeen-year-old boy who had mailed writings Comstock declared to be obscene—Comstock fell ill with pneumonia, and on September 15, 1915, at the age of seventy-one, he left for a more wholesome world.

William Randolph Hearst went on to establish a media empire that came to include newspapers throughout the country, magazines *(Cosmopolitan, Good Housekeeping, Harper's Bazaar, Town & Country,* and others), a major comic strip syndicate, a newsreel production company, and one of the country's first television stations. His political career never materialized. He died on August 14, 1951, in Beverly Hills, California.

J. Edgar Hoover became the director of the Federal Bureau of Investigation in 1924, where he served until May 2, 1972, when he died in his sleep.

A Note on Sources

Most of the characters and events described herein are real, but as this is a work of fiction, with no pretenses at history, some explanations are in order.

For the most part I have described how things might actually have been, attempted to offer explanations of inner lives and motivations that history cannot explain. I have drawn lines where history supplies only dots.

The bulk of the events described involving McKinley, Ida, Emma, Berkman, Bierce, Hearst, and Hanna are historically accurate. Much of McKinley's and Emma's speeches, Hanna's statements, and virtually all of Bryan's speeches, are taken verbatim from the originals, as are the speeches of the Haymarket martyrs.

James Parker did prevent Leon from firing a third shot at the president, but within weeks reporters and witnesses at the trial denied that he had done it. The rest of his life is my creation, though the account of the lynching near where President McKinley was staying in Georgia was described in a petition sent by Negroes to McKinley while in office.

Little is known about Leon Czolgosz other than the basic outline of his life. His mother was pregnant with him when she and his father came over to America; she later died, at the age of forty, after giving birth to her eighth child. Leon was forced to leave school to work at an early age. His jobs described in the book, his education in radical politics, his leaving the workforce, his meeting of Emma Goldman, are all reported in histories, as is what he says to the police and on the chair. Although his relationship with Megan is not reflected in histories, there are enough blank spaces in Leon's life to allow for the possibility. And while contemporary alienists did write that he had no female relationships, a West Virginia newspaper recently reported that Leon did father a child who lived, with its mother, in Kanawha. Leon was known to disappear into Cleveland for days on his own. What he did there—or in the months in 1901 after he left his family's farm—is not known. He left behind little in his room in Nowak's saloon. After his arrest the police found a little change and the rubber nipple of a baby's bottle.

I have utilized many sources to research these characters and events, including newspapers, books, and websites (at http://lcweb2.loc.gov/ammem/papr/mckhome.html one can view Thomas Edison's films of the Pan-American Exposition of 1901, McKinley's last speech and funeral, and a fake execution of Leon Czolgosz). Among other books, most helpful were the following: *Living My Life*, by Emma Goldman; *Anarchism and Other Essays*, by Emma Goldman; *Rebel in Paradise*, by Richard Drinan; *The Homestead Strike of 1892*, by Arthur G. Burgoyne; *Prison Memoirs of an Anarchist*, by Alexander Berkman; *The Man Who Shot McKinley*, by A. Wesley Johns; *The Trial, Execution, Autopsy and Mental Status of Leon F. Czolgosz, Alias Fred Nieman, The Assassin of President M'Kinley*, by Carlos F. MacDonald; *The Manner of Man That Kills*, by L. Vernon Briggs; *The Trial of Leon F. Czolgosz for the Murder of President McKinley, American State Trials*, edited by John D. Lawson; *The Assassins*, by Robert Donovan; *In the Days of McKinley*, by Margaret Leech; *William McKinley and Our America*, by Richard L. McElroy; *William McKinley and His America*, H. Wayne Morgan; *The Presidential Election of 1896*, by Stanley L. Jones; *McKinley, Bryan and the People*, by Paul W. Glad; *The Haymarket Tragedy*, by Paul Avrich; *Citizen Hearst*, by W. A. Swanberg; *Traps for the Young*, by Anthony Comstock; *Anthony Comstock: His Career of Cruelty and Crime*, by D. M. Bennett; *Marcus Alonzo Hanna: His Life and Work*, by Herbert Croly; *Resurgent Republicanism: The Handiwork of Hanna*, by Clarence A. Stern; *Mark Hanna: His Book*, by Mark Hanna; *Hanna*, by Thomas Beer; *Ambrose Bierce*, by Richard O'Connor; *Henry Clay Frick: The Man*, by George Harvey; *J. Edgar Hoover: The Man and His Secrets*, by Curt Gentry; *The Boss: J. Edgar Hoover and the Great American Inquisition*, by Athan Theoharis and John Stuart Cox; *How the Other Half Lives*, by Jacob Riis; *The Rise of Industrial America*, by Page Smith; *Our Times*, by Mark Sullivan.

One more thing. The assertions made by the professor at Morris Vandeveer's dinner party, about the arrested mental development of Negroes? Word-for-word from the famed eleventh edition of the *Encyclopaedia Britannica*, published in 1911. That was science. That was the truth of the day.

About the Author

JONATHAN LOWY is the author of the critically acclaimed novel *Elvis and Nixon,* which won the Dictionary of Literary Biography Yearbook Award for Distinguished First Novel and the Towson University Prize for Literature. *Time* magazine recognized him as one of six promising first-time authors in 2001. He was born in New York City and now lives in the Washington, D.C., area with his wife and two children.